THE DAY OF THE NEFILIM

DAVID MAJOR

A DISTANT MIRROR

THE DAY OF THE NEFILIM

by David Major

Copyright ©2020

ISBN 978-0-9802976-8-3

This book is a work of fiction. Any resemblence, etc, etc... Any bits that are too ridiculous to be true might be true, however.

A DISTANT MIRROR

web – adistantmirror.com.au
email – info@adistantmirror.com.au

Praise for *The Day of the Nefilim*

"I have been reading SF since about 1970, when I was ten years old, having inherited a bookshelf of the greats – Heinlein, Herbert, Azimov, Bradbury, Vonnegut, etc, when my family moved in to a new house. Since then I have devoured just about everything in most of the genres that have populated the print and electronic worlds as they have matured along with the realities of hard science. I have also been a fan of conspiracy lit, be it templar, illuminati, or of the X-Files sort.

In the last year, as a result of having an iphone and discovering *manybooks.net*, I have started consuming more and more SF from the 'unknowns' and 'unsigned' which have been showing up with a greater frequency, and the fact of the matter is:

The Day of The Nefilim is one of the best SF novels I have read since I began reading.

Maybe that's just because all of what I have read until now provided the knowledge and context to appreciate the depth of David's work, which didn't allow me to put it down until I finished it. Straight through, in one sitting. Yeah, that's right, I did not put the book down until I finished reading it. Couldn't.

Well done David. Keep writing. Can't wait to read your next book… You would make Robert Anton Wilson proud, and Douglas Adams smile." *— exiledsurfer* on *Manybooks.net*

"...I love this book as much as I love all of my favorite science fiction books, and that's a quantity that defies quantifiers. Everything in this book is perfect. The ending is perfect; the villains are perfect; the characters and images and settings are perfect. I, too, could barely put it down. And I want to also say, thank you." *— P. Deering*

"I've read a lot of SF and conspiracy theories in my time, watched thousands of SF movies and documentaries, but I've never come across anything with the likes of your imagination. I was only able to understand it because of all I've read and watched in the last twenty years. I've never read any of your work before, but I believe you stand out." *— E.V.*

"This was an excellent read. Elements of Moorcock, Heinlein and Barker. Deserves serious consideration for the avid SF reader. Hopefully will spawn some more installments in the story line. Also feel it has the makings of a good screenplay. Thanks for the great writing David!" *— Ron W.*

"And just as Pig 'was going to have a crap in the grass, then a roll in the mud', it finished. Great read, I hope to see more. Reminds me a lot of that Triffids book which sticks in my mind from about 40 years ago. Good read :)" — *be1952*

"Loved the book. It ranks, in my mind, with L. Ron Hubbard's *Battlefield Earth*. Would be a great movie. Please continue." — *LG*

"…this is an excellent full-on fantasy sci fi that incorporates current parallels and a unique and engrossing universe. An interesting blend of 2D and 3D characters and an interesting 'life in the interior' scenario. When's the movie coming?" — *RS, PalmGear*

"Well I just finished the first half of this fine story, what can I say other than I'm hooked!!!!!! Who's the blue mutant woman, does Bark get with Reina?!?! Can the rebel mutants shut down the Nefilim grid and engage theirs before it's too late?!?! Hmm, I guess I won't find out until you release the second half. A big New York City thanks to you and some fine SF writing." — *LC, Palmgear.com*

"Thank you for publishing the *The Day Of The Nefilim* for the Palm. I have enjoyed the imagery that you have provided in the story and think that your style of writing is very captivating. Keep up the good work, and thank you again. I have enjoyed the reading MUCH so far!" — *WP, Palmgear.com*

"Wow!!! Oh my. I almost quit work to finish the first part. I got lost in the awsome surrealism of this novel. When I started reading, I couldn't put it down. Please (I beg), for humanity's sake, make Part 2 available in the .lit version. I'll pay for it. I'll almost buy a Palm Pilot just to read the second part." — *lawalty, Handango.com*

"Great story! One of the most original I've read in a lonq time! Brilliant use of characters and current events. I couldn't put it down." — *MF, Palmgear.com*

"Okay, okay. That was coooooooooool."
— *MP, Branch Manager, West Indianapolis Branch Library*

"It's an odd book…" — *DS*

Prologue / 1

The sun darkens. At first imperceptibly, and then with greater speed, it casts an unfamiliar veil over itself. It is the first eclipse in years.

The people look up at the sky, where some of them notice to the east a star falling to its death, and others watch the hulking disk of the moon that obscures the sun. It was all there in the sky that day, above Barker's Mill.

After a few minutes, the eclipse is over. The planets creak slowly along their orbits, and soon everything is as it was.

On the ground far below, life teeters on the edge of changing forever, but for today at least, it changes its mind and proceeds as it always has, grinding along the rusting tracks of its normality. It forgets quickly the strange orange dusk that had descended from the middle of the day.

On the edge of a tree-lined bay, with water the same deep green that you find in the glass of old bottles, stands Barker's Mill. The town has been laid out with the same care that a child gives to the arrangement of a new set of blocks. Its houses sit solidly, arranged in neat rows, portly squires gathered around a dinner table on their foundation seats of brick and bluestone. It is a most respectable gathering; everyone is well behaved.

It has been like this since the town began. To the people who live there, it feels as though it has been like this since the beginning of time. Which, of course, is not the case.

Meanwhile, far away, the General dreams, and Bark dreams.

For now, they don't remember the things they dream, but in time that will change; for one of them at least, and for the other it won't matter.

Their paths are linked, like the curls of a tattoo of snakes; but also like a tattoo, the effect will not be to everyone's taste.

These things happen.

The planet had been traveling through the cold, deathless silence for a long time. Like a marble worn smooth with age, it rolled across the black expanses of deep space, patiently following its preordained path. The planet's orbit was a huge ellipse, and the sun that held it in its sway was growing closer now as the planet tumbled into the star's inner system, towards perihelion.

The star's radiance began to heat the frozen orb. The liquid and gas that had long since been frozen solid by the unyielding cold of the vacuum of space began to thaw. If there had been anyone on the planet's bleak surface to see, the approach to its star would have been greeted first with wisps of vapor as the atmosphere began to return to its gaseous state. Then clouds of mist formed, covering the entire globe in wreaths of swirling white. As the approach continued, continents of ice crumbled, disintegrating into the seas that had begun to form.

Life that had been suspended in the death of absolute zero began to stir. Life cycles resumed as seed found sustenance in the chilled tundra, and creatures emerged from eggs hatching in the slight warmth of the sun. Spores drifted through the reconstituted atmosphere, seeking and finding refuge.

Deep in the frozen earth, other processes were set in motion.

Ice fell from hollowed, gaunt faces; deep black eyes flickered and opened. Muscles that had been as solid as ice for eons flexed and moved again. Tall forms moved through dark caverns.

Nefilim, they called themselves.

PART 1

The New World Order comes to town.

For Reina, Barker's Mill had been home since the day a few years ago when she had got off the bus that stopped here on its way north. It was coming up to eight years since she had left the city, and she had no nostalgia for any part of it. She had been on the dole when she first arrived in Barker's Mill; she had worked as well, of course. This place didn't suck money out of you with the same unrelenting efficiency that the city did. And you can't spend your whole life on the dole, she had thought, so she gave it away, and got a couple more part-time jobs instead. Her life had soon settled down into the comfortable rhythm that the place encouraged in everyone who lived here.

One of the several jobs she held was driving for an old farmer who came into town only when he had to. Which meant almost never these days, because Reina did his driving and ran his errands. Her job was to load her pickup with produce and drive it into the buyer in town. She and the old man had piled the crates of vegetables and fruit into the back. It was a fine afternoon for a drive; she had the window down and the breeze felt good.

While Reina was driving into town, the government was doing the same.

A couple of miles out, just as she was coming up to the creamery by the bridge over Old Goat Creek, the familiar shape of an army truck, painted white with its metal and glass all shiny and its headlights burning hot in the midday sun, filled her rear-vision mirror. As she rounded a curve, she saw that the truck wasn't alone. She pulled over into the gravel and started rolling a cigarette as the convoy went past. Damn, it was hot. She felt like a drink.

There were half a dozen trucks, followed by heavy transport vehicles that carried earthmovers, and other equipment covered by huge tarps. Everything was painted white and bore the letters 'UN', large and blue. The soldiers, of whom there were many, all wore the familiar blue helmets.

This wasn't new. There had been soldiers and other strangers all over the area for the last few months. They kept to themselves, in the base they had built among the sand dunes on the other side of the harbor. They didn't have much to do with the town, and when they did, they hardly said anything, which only encouraged speculation among the locals.

At the rear of the convoy were two long shiny cars, black instead of white, with windows of dark tinted glass and little blue flags that fluttered daintily on their front guards. Inside, the General and the other officers sat in air-conditioned comfort and watched the rustic world outside glide past.

A broken rudder.

Far, far away, within the curled and convoluted folds of a place and time far removed from Barker's Mill, Onethian and Sahrin are becalmed, and although they've been becalmed for quite a while now, they're happy.

They are happy because finally they have a solution to the problem of the broken rudder. Using material scavenged from crates that tumble out of the cargo hold and over the deck, they've replaced the old rudder with a new creation of wood and rare metals and some strange pieces of ceramic, the original use of which is a mystery to everyone and of consequence to no one.

The result of their labor more closely resembles an artifact from some exotic culture than anything as mundane as a rudder, but there is nothing to lose, and they had to do something about their predicament. They couldn't assure the Captain that it would work, but he gave his assent to the exercise, there being no reason not to try, and besides, Bark is as eager as any of them to get under way again. They have been aimlessly adrift for long enough, he thinks, lying idly on a pile of sacks and eating a piece of dried fruit from one of the barrels in the hold.

He looks up at the bare masts and imagines the sails unfurled and full, the ship once more making its way through the clouds and nebulae of deep space.

But the ship sits idle. The clouds of space scud slowly around them, and until the rudder is fixed, they are going nowhere. Until then, here they must stay, suspended in an azure limbo of no time and no space.

And until then, they have all the time in any world.

Bark slowly calculates a trajectory, and then watches as the piece of fruit follows it, up, and then down, over the side of the ship, into the void. He idly plays with one of his earrings for a minute, then goes back to sleep. Bark has never been in a hurry, and he's not going to start now.

Thirsts are slaked.

Passing Reina, the UN convoy drove into town. People stopped to look. The only time there were so many vehicles on the main street these days was when the army was passing through.

The vehicles, and the soldiers in them, were from all over the world. There were Syrians, Israelis, Russians, Koreans and Africans, and there were Americans. Months ago, the children had run to hide, but now they gathered in small groups and pointed and waved at the soldiers. Some of the soldiers waved back, and threw sweets to the children. The adults stood and crossed their arms and looked on with expressionless faces.

The main part of the convoy – the soldiers and their heavy trucks and all their equipment – drove straight on without stopping, heading along the road that would take them around the harbor to the sand dunes opposite town.

The officers consulted between the two black shiny cars on their cell phones, and decided to stop for a break. They pulled into the parking lot beside the Red Lion, and the officers emerged from behind the tinted windows, blinking in the sunlight as they put on their sunglasses.

They went into the bar and sat around one of the white plastic tables in the beer garden. From here, they had a clear view across the water, where outcrops of volcanic rock dotted the sand dunes like raisins on a cake. From here, the only sign of human activity was the small dark mass of tents, buildings and fences.

It was a hot day. The sun was strong, and despite the shade provided by the umbrellas of the beer garden, the half dozen starched white collars quickly became limp with perspiration. The talk was of politics and careers.

After a while they leaned back in their seats and marveled, each one to himself, at the wonderful and important things that were happening beneath the sand and rock across the water, and how fortunate they were that history had chosen them to do this work.

Except the General, of course; he had chosen himself. He sat silently while his subordinates talked, tapping his fingers lightly against the side of his glass. If there weren't appearances to keep up, he might even have been smiling to himself.

A map gives up its secrets.

A long way from the garden bar at the Red Lion…

On the ship, Thead is unconcerned by the fact that they have been unable to continue their voyage, and is equally uncaring about the success of Onethian and Sahrin. He has his own project to think about, and he feels one of life's important moments approaching. It is the crossing of a threshold – a tide reaching its high-water mark. This has been a long time coming, and the moment belongs more to him than anyone else; it is the unraveling of the secret of the map.

Thead sits back and runs his hands though his thinning shoulder-length hair. His skin, rough and pockmarked, is shiny with sweat from his exertions, even though they have all been cerebral in nature. His eyes, normally thin and constantly shifting, widen momentarily as he makes a connection on the maze before him. He smiles to himself and leans back over the map.

It was given to one of the ship's former crews, at a place they visited so long ago that its name has long been forgotten. Since then, it has taken on great importance to all the crews of the ship, from those whose names are lost in antiquity down to the six who make up the crew of the present day. A rich mythology has formed around the parchment. The mysterious territory which has its features drawn on the faded surface is part ancestral homeland, part legend.

The map has long been Thead's obsession. Long after the curiosity of others has turned away and settled down into a collection of comfortable and reassuring myths, he still studies it relentlessly.

He crouches down among the tall, gangling structures of the ship's foredeck, in a makeshift study created from barrels and boxes and sheets that he has taken from the cargo hold. Here he spends his days, and here he is today, sheltered from the wind and the distraction of his crew mates, bent over his precious parchment.

When he is sure of a new realization, he makes the faintest of marks on the parchment – a circle, a line, an arrow – in soft graphite that can easily be removed, his touch is so deliberate and light.

The maze of symbols and labels are sometimes in a language familiar to him, but most of them are in a foreign script, the slow deciphering of which has been his work. Its flourishes and curlicues never cease their whispering to him; sometimes he hears the voices through the night as he dreams. Sometimes his dreams have form, as though they are populated by entities, and those nights are not easy. It is better when the dreams don't come.

The rest of the crew is happy enough to leave Thead to his musings. And Bark, of course, is happy with things that way as well. There are members of the crew with whom he has easier relationships.

It makes sense that there should be someone working on the map, and it is as well that it is Thead. Practical tasks have never suited him, and the rest of the crew would be distracted if Thead were to spend too much time with them. There is something about him that makes them uneasy.

The hull of the ship creaks as it floats, moving listlessly in the gentle current.

Apart from Onethian and Sahrin, who are busy with the new rudder, the crew has nothing to do. Bark is still asleep on his pile of sacks. The Senator is working on another one of his speeches that he will never deliver, and Kali is below decks, in the galley.

Thead feels a rush that surges through his whole body. Steadying his hand to keep it from shaking, he makes a faint mark on the map.

The final piece of the key falls into an ancient lock.

He has it! He leaps up and runs the length of the ship, shouting, waving the map above his head. Idiot, Onethian thinks.

At first no one else understands the reason for the disturbance, but they soon recognize what he is holding. They drop what they are doing and follow him, even Onethian. This must be a good day. First the rudder being fixed, and now this...

Thead crouches down beside Bark and spreads the parchment out on the deck. The others gather around and watch intently, without understanding, as Thead guides Bark through the glyphs and symbols.

When Thead finishes speaking, his finger is slowly circling a small and insignificant looking set of marks on the map.

Bark straightens and looks up. He is wide awake now. He stretches as he contemplates the clouds wrapping themselves into cool wreaths around the ends of the ship's masts. All around them, hills of denser cloud lie stacked one upon the other, reaching as far up and as far down into the depths below them as anyone can see. The more distant clouds move slowly, carried by the most gradual and impartial of tides.

But something apart from the clouds is moving. Bark can feel it. It is their future that is spread out before them on the deck.

But do they complete their mission, and deliver their long overdue cargo, or do they follow the course that Thead has discovered on the map?

All of them feel the answer. It isn't long before the rudder is in place, and as soon as everything is ready, they set sail.

It exhilarates them to be moving again. The sight of the billowing mountains of cloud in movement lifts their spirits, and even the ship itself seems to rejoice as it carries them along.

They follow Thead's directions. The seductive joy of submission to a higher purpose spreads through the crew. The wind seems to catch their enthusiasm, and it picks them up, bearing them along confidently. They sail down narrow byways and across vast uncharted wastes of space. They cross darkness and light, places where there are no clouds, and places where there is nothing but cloud. They see strange creatures in even stranger skies, such that no one would believe. They see signs and wonders. The cargo lies forgotten in the hold.

Finally, after a long time, and several adventures that in normal circumstances would themselves be considered sufficiently unusual to warrant retelling, they arrive above a new land.

A brief history of Barker's Mill,
and Reina makes plans for the weekend.

A century ago, the hills across the harbor from Barker's Mill had been covered with forest. Giant trees, hundreds of years old, towered over dense confusions of bush. Then a new type of human arrived, different from the ones who had lived there before. The original inhabitants' small numbers and simple lifestyle had not lain heavily upon the land, unless you counted the extinction of a few species of large flightless birds that were good eating and easy to catch.

These new humans wore heavy clothing to protect themselves against the weather, and they wore boots on their feet. Their horses pulled carts through the mud of the paths that they cut through the forest. They chopped down the trees and cut them up and put the lengths of wood on the carts. They left behind piles of burning branches, and all the rubbish that followed them everywhere. The hills were soon becoming bare.

They took the cut wood around the harbor, to where an individual named Barker had built a timber mill and where houses were appearing in clearings carved out of the forest. Soon there was a town, with a store and a school. The town came to be known as Barker's Mill.

The people of Barker's Mill built themselves a church in which they gathered to celebrate their good fortune.

For the next few decades, the town amassed a degree of wealth by removing the rest of the trees from the hills around the harbor and selling the timber to anyone who would buy it. When the forest was gone, the mill closed down. The sons and daughters of the Barker family, now rich, moved elsewhere.

Where the forest had once been and where there was now none, the hillsides gave way under the rain. The topsoil, now dust, muddied the water as it ran down to the sea, or it was lifted by the wind and carried away, falling to the ground as a fine layer of annoying gray dust that discolored everything. After a few years, the sand and rock that had supported the topsoil were totally exposed.

Once the sand was uncovered, there was nothing to stop it from sliding off the hillsides. Streams became choked and then dried up altogether. Their beds disappeared under the sand. It was said by the locals that somewhere under the sand were buried the remains of an old village in which a few natives and settlers had lived together even as the forest was disappearing. No one knew the identities of the people who had lived there, just as no one knew where they had gone after the sand had flowed over their houses. There were stories, though.

There was another story as well, a much older one, which belonged to the indigenous people. Their legends told of another race that had lived in the area, long ago. But those stories were ancient now, and almost entirely forgotten. A few of the old people remembered fragments of them, and the young didn't care.

They didn't care because the legends were from the past, from the old world of spears and weaving flax and cooking food in the ground, and this was now. Most of the young people moved to the city and never came back. The area had its own history now, and the people who lived and worked there were fourth, fifth, and sixth generation. They were the locals now, and anyone who rolled through here in a convoy, army or otherwise, in trucks or shiny cars, was an outsider.

When she got into town, Reina pulled up outside the Red Lion. It was hot and dry, and she had time for a drink before unloading at the buyer's. Crossing the street, she saw the black cars sitting in the car park. If it weren't for the two uniformed drivers leaning against the side of one of them, talking and smoking, it would have looked as though the mob was in town. She went in.

Bryce was sitting at the bar.

Reina sat beside him. She dropped a note on the bar and pointed at one of the taps. The woman behind the bar put a beer in front of her. "Thanks, Denise."

"What do you make of these?" Bryce nodded towards where the officers sat, sweating in the shade.

"Their trucks passed me on the way in. Big ones, covered with tarps. Machinery or something," Reina replied. "I suppose they've gone over to the dunes?"

"Yeah, the trucks and the other stuff shot straight through. This lot must think they've earned a break. Pretty, aren't they? Nice braid, shiny medals..." He was talking deliberately loud. A couple of the officers turned and looked coldly in their direction.

"Jesus, keep it down..." Reina laughed, not really caring whether he did. She was well acquainted with his ideas about the military, authority, and the system in general. He was an anarchist, and he didn't mind who knew it.

Bryce stared back at the officers, goggle-eyed, daring them.

Reina picked up her beer. "Give it up, shithead. What do you think it's about?"

"You mean none of the theories we've come up with have impressed you? You're a hard woman to please. Shall we go over and have a look?" He nodded towards the open doors. Through them, the dunes on the other side of the harbor were visible.

"Yeah, we haven't been over for a while, have we. Not now, though. I'm working, as we speak. What about this weekend? After netball?"

"After netball it is, then. A bit of fascist-watching to round the afternoon off. We'll take lunch and a bottle."

The officers were about to go when their trucks came into view across the water. From where they sat, the vehicles looked like tiny matchbox toys as they entered the compound, but the comparison never occurred to them. Such thoughts do not commonly exercise themselves in minds such as these. The officers finished their drinks and watched as the compound's gates closed behind the last of the trucks. Then they got back into their black cars and set off along the road around the bay, leaving clouds of dust hanging in the air behind them.

In the leading car, the General, permanently assigned by

his government and his uncle (in this case, the same thing) to the standing army of the United Nations, turned up the air conditioning and loosened his tie. The gin had made him sleepy.

His lethargy was due to more than just the drink, though. He had been feeling haunted all day. The previous night, while he slept, he had dreamed.

He was in a huge room… It had walls of dark, finely carved stone and a high ceiling lost somewhere in a darkness that seemed to gather around him like a cold, shifting fog. In the dim light he saw obelisks, twice as high as a man.

There was no one in the room, but it lacked the stillness that it should have had. There was a sense of being, of something, which slowly coalesced, taking on a form that was invisible but palpable, that brushed against him like seaweed swirling in a tide. The sensation of voices, a hot, dry rustle of moth wings, fluttered around his head…

When he woke, he couldn't remember anything of what the voices had said. That had frustrated him at the time, and the memory of it frustrated him now. There was an urgency, he could recall that much. He felt, in his dream and afterwards in the shower, and as he put on his uniform, that they – whatever *they* were – were trying to tell him something. There was something in the whispered dialogues that made him feel uncomfortable.

In the end he gave up, as practical men should do when confronted with dreams. He had a lot to do.

The General was the only person here who knew everything about the operation. Everyone else, including the archaeologists, knew enough to do their job, and no more. The bigger picture was not their concern.

Of course, there had to be some people whose jobs demanded that they know more than they could be trusted with. It was unfortunate. Sometimes it was possible to clean their brains out – there was technology more than equal to the task; but sometimes memory removal wasn't possible or appropriate. Sometimes it was necessary that someone disappear. But the

General was a reasonable man, and he tried to keep those losses to a minimum.

They were approaching the gates of his new command.

An arrival.

"This is the place," exclaims Thead, checking the map, then looking through his sextant, and then through his telescope again, checking and rechecking.

Thead is used to the idea that he is doing an important thing. This place was promised to them a long time ago. They might not know exactly what awaits them, but over successive generations, the ship's crews have made up stories among themselves. It is those stories that have kept their faith alive through the centuries, and it is those same stories that stir their blood now.

In the direction of the sun, an ocean reaches out towards the horizon. Below them, a coastline meanders slowly away in both directions, indented by bays and inlets. A town, sheltered by the surrounding hills, hugs the edge of one the larger bays. In its streets they can see life, tiny, like fleas crawling through the fur on a dog's back.

"Thead," says Bark after they've spent a few minutes looking in silence, "where are we? What does the map say? Where should we look now?" He wants to ask what they should look for, but no one knows, and they all know that no one knows, so there is no point in asking.

Thead is happy now that his opinion matters. "I can't be sure. We're in the right area, according to the map. More, I can't say. There is nothing more on the map that can help us. Nothing that I can see, anyway."

"We'll moor the ship there," says Bark, pointing to the opposite side of the harbor. "Away from the town, above those dunes."

They cross the harbor. Bark is enjoying himself. This is a great moment in history, even if it is just the history of the ship, not Big History. It's as close to a Great Moment as any of them have ever been, with the possible exception of Bark himself, who can recall from somewhere the investiture of some kind of emperor, sometime in something called the Middle Kingdom. Something like that. It *was a long time ago, in one of his other pasts.*

Near the dunes, Onethian, always first in line to do any physical work, flexes his muscles and leans into the winding gear, letting the anchor descend to the ground. It lodges in the branches of a tree, and the Senator and Sahrin join Onethian as they begin winding the chain in.

The ship descends towards the ground. The three of them strain at their task, and it isn't long before their skins shine with sweat. "Get lost, old man," grunts Onethian. "You're getting in the way."

"Leave him alone," says Sahrin as the Senator puffs obediently away and sits down.

Kali, drawn from below deck by the sound of the winch, goes to one of the viewports and immediately calls out.

Below them, sitting on a ledge of rock among the sand dunes, are three people.

The ship, along with themselves, is invisible to the local inhabitants, so they aren't concerned about being noticed by the three on the ground, but there is still an element of surprise in seeing some of the locals so soon. And for them to be, from this distance at least, the same as the crew; that is to say, human, or at least the same basic shape – that in itself is unusual.

Now they need to make another decision.

The view from the dunes.

A few days later, after netball and as arranged, Bryce and Reina stopped at Tommy's place on their way to the dunes. We've got a couple of bottles, they said, and bring some smoke, some of that leaf you had the other day, and we'll lie in the sun and watch the boys at the camp work. Good enough, said Tommy, who wasn't doing anything anyway. He'd just had a couple of tattoos removed, and didn't feel like working.

"More bloody army, mmm. Foreign again, yeah? Or were they ours?" Tommy was saying a short time later. He was pretending to be interested for Bryce's sake, and as usual he wasn't doing a very good job. They were in Reina's pickup, heading around the bay towards the dunes. Tommy was sitting between Bryce and Reina, trying to roll a smoke, and failing because the road was bumpy. "Ah, fuck it," he said, folding the plastic bag back into his pocket.

"There's no such thing as *our* army, mate," said Bryce. "You should know that by now, with all the bloody lectures I've given you. They all belong to the ruling class. The elites, if you want to use the modern term. Armies always have, always will. These guys are UN, they belong to the big State, the new one. They've got zip to do with us, that's for real."

"Yup," replied Tommy.

"Yeah, yup," said Bryce. As usual, he was frustrated by his friend's indifference, but he'd gotten used to it when they were in the army together. "I suppose you won't care about them until they do something that fucks you up personally."

"Fair guess, mate. Do you want some of this?" Tommy had found a joint somewhere.

They turned off the main road and took a smaller track. After a couple of minutes, the track ended. They got out of the pickup and walked into the sand dunes.

After a short walk across the sand, they reached their favorite outcrop of rock. It was easy to get to, comfortable, and gave them a good view of the military encampment. Once they were settled, Reina pulled a pair of binoculars out of her pack.

A few of the soldiers were still unloading equipment from the trucks, even though it was a few days since the convoy had passed through town.

The stuff was being taken into a tunnel that both Bryce and Tommy knew well. For as long as they could remember, it had been a local landmark, where the local children would play all the games that children play anywhere when such a wonderful resource as a cave is available. It was – or at least it had been before the soldiers arrived – a short cave, about fifty feet long, with a gently sloping floor that ended with an impassable rock face where the roof had collapsed some time in the distant past.

Things must have changed. They had watched from their hiding place over the last few months as the cave had swallowed huge amounts of equipment. Building materials were taken into the tunnel and never reappeared. They had seen tons of tailings being taken in trucks to the water's edge and dumped.

They had all sorts of theories that came and went, depending on what they saw, what the latest whisper in town was, or what their mood was. Tommy's interest was casual. If Reina and Bryce hadn't been interested, he wouldn't have bothered coming out here. Reina agreed with Bryce; there was something going on. Whether or not she cared much about it was another matter.

The General peruses some artifacts,
and we meet Bisset.

Past the point where the rock fall had been cleared, a string of lights illuminated ancient walls, sloping down and fading into the distance.

They had found a lot, but as for knowing what the tunnels meant – the answer, it was hoped, was somewhere below them. That, at least, was what the drones had been told. As far as they knew, they were here to dig up the secrets of the past, to move long lost knowledge to the surface in container loads of rubble and artifacts.

A new tunnel had been built near the entrance. It branched off from the old one and housed the offices and research areas. The rooms here were lit, heated, sealed, and entirely functional. This was the General's first stop.

He stopped briefly at a door that bore his name. He went into his new office and dropped his case on the desk. So, this was going to be home for a while. He looked around. They'd set it up well enough. It would do. He turned and left again, heading further down the corridor to the research labs.

The archaeologists were there, sorting through artifacts that had been brought up from the lower levels. The objects were piled together on long tables, waiting to be classified according to whatever system had been contrived for the exercise; an intellectual folly which the General was happy to have no part of.

Bisset, the chief archaeologist, was there. Middle-aged and paunched, he usually made up for a lack of hair by using too much oil, but working here must have been getting to him, and he had let what was left of his hair do as it wished. It was sticking out like a frizzy gray halo, making him look like the mad scientist he almost was. He was holding a fragment of something up to the light and turning it around slowly, dictating notes to one of his staff.

He glanced up as the General approached. "You've arrived,"

he said, dispensing with formalities. "You'll want to take a look at these. They're only the small ones. Here are some photos of some of the larger pieces that have had to stay down below because of their size." He indicated a pile of prints. "There are thousands of the things, and we've only just scratched the surface."

The General thought back to when the first samples had been put in front of him. It had been several months ago, in Bisset's office at Mount Weather.

"This is strange stuff. I've never seen anything like them. What do you make of them? Not a fair question, I suppose," he had asked the archaeologist.

"On the contrary, it's a very fair question," Bisset had replied. "Mysteries like this have been around for a long time, though they never get much of an airing in public. The Smithsonian's got a lot of it, but only our own people have access to it. As far as we know, this is the largest collection that's ever been found at a single site. Even Acambaro is nothing compared to this."

Bisset had shifted his attention to a small group of clay figures. Two human figures, male and female, were standing side by side, facing a lizard-like creature slightly taller than them and standing on its rear legs, supported by its tail. The three of them could have been having a conversation.

There was enough knowledge on this table to rewrite all of human history. But history, of course, could not and would not be rewritten. The future was more important than the past, and the present would take whatever shape was needed to provide the required future.

"We're going to have a strange few months, aren't we, Professor?" The General picked up a ceramic of a stegosaurus.

"It looks that way," Bisset replied. "The items on this table, including the one you're holding, were found under rock at least two million years old. And the tunnel system itself is at least as old. This changes a few things."

An encounter in the dunes.

Bark, Onethian and Thead have joined Kali to see what has attracted his attention. Sahrin and the Senator come over as well. The whole crew is there.

Below them, the ground appears to be alive. A pulse rises and falls, like heat existing on some other scale of temperature. Trails of comings and goings are almost visible, as though what is happening is just around the corner of perception, asleep in a dream of its own. Bark feels something familiar in the scene.

The activity on the ground surrounds a cave entrance at the bottom of a cliff.

"Playtime?" Onethian rubs his muscular hands together like the idiot he can be sometimes.

"You could try being a little more serious," the Senator says, displaying a rare moment of resistance.

"I could," grunts Onethian, "but I'm not going to."

"Shall we take a look?" Bark remembers that he's the Captain.

Onethian and Sahrin return to the winch. The ship soon starts to move again, swaying slightly in the wind as it descends. When the bottom of the hull reaches the treetops, Bark calls for the winding to cease. Thead finds a space among the branches, and lowers the ladder to the ground.

A short walk across the sand dunes separates them from the site of Kali's discovery. They set out, and are about to descend an incline when they notice below them the three people that they had seen from the ship. The strangers are watching the same area that has caught their own attention.

As Bark expects, Bryce, Reina and Tommy fail to see the new arrivals, who are now standing directly in front of them and inspecting them with great interest.

The visitors and the locals are in the same space, but like two signals traveling down one wire, they are out of phase with each other. They are in different versions of the same world.

"They're a strange color," says Sahrin. She looks at Reina's dark coffee-colored skin, and then at Tommy, who is an even darker shade of the same color. Bryce is more her own color. "I like her," she says, looking back at Reina. "She's gorgeous."

"She's impressive, yes, but this one's dress sense is winning the battle for my attention. Just look at this," Bark says, nodding towards Bryce, who is shading his eyes against the sun as he peers down into the encampment. Had he known that his grip on fashion was being questioned, he wouldn't have been able, let alone motivated, to defend himself. As usual, he was in jeans, tired runners and a torn denim jacket with a big yellow smiley face on the back. "Shocking," says Bark, feeling suddenly pleased with his own choice of a loose red and purple striped silk shirt, burnt orange tights, and embroidered canvas boots. Bark can always be relied on to dress for an occasion, even one that has little chance of happening.

"Could you tell what rank he was?" asked Bryce.

"What rank who is?" says Thead. The local's speech warbles slightly, as though he is speaking under water, but it can be understood.

"Remember," says Onethian. "They can't hear us."

"I know that!" snaps Thead, who has a problem with Onethian and his unending helpfulness. "I wasn't talking to him, I was talking to us. Even you, if you've got anything sensible to say."

"A general, I think, I don't know. Do you want a turn?" Reina handed Bryce the binoculars.

"They'd be handy," says Bark.

"We don't need more crew," Sahrin says.

"The glasses, not the locals."

"Oh, the glasses… yeah, I guess."

"It's guarded all the time, and now that there are more soldiers, we'd never get in, no way," said Bryce.

"Did you hear that? They want to get in there," says Onethian.

"It's not as though we want to get in, anyway, right?" said Reina, suspecting that Bryce might be missing his soldiering days.

"Nah," replied Tommy, watching a bird in a tree and at the same time feeling relieved that neither of his friends were sounding serious about going down there.

"These people appear to have the advantage of a bit of local culture," the Senator says. "And if they've been watching this place for a while, they might have some useful information."

"That may be," replies Bark, "but I'd prefer that we rely on our own judgment." The others agree, and begin to move down the hill.

"But why don't you stay, Senator, and see if their conversation sheds any light our situation. We'll be back soon," Bark says, turning to follow the others.

The Senator, never one to argue (at least that is how he sees himself) finds a space on the rock ledge and sits down.

It doesn't take Bark and the others long to reach the perimeter fence. They stop in front of it, and look along its length and then at each other. They shrug, as if deciding something not very important at all, and then walk through it. It flickers briefly, creating a brief nimbus of fairy lights around them.

* * *

Underground in the control room, a private currently more interested in a recent earthquake in the Ukraine than anything else was making a coffee when he was drawn back to his computer by the beeping of an alarm.

On the screen he saw that the fence's field had been breached in five places, all close together, as though a group of something was moving together.

"Shit," he thought and said in Ukrainian. "Intruders." He flicked through the cameras along the fence. There was nothing there. Everything was fine; the fence was intact.

Damned machine. It hadn't acted properly since they hauled it off the truck. Private Dosteyin went back to his coffee.

Archeology 101.

The General and the archaeologist were standing with a group of engineers in front of a wall, surrounded by the crumbling remains of subterranean buildings. The General reflected, not for the first time, on the attraction of archeology. To unveil these things that had been buried, unseen and unsuspected, for so long that no human had any idea of the time involved...

The original inhabitants of the excavations had been human, or at least humanoid, judging by the architecture. Whoever they were, they had been tall; the doorways and steps suggested a height of seven or eight feet. They didn't yet know how many kilometers of tunnels there were, but it was a large system, bigger than the others that had been found in other parts of the world.

There were three other locations that were known of. One was in the jungles of the Yucatan Peninsula. Another was in the Himalayas, inside the Chinese border, which had meant that some high-level and very careful cooperation was going on. The third site had been found under the sand in Saudi Arabia, at a place where nomads had gathered for rituals for as long as they could remember, and where earthmovers and trucks and scientists and soldiers now gathered.

And there was this site, near the northern tip of the North Island of New Zealand. It was the fourth site, the last to be identified.

Time was short. The other three sites were ready and waiting. Everything was in place.

The UN had been sure that there was something to be found when they sent the first party of surveyors here. The ruins had been found exactly where they had been expected; at the point which, combined with the other three sites around the world, formed an irregular but very precisely shaped tetrahedron, the four corners of which were occupied by these impossible ruins, buried under rock that was millions of years old.

The workers who had been involved in the initial exploration had been given all the normal mind-clearing drugs, after which all memory of the excavations had been removed. As always, there were a few in whom the suggestion didn't take, so there had been some accidents to arrange. Training mishaps, the odd helicopter crash, that sort of thing.

The New Zealand site was the last piece of the puzzle. There had been some tension in the air at Mount Weather when the General had left to come here. There was doubtless a lot more now.

The wall in front of them was at the end of one of the labyrinth's main tunnels. They were almost a kilometer underground.

Both men could feel what had been described in the reports. The soldiers and engineers who were with them stirred uneasily. The first people to stand here three months ago had described it as a feeling of apprehension that grew stronger the longer you stayed in the vicinity of the wall. Eventually, it became so strong that it was impossible to remain there. It crawled at the base of your brain, physical and thoroughly visceral. An unnamed dread of *something*.

They could feel it now.

"Amazing," the General said, his flesh gathering into cold goose bumps. His breathing had become shallow. "I found it hard to believe the reports."

"It gets worse than this, sir," one of the soldiers said, moving back a step.

The archaeologist moved closer to the wall. He was sweating heavily. Fumbling, he pulled an implement from one of his pockets and picked at the surface of the stone. After a few seconds he interrupted his scratching and paused, seeming to pay attention to something in the air. Then he leaned closer to the wall and placed one ear against the surface. He turned and beckoned.

The General went over and put his ear against the wall. A deep humming sound was audible somewhere behind the rock. The feeling of apprehension was getting stronger. They moved away, putting welcome distance between themselves and the rock face.

The General turned to a sergeant. "Get a team down here with a resonance cutter and get to work on it. Keep me informed. If there are any problems, I want to know. And I don't want anyone going through there when the wall is breached. As soon as you've made it through, call me."

* * *

A kilometer above, the three locals were still there, but their vigil had entered a familiar and relaxed stage. Reina was rolling a joint from Tommy's leaf, while Tommy himself lay on his back, hands behind his head as he dozed, smiling, in the warmth of the afternoon sun. Bryce was pushing the cork into a bottle of wine with the handle of a knife.

The Senator, deeply impressed by this capacity for luxury, and warming to the three of them, decides to join in by chewing a few bindoo leaves. They soon have the desired result.

"You seem to have a relaxed attitude towards things," he says out loud, not caring that they can't hear him. "You would probably enjoy bindoo," he smiles dreamily. He offers them a sample from his pouch, and shrugs happily when they ignore him.

* * *

Having passed through the perimeter fence and interrupted Private Dosteyin's routine, the others arrive at the mouth of the tunnel.

"What is it?" asks Sahrin, who has never seen a cave before.

"It's a hole," replies Bark. They move forward, tentatively edging into the mouth of the cave. It looks as though it goes on forever. "It's a strange thing indeed," says Bark. A guard standing nearby remains oblivious of their presence.

This is the place that Kali had seen from the ship. The movement in the air that had drawn his attention is barely visible now; like smog over a city, it exists only in the distance.

Even so, they can still sense that there is something going on. There is an energy here that twists like a trapped animal, caught somewhere between the space that the travelers occupy and the local space. Like a sheet of rubber stretched taut and thin, it threatens to tear and reveal the entities they know are here, moving and skittering around like the rats in the ship's cargo hold.

They enter the cave. Ahead of them, lights strung along the ceiling offer a dimly lit path into the depths. To their right is the entrance to the offices and labs.

"Let's have a look in here," says Bark, "before we go any deeper." The truth is that like all of them, he finds the prospect of going underground daunting. It is a new idea, after all. They are all accustomed to open space, with its fields of clouds and stars and nebulae, and its winds that keep changing everything, over and over again.

They go through the locked door and into the administration area. At the end of the corridor they come to a large room, in which a great number of objects have been laid out on long tables. People, some in white coats and some in uniform, are studying the artifacts.

Onethian leans over one of the tables. He watches as one of the whitecoats picks up one of the ceramics. "You should see this."

The rest of them gather around. The figurine the scientist is holding has a human face from which a bird's beak protrudes, and there is some kind of comb on the top of its head. Bird's wings sprout from a hunched back, and it has the legs and tail of a reptile. It is rearing up on its hind legs, using its tail for balance.

They look at the other figures on the table. It is a collection of monsters, mutants and half-breeds. There are combinations of human and non-human, non-human and non-human. One of the figures stands intact and larger than the others, dominating the center of one of the tables. As they recognize it, their spirits fall. The figure, skeletally thin and insect-like, is almost as tall as any of them. The dome of its skull is large, as though it contains great intelligence, but it is obvious from the face that there is no place here for compassion. The eyes, cruel and heavy with black shadows, have been carved deep into the head. The smooth stone gazes coldly at them all, asserting its authority across the ages.

"They've been here."

"And I hope they're long gone," says Kali, disconcerted.

"Do you think these people know what they're dealing with?" asks Sahrin.

"I have a strange feeling," says Bark, "that they don't. And that they will."

A decision is made.

The General left the wall to the exertions of the engineers and returned to his office, where he found the pile of photographs that had been left on his desk.

They were of a chamber, just discovered, in another part of the system. The report with the photos said it was about a hundred meters long, fifty wide, and about ten meters from floor to roof. Big, in other words. It wasn't natural, of course; it had been carved out of the stone using the same heat process that had produced the rest of the tunnel system.

The megaliths he had been expecting were there, arranged across the expanse of the chamber's floor. Massive heavy-roofed porticoes squatted against the walls of the chamber, looking like theatrical props in the stark, high-relief lighting of the engineers' equipment. This was a good find. Mount Weather would be pleased.

And there was something familiar about it... but he was too busy and his mind too distracted for him to connect it with his dream of the night before. It was the fleetest of impressions, coming and going in an instant.

Someone had drawn a map of the chamber. Opening his briefcase, he took out a large map of the tunnel system, found some tape, and stuck it up on the wall. Getting the smaller hand-drawn map, he picked up a pen and marked the location and orientation of the new chamber on the large map.

The addition of the new chamber completed the pattern. The only thing missing was the area beyond the sealed wall, but if he extended the symmetry of the known areas, he could fill in the missing parts there as well. This site was just like the others. Excellent. He picked up a phone and keyed the Secretary-General's private line.

Although he is unaware of the fact, the General has an audience. The five travelers have left the room full of statues, and have come into his office, where they found him contemplating the maps on his wall.

Now they are looking, open mouthed, at the photos spread out on the desk. The shapes, the architecture, and the hieroglyphs are all familiar to them.

Bark is thinking that his strange feeling has been vindicated, and that this is probably not a good thing. "It's them, for sure."

"Yes. Nefilim…"

"If they wake…"

"I think they're already awake," Bark replied. "That's what we saw from the ship. The movement. They're just not on the physical plane yet."

"Do you think these people know?"

"This one doesn't, from the way he looks at the map."

"But how did they know to come here? Somewhere, someone must know."

"Either that or they're about to find out."

"You know, I've never seen Nefilim in the flesh."

"None of us have. The sections of time that they escaped to have always been closed to us."

"Why are we here? Why did the map bring us here?"

"Maybe we should go. I don't care what the map says."

"But there has to be a reason for us to have come here."

"Does there? Just because the map fell into our hands doesn't mean it was meant for us. And just because Thead decoded it doesn't mean that he was meant to. It might have been nothing more than an accident."

"Maybe. Maybe not. Even if it was meant for us, that's no reason for us to accept our lot without question. It's up to us, not some piece of parchment that's been around so long that we're not even sure where it came from."

"True. It's our decision. It's up to us."

"Exactly. In view of which, we should decide what we're doing."

"Well, it does seem interesting."

"Any situation which has something to do with the Nefilim will *be interesting. That might be a slight understatement.”*

“Leave me alone. There’s no need to be sarcastic.”

“With you it’s hard not to be. This could be a bit dangerous, you know. We’ve all heard the legends.”

“The legends are bad enough, aren’t they?”

“The Nefilim legends, you mean? …they’re not pleasant.”

“I’m still curious, though.”

“Curious enough?”

They are curious enough, it seems. They head for the door.

“We’ve come all this way…”

“We can’t turn back now…”

“But…”

“But nothing. Don’t give me the shits, Thead.”

Archeology 102.

Deep underground, the wall was starting to give. It started to crack, then resisted for a moment, swelling with internal heat caused by the waves of sound. Finally it gave up, exploding outwards and sending rock fragments showering into the tunnel. There was a heavy, audible sigh as different air pressures met.

The engineers smelled something stale. Before they could do or say anything, they slumped to the ground. An invisible cloud streamed out of the opened chamber, heading upwards through the caverns and tunnels as surely as if it possessed a conscious purpose. It rendered unconscious everyone in its path.

Undeterred by the plight of their operators, the machines kept digging or dusting or grinding. The cloud snaked through the kilometers of tunnels, backed out of blind alleys, retraced its steps, sought out the surface, turn by turn.

For the General and the others in the administration section, the first sign that something was wrong came when the alarms on the machines started sounding because of the inactivity of their operators. They opened a channel to the crew at the wall, but got only silence. They tried to contact other work sites, but there was nothing there either.

Then from a site closer to the surface, they heard incoherent speech; "the air... strange... what the f..." the voice faded into nothing. Whatever it was, it was heading towards the surface.

The General went to the door that led out to the main tunnel. The only person in sight was a single guard.

"In here, now!" he yelled. The soldier turned and started towards him. He was about twenty feet from the door when the General heard a confusion of voices and the unmistakable thud of falling bodies coming from somewhere down the tunnel.

Without a second thought, he slid the door across. The guard stopped and looked towards the depths. His eyes widened, and he dropped his gun and put his hands to his throat. He gulped air like a goldfish, then fell to the ground.

The door was airtight, as was always the case with operating command centers, so if this was some kind of gas, the area would be safe. The General went to the monitors and flipped through the cameras. One of them was trained on the breach in the wall. He paused when it came up, leaning closer to the screen. He couldn't tell whether the crew were dead or unconscious, but they weren't moving.

The wall was mostly gone. It had been reduced to a pile of rubble, and the area behind it was open but concealed in darkness. As he watched, he saw the shadows begin to flicker with traces of light.

He went to the research area. There were three people in the room: Bisset, a corporal and a young female archaeologist.

"What's going on?" Bisset looked nervous.

"We have a slight problem." The General closed the door and checked the seal. "The team that we left at the wall have broken through…"

Bisset nodded. "Well, that's good…"

"…but there was something down there. Some type of gas. From what I've seen, it's floored everyone down below. How many are there outside? Above ground?"

"Not many, sir," the corporal answered. "I was up there a few minutes ago. A few at the gate, and some engineers in the vehicle section. And the kitchen staff, I guess. Pretty much everyone else was below ground working."

The General called the guard post at the main gate. It was the point in the compound that was furthest from the cave mouth, so if anyone was still on their feet, it would probably be there. The phone at the other end was answered immediately.

"Main gate." The voice was young and scared.

"What's going on up there?"

"Everyone just dropped like flies, General. Men came running out of the workshop and collapsed, and everyone else as well, and now there's just three of us left here. We must have been too far away, or something. I dunno. What's going on… er…sir?"

The General thought quickly. "Two of you stay where you are. One of you come to the admin section. I don't care which one. The door's shut. Just wait outside it. Do it now. No, wait. What ranks do you have there?"

"I'm a sergeant, and the other two are privates, sir."

"Send one of the privates." If it was some kind of gas, it would have only a limited life. It would probably have dissipated by now, but he had to know for sure, and given the absence of a canary, a grunt would do.

* * *

Up on the rocks, Bryce had watched it all happen. Soldiers staggered around for a few seconds then collapsed to the ground, where they lay twitching peacefully. A few minutes later, one of the guards at the gate ran towards the tunnel and disappeared into it.

"Something's on, eh?" Tommy sat up.

"I reckon. Something's on for sure. Don't tell me you're going to get interested, mate."

"Oh, absolutely." Tommy reached for a cigarette.

A few minutes later, they saw one of the two remaining guards talk briefly into a cell phone, and then they both ran towards the tunnel. The gate was left unattended.

* * *

With the guards from the gate with him, the General felt a little less exposed.

He told Bisset to stay in the lab, but the archaeologist insisted on coming along. His assistant, the young woman, would come as well. The General didn't argue. It didn't matter that Bisset would be there. And the woman would be needed.

He led the group down into the tunnels. Led was not quite the right word, of course; one of the grunts walked point. They all wore gas masks, in case there was a repeat of whatever it was that

41

had floored everyone.

Behind the scientists, five unseen visitors follow in single file.

When they arrived at the remains of the wall, everything looked as it had through the security camera. The soldiers started to check the bodies on the ground.

"Don't worry about them," the General said as he stepped into the chamber.

The air was heavy with something that smelled sour, even through their masks. The floor was shiny and wet.

"Spread out, so we can see what's going on. This should be one room, about a hundred meters long and about fifty wide." The General stayed where he was while the archaeologist, the assistant and the four soldiers entered the cavern, their lamps cutting wide swathes in the gloom.

Like the other room in the photographs, this one was full of megaliths. As the columns of rock emerged from the darkness, the General saw that they were about ten feet tall and three feet wide. The walls were covered in alien script and markings.

"This all makes sense. Every site so far has had two of these caverns." The archaeologist moved towards one of the walls. "And this chamber has these…" He held his lamp up so that its light crawled up the wall in front of him. Designs covered it from floor to ceiling. "This is new."

The General went to where Bisset was standing. The patterns weren't painted on to the walls; they were made of a colored resinous substance that glowed with internal color at the slightest encouragement from the lamps. The archaeologist was right. This is what would make all the difference in the months to come. It was the user's manual.

This had been – and would be again – a command center.

The archeologist's young assistant was standing in front of another wall covered with what seemed to be a map of landforms. "Another planet," he said, joining her.

"No, look," she said, running her light along the edge of a continent. "That's part of the western coast of Africa. And see…

there's the east coast of Australia… there's New Zealand… before they all moved apart. This is ancient."

"My god, this is old," said the archaeologist, shaking his head.

Bark and the others don't follow the General and the other locals into the room.

To them, there is no darkness at all; the room is full of light even before the halogens are turned on. Up near the smooth dome of the rock ceiling, they can see more of the entities that were gathered around the mouth of the cave, flitting around in the stale air, like beetles with wings that are brittle and dry and make a hard rustling sound that make you want to shrink away. There is an urgency in the movement; a deep hum below the hysteria, a frequency lower than the human ear can detect.

Kali sits down on a piece of the dismembered wall. "I don't like this." The whine in his voice is familiar. "I want to go back to the ship."

"Well, go back to the ship, then," snaps Bark. He has trouble with Kali sometimes.

"Only if we all go." Kali looks up towards the ceiling.

"Well, we aren't all going to go, so shut up!" says Sahrin. There has never been much love lost between them. "The Senator's outside, why don't you go and wait with him."

"Leave me alone," says Kali, but he doesn't move.

Thead shares none of Kali's misgivings. He has joined the locals inside the chamber. He stands before one of the walls, where he instantly recognizes the script as the one that adorns his precious map. One of the beetle-wings whispers in his ear.

He reads the script, and understands it as words roll off the entity's dry tongue. It and its kind have a mission that has been assigned to them by the history of their race…

Thead feels the thrill of exhilaration as the knowledge grows in him. It is an exhilaration mixed liberally with fear, which makes him feel it all the more keenly. And he enjoys it.

Bryce and Reina go exploring.

Outside, the wine and the smoke were forgotten. Bryce, Reina and Tommy were discussing what to do.

"It's got fuck all to do with us, man." Tommy was as keen as ever on getting involved.

"And that fact has got nothing to do with anything," said Bryce. "I say we have a look. What are they going to do? Shoot us?"

"Umm…"

"Look, there's no one at the gate, is there? If we get sprung we can just say we've never seen this place before and we thought it was deserted, and we're just having a look."

"Yeah, Tommy, don't be a wus." Reina was high.

"Yes, Tommy, whatever a wus is, don't be one," says the Senator dreamily, high on bindoo leaf and not at all worried about being shot.

"Nup. You guys are nuts. I'll wait here and finish the wine. You won't be taking the bottle, I guess?"

"Wus."

"Yeah right. Someone has to look after home base."

"Just means more weird shit for us," said Reina. "Can we take the smoke? There's another bottle in the truck. See you soon." She and Bryce set off down the hill.

The Senator wonders briefly what to do and then follows them.

* * *

Bryce and Reina found the gate open. Reina stopped at the first body, a tall, skinny soldier lying like a dummy discarded from a shop window. His helmet had come off his head. She bent, placing a hand on his throat. "Hey, he's alive."

Just inside the tunnel, they found the entrance to the offices and labs. It was locked. Bryce dragged the unconscious guard over to the door and held his thumb up against the security lock. The door slid open.

Reina was impressed. "Cool! How did you know to do that?"

Bryce laughed. "They're planning on introducing that sort of stuff all over the place in the next year or two."

In the first room, they found the photos on the desk. "Here's something…"

"Check this out." Reina had found the map on the wall.

Bryce came over. "This must be what's down below."

"There's enough of it. It's humungous."

"Let's see what else is here."

They left the office and went down the corridor to the lab. They had never seen anything like the artifacts that were laid out on the tables. The hybrid animal-humans, lizard men and dinosaurs looked like props from a B-grade movie.

"What are these doing here?" Bryce picked up a small brontosaurus. "No prehistoric human ever made an image of a dinosaur. It's impossible. There's the slight matter of a few million years…"

"Oh, wow." Reina had found a meter-high ceramic of a woman having sex with something that looked like tyrannosaurus rex. "That's bent."

"How can you tell?" asked Bryce.

"Idiot. This thing's fucking her, look…"

"You're too kind. And so it is. Now concentrate, we have to think. We've got photos of some ruins, we've got a map, and now we've got some strangely amorous garden gnomes…"

"We have indeed, Sherlock. You're quite brilliant. There's something weird going on here."

"Too right there is. They've been digging all this stuff up. That's how come all the equipment, and all the guys. Shall we go and have a look?"

"Absolutely. Let's have a smoke first."

Underground.

The General and the archaeologist stood before one of the panels of hieroglyphs, unaware that Thead was observing their deliberations. In the center of the wall was arranged a large spiral pattern of circles, some hollow and others solid.

"That's this room," says Thead.

"That's this room," said the archaeologist. "You see, that's the tunnel leading to it, and that's where it was sealed by the wall. And you see the circles? They show the locations of the megaliths in the room. You can see from the diagram that they're laid out in a pattern, in two joined spirals with the centers towards the ends of the rooms. Those marks to the left and right of the rectangle are their writing. It's the same script that we've seen in the other sites."

The General knew this. He also knew that the rupturing of the wall had started the process. The crystalline structures inside the rock had begun moving, flowing like fluid through the half-formed veins of an embryo.

Thead knows much of what is happening, having read the writing on the wall. He congratulates himself on his facility with the language, and briefly has a chance to feel smug about this payoff for his preoccupation with the map.

The General moved towards the entrance. He knew, at least to some extent, what was about to happen. More was known than had been admitted to anyone – more than the archaeologists knew, and much more than any of the lower ranks realized. One of the advantages of his position was that he could watch history make itself, and know what he was watching.

He looked at his watch. It was approaching time.

The final phase should begin about eight and a half minutes – two of their time units, if the translation had been correct – after the introduction of biomass into the room.

It was a pity that his hand had been forced. The original plan had been to breach the chamber, establish that it was what they believed it was, then seal it up again. The excavation of the caverns could then have proceeded at a leisurely pace, and when they had learned all there was to know from the artifacts and ruins, the main force of soldiers and archaeologists would have been shipped out, and replaced by specialists from Mount Weather.

At that point, the Nefilim would have been revived, using what had been learned over the last few months. But events had overtaken them already.

The ground shook.

Somewhere, something moved. The halogens tumbled and all but one of them went out, their filaments shattered.

Without warning, the obelisks exploded. Fragments of stone flew everywhere. One of the soldiers made a small, surprised sound as he disappeared beneath falling pieces of rock. Bisset expired without a sound, crushed against a wall by a collapsing pillar.

The General stepped back and drew his gun. He waited out of sight until the woman and the three remaining soldiers appeared, running towards the entrance.

He stepped in front of them. "Back in there." He leveled the gun and pointed it over their shoulders at the blackness behind them. "Now."

"But why… you saw…" The sergeant was bleeding from a gash in his forehead.

The General shot him, then pointed the gun at the others. "Do it now."

Silently, eyes wide, they edged back into the cavern. The explosions had stopped. Columns of shadow began moving among the piles of rubble, like dark searchlights shining down from the ceiling.

The panels in the walls disappeared, revealing banks of controls that pulsed with light in the same way that the designs on the rock faces had.

The columns of darkness began to move together.

Figures became visible in the dark mist. They were humanoid, but definitely – most definitely – not human. The General held his breath and took another step back.

The creatures were tall, with long gangling limbs. Their elongated skulls were devoid of hair, except for long strings of braids attached to the sides and the back that hung down over thin bony shoulders. Large coal-black eyes looked out from between heavy brows and hollow, bleached white cheeks.

The General knew that the same thing was happening at the three other locations around the world. All the signs had pointed towards this site being the key – the center – the revival of which would be the spark that brought the whole system to life.

He thought of calling Mount Weather, but decided against it. One thing at a time. It wouldn't do for things to get out of control. The General's superiors weren't famous for their tolerance of failure. The fate of his predecessor had been proof enough of that. He would get things in order here first.

The woman and the two soldiers were standing, stupefied, between the entrance and the nearest of the creatures. A low throbbing reverberated through the walls and the floor.

Kali is whimpering again. Shut up, thinks Bark. We've got enough to deal with. He looks around. Sahrin is watching calmly, but Onethian looks worried.

The creatures moved forwards. The three humans were frozen, gripped by some unseen force. Long fingers wrapped themselves around the woman and one of the soldiers and lifted them off the ground.

At that point, the spell that had been holding the remaining soldier seemed to break, and he turned and ran from the room, past the General. He stopped and turned. When he saw that the General had turned as well and was aiming his gun at him, he disappeared around the nearest corner, a bullet cracking the rock near his head.

Onethian, the example set for him, follows suit. This is too much for him. Physical dangers that he can understand are fine; he'll mix it with anyone. But this... he can't put a handle on it at all. Onethian, a traveler of much spine but little imagination, is out of here.

* * *

Bryce and Reina, descending into the caverns, marveled at what they saw. They gazed in silence, their mouths hanging open at the scale of the ruins.

The Senator's reaction is more specific. "Oh," *he says, recognizing the style.* "Nefilim… It has to be Nefilim."

He wishes he could tell the two locals about the Nefilim, and how their dark reputation has spread through the furthest reaches of space and time. But then, he thinks to himself (knowing that he is wrong), these are just old ruins, dead, cold, and there is nothing here except dust and dissolution. There's nothing at all for these people to worry about, and certainly nothing for him to worry about...

* * *

Meanwhile, Bark, Thead, Sahrin and Kali are feeling strange. Something is happening.

A wave passes through them all. They might not understand that anything has changed if the General was not staring at them. They have shifted frequencies, they realize instantly.

They are on the physical plane. Unheard of...

* * *

Suddenly, they were there…

The General saw four strangely dressed and confused people snap into existence a few feet from him. Everyone stood still, forgetting for a few seconds about the Nefilim.

The General came to his senses first. He turned his gun on the group. If he hadn't witnessed their unusual arrival, he would have killed them straight away.

"I don't know who you are, but right now it doesn't matter. All of you stay exactly where you are. I'll kill anyone who either interferes or moves. Got it?"

49

Bark nodded and said nothing.

The General took his phone from his belt and keyed Mount Weather. Screw waiting for anything. The small screen came to life as the UN logo appeared, and then faded away to reveal the face of the Secretary-General.

The fat face was contorted with rage. "What the hell is going on there? The monitors are down, we're getting no feedback at all from your site. And the process is starting ahead of time at the other sites! It's chaos; we'll be lucky if we can maintain control. What the fuck have you done?"

"My hand was forced, Secretary-General," the General said in his best voice. "The seal was breached as planned, but we couldn't close it off. Virtually everyone here is down, in some sort of coma. The creatures have arrived here, what about the oth—?"

"Yes, they have." The Secretary was sweating. "We'll have to make the best of it. Do they have what they need?"

"They have the two sacrifices. We were extremely lucky; there was a woman here, one of the scientists. They've taken her and a private. Is everything set in the other sites?"

"Yes, no thanks to you. You're pushing your luck on this one, General. But we'll discuss that later. Don't screw up again."

Shit. "I've got four uninvited guests here," he replied. "Are they anything to do with you?"

"No. If they're not with you, I don't know anything about them. Kill them." The Secretary-General closed the connection.

The General pointed his gun at the group.

"Now that wouldn't be a good idea at all," said Bark, not sure how far their new corporeality went, and how susceptible to bullets they would be.

"You might well think that," the General replied, and shot Kali.

Their physical status was established beyond all doubt. Kali was thrown against the wall and slid to the ground, thoroughly and completely dead, a small hole in his chest and a much larger one in his back. Blood spread into a pool on the ground beneath him.

Bark grabbed Sahrin by the arm and pulled her around the same corner that had saved the corporal.

The General swore. Pursuing them through the darkness was not an option.

Thead, too close to the General and his gun to consider the same maneuver, cowered back against the rock. He was trapped.

The General was about to send Thead the way of Kali when his potential victim had the brainwave that would not only save his life, but also open up a new career path for him.

"I can read their writing. I've studied it for many years," he blurted, gesturing towards the Nefilim, who were busy with an array of devices that had appeared from somewhere. "I'm fluent in it." At this point, Thead had not much else going for him.

The stranger knows something, the General thought, *and he's scared as well. He won't be trying anything.*

"You stay in sight," he said to Thead, who nodded vigorous agreement. "If you move – if you do *anything* – you're as dead as your friend there."

If this new arrival could in fact read the Nefilim writing, he might be useful. And delivering him to the Secretary-General would help the General's return to favor. If not, the stranger could always be executed.

Thead slid down the wall onto the floor. It was infinitely preferable to death, he reminded himself, sitting as he was only a few yards from the cooling corpses of Kali and the soldier.

The General turned his attention back to the chamber. There were at least a dozen of the creatures, and they had been busy.

The female archaeologist (whose name he had never bothered to learn and which now mattered to no one) and the equally nameless and hapless soldier had been placed on large stone slabs that had risen from the floor. The slabs and their occupants were surrounded by columns of intense silver light.

It was time to meet their new allies. He gestured with his gun to Thead, indicating that he should stand up and walk in front of him. Slowly, with an unwilling Thead in the lead, they entered the chamber.

Each of the humans was being attended by two of the Nefilim. They were having some sort of probes or terminals attached to their heads, their limbs, and their torsos. They weren't temporary, the General noticed. They were being inserted deep into the two bodies.

The subjects had been paralyzed. The only control they had was over their eyes, wide with panic and staring in terror at what was happening.

At each of the three other sites around the world, a male and female had been kept on hand for precisely this moment, and in the last few minutes they would have been delivered over to the Nefilim for this same procedure. The soldier and the woman were being wired into the Nefilim grid. The earth would once again pulse with the power that had maintained and invigorated it in distant times – except this time, the Nefilim would have an ally. The world's governments and the inhabitants of the distant past would be of much use to each other. Combined, they would be invincible; something which the uncooperative parts of the planet would soon come to appreciate.

Thinking this, the General felt invigorated as he stood among the Nefilim.

One of the creatures turned to him.

'You are early.'

"It was not something we could avoid. And surely not a problem?" His conditioning was working well. No sign of panic; he felt totally in control. The trickle of sweat running down the back of his neck was due to nothing more than the heat.

The Nefilim laughed, if you could call the sound that, as it tightened an attachment connected to a tube inserted into the thorax of the archaeologist. Her head twitched slowly in response. The Nefilim leaned over, making small clucking sounds, and tightened something. The twitching stopped.

'There is no problem,' it replied. *'You have done well. We will be able to work efficiently together, your species and ours. We hope*

that your race will last longer than our last... friends. But then, they didn't have the pragmatism of you humans. You have been watched, with great interest.'

The General wondered how these creatures could have known anything about humans if they had been in suspension for millennia, but this was not the time to be distracted by minor details. The connection of the two humans to the Nefilim grid was the important thing.

How his superiors had come to know that all this was going to happen he didn't know – he didn't want to know – but there had been whispers at headquarters of experiments with psychics and remote viewing, and a lot of work had gone into deciphering the strange inscriptions and diagrams that had been found at the other sites. They were methodical, the Nefilim – and their written language reflected the fact – but humanity was no less methodical.

The hows and whys were of no concern to the General. Get the two bodies plugged in, and get above ground, out of here, and wait for the reinforcements to arrive.

"What about my men?" he asked. "How long are they going to stay unconscious?"

'Perhaps forever. There is no way telling,' replied another of the Nefilim. *'There had to be some difference between the air of our time and that of yours. We can breathe almost anything, our history is long enough, but your race, it seems, has a more delicate constitution.'*

The General's skin prickled at the sight of the Nefilim's smile. Thin lips peeled back over flat teeth that curved back into the creature's mouth, like rows of tiny fishhooks.

It was at that point that the General realized that the Nefilim wasn't speaking. The pupils of its eyes, marble-small and red, were fixed on him, unwavering. It was using some kind of telepathy.

'Quite so,' the Nefilim answered the General's unvoiced question. *'Your own mind is doing the translating. Wherever possible, we prefer that others, you in this case, do the work...'*

One of the other Nefilim made a sound, which for no particular reason the General took to be their equivalent of laughter. "How long until you will be ready to start the grid?" he asked stiffly.

'The point of the alliance between our two races, yes,' replied the one that had been doing the talking – no, the thinking. 'Not long. Then we can all begin the real work.'

The real work… *Something else for later,* the General thought.

Various people meet each other.

Bryce and Reina, accompanied by the invisible Senator, could easily have encountered Onethian or the fleeing corporal as they found their separate ways through the maze of unexplored side tunnels, but they didn't. Their paths never crossed.

Onethian and the corporal did meet each other, though, near the compound's main gate. Onethian, out of breath and gasping, found Corporal Ortega sitting on some rocks not far from the gate, looking into the middle distance with a dazed look on his face.

Both being too disorientated to be scared of each other, and not at all sure what to do, they set off on the road towards Barker's Mill. In time they arrived at the Red Lion, where they got drunk.

* * *

Bark and Sahrin soon found themselves back in the main tunnel system. They were trying to decide what to do when they walked around a corner and into Bryce and Reina, who were making their way towards the source of the noises they could hear.

"Bark! Sahrin!" cries the Senator, overjoyed at the sight of them. Their new physicality, however, renders him invisible to them, so that Bark and Sahrin see only the two humans in front of them. The Senator fumes in frustration.

"Are you going to try to hurt us?" asked Bark.

"…because you'd better not," added Sahrin, doing her best to sound dangerous.

"Chill, whoever you are." Reina wondered who the two strangers were. She'd never seen clothes anything like what they were wearing. Whoever they were, they liked color, texture and accessorizing. And fur.

"As far as we know, we're safe to be around," said Bryce. "Which, I think, is more than can be said for *some* people around here." He pointed towards the depths of the tunnel, from where a low hum was audible. "We heard shots from down there somewhere."

"The Senator should be with these two," Sahrin said to Bark, looking around. "These are the locals we left on the hillside. There was another one of them as well."

"That would be Tommy," said Reina, "but you didn't leave us anywhere. We've never seen you before."

"I'm here!" cries the Senator, waving his hands in Bark's face. He tries to touch Bark on the shoulder, but his hand passes through him.

"Maybe he is, but we just can't see him," said Bark. "Remember, we've shifted, and we're physical now."

"Who are you talking about?" Bryce asked. "We were with a friend of ours, but he stayed on the surface."

"Never mind," Bark replied, realizing that they knew nothing about the Senator.

"One of your people has gone mad," said Sahrin, pointing down the cave. "The Nef… there are some creatures down there, and the people who have been occupying this place…" – Sahrin indicated the unconscious body of a soldier lying not far from them – "are responsible for bringing them here. One of our crew has just been killed, and another one is being held captive. A third one is missing, somewhere in these tunnels. And we left one watching the compound with you people. I don't suppose you've seen him?"

Bryce was impressed. "No, sorry, we haven't. Creatures… you mean, like, aliens? No shit… You guys aren't with the soldiers?"

"They're not from here, that's obvious," said Reina. "What's happening?"

"Later," said Bark. "I'll explain later."

* * *

The leader of the Nefilim stood in front of a wall covered with controls. Lights and shifting shapes danced around the images of another three of the creatures that had appeared in front of him.

They said nothing; they were using the same technique that had been used to communicate with the General.

The Nefilim seemed to come to some conclusion and ended their conference. One of them adjusted a control and the stone slabs that were supporting the humans descended back into the ground, leaving their occupants at floor level.

The rock beneath them shifted and became fluid. It started to claim them; first their limbs and then the rest of their bodies began to melt slowly into the floor. The General could tell by their eyes that they knew what was happening.

Good. He opened his cell phone and keyed the Secretary-General's number.

The fat man came on. He'd been drinking. "Aaah, General...." He chuckled happily.

The General had never liked the Secretary-General. He'd seen him drunk before, during the Turkish thing. He hoped it wasn't a sign that something had screwed up this time as well. "How are things going down there with our new friends? You haven't offended anyone, I hope?"

"No, Secretary, everything is going according to plan, apart from the slight inconvenience of me being totally alone here. All of my men are down, and according to the Nefilim, it could be permanent. I need replacements here immediately."

"Fine." The Secretary-General leaned closer, his bloodshot eyes staring directly into the camera. "We'll get some more men there in a couple of hours. Just a few at first, and better numbers later. But I want you back here on the first helicopter that gets there. Your new boys will be reliable, totally mindfucked, no security risk at all. As you'll be their new C.O.," – the General breathed a quiet sigh of relief – "they'll think you're God. What happened with your mysterious interlopers? Who were they?"

"I don't know, Secretary, but they've been neutralized." He wasn't about to admit that two of them had escaped. "One of them was interesting, though. He claims to have some knowledge of the Nefilim, so I'm bringing him back with me."

"As you wish." The SG was quite affable when he'd had a few. He should do it more often, the General realized. "Bring a couple of the Nefilim back with you, if they're agreeable. Tell them we need to meet personally. There are some decisions to make. I'm just sitting here having a drink with President Veal, we'd both like to say hello, wouldn't we, Helmut? Yes, of course we would. See what you can do, there's a good General…"

The Secretary-General reached forward and cut the connection, already turning, laughing, to continue his conversation with the President of Europe.

* * *

Bryce had been surprisingly hard to persuade, but descriptions of creatures with multiple rows of sharp teeth and coal-black eyes with glowing red pupils, combined with Bark's retelling of the General's capacity for immediate and terminal discipline, finally did the trick. They turned back towards the surface.

"I suppose that means we'll never get to see one of these creatures," Reina said.

"I'll draw you a picture," replied Bark impatiently.

"What about Thead?" broke in Sahrin.

"Yes, what about your friend?" asked Bryce. "You aren't going to leave him down there, are you?"

"Oh, yes, Thead," replied Bark, not sure that he wanted to be reminded. He cursed quietly to himself. They turned back, not at all sure what good they could do. The two locals, not about to be left alone, followed.

"Just as you should, without a doubt," fumes the Senator, who for some reason regards himself as the closest thing to a friend that Thead has got. Frustrated by his inability to talk to anyone, the Senator is beginning to feel alone, surrounded by the ghosts of the present.

* * *

The General noticed that Thead was getting active again, recovering from the stupor of terror that had been keeping him conveniently immobile. He gestured, telling Thead to come and stand where he could keep an eye on him.

Thead got to his feet and came over, not happy at lessening the distance between himself and the Nefilim. One of them sensed his fear and snarled, eyes flashing, thin lips sliding back over its teeth.

The General watched as the floor slowly claimed the soldier and the female archaeologist. After a few minutes, the only sign of them was a few irregularities in the rock surface. Finally the stone crept over them, like moss growing over something rotting on a forest floor. There was no trace at all left of the two victims.

A new, more urgent tone entered the sound that had been pulsing through the room. Visible aethers moved around the Nefilim as they communicated between themselves.

So this is how it is done, then, the General thought to himself.

So they're doing it again, Thead thought to himself, recalling the legends in which other races served as the catalysts for the Nefilim grids.

Thead could see from the General's face that he had never seen this before.

"Like a crystal, in a radio set," Thead said, moving closer. "Their energy will be used as a tuning device by their grid. I hope you've done some research on your new friends. It is never a good idea to enter into an agreement with an unknown quantity. Or that's how it is in most places I've visited. Perhaps you do things differently here." He was prattling. He stopped when he saw the General's face darken.

The General didn't reply, but he understood what Thead meant.

The lines of energy and force that covered the planet's surface formed a geometric pattern of finely tuned links, each of which was allocated a function in the grid. This was the source of the mythology surrounding ley lines, sites of power and gravity anomalies. Sometimes there was some science involved, but usually it was too heavily rooted in folklore to mean much.

But this was the real thing. As Thead had said, the life forces of the victims would act like crystals, focusing the earth's raw energy and sending it, in a purified and concentrated form, to other points on the grid. Other points would become communication nodes, and yet others would monitor and survey, refine and redirect.

In short, the demands of a power structure, both political and physical, would be met with ease.

Over time, the influence of the eight victims, two in each of the four sites, would dissipate, like batteries going flat, and they would need to be replaced, the whole ceremony being re-enacted. And thus, the General reflected, was born, among all the races that the Nefilim had dominated, the copycat ritual of sacrifice; the necessity of providing the earth a yearly offering of blood and life energy.

He remembered that the Secretary-General wanted to see some Nefilim. He went to the one that, for want of better instruction, he regarded as their leader, and passed on the request for a meeting. The Nefilim studied him for a few seconds, as if seeking information from his physical appearance, then accepted.

He made sure that the creature knew that more soldiers were on the way. For some reason, it made him feel better.

* * *

The General led his party straight to the surface, expecting the helicopters to arrive at any moment. As it was, they were late, and it would be an hour before the black shapes came floating over the horizon like dark wasps, hugging the treetops.

Thead used the time to think. There could be a career opportunity here if he played it right. The natives were obviously bent on making some sort of deal with the Nefilim.

It was a new angle, he had to admit. Over the years, he'd heard of different ways of dealing with them, but an alliance of equals was a new one. Maybe there was more to these humans than met the eye. Or less. They were either very smart or very stupid.

He was sure that he didn't like the General, who was far too rough for a scientist and intellectual such as Thead. Still, for the sake of science, you do what you must do, he thought. No sacrifice is too great.

He hoped he wouldn't have too much direct contact with the Nefilim, who had a habit, he'd heard, of not distinguishing between their friends and their enemies. Whatever. Science and scholarship, they were the main things... he had responsibilities to truth and knowledge. He was above politics.

'*You may well be above politics...*'

The words leapt from nowhere into Thead's mind. He started, his heart jumping. He looked around and saw the glowing eyes of one of the Nefilim mocking him. Thead felt disconsolate at the thought that he didn't know how long he had been the object of the creature's attention.

'*But I shouldn't worry,*' the voice in his head continued. '*Someone will find a job for you.*'

Thead said nothing and looked away.

Sahrin goes exploring,
and finds some company.

Below ground, they had arrived at the area where the Nefilim had appeared. Sahrin stayed near the entrance to the chamber, keeping watch in case anyone came down the tunnels.

The floor was carpeted with shards of broken rock. Whatever substance had covered the arrays of controls had peeled off the walls like paint blistering in heat, and slumped onto the floor in pools of slime.

The room was empty. The Nefilim had gone, as were the corpses of Kali and the sergeant. There were marks in the dust, left by their heels as they had been dragged away. The trails disappeared into the darkness, into which Sahrin looked uncertainly.

In the chamber, the control panels, still alive, flickered coldly. There was no movement and no sign of life.

"What's all this about?" Reina asked, looking in wonder at the hieroglyphs and lights.

"This room contains the mechanisms with which the Nefilim control their energy system," Bark answered. "As for why they would want to do that, we definitely don't have time to go into that, except to say that it's in their nature. There's no sign of Thead here. He was here with one of your soldiers and some of the Nefilim when we left. I'd guess that he's most likely with them now."

"They're not *our* soldiers. Who are the Nefilim?" Bryce asked.

"Can we do this later?" Bark had become impatient. "Or am I alone here in having an appreciation of the immediate danger of our present situation?"

Having satisfied themselves that Thead was nowhere in the chamber, they went back to the breached entrance where they had left Sahrin.

She was gone. Her footprints led off into the darkness, in the same direction as the scuff marks left by the transport of the two bodies.

Bark swore softly. "Marvelous, this is just marvelous. We'll have to go after her…"

* * *

Sahrin had gone in search of the source of the noise.

It was the faintest of sounds, quite distinct from the humming that was coming from somewhere in the chamber. It was muffled by the turns of the winding tunnels and walls of heavy rock, but it had still been loud enough to catch her attention.

She knew she should have called the others, but something stopped her. Whether or not that something was just stupidity would remain a point of debate for some time. She edged her way along a wall, following its turns through the darkness. Something glowed ahead of her. As the wall veered to the left, the source of the light came into view.

She was at one end of a long cavern. In row upon row of cubicles, she saw creatures, scores of them, lined up in transparent coffins, like corpses awaiting burial. She edged closer, her surroundings now visible in the pale green glow that came, she saw now, from the containers that housed the bodies.

Rows of the cubicles receded into the distance. There was movement among the ranks of sepulchered bodies.

One of the Nefilim was moving along the aisles. It was working methodically through the ranks of its immobile companions, operating controls, repeating the same movements each time. Then she saw another of the creatures, and a few seconds later a third, all engaged in the same activity.

They were moving away from her as they worked. When she thought it was safe, she moved out of the shadows, and crept towards the nearest of the bodies.

It looked like a monstrous, premature infant in its incubator. Some kind of tape had been wrapped around the torso and head, making the creature look like a half-completed mummy. The ends of the tape were attached to terminals at the foot of the sarcophagus.

They did have a certain nobility, and it wasn't just because of their height, she thought. The creature's head was larger than a human head, and covered with pale leathery skin stretched taut over high cheekbones and wide temples. Its eyes were shut. She looked closely, noticing the almost imperceptible rise and fall of the creature's chest. Its breathing was slow and slight, barely happening at all.

Then she saw that the tape that was wrapped around its body was moving, almost imperceptibly, like a slow flatworm. She leaned closer. It seemed to be alive. It was using some kind of peristaltic motion, gradually inching its way around the alien's body. Perhaps there was some symbiotic relationship at work here. A parasite/host thing.

She was standing with her face only a foot or so from the entombed creature's head when two things happened at once.

Inside the case, the creature's eyes snapped open without warning. It breathed out loudly, made a high-pitched squealing sound, and turned its head towards her.

At the same time, outside the sarcophagus, the Nefilim that had quietly come up behind her, seeing that the motion of its waking companion would scare her and send her running, quickly reached out and placed a heavy hand on one of her shoulders and another over her mouth.

A shriek died in her throat as she realized instantly that there was no point in alerting the other Nefilim to her presence, if that had not already been done. Besides which, the hand over her mouth was irresistibly strong.

She knew even before she was turned around that the owner of the powerful grip wasn't human; the pressure on her shoulders was entirely alien, like needles that wanted to break her skin.

'*Be quiet.*'

The message came into her mind softly, as though the Nefilim was trying not to alarm her. It bent forward, lowering its face towards hers.

'*You are in no danger from me. The only immediate danger to you is from the others of my kind who are here. And perhaps this one.*'

The Nefilim reached behind Sahrin and did something to a control on the side of the case. She heard a brief scuffle of movement, and then silence.

"What are you going to do to me?" she whispered.

'*No harm. For now, you must trust me, even though you know nothing of me, apart from what you think you know of my race. Both of us are in danger as long as we remain here. Now please, come with me.*'

The creature turned and walked into the darkness.

It had not been threatening; there might even have been a pleading tone in the words that had appeared in her head. In any event, given her present situation, she seemed to have little choice but to go along with it, for the moment at least.

She looked around, and saw no sign of the route that had brought her here. She followed the creature, stumbling through the gloom to catch up.

Once they were some distance down the tunnel that the Nefilim led her into, her eyes became accustomed to a soft gray light that seemed to come from the walls. It was a narrow passageway, and apart from the smooth and level floor, it seemed to be natural. Cave moss clung to the walls. Something brushed against her face and buzzed lazily away.

'*I should return to my friends,*' she thought at the Nefilim's back.

'*That is not possible right now,*' came the reply.

She was being led deeper into the earth, down gradients that became steeper as they went, through tunnels that soon became even more rough and narrow. The artifacts that she'd seen in the tunnels above were no longer in evidence. These tunnels appeared were purely functional, only to be used if you were going somewhere.

Finally, the Nefilim stopped in front of a bare piece of wall and touched it in three different places. The surface dropped away to reveal another tunnel, bathed in the same gray light. *Secrets?* she wondered. *From who? From the locals? Or do they have secrets among themselves?*

The Nefilim turned and looked at her. '*A few.*'

They entered the tunnel. Sahrin made no more attempts at conversation, vocal or otherwise.

Good morning.

Bark, Bryce and Reina had followed Sahrin's footprints, and were gazing in silence at the rows of unconscious giants. The glow cast from the coffins bathed the whole scene in an eerie light, from which they sheltered in the same shadows that Sahrin had relied on.

Bark was whispering to the other two. "I doubt that these are corpses. They are probably asleep, and nearing the end, I suspect, of a long rest. This is probably not the only place on this planet where this is happening. We should be careful."

The light from the coffins had grown brighter. In the distance, a group of Nefilim ascended a staircase and disappeared through a door.

They heard a sound, or felt a vibration, it was impossible to tell. It seemed to come from the walls themselves. The occupant of one of the closest cabinets stirred suddenly. The Nefilim lifted its hands to its face, and lurched over onto its side. It tried to lift itself up onto its elbows, but it seemed to lack co-ordination and fell back, its limbs moving slowly as though it was a newborn baby.

There was movement in the other chambers. Long limbs stirred slowly, then their actions became more coordinated as the inhabitants became aware of their surroundings and began to orientate themselves.

Without warning, the cabinets filled with clouds of gas.

As quickly as the gas arrived, it cleared. The top of each pod slid back, exposing the inhabitants to the air.

As the Nefilim emerged from their long sleep, the three intruders, without concurring and without hesitation, turned and disappeared back into the shadows of the tunnel they had come down. For now at least, Sahrin was out of reach, and would have to look after herself.

PART 2

Welcome to Mount Weather.

The helicopters flew along the water's edge, following the curve of the coastline. The beach below would have made an ideal holiday resort, were it not for its isolation. Although part of the North American mainland, it was guarded at its various edges by the sea, mountain ranges, and an intractable stretch of desert.

At a point halfway along the length of the undulating ribbons of white sand, the helicopters turned away from the ocean and headed inland, following the path of a stream that flowed towards the sea.

They were heading for Mount Weather. A huge complex carved out of the interior of an old volcano, it was the operational headquarters of the United Nations. Military, scientific, and communication facilities were maintained by a resident population of more than nine thousand. It was the site of the world's real government, even though the world's population didn't even know it existed.

Mount Weather soon appeared among the clouds. One by one, the helicopters descended into a crevice halfway up its northern face. Along one of the rock faces that were formed by the incision in the mountain's side, hidden under heavy brows of overhanging rock, were arranged a dozen or so landing sites, each one large enough to accommodate several of the helicopters. Arc lights illuminated the landing areas, leaving the depths of the chasm below lost in darkness.

The helicopters landed in front of a group of waiting officers and civilians. Guards surrounded the area.

An overweight, over-jowled man in a finely tailored suit was waiting among the officers. It was the Secretary-General himself.

"General," he said warmly – half a bottle of gin's worth of warmth – as he came across to meet the group. He was accompanied by the President of Europe, who kept glancing nervously in the direction of one of the other helicopters. The two

Nefilim were crossing the landing area towards the group.

"Are they sociable, General?" asked the Secretary-General, lowering his voice. "You've had more exposure to them than I have... are they easy to deal with?"

"They're... *alien*. Don't expect it to be like talking to any human you've ever met. And they can read your..." The arrival of the Nefilim cut him short.

'...mind. We can indeed. And you will find us firm, but fair, I think is a phrase that you might understand, Secretary-General.'

The creature spoke to its companion. Their speech was a thin rasping sound, with none of the resonance of their telepathic communication. It was hard to listen to.

"As you can see, Secretary-General," the General persisted, not caring whether they heard him, "our guests appear to possess the ability to read minds, and they can communicate directly with us on that level as well."

The Secretary-General nodded and reached up to offer his hand to the two creatures. They seemed to know what was required and offered theirs in return. *The first physical contact,* the General mused.

'Not quite the first.'

The thought appeared in his brain, and he realized that the second Nefilim was looking at him again. He turned away. He was beginning to develop a dislike for them.

Later, in the hallway outside the offices of the Security Council, Thead was shown – as one parades a slave or a horse in front of a prospective buyer – to the Secretary-General. Thead's red and white overalls and collection of earrings dangling from one ear combined to convince the Secretary-General that he was some sort of freak.

"Oh, Jesus. Have him questioned. Get everything he knows," the Secretary-General sniffed, and turned away towards the Council chambers, where the two Nefilim were waiting.

A pair of guards led Thead through the labyrinth of corridors.

"I hope they know what they're doing," Thead said to the

stone-faced soldier next to him.

The guard said nothing.

An alliance.

Several thousand miles away, Bark, Reina and Bryce stood at the top of a sand hill, looking up into the sky. Bark had just told them that the ship was moored above them.

"Where?" Bryce and Reina both asked, squinting into the sky, seeing nothing.

"Just above these trees," Bark replied, feeling better now that they were above ground. He pointed to a group of pines on a small plateau of rock.

Bryce and Reina looked up beyond the tops of the trees, but there was nothing to see except a glimmer of light in the atmosphere, which might have been something. Or not.

Bark reached out and held onto something. "Like this," he said, and swung himself upwards. He began climbing, supported by nothing. A few feet above the ground, he started to flicker, then disappeared.

"No shit!" Bryce went to the spot where Bark had been standing and felt around in the air.

His hands encountered something that swayed under his touch. It startled him for a moment, feeling something that he couldn't see, but he soon deduced from Bark's actions and the texture of what he could feel that it was nothing more sinister than a rope ladder. He took a firm grip on one of the rungs and swung himself up.

"It's OK," he said to Reina, before he disappeared. She watched in silence for a few seconds, took a deep breath, and followed.

As they climbed, the ladder gradually became visible. By the time Bark disappeared over the side of the ship, Bryce could see the dark underside of its hull. He looked down at Reina. They both shrugged their shoulders and continued.

Bark was waiting on the deck. He took Reina by the arm and helped her over the railing.

"Welcome… and what do we have here?"

The Senator was climbing up the ladder behind Reina, grumbling to himself and to anyone who cared to listen. The group's failure at finding Sahrin was still bothering him, and his experience with invisibility, temporary though it was, had not helped his temper. He communicated his feelings on both matters to Bark. At length.

"I suppose you were there when the Nefilim were revived," Bark sighed when the Senator finally finished. "You would have to agree, wouldn't you, that our options at the time were limited?"

The Senator reluctantly grumbled something approaching agreement, and reached into his pouch for a bindoo leaf. He sat down heavily on one of the ceramic converters near the base of the main mast.

"I'm Senator... oh, never mind," he said to Bryce and Reina, who were looking confused. "And you two are locals. You must have had an interesting day." The bindoo was already painting a glaze over his eyes.

"We sure have." They nodded agreement, but their attention was already turning to the ship.

Whatever its position might be in the pantheon of space-going vessels, the ship was a mess. It had been added to relentlessly over the ages, with cabins and decks and masts attached at random, so that they protruded in all directions. It was a floating maze. What little of the original deck that was left was littered with furniture and effects, as if the crew were accustomed to living outdoors. The contents of the hold were bursting from the hatches. Some of the crates had been opened, and their contents gone through.

"Mmm... ok... this is a relaxed looking place," said Reina.

"Well, we are relaxed about most things," replied Bark. He looked over the rail, half expecting to find that they had been followed. Satisfied that they hadn't, he turned back to his guests.

"As you might have guessed, we're not from your world. Some might call us aliens, but actually we're more what you might call distant relatives."

"Relatives?"

"Well, as you can see, there's no physical difference between us. We are just from a different place, and slightly better traveled as well, that would be right, wouldn't it, Senator?"

The Senator hummed happily in agreement. "Oh yes, we get around, all right." He offered Bryce a strip of Bindoo. Bryce took it and started chewing.

"Do you know what's going on?" Reina asked Bark. "Why all the excavations and drama with the soldiers? And what were those creatures, the ones you call Nefilim? Whatever's going on, it must be serious if people are getting iced."

Bark weighed his options for a few seconds. "Why don't you come with us? In fact, you should come with us. Yes. I could use the help, as you can see…" He gestured towards the Senator, who had retreated into a world of his own. He was nicely relaxed, adding to his notebook of speeches that would never be given.

"I can't sail the ship on my own, and I'll explain on the way."

Reina thought about the vegetable deliveries she was supposed to make the following day. She couldn't see how there was much contest.

"Sure. How long will we be?"

"What do you mean?" asked Bark, releasing the anchor and gesturing to her to help him wind it in.

What the hell. Reina began winding and forgot to reply.

Thead's career path opens up.

In the depths of the Mount Weather complex, Thead's interview had gone well. They had gone now, leaving him alone in a room containing nothing but a table, a few chairs, and a camera that stared unblinkingly down at him.

He had told them everything he knew and, not wanting to leave any room for doubt, a few things he didn't as well. They had listened intently and asked questions as he described the ship, the crew and their travels. He told them how they had been guided to Earth by the map. They had shown great interest as Thead told them how the ship sailed through time as well as space.

When they had finished, they took their notes and their recorder, and told him nothing. A guard brought him something to drink. It was hot, and tasted bitter and sweet at the same time. It made Thead's head rush. He liked it, of course.

He waited patiently, idly wondering about what had happened to the others, when the door opened and a pair of guards walked in.

"You're in luck, freak. He wants to see you."

"You don't want to know what the other option was," the other one added. "Now move it."

They led Thead through long and identical corridors until they reached an elevator. A few seconds later they emerged into a foyer more plush than the bare functionality that Thead had seen so far. They stopped in front of a secretary, who spoke briefly into a headset and then nodded at the guards.

Through a heavy hardwood door, Thead found himself in the presence of the Secretary-General, the President of Europe, the General, and a few others whose jobs seemed to consist of hovering.

"Please sit down, Mister Thead." The Secretary-General nodded towards a seat in front of his desk.

Thead sat.

"Your story is an impressive one." The Secretary-General tapped the recorder sitting on the desk in front of him. "You are either mad or a liar – and about to get a bullet in the back of your head in either case – or you are a young man with some interesting career prospects. What do you think?" He sat back in his seat, fat rippling, and waited for an answer.

Thead's heart raced at the idea that the white lies he had used to decorate his stories might be found out. "Everything I've told your men is just as it is. I have much experience."

"That may be so. Do you know who I am?"

"Not really, I must admit," replied Thead. "Every place in the universe, planets and otherwise, has its own way of doing things. But I assume that you are a person with authority. And that your opinion matters."

The President of Europe sniggered. He was thin, with a long face and slight, shifting eyes that could never hope to conceal his sycophantic nature. "Oh, ze Secretary-General's opeenion matters, all right."

"Yes, thank you, President Veal," the Secretary-General interrupted. "Why don't you pour us all a drink, Helmut."

The President went to a cabinet at the side of the room and started sorting through bottles.

"President Veal is a trusted ally of mine, and I very much value his assistance in keeping the various autonomous regions of Europe in line. But you don't need to know that, Mister Thead. All you need to know is that I am the Secretary-General of the United Nations, and therefore what I say goes. Conditional upon the approval of the Security Council, of course." He looked in the President's direction and both men smiled.

"Of course, Secretary-General," said Thead. "Order is a necessary component in any society. This is something that I've found to be true in every place I've visited," he lied.

"Have you now? Well, you can leave the sociology to us." The Secretary-General took the glass that Veal was offering him.

Thead picked up the drink that had been put in front of him.

He sipped the dark amber liquid and felt a burning taste in his mouth, which he liked instantly. His pleasure increased when the warm sensation extended to his stomach.

"We've gathered from what you said to the officers downstairs that you do indeed seem to know something about our new friends. Some of it supports what we already know. The rest, if it is true, is interesting indeed. Such information, of course, is welcome at any time, but especially so now, given the… well, innovative nature of our relationship with the Nefilim." The Secretary-General paused to adjust his bulk in his chair. "We've decided to put you on probation. Let's see how you go. I'll be watching, of course."

Which was what Thead had been waiting to hear. That, or something equally reassuring.

"Of course, gentlemen." Thead made sure he got in some subservient eye contact with President Veal as well as the Secretary-General. "You can rely on me, Secretary-General. Don't worry."

The Secretary-General laughed. "Oh, I'm not worried. Now, you can accompany the General on a little mission he has to undertake. He will explain all the details to you. I'm not really a details person, Thead. I'm more inclined towards the big picture. The grand strategy, if you like. History. I'll look forward to seeing you again. One way or the other. You can go now. The General will show you the way."

The General stepped towards the door. "Come with me," he said flatly, not bothering to look in Thead's direction.

They took some elevators and walked in deliberate silence along more featureless corridors until they came to a large room with no windows. There was a whiteboard on one wall, and benches arranged in rows. On the benches sat thirty to forty serious and fit-looking young men and women in full battle dress, waiting for something to happen.

The General went to the front of the room and started talking.

They were going to a place that the UN had only just found

out about, and they needed to be ready for anything. They had learned of its existence from the two Nefilim who had spent the last few hours with the Security Council. It hadn't been scouted, and no one knew what to expect. The place was some kind of navigation or communication center, and the Nefilim wanted to be taken there. They said it was important.

These soldiers were the General's special boys and girls, which was why he was telling them everything. Totally reliable, totally conditioned, they were his pride and joy, his Praetorian Guard. They fought like hell and he could rely on them in any situation.

Thead suspected that he knew the place that the General was talking about.

It had been common practice, for as long as the history of the universe had been recorded, for there to be on every planet a place that could be used as a way station. A cross between a first aid post and a command center, it contained facilities for navigation and communication, as well as a place of refuge for weary or endangered travelers. In a variable universe, the Pilots' Stations were beacons of stability.

It wasn't surprising that the Nefilim knew about the station, even though they almost certainly hadn't built it. As for the fact that they knew where it was; that was interesting as well, but if they had maintained some sort of presence on this planet for a long time, Thead thought, it was logical that they should know what went on here.

The General had started talking logistics. The talk got technical, and Thead's mind drifted forward, to a panorama of possible futures that was somehow simultaneously dark and glittering. He didn't understand any of the talk, and there was not much point in trying. He let it continue, unattended by the profound depth of his understanding.

The briefing finished, and the soldiers collected their equipment and filed out of the room. Thead followed them to one of the landing pads.

Five sleek black helicopters sat in a row, facing the dark interior of the volcano. They were stylish machines, Thead thought, the way they were slung close to the ground, with their sinuous black curves, and the tasteful, rhythmic arrangement of their rows of cannons and lasers.

"What's down there?" Thead asked the soldier next to him. He pointed towards the edge of the landing pad, where it gave way to the darkness of the pit.

"No one who goes down there comes back," the soldier replied. "Only bad people ever see the bottom of the pit," he laughed. A couple of soldiers standing nearby joined in.

The flight crews were waiting beside the helicopters. Like their machines, they wore no markings or insignia, just plain black. Thead looked around at the soldiers and saw that they too had no markings on their uniforms.

The General came up to him. "You travel with me. I want to keep an eye on you. Let me down, and you're in trouble. Here." He handed Thead a pistol. "We may as well see if you know how to handle one of these."

Thead took the gun out of its holster and weighed it in his hand, enjoying the feel of its solidity and the immediate sense of purpose that it gave him. He'd never had much to do with weapons, but if it would help his career as an intellectual and a scientist, he would happily acquaint himself with whatever hardware was necessary. He strapped the holster around his waist.

The two Nefilim had arrived, escorted by some MPs. They climbed into a helicopter and sat waiting.

The General's cell phone buzzed at him. He answered, listened without speaking, and then put the phone back in his pocket. He was angry.

"Shit! Fucking shit!" he said quietly to himself, but within earshot of Thead.

"What is it?" asked Thead, who had yet to learn that here a subordinate only spoke to a superior when spoken to, or when there was a good reason.

The General looked at him coldly, but replied anyway. "We're going to be accompanied by the Vice-Secretary Gores. Both of them," he snarled, then walked away.

Thead's imagination didn't have much time to exercise itself on the matter of who the two Vice-Secretaries might be. A few seconds later, a jeep came careering noisily onto the landing deck. It screeched to a halt and a man and a woman jumped out.

"That'll do boy, you get on back, now," the one who had been driving said to a private who was sitting in the back, gripping the edge of the seat with white knuckles.

"Now there's no need to go all troppo, boy. Just know a driving lesson when you see it, that's all," the man laughed as the youth clambered into the driver's seat and drove slowly away.

So these must be the Vice-Secretaries Gore.

They both wore full dress uniforms, as though they were about to attend a formal parade. They were obviously twins. Average height, no more than forty years old, round cherubic faces topped with sandy-colored hair and punctuated with green eyes that sparkled, bright and friendly, taking in everything with a childlike enthusiasm, free from any taint of conscience.

"And you must be… the… neyoo… boy," said the female Gore, accentuating every word so that the sentence seemed to become some kind of joke. She grabbed Thead's hand between both of hers and shook it vigorously.

"Welcome to the only team in town, Thead, what sort of a goddamn name is that? Never mind boy, we're just here to do the lord's work, aren't we now, Theo?"

"Damn right, Alexis, damn right," the other Vice-Secretary replied. "Why don't the new boy come with us? C'mon boy, come in our chopper. We might find some interest in such a forinner as yourself. Ain't that so, Alexis?"

"Damn right, brother."

"Thead is traveling with me," said the General, who had been pointedly ignored by both Vice-Secretaries.

"Is he now? Oh well, boy, you just have a good time with the old man," said the male Gore, winking in Thead's direction.

"Where's our baby?" The sister was looking around for something.

"Isn't she here..? Our baby is not here?" Vice-Secretary Theo's face turned red and his voice lifted to a screech. His eyes were beginning to bulge when the General, to whom this was nothing new, and who knew the value of cutting their temper tantrums off at the pass, spoke up.

"Relax. Your helicopter is on its way. It had to go down for a refit after the last thrashing you gave it." He sounded exasperated. "You should try to be a little more careful. These are expensive machines. And delicate. You should use one of the pilots."

"But flying is just such a spiritual experience for us, General," Vice-Secretary Alexis smiled beatifically.

Her brother's face had retreated back down the color scale. "Well we'll just have to stand ... here ... and ... wait ... won't ... we ..?"

"Oh, there now, boy," she massaged her brother's shoulders. "The ol' avengin' machine'll be here real soon."

At that moment the whine of an approaching motor heralded the end of the scene. The General muttered gratitude under his breath.

A helicopter appeared beyond the edge of the landing pad, swimming up from one of the levels below. It was smaller than the other machines, with an even sleeker form. It was painted a multitude of shades of red, like an angry insect. Directional turbines and a double row of heatseekers were slung discretely beneath the fuselage.

"Aah, baby," cooed the Vice-Secretaries as the pilot saw them and maneuvered in to land.

"Christ," muttered the General, gesturing his soldiers on to the helicopters. "Whenever you're ready," he said in the Vice-Secretaries' direction, not caring whether they heard him or not.

A few minutes later they flew away from Mount Weather, across the rain forest and then a desert that stretched beyond several horizons.

Thead was puzzled by the scene at the landing pad. "Who are the two in the red helicopter?"

The General was more talkative now than he had been on the ground. "Theodore and Alexis Gore. The two Vice-Secretaries of the Standing Committee of the United Nations. They're id… extremely eccentric. I would suggest that you don't upset them. They're very tight with the Secretary-General. Don't upset him, either. Or me, for that matter," he added, as an afterthought.

They continued the journey in silence, Thead wondering only slightly less than the others what they would find at the Pilot's Station.

The Pilot's Station.

The currents on this planet suited the ship well. They were making good time.

Reina and Bryce kept quiet until they were well underway, but once the course was set, they started with their questions. First Bark told them how he, the Senator, and the rest of the crew had come to their planet.

The two locals sat and listened with such open-mouthed attention that Bark couldn't resist throwing in a few adventure stories from his travels.

By the time he was ready to deal with the matter of their destination, it was dark, and they were sailing high above a black sea shot through with glittering phosphorous. The breeze had stayed warm, and Bark had taken a bottle of something old and expensive from the hold.

"Every planet has a Pilot's Station." He filled their glasses.

He was holding the map that had led them here. Concentrating hard, he studied it in the light of an oil lamp, trying to remember what Thead had told him, piecing together the few symbols that he knew or could decipher. Helped by the fact that he knew what he was looking for, it wasn't long before he found it, in some highlands on a peninsula between two larger land masses.

It meant nothing to Reina when he showed her. "So what's in this place that we need to see?"

"Convention requires that every vessel that visits a place must register its passage with the Pilot who has been assigned there. It is his job to keep a log of the comings and goings of ships and other vessels, but that is not his only function. He also collects information about the planet, from travelers and from any other sources that he can, so that anyone wanting assistance or guidance can usually do no better than to start at the Pilot's Station. If there is something to be known, the chances are that the Pilot will know it."

"You mean there will be someone there?"

"There might be. There should be. I don't know, really. The Stations are supposed to be maintained continuously, so for as long there is a station, there should be someone there. It depends on how well-traveled these parts of time and space are. If there's someone there, we should be able to get some answers."

"Answers to what questions, exactly?"

That was a good question in itself, Bark had to admit. "We need to know what the Nefilim are up to," he said, sounding more confident than he felt, "and we should also find the best place to start looking for Sahrin."

"Wasn't there another member of your crew? Onethian? Was that his name? What about him?"

"Ha! Yes, Onethian. He ran away. He can take his chances wherever he likes." Bark was quite happy to be rid of him. The antipathy between them had its origin back in the time when Onethian had been the ship's captain, and in the reasons behind his replacement by Bark. That, however, was another story, and not one for the moment.

In the space of a few hours, Bryce's liking for bindoo leaf had become a character trait. He was still chewing on it. "Do yink thu ... d'th ... d'you think we'll find this Sharon woman of yours?"

The Senator and he had strung a couple of hammocks up in the rigging. The Senator had found the whole day rather tiring and had dropped off to sleep, a blank piece of paper in one hand and a newly sharpened pencil in the other.

Bryce relaxed into a bindoo-induced reverie, during which he maintained a conversation of sorts with Reina and Bark, but kept his eyes turned towards the black masses of the clouds as they floated past the ship. Or as the ship floated past them. Bryce was trying to work out which.

"It's *Sahrin*. Who knows?" Bark's mind went back to the caves beneath the sand dunes, Sahrin's footprints in the dust, and the rows of Nefilim they had seen. "I hope so. I hope she comes back."

"Are you a couple?" Reina asked.

"Oh, no. Well, *once*, after too much of this." Bark nodded at the bottle they were drinking from. They talked a while more, and slowly drifted off to sleep, so gradually that none of them could be sure when they stopped talking.

* * *

When they woke, it was late morning, and the sun was well into its journey through the sky. The clouds of the previous night had passed, leaving the sky empty and blue in every direction.

As the day progressed, the desert below them gave way to dense vegetation. They took the ship down so that they were sailing only a few mast heights above the treetops. Brilliantly colored parrots and large dark monkeys with flashes of gold and white in their fur darted around in the foliage.

Bark and the Senator had never seen anything like it.

"It's beautiful," said the Senator.

Bark had been considering other matters.

"As Captain of this vessel, it's my duty to oversee the appearance of my crew. Temporary you may be, but crew you are, nevertheless. As your Captain, I feel obliged to point out that your clothes are dirty, bordering on unpleasantly aromatic, and by far worst of all, they lack any style whatsoever. So unless it's against your religion, I would like to see you outfitted with new and more suitable attire."

"Well... sure, I guess."

"Yeah? Whatever..."

"Senator, would you mind showing the crew to the wardrobe?"

"So you're really a Senator then?" asked Reina as they went below deck.

"I was, and I would be now, if there was any justice; I would still have my seat in the Senate." The Senator had become grim, his lips pinched into lines as thin as lemon rinds. This was not a line of conversation to be pursued, obviously.

He opened a door in a corner of the bunkroom. It led into

a smaller room overflowing with clothes. They were piled on shelves, hung on hangers and hooks, packed into drawers. There wasn't an inch of room to spare.

"Overkill," said Bryce.

"It's like a theater, isn't it," said Reina.

"A what?" asked the Senator.

"A theater. A place where people make believe, where they agree to help each other pretend to do things and to be people they're not," Reina replied.

"People do it for fun, among other things," added Bryce, sorting through a rack of shirts. "It's part of what we call culture."

"Oh," said the Senator, losing interest.

Reina started looking through a row of flowing ankle-length dresses. The Senator reached out to stop her.

"Not practical. Fine for deck wear on a day of leisure, but we don't know where we'll be or what we'll be doing. Leggings, a short skirt, or maybe shorts, and something warm for your top, a jacket like this one here, here we are, this is you…" He reached into a closet and pulled out a jacket which was made of something similar to wool, but had the sheen of silk as well. Dark green and black stripes started wide at the bottom, and became thinner as they went up, so that by the time they had reached the shoulders, they were so fine that to the casual glance they seemed to have merged into a single color.

"Done," said Reina, slipping into the jacket.

When they emerged an hour later, they had been totally refitted. As well as the jacket, Reina had chosen a loose top with a stylized paisley design in blue and black, and black tights, over which she wore a short skirt made of some clear material that felt like silk. She had finished the outfit off with a pair of lace-up boots with sensible heels.

Bryce was wearing a shapeless pair of black trousers and a gray top. Around his waist, he had tied a belt studded with colored gems arranged in the shapes of skulls and other bones. He had wanted to take a pair of shoes that matched it, but Reina wouldn't let him, so he went for a pair of boots similar to hers.

He wouldn't accept any argument, though, over his choice of jacket. It was deep blue, waistcoat length, and adorned with braids and insignia that meant nothing to him. The back and the lower halves of the sleeves were covered in beads and gems. He had to have it.

"It's a theater prop," laughed Reina.

"Oath it is. But a good one," he retorted, determined that the shoes were going to be his only compromise.

They went back up onto the deck. Bark was at the wheel. "Much better! I approve. Now, look there."

They looked, and saw a mountain of bare rock looming in front of them. Its top was lost in mist, and its foundations were lost in the jungle.

"The Pilot's Office is somewhere there."

"They're not worried about catching the pedestrian traffic, are they," said Bryce.

"How do we find it?" Reina asked. They both pulled their new jackets around them. The air was getting cold.

"Pilot's Offices are always marked by a particular symbol. Depending on the terrain, it can be inscribed in any of a number of ways, but it will be visible from the air and at a distance, you can be sure of that. Look for anything that resembles a spider. It might be a sculpture, a carving, or even part of the landscape. But it will be obvious."

The ship rose as Bark steered it into a course that would take it around the mountain. Dwarfed by its scale, Reina thought that they must look like insects as they passed in front of the great slabs of rock and the cracks and chasms that corrugated its surface. The air grew still colder as the mist gathered in around them.

With Bark at the helm and the other three leaning over the side looking for a spider, they had almost completed a full circuit of the mountain when a cloud of fog shifted in a sudden gust of wind.

Bryce saw it first and called out. Then they all saw it, carved into the rock, fifty or sixty feet high, near the top of a cliff face.

Eight legs, four pointing up and four down, and a small head at the top of a large bulbous body, with antlers or mandibles protruding from it, had been carved deeply into the rock.

"That's it. That's our spider," said Bark.

"Why a spider?"

"No idea. It's always been that way."

They fastened the anchor among some rocks so that the ship was floating beside the gigantic carving. Above the spider's head, as though it was a precious object delicately clutched between two monstrous claws, was a cave mouth, a perfect circle, maybe a dozen feet in diameter.

Bark walked to the rear of the ship and pulled a tarpaulin from a jumble of knotted ropes and sails.

"Damn." He moved an armful of the tangled mass aside. "We haven't used this for years. I'll need a hand."

They went to help him, and in a few minutes had uncovered a small boat.

"At least one of us should stay here," Bark said. "I don't like leaving the ship unattended."

"It should be me, I think," said the Senator. "These two know nothing about the ship."

"Well, we've learned how to use the sails," said Bryce.

"A bit, anyway," added Reina.

But Bark agreed with the Senator, and Bryce and Reina were drafted into the shore party. Soon the small boat was afloat beside the ship, suspended over depths lost in mist. It rocked lightly as they climbed into it.

They crossed the space separating them from the Pilot's Station. The boat was light, and more difficult to handle than they had thought it would be. It took all their concentration to keep it steady, but Bark knew what was needed, and taught them as they went.

They made a bumpy but safe landing at the entrance. Bark secured the boat, and telling Bryce and Reina to be quiet and careful, he pulled a small crystal from a pocket. It glowed gently, casting a soft light over their surroundings.

They were standing in an area about thirty feet square. It was bare, with no features to distinguish it from any other empty room carved into the side of a mountain. In the dim light of the crystal, they saw a flight of stairs at the far end of the room, leading upwards into more of the heavy gloom that sat around like large piles of coal.

Bark passed Reina and Bryce a crystal each. They began to glow as soon as they took them. The light helped. The floor was old, with cracks and missing pieces, and wet with slime and water. They crossed the room without comment, each of them in the center of a cloud of blue light and disturbed insects, and climbed the stairs.

"This is it," said Bark, his voice sinking. "The Pilot's Station."

"It's a mess," said Reina, holding her crystal higher so she could see.

"It's the pits," agreed Bryce.

"I have to admit, it isn't what I was expecting." Bark was disappointed.

The place was a ruin. If anything had ever been here, it was long gone, apart from some broken and crumbling pieces of rock that looked to have been once shaped to some purpose. They had fallen apart, disintegrating under the relentless touch of water and time, so that now the place looked like some recently dredged prehistoric ruin brought up from the bottom of the sea. It even had the right smell; dark and dank, as though there should be gulping fish flopping around in the water on the floor.

"This is no help to us at all." Bark sat down on the edge of a granite block.

Bryce and Reina walked around, looking behind rocks and in corners. There was nothing but water, slime and darkness. Something small slithered out of a corner and along a wall, its claws clattering.

Bark was about say that they may as well return to the ship when a sound caught his attention.

"What's that?"

Bryce heard it next, then Reina.

"Motors," Bryce answered. "Planes, maybe helicopters. What would anyone be doing here?"

"Nothing that will benefit us, I bet," said Reina. "Back to the ship?"

"Back to the ship." Bark replied.

They ran back down the stairs and were almost at the boat when the sound suddenly became louder. Beyond the mouth of the cave, a searchlight swept back and forth across the cliff face.

"Helicopters," said Bryce.

"Can they see the ship?" Reina tugged on Bark's sleeve to get his attention.

The searchlight had found the entrance.

"Not the ship, that's not on their frequency," Bark replied. "But they'll be able to see the boat. And us." They edged back into the shadows, taking care to stay out of the light.

"If we get back in the boat, they'll be able to see us?"

"Yes. Once the boat is away from the ship, it resonates with the local frequency. It's just a boat, after all. You'll be visible, of course, and so will I, going by my experience in the caves."

"We're in deep shit then?"

"If that means trouble, yes."

One of the helicopters had approached the entrance. Against the darkness, the flame of a jetpack's exhaust became visible. As it crossed in front of the helicopter, the searchlight's beam fell on a soldier, flying in their direction. Then they saw another, and then two more in quick succession.

"Oh. Deeper shit, then. Back up the steps."

They ran back up the stairs to the other room.

"Look around for another way out. Anything we might have missed," Bark said, but he didn't have to. Bryce and Reina were already doing it. Bark crouched down out of sight of the entrance but close enough, he hoped, to hear what was going on in the lower room.

The whine of the jetpacks stopped as the soldiers landed.

"What the fuck is that?"

"A fucking boat! Bullshit!"

"Hang on, I'll radio the boss and tell him."

There was a brief pause, and some talking, followed by a muffled response.

"He says to throw it over the edge."

Bark groaned to himself. Getting out of here was looking more unlikely every minute. He heard the sound of the boat being dragged to the cave's entrance. One of the soldiers whooped, no doubt at the successful launch into space. Lacking a crew, it fell like a stone, and in a few seconds would be lying in pieces on the rocks below.

Torchlight flashed around the lower room. "Two of you up those stairs," a voice said.

Bark was turning to the others, ready to tell them to hide, when Reina arrived quietly at his side. "There's a door or something," she whispered.

She led him to where Bryce was waiting. They crouched down, and he saw, partially obscured by a fallen arch, the remains of a doorway.

"Hurry. They're coming this way."

Dropping to their hands and knees, they crawled through the gap and then stopped. The way was blocked by a rock fall.

"Shit!"

"You're not wrong."

The soldiers were in the room behind them. Bark could see the light from their torches swimming across the walls. There was more talk on the radio, and then one of them spoke to the other.

"The boss says to turn the place upside down. Soon as we're done here, they'll frag the place."

"Don't those aliens want something here?"

"Yeah, that's probably why they're gonna ice it."

One of the soldiers had moved to the opposite side of the room and was inspecting the wall.

The one that was looking among the debris on the floor found something and called out. They both crouched down and a radio conversation began.

Bryce turned to the others. "We've got to move. They'll find us here. There are jetpacks at the entrance…"

"Yeah sure," whispered Reina, but she was already following Bryce and Bark.

They crept out of their hiding place and along the wall to the top of the stairs. The two soldiers were still engrossed in their find.

As silently as they could, they crept down the stairs. The other two soldiers were at the cave entrance. One of them was leaning against the wall, and the other was kicking at something on the ground. Neither of them had their torches turned on. Outside, the helicopters buzzed like impatient hornets.

Bryce reached out and pushed Reina back, just enough so that she understood. He and Bark kept walking.

The soldiers heard their footsteps when they were just a few strides away.

"What's happening? Did you find anything?"

"We're out of here," said Bryce, trying to sound enough like a soldier to gain them another second or two.

A light clicked on. They were two strides from the soldiers. The pretence was over.

"Fuck you, asshole!" The soldier lifted his rifle.

Bark leapt forward. He grabbed the soldier by the arm and pulled him forwards. Trying to regain his balance, the soldier fell sideways onto the knife that Bark had pulled. They fell to the ground.

The one holding the torch dropped it. He was scrambling for his rifle, then saw that Bryce was almost on him. He swung his weapon like a club, hitting Bryce in the chest.

Bryce went down. He swung a leg around as he fell, his foot connecting with the soldier's ankle. They landed together in a heap. The discarded torch cast an unreal, theatrical light over them as they struggled.

Reina ran across the few feet that separated them and pushed as hard as she could. The soldier reeled back.

Bryce rolled with the motion, sending the soldier a bit further. At the same time Reina pushed again, catching him on the shoulder. He stumbled and reached for support, but his balance was too far gone, and he put one foot out into empty space. He went over the edge without making a sound.

Reina grabbed Bryce and pulled him back into the shadows.

"Man, I didn't know I could do stuff like that." Her heart was pounding.

The helicopters were still hovering outside. There was no sign that anyone on them had noticed anything.

Bark had picked up his victim's gun. "How does this work?"

"Give it to me," said Bryce. "I know how to use it." He took the gun and checked the magazine and the safety.

Reina picked up the torch. She and Bark leaned over one of the jetpacks. "How does it work?"

"I don't know. Don't you know? This is your planet."

"Well that doesn't mean I know shit about these things…"

There was a sound behind them. One of the other two soldiers had come down the stairs while they were talking.

"Hey guys, come and give us a hand with th…"

Bryce fired.

"No shit," he said, hefting the gun, admiring its balance. "No recoil."

"There's another one up there. He will have heard," said Bark. "Bryce, do you know how to use one of these jet things?"

"Nah. Does that mean we're screwed?"

"Never mind about that," said Reina. "What's this?"

A rope was hanging in front of them, directly outside the cave mouth. Only a few feet of it was visible; the rest of it faded out gradually, like a parlor magician's trick.

"One of ours, I should think," said Bark. "Shall we?" He reached out into the void and swung onto the rope.

"You go," Bryce said to Reina. It was literally a leap of faith to jump out into space to grasp a rope suspended from nothing, but there was no choice. She followed Bark's example.

Bryce crouched down, rifle ready. The last soldier came running down the stairs. Bark was gone. Reina was almost gone. He fired, and the soldier retreated, swearing.

It was Bryce's turn. Without hesitating, he shouldered the rifle and jumped. Grasping the rope and swinging precariously in space, he discovered that their departure had finally attracted someone's attention.

A searchlight fell on him. A machine gun came to life, firing tracers that were wide, but began closing in on him as he climbed.

He felt a pain in his leg, sharp and intense, like a wasp sting. He faltered, and in the instant in which he might have lost his grip, hands appeared from nowhere and seized his arm. He was dragged up over the rail and onto the deck.

Someone on one of the helicopters made an executive decision. As Bark and the Senator pulled Bryce to his feet, there was a flash of light from the closest helicopter. An instant later, an explosion ripped apart the entrance to the Pilot's Station. The cave mouth they had been standing in a few seconds ago disintegrated in a fireball.

The helicopter moved away, and fired again. The other two helicopters joined in, firing a small storm of missiles. The light from the explosions illuminated the pieces of mountain that were flying everywhere.

"Should we move the ship?" Reina wasn't sure how much their invisibility would protect them.

"We should be all right," the Senator replied, leaning on the rail and enjoying the show. A piece of rock disappeared into the side of the hull and emerged through the deck, without causing any damage. "Different frequencies, remember."

A section of the mountain was collapsing in on itself. Something in the Pilot's Station must have been combustible; the explosions were continuing and spreading. The helicopters backed off and continued firing.

Soon most of the cliff face was gone, and with it the carved spider and any sign that the Pilot's Station had ever existed.

"What a result," said Bryce. "Massive." He was lucky. The wound on his leg was just a scratch. His chest hurt a bit from its encounter with the rifle, but it wasn't about to slow him down.

After a few minutes, the flames subsided and the mountain stopped collapsing. A wind had sprung up.

"What's this?" Reina wondered aloud.

"It's not blowing," said Bark. "It's sucking. Look."

A huge hole had appeared in the side of the mountain. Wisps of smoke and ash and trails of sparks were disappearing into it, spiraling like water down a drain. The helicopters had moved in closer again, milling about the result of their handiwork like flies around a carcass.

Bark and the Senator raised the anchor and made the sails ready. "Whatever happens," said Bark, "we'll be going somewhere. I don't know why, but this wind appears to affect us. Strange. It must be aetheric, as well as physical."

Three more helicopters were arriving. Rounding a distant spur of rock, they grew in size as they approached, their lights sparkling in the darkness like festive decorations. Two of the new machines were large and black like the others. The third was small and red.

One of the new arrivals moved straight towards the ship and started circling it slowly. From an open side door, a figure was looking intently in their direction.

It was a Nefilim. Another one appeared beside it, pointing at the ship.

"They can see us," said Bark.

"Is that supposed to happen?"

"No!"

The breeze had become a swirling vortex, pulling at everything in its wake. They ran to lower the sails, now straining and distended, threatening to tear themselves apart.

They couldn't have avoided it, even if they had wanted to.

Slowly at first, and then with increasing speed, the ship was drawn towards the gaping breach in the side of the mountain, as surely as if it was a piece of flotsam on a raging river.

Clutching anything that would give them a handhold on the reeling ship, they were dragged into the darkness of the underworld.

The island of the mutants.

The helicopters carrying the Nefilim and the Gores arrived as the Pilot's Station was being destroyed.

The General pondered his next move. The point of their expedition no longer existed; it had just been blown up. And he'd lost four men. He was lucky that they were his own private boys; he wouldn't have to explain anything.

He turned to Thead. "Were those people friends of yours?"

"I've never seen them before," Thead lied convincingly.

A new voice joined the radio chatter. It was the pilot of the helicopter carrying the two Nefilim. The aliens were saying that there was something there, he said. Some sort of ship, floating in the air.

The General couldn't see anything, but he wasn't about to argue. He didn't know how pissed off the Nefilim would be now that the point of their journey had been trashed, and he was going to be careful. The wind was picking up. It was swirling, disappearing into the hole in the mountain.

"They're moving… the ship I mean… going down, through the hole…" said the radio in the General's ear.

"What do the Nefilim want us to do?"

"I'll ask." There was a pause, then "They say we should follow."

"Of course they do." *Damn.* "Lead the way."

They passed through the gates of broken rock, into total darkness. The air stream was fast. It caught the helicopters and propelled them along, the corkscrew motion of the air keeping them away from the walls and in the center of the tunnel, where the airflow was smoother and faster.

The General kept his attention on the sonar. They were in a shaft about fifty meters wide that descended straight down, with no twists or turns.

"Where's this damn ship of theirs?" he yelled into his headset above the howl of the wind.

There was another pause.

"Below us, sir. We're all traveling at the speed of the air current. We're not gaining on them, or losing ground."

The General grunted and sat back. All they could do was wait it out. He wondered if the Nefilim knew where they were heading, or whether they were just stupid. And as for a ship that no one could see… He tried to contact Mount Weather, but it was useless. The rock around them was blocking everything.

After half an hour or so, their motion in the air current became smoother and slower. Light appeared ahead of them. It was soft, glowing gently in the darkness like radiation. Their advance became still slower.

* * *

They entered the light and emerged into the underworld.

It stretched away so far that its outer limits, if there were any, were hidden in the haze of distance. Below them stretched a sea, as flat and gray as slate. The helicopters floated in formation, their pilots and crews pausing to take in their new surroundings.

"What is this place?" someone asked over the radio.

"Fuck knows," crackled one of the Gores from the speaker. "What are we going to do now?"

A good question, the General thought, opening the channel to the helicopter with the Nefilim in it.

"The ship?"

"They say they can't see it, sir."

"Never mind some ship we can't see," interrupted the female Gore. "Let's see what's here." Their helicopter, a flash of red in the gray light, dropped away, descending towards the subterranean ocean.

Wishing that the Gores would ask his opinion about something just once, the General ordered the other pilots to do the same.

"Most planets have some kind of underground formations," Thead was saying a few minutes later as they flew along a coastline. "Usually there's something living there. Lowlife of some kind, as a rule. It's strange, don't you think General, how nature fills in every available corner? Usually with rubbish, for some reason."

The General's attention was on the island that was emerging out of the haze before them. Soon he could make out structures on it. "Shut up," he said quietly.

Thead, who had begun telling the General his ideas on the purity of species and the desirability of its maintenance, stopped talking.

"Buildings," he said when he saw what the General was looking at.

"Yes, Einstein. Buildings." He called the other helicopters.

There were yelps of glee. It was the Gores, of course. The General felt a surge of intense dislike for them. If those bastard twins didn't share the post of Vice Secretary-General and a long list of other titles between them, he would have long ago taken great pleasure in organizing an accident for them. The patronage and protection of the Secretary-General had served them well.

Thead noticed the General's expression of disgust.

"You don't have much time for those colleagues of yours, do you?" he asked, at the same time peering towards the island.

"It's not your concern."

They flew over a jumble of buildings and looked down on the inhabitants, who were either scurrying for shelter or standing looking up into the sky at the new arrivals. Near the center of the town was a square or market of some kind. The crowd in it didn't look even remotely human.

"Mutants!" said Thead. "So you have them as well."

"You know them too? Well, now we know where at least some of them live, don't we?" said the General, looking around to see if any of the other helicopters had arrived.

At the same instant, the Gores' helicopter flashed past them, the chatter of gunfire and the smoking trail of an air-to-ground missile in its wake.

The General swore and opened a channel. "You have my permission to open fire."

"Well, thank you, General sah. Thank YOU!"

The General grimaced again. Thead said nothing.

This would surely serve the General well back at Mount Weather. Mutants had been a source of major frustration for as long as anyone could remember – for as long as history had been recorded, in fact. It wasn't so much anything they did, although they did meddle when it suited them; it was more that they kept themselves separate, and so little was known about either them or their agenda. They were beyond the jurisdiction of the surface. Whenever they were hunted or pursued, they disappeared underground, and no one had ever known exactly where they went. Until now. He wondered how many places there were like this.

The General imagined the Secretary-General's beaming face in front of him as he pointed the helicopter's nose towards some buildings. He was still smiling as he pressed the fire button.

The other helicopters arrived. "Leave a few of them alive," he told them. He needed a half-dozen or so for questioning. And something to show at Mount Weather, of course.

Soon the sound of his men, happy in their work, filled the headphones. The General flew above the length of an alleyway, herding a group of mutants before him. When they were cornered, cowering against the end wall, he turned to Thead.

"Have a turn, boy. All you need to do is press this." He tapped a red button and looked Thead straight in the eye, waiting. This was a test.

Thead looked down at the cowering group. They were all the same, with insect wings and heads half the size of a human head, but they were different sizes, with the larger ones trying to shelter the smaller ones. A family, maybe.

Thead pressed the button without hesitating. There was a soft thudding sound, and the mutants were engulfed in a ball of fire. It dispersed almost immediately, but the flames clung to them. After a few seconds, they stopped moving. When the flames subsided, nothing was left but a collection of blackened husks.

"The joys of anti-personnel air-to-ground DF-3 incineration accelerant," said the General. "Well done, Thead."

"A pleasure, General." Thead smiled.

The other helicopters were flying over the rooftops, dropping incendiaries among the buildings. Smoke and flames rose from the crowded streets, in the way of wars everywhere.

The Gores were hovering above the marketplace, firing their machine guns happily and randomly into the crowd.

"But ain't this the life, sister," said the brother, pausing to lob a grenade into a group of fleeing mutants.

"Makes you feel it's all worthwhile, don't it? Sure as heck gives you that warm useful feeling," Alexis replied, taking aim at a bird hybrid and squeezing the trigger carefully. Its head exploded in a shower of blood, beak, and brains. "Yup. Sure does," she agreed with herself, taking aim again.

Finally bored with the marketplace, they went roaming above the houses, setting fire to them. Pausing in front of one of the larger buildings, they saw someone running into it.

"Let's try the laser. Have we tried the laser yet?"

"No, brother, we haven't tried the laser yet. And I'm of the opinion that we most definitely should."

The brother armed the laser, waited until it was charged, and fired. The beam sliced through a door frame in the front of the building, along the front wall, and then took out the upper half of a window, setting old wood alight as it went.

"Not bad," he said, "but I prefer the kick of the machine gun. Call me old fashioned, but there you go!"

"Aw, you're just an old romantic," replied Alexis, at the controls. "Let's hear that little baby fire up, boy!" Her brother obliged by swapping weapons and opening fire on a group running into the building.

A few seconds later, the General's helicopter came up beside them. Without saying anything, the Gores flew away.

The General flew over the building and made towards the beach.

"Two there!" Thead yelled. "We just passed them!"

The General looked down and saw two figures. One was a female, normal enough. The other was a Nefilim. What was a Nefilim doing here?

He swung the helicopter around in a tight circle. "Get on these two," he said to the side gunner.

As soon as they were in his sights, the gunner opened up. The bullets skittered harmlessly around the girl, but the Nefilim was hit and fell. The helicopter overshot them. The General swung it around as fast as he could.

"I know that female!" Thead yelled above the sound of the turbines.

"In that case, when we find her, I'll allow you the pleasure of dispatching her."

But the female was gone. "Time to get on the ground," said the General. He ordered two of the helicopters to continue looking for survivors, and sent the others to the marketplace.

The Gores were meticulous about certain things; documentation was one of them. "History must never forget our work," they said as they filmed their exploits, taking great care to capture the most telling and graphic moments. Alexis was particularly adept with a camera, probably because she lacked her brother's tendency to get carried away in the heat of the moment.

"We'll get just the finest shot of yourselves landing there, General," Alexis said into the radio. "Looks mighty fine, all that burnin' shit and those dead mutants lyin' all round the place. Be right fine with some choppers comin' down, ain't that so, Theo?"

"Damn right, sister."

There were occasions when the Vice-Secretaries, in spite of themselves, made sense. Some film of the General and his boys in action on the ground might be useful later. One always had to consider the media. And the troops inside the helicopters had been unable to take much of a part in the festivities so far. They had been cooped up for several hours, and were getting jumpy. It was the compassionate thing to let them have a run.

The helicopters headed in to land. Thead was hanging out the side window, firing his new pistol at anything that moved. He was missing everything, but he was enjoying himself. Then he saw Sahrin. She was standing in front of a cowering mutant, and she had her arm drawn back, preparing to throw something.

"Bitch!" Thead had never had any reason to dislike her in the past, but now that he found himself on the opposing team he wasn't going to let details obscure his appreciation of the big picture. He took aim, but the other helicopter was coming down between them. It blocked his view a second before Sahrin's grenade took flight. Another couple of seconds after that, it erupted in a ball of flame.

The General, who had seen nothing, felt the blast. Even as he turned to see pieces of helicopter being scattered by the blast, he was considering his options. He didn't know what type of weapon had taken out it out, or from what direction, so there was no advantage in going back up.

He landed and ordered the soldiers out, but it was unnecessary; they were on the ground already and spreading out across the square, killing wounded mutants and apparently forgetting the order to take some prisoners. The General and Thead followed. The General was half expecting another attack, but it didn't come. Whoever had wasted the helicopter would be foolish to have stuck around.

"It was her," Thead said. "The female from the beach. I saw her again, just now. Over there." He pointed to a building beyond the burning carcass of the destroyed helicopter.

The Gores had landed as well, and came running over. The sister was still filming as she stumbled over pieces of debris and bodies. Theo was carrying a rocket-propelled grenade launcher.

"RPG for short, boy," he offered when he saw Thead looking at the weapon. "A fine companion when no argument or contradiction is to be tolerated. Jesuz, what a freaking mess!" He looked around at the remains of the helicopter.

"I was just saying," said Thead, "that the one who did it was over there. I saw her." He pointed again to the spot where he had seen Sahrin, happy to demonstrate that he knew something of value.

"Well, no shit." Theo raised the RPG to his shoulder and before anyone could say anything, fired a grenade towards the doorway Thead was pointing at. He didn't use ordinary grenades. These were souped-up versions, made especially for him by the weapons techs back at Mount Weather. When the projectile exploded, it demolished an entire side of the building, and set fire to the buildings on each side of it. The upper floors promptly caved in, collapsing onto the shattered remains of the ground floor. Fire spread, and within seconds the row of buildings was an inferno.

The Gores laughed and slapped each other on the back. Alexis got the whole thing on film.

The General went back to the radio and called in the other helicopters. It was time to clean up.

After a few minutes, they arrived, and their cargo dispersed through the streets of the island. The gentle, meditative sound of occasional gunfire wafted through the air.

How Sahrin came to be
on the island of the mutants.

Sahrin woke. She lay still for a moment as the dream she had been having faded away. She sat up and stretched her arms, then with a start remembered where she was. She was underground, and it was now many hours since she'd followed the creature into the depths of the tunnels, away from the cavern full of the other sleeping Nefilim. *Good call,* she thought to herself. That was real sensible, to have gone there in the first place. *Idiot!*

Sleeping soundly a few meters away was the Nefilim, whose name, she had learned, was a strange sound, the best rendition of which she could manage was something like *Obirin.* Its full name was a lot longer than that, but Obirin would do, it had said.

"Where are we going?" she had asked.

'*We're going to meet some others,*' was the reply. '*It is some distance, and you must trust me.*' Until then, Obirin had said, he would explain as much as he could. And he did. As they walked and climbed through tunnels and rock formations, some natural and some artificial, Obirin had begun Sahrin's education in the prehistory of the Earth.

'*Not all the Nefilim are united. Also, not all of us have been hibernating for the last few thousand years. There have been others, who have lived their lives deep underground. If everything has gone according to plan, they will have been alerted to the awakening that has happened, and they will be expecting me and some others of us who think the same way to come and meet with them. We will decide there what must be done next.*'

"Done about what?"

'*The awakening means that this world, which is as much ours as anyone's, is about to experience great changes. Much is about to happen, but it is doubtful that the rulers of the surface, the human leaders, will want the masses of their people to know the truth of what is happening. They have never been able to admit that this planet has a history that is much longer than is generally known, although the rulers themselves have known of it for a long time. Much less so will they want the populace to know that it is not a dead history but a living one, and that that history has awakened, and is about to assert itself.'*

Sahrin thought that Obirin was assuming that she was a local, that this was her planet.

"I'm not from here, from this planet, I mean," she said. "I came here with some others in a ship. We sailed here…"

'Yes, you're one of the aether pilots, aren't you. You were seen arriving. Your presence here aroused much interest.'

"I am. And were we? And among whom? We followed the directions on the map that one of our crew had been deciphering, and it's been our undoing. Unlike the locals, we have an understanding of your race, even if it's a second-hand one. Your species traveled widely in the past, and there are traces of you in the myths and legends of many races."

'True,' replied the Nefilim. *'And the contribution we made to the affairs of those who we ruled was not a happy one, unfortunately. At its height, we ruled many systems and many cultures, and the Nefilim were harsh masters.'*

"While it lasted it was effective, I guess. But it was cruel, judging by the tales that outlived your empire." Sahrin changed the subject. "I remember hearing a story once, when we were trading in the Enstrai Cloud. According to the legend, there would be a time when the Nefilim would be resurrected, reborn, and that it would happen when their two homes moved together. Has that got anything to do with what's happening now? And if the Nefilim are being reborn, does that mean that they're going to want their empire back as well? And what homes? Why two?"

'So many questions. How human.'

They were walking along a narrow path. The top of the cliff it was cut into disappeared into the darkness, but its lower reaches were very visible. A hundred or so feet below them, a river of molten lava flowed into a sinkhole at least two hundred feet across, forming a lake of fire that spat and boiled furiously. The air burned. Her lungs felt scorched.

'*Yes, the two homes are moving together. This planet is regarded by our race as part of our heritage. Earth, as the humans call it, was the first planet we ever traveled to. It was the first because periodically it is the closest habitable object in space to Marduk, which is what we call our own world. Marduk has a long orbit that takes it out on a huge arc into the coldest and blackest space. It spends three and a half thousand of this planet's years in space, after which time its orbit brings it back into the reaches of this system. The last time this happened was three and a half thousand earth years ago.*'

"Then it's about to come again? Or it's here already… do the Earth-humans know?"

'*Some of them know. The ones that rule know, of course. They have always known. Those that study know. The scientists will know that something is coming.*'

"And what is going to happen?"

'*The Nefilim population on Earth have been sleeping for twenty eight thousand of this planet's years. The two planets have been in close proximity to each other eight times during that period, but now, there are other factors in play which are causing the awakenings to happen.*'

'*The earth-humans might like to think that they alone have instigated the process, but there is more to it. The humans have been watched and guided in everything they have done.*'

They had passed the lake of fire several days ago, and had traversed several caverns lit by small ferocious-looking creatures that looked like a cross between a bat and a firefly which flew far above their heads, making strident shrieking noises but never coming near them.

Finally they emerged from the caverns onto the coast of an underground ocean.

Small waves of clear water lapped quietly at a long shoreline. Sahrin tasted it, and found it fresh and cold. They had both been hungry in the small tunnels, and had wiped condensation from the walls to slake their thirst. Now, beside the underground sea, they found strange fungi, all different shapes and sizes, like nothing that Sahrin had ever seen before. They stopped and rested, and ate their fill. The flesh was sweet, even if the appearance of the fungi did little for her appetite.

"Why did your race go into hibernation?"

'The answer to that lies in the changes that are about to befall this part of the universe. Eight orbits ago, our scientists found an object in space which puzzled them greatly. It was far away, so at first, their interest was merely academic. They identified the new object as a massive cloud of photons, stretched across a vast area in a belt. They set about analyzing this phenomenon, and soon found that it was heading, at great speed, in this direction. Towards this system. As you might expect, this lent some urgency to their investigation of its qualities.'

He stopped, and thought for a few seconds. Sahrin bit into a piece of fungus.

'When its path was calculated more precisely, they found that the photon cloud was going to arrive in this planetary system at the same time that Marduk would be at the perihelion of its orbit, and at its closest aspect to earth.'

'The research that we – for I was one of the scientists who worked on this project – undertook indicated that the photon belt had some unusual qualities. It would absorb any light it encountered, both from the stars and our own sun. We calculated that both planets were going to pass through the cloud, and that it would take three Earth-days. Both Marduk and Earth would experience total darkness during this time. Of course, without sunlight, the temperature would plummet. But the real effects would be on the living creatures that were exposed to the photons. DNA would be subjected to a shifting range of frequencies, stimulating a resonance effect...'

"I'm not understanding you," Sahrin broke in. "I'm not a scientist."

'The photon belt was going to effect some changes on living creatures – _all_ races of creatures. We recognized straight away that this would have implications for our own race, and also for the humans and other life of Earth.'

'When Marduk is moving through the far reaches of its orbit, far from the warmth of the Sun, Nefilim hibernate. We freeze solid, so that all our physical life processes are suspended. Out of the three and a half thousand earth years that equal one of Marduk's cycles, we spend all but five earth years in this frozen state. For those five short years, the Nefilim can live like any other creatures.'

"Are you asleep?"

'During the hibernation? No, I don't think you could call it that. We are still conscious, and we live on the mental plane while our bodies have returned to the ice. Marduk becomes a planet of ghosts while it travels in distant space. When we realized that the photon cloud would transform all life by raising its frequency, we decided that we wanted to see it for ourselves, and not leave it for our descendants. Since it was possible, we did it.'

"How long do you live?"

'We don't age while we are in suspension. However, we age very quickly when we are awake to the physical world. Four or five cycles is an average life span. So, we tend to value highly the time that we spend out of the mental plane, as it is literally killing us.'

'We were curious, like scientists anywhere. So, the race allowed its natural ability to hibernate to be augmented by technology, so that we would be suspended for the eight cycles, and would awake when the cloud was almost upon us.'

"And no doubt it's almost upon us?"

'Yes. This planet will enter the photon belt in a few days. Marduk will enter it soon after.'

"And where is Marduk now?"

'It is coming. At the moment it is on the other side of this planet's moon, but it should be visible after the photon belt moves on. It is a most unusual coincidence of astronomical phenomena.'

"Sure sounds that way."

'But don't think that the interest that the Nefilim have in the photon belt is purely for the sake of science. We – they – haven't become ghosts for the last twenty eight thousand years for the sake of knowledge alone.'

Sahrin wondered what other reason there could be, and what Obirin's role was in all this. He was a renegade of some kind, but for what cause? If he was a rebel, what was he rebelling against?

Her questions would have to wait. Obirin was indicating that they should be moving again, and now he preferred to walk in silence.

They saw no signs of life initially, but that was about to change. Obirin told her that they were making their way to an island. After a long walk along the black and red sands of the beach, she saw it, surrounded by a cold mist that had settled on the surface of the water. As they approached, she made out the dark shapes of buildings piled together like stacks of wood and stone awaiting some more organized use. By the time they had reached a pier where someone seemed to have had the foresight to leave a boat, they could see figures moving among the buildings and along the beaches of the island.

They climbed into the boat and Obirin began to row in long, powerful strokes. As they drew closer, Sahrin saw that the people on the island were not necessarily people at all, or rather, that while a few of them seemed normal enough, many of them seemed to be mutations, incredible mixtures of animal and human life.

She felt a shiver of apprehension pass through her. In all her years of travel through the distant reaches of time and space, she had never seen anything like this. What was going on here?

Which is the question she asked Obirin.

'There is nothing to fear,' he replied. *'You will soon see.'*

Not given a lot of choice, Sahrin quashed her fears and turned back towards the front of the boat. Three creatures were coming down to a pier to meet them. When the boat was close enough, one of them threw a rope. Obirin caught it and tied it to the prow.

The creature that threw the rope was perfectly and utterly

ugly. Its head was sunken deep into a barrel chest, so much so that its eyes, no more than deep red gashes in its skin, were the only features of its face that were elevated above its square shoulders. Its nose was missing, the holes of its nostrils flush with the skin, and its mouth, no bigger than its eyes, worked ceaselessly, shaping words which, Sahrin realized as the boat was made fast, were quite understandable.

"You must hurry," it was saying. "They have been waiting for you. Waiting for you, yes, they have, now hurry, we'll show you the way, yes we will, although you could no doubt find it yourself, yes, yes you could, it's not a big place, this, and there are people to ask by the hundred, there are…"

The speaker's two companions were no less strange. One of them, who stood back and fidgeted restlessly, had the head and naked torso of a young woman, but the legs and feet of a large bird, with which she continually scratched at the ground.

The third creature had the normal features of a human male, but in the center of its torso, where its chest and stomach should have been, there was a large oval hole, through which Sahrin could see figures in the distance. With a start, she realized that she had been wrong in thinking that the small figures she could see were behind the creature. In fact they were about ten inches tall, one male and one female, and she saw now that they were sitting in the hollow of the gap in the torso, where the pit of the creature's stomach should be.

I don't know what's going on here, she thought to herself.

'But,' the reply came to her, '*you don't need to know, do you? Just treat everything you do know as a gift, and all the things you don't… well, leave them for now… this is a place of unusual things; it always has been…*'

I don't think like that, she thought, and looked at Obirin, expecting to see him looking at her, but he wasn't. She climbed out and followed him onto the pier.

Her eyes fell on the two miniature creatures that inhabited the hollow mutant's torso. They were looking at her, smiling.

The words had come from them. *Great, more mind games,* she thought. She smiled thinly and turned away.

Without anything more being said or thought, the trio led them up a short path, into the maze of alleyways and pathways that wound through the jumble of buildings that covered the island. It was chaos. The air was hot, and thick with smoke and the heavy smell of unwashed bodies. Sour cooking smells and other more obscure odors wafted out of dark doorways.

Sahrin realized that she was walking close to Obirin as they made their way through the narrow alleyways. It was strange, she thought, that she should be relying on one strange creature for reassurance in the midst of a mass of even stranger ones. A dark face peered out of one of the doorways as they passed. Red eyes narrowed. There was a hissing sound, and a long tongue darted out and wrapped itself around her arm. She shrieked and jumped back. Something made a laughing sound in the shadows, and the tongue fell away, leaving her even more apprehensive about the locals as they moved on.

They passed through a square in which some creatures, which she decided might be children on account of their size, were playing a noisy game that involved spinning a skull and keeping a record of how it came to rest.

Near the edge of the square, stallholders were offering goods for sale. She slowed as they passed. On one of the tables were artifacts that, if she had known, she would have realized could only have come from the surface. There was a soldier's helmet, and she recognized a belt of grenades. There were pens and pencils, some rolls of clear plastic, a jumbled pile of shoes, some sunglasses, a compass, and a small piece of mirror. Most of it was old junk, suffering much from the effects of time and neglect, but a few of the items were in good condition.

They were quickly through the square. Wherever it was that they were going, it was clear that time was not to be wasted. They came to a dark alley in which the air was heavily scented with the sweet acrid smell of something burning. Something crippled scuttled out of their path as the three locals led Sahrin and Obirin into an open doorway at the end of the street.

They walked into the ground floor of one of the larger buildings. The back of the room was open. They were on the edge of the town, and the missing wall provided a good view of the sea around the island. Its waves, small as they were, had subsided, and the surface of the water was now smooth. The fog had evaporated, and a light rain was falling.

But Sahrin's attention was not on the rain, or the dead sound it made as it hit the ground outside.

Around a large table in the center of the room were arranged a dozen seats. Four of them were empty. Obirin and the three creatures who had met them on the beach sat down.

The other eight seats were occupied by a collection of mutants. There were feathers and scales, hands and claws, human flesh of all colors, combined in physical and anatomical combinations that Sahrin could never have dreamed of.

She became aware that she was the only one standing, and that several of the creatures were looking at her. Suddenly self-conscious, she edged back into the shadows of one of the room's corners. It seemed to have the desired effect. They resumed their conversations.

After a few minutes, one of them slapped its hand on the table and the room fell silent.

A short creature, which seemed to be a cross between a dwarf Nefilim and a female human, with the addition of a pair of leathery wings that hung limply from her back, leaned forward in her seat.

"We were thinking you might not be making it, Obirin. We were about to give up waiting and begin."

"I came as quickly as I could, but there were a few problems I had to deal with before I could leave."

It was the first time Sahrin had heard Obirin use his voice. She could tell that it didn't come easily to him. He had difficulty forming the words, and his voice had a thin, scratchy tone that was flat and unmodulated.

"Of course. This is a time for problems. There will soon be problems enough for everyone," said a creature whose skin was incised with deeply engraved tattoos. It had a sloping forehead and tiny pinhole eyes, which at first gave Sahrin the impression of imbecility, until she reminded herself that this didn't seem to be a place where appearances counted for much.

"You can vouch for your companion?" another one asked.

Sahrin cast a quick glance at the Nefilim. After a few days traveling underground together, they had begun to read each other's actions and expressions with a degree of success. She saw him look in her direction, and then say something quickly in another language. No one looked at her again. Whatever he said must have satisfied them. She listened in silence as they spoke.

"The Nefilim have activated the control points of their grid," Obirin was saying.

"We suspected as much. We felt the signs among ourselves." The speaker, the woman with the ostrich legs, passed a hand lightly across her brow as though to indicate that she was reporting a mental impression that someone had received. "It hasn't been fully brought online, though, as far as we've been able to tell. We still have some time, but it would be unwise to think that we have much…"

A thing with four arms, gray fur and no discernible eyes spoke. "We are not sure of the degree of co-operation between the Nefilim and the human rulers on the surface. Do you have any information?"

"Only to say that there must be some," Obirin replied. "Humans were at the site that I've seen. As to the exact nature of their involvement, I do not know."

"We must assume that there is some co-operation between the two races. For the present, at least." A murmur of agreement went around the table.

"The humans obviously think that there is something in it for them – or *some* of them, at least," somebody said.

"And the Nefilim must be letting them think that," said the one with the incised skin.

"Or it could be that we've misjudged the humans," said the dwarf Nefilim-woman hybrid with wings.

"I think we've known them long enough, even if at a distance, to know that that could well be true," said Obirin. There was more agreement.

Sahrin was watching the one with the hole in its torso. The two midgets were acting as its hands. The male climbed out onto a chair leg, and down to a bag that lay on the ground at the creature's feet. It rummaged through the bag's contents for a moment, then climbed back up to its host's shoulder. There, like a trained monkey, it fed a morsel of food into the creature's mouth. After its chore was done, it climbed back down to its place with its partner.

After a while Sahrin realized with a start that not only had she been daydreaming, but that they had been talking about her. How conversant was she with recent developments? Did she know about their plans? Could she be trusted?

They seemed to have realized that she wasn't paying attention, and if they had been talking to her, they'd given up, and were now talking between themselves.

"I know nothing about your intentions," she interrupted, recovering quickly. "I came to this planet with friends, but we've become separated. I would like to meet up with them again, but I suspect that by now there's a great distance between us. As for what's happening on the surface, I know nothing. And as for the Nefilim, Obirin here is the first one I've ever met."

"But you've heard of them before?"

"Heard of them? Yes, of course I have," she replied. "Their race is part of the folklore or mythology of any place you visit, anywhere or in any time..."

"Time..?" A ripple of attention went around the table. "Are you saying that you can travel through time?"

Instantly, she regretted what she had said. Had she let them know too much? "In a sense," she replied, hesitantly. "There are some places that we can go, there are others that we can't. It's like going anywhere. Sometimes the passage is easy, sometimes difficult, sometimes impossible. But there are maps..." She stopped. *Damn...*

"Maps? Maps of time?" It was the one with the two helpers in its midriff. "Do have any with you?"

Sahrin noticed that the two midgets were following the conversation. They saw her looking at them, and the female broke her gaze and whispered something to the male.

Sahrin realized that these people, or whatever they were, were in trouble, and anything that could help them would be of interest. But what, exactly, was their predicament?

"No, the maps are on the ship. And I don't know where the ship is," she added quickly, wanting to end this line of conversation.

"Your vessel... it doesn't work on electricity or magnetism, does it?" asked Obirin.

"I don't know those words," she replied, quite truthfully. "What are they?"

"What powers your ship?"

"The currents... the wind... in time, and space..." She was hesitant, not sure how to describe it. "Why is this important?" she asked. No one answered her. They whispered amongst themselves, and after a few seconds appeared to reach some agreement. The one with its head sunken into its chest turned towards her.

"It seems to us, it does, that it might be good for everyone if you knew just what was happening, and what is planned. Yes. It could be useful; well, *you* could be useful. We know you are telling the truth, or rather Distere knows you are telling the truth..." He indicated the woman with the ostrich legs. She was slumped in her seat, her eyes half-closed, head tilted in Sahrin's direction. A low thrumming noise came from her throat. The whites of her eyes flickered, and Sahrin saw the pupils behind the half-lowered lids, glazed over, looking at something that didn't exist. Something both far away and very close.

The one with the carved skin and the dwarf were rising from the table.

"These two are going to get some items that we need," continued the sunken-headed one. "They won't be long. No, they won't. While they're gone, come for a walk with Obirin and Distere and myself, and we'll explain what we can to you."

The dwarf and the one with the chiseled skin left, the dwarf hurrying to keep up with the long strides of the other.

Sahrin followed the headless one out through the open side of the building, down to the shoreline. Obirin and the ostrich woman followed, talking between themselves.

"Who are you people?" she asked the headless one. If she was going to get involved in the affairs of this collection of misfits (although they seemed to fit in well enough here), she wanted some background.

"A fair question. And since you're not a native of this planet yourself, the answer will not offend or shock you. No, it won't. We are the refuse, the rubbish left over from experiments in genetics and breeding that were undertaken many thousands of years ago. The aim of the program was to create humans. A slave class."

"The experiments were undertaken by my species," said Obirin, speaking aloud. "The Nefilim are accustomed to having the upper hand. A long time ago, my race was the dominant one on this planet. That is not a fact that is generally known, but there are humans that are aware of it, although they keep quiet about it. Those who would speak out are discouraged from doing so. It is in no one's interest for real history to be widely known. It seldom is."

"I know a little about the Nefilim from my travels," said Sahrin. "Your adventures in the distant past have left you with a reputation. From what I've heard, you made sure that you got what you wanted. Ruthless and warlike, according to the stories."

"True enough," replied Obirin. "Most of our race regard war and conquest as noble occupations. But to return to the point... As you know, this planet, Earth, is a special one, in that it is part of the system which contains our own home planet. And there was no intelligent life here when our race first arrived, over two million years ago."

They stopped. Obirin sat down on the sand. Sahrin stood at the water's edge, enjoying the way the water played over her toes. The ostrich woman stood a little distance away, her eyes closed. The one with no head walked into the water, moving out so that it reached up to its knees.

"The Nefilim plan to re-establish their control of this planet. Obirin has told us that you know about the discovery of the photon belt twenty eight thousand years ago, and how many of the Nefilim put themselves into suspension so they could be here when it arrived. However, there is more to the story than just that."

"The last time the Nefilim had a real presence on Earth was more than two hundred thousand years ago. It was at that time that their slave class, the humans, got out of control. There was a rebellion, encouraged by some elements of the Nefilim for their own purposes; they wanted to have the power here all to themselves. It took a long time, and there was much bloodshed and suffering, but the rebellion was finally successful. Contact with Marduk was broken. Once the planet's orbit had taken it out of the solar system, safely away from Earth, humanity turned on the Nefilim that had helped them to rebel."

"Outnumbered, they were either destroyed or escaped underground, to live in the web of caverns that stretches around the planet. There, they found that they were not alone."

"We, the freaks, had sought safety in the caves long before that. Our… peculiarities… meant, and still do mean, that we are safer away from the gaze of humanity. On those occasions when we have been seen by the surface dwellers, we have provided the basis for their myths, legends, and horror stories. Contact with humans usually doesn't go well for us, so we have made a habit of keeping to ourselves. For the same reason, the Nefilim that have been living with us, for many thousands of years now, have adopted our liking for privacy. They have become part of us. They have become mutants as well, if you like."

Obirin took over.

"Among the Nefilim scientists and others who came here secretly when the photon belt was discovered – and among the population on Marduk itself – there have been those who sympathize with the inhabitants of the underworld, both Nefilim and mutant. I am one of those."

"We see no real benefit for anyone, Nefilim or otherwise, in reviving the old order. We abhor the old barbarisms. We should be striving to evolve beyond our history, not attempting to restore it. The old Nefilim empire was merciless in maintaining its control over its subjects, and there was much suffering and cruelty. Even among our own, the suppression of dissent was ruthless.

"It was a good thing that their influence declined, and their empire retreated to this, their home star system. It was a better thing when the human rebellion ended their control of Earth. But as a race, we have never liked the idea of losing what we hold to be our own. The Nefilim state seeks to re-establish its old empire, and it intends to start with Earth.

"They plan to take advantage of the confusion wrought by the photon belt. As the planets pass through it, anything that requires an electric current to operate will cease functioning. Motors, computers, everything with a circuit, will all fall silent. And there will no doubt be other, unexpected effects. The consequences for human civilization will be devastating, of course. And permanent."

"I've seen technology and how it works for some of the races we've encountered in our travels," said Sahrin. "I can imagine how things could fall apart if that happened."

"They will," said the one with no head, who was now standing waist-deep in the water.

"But won't the Nefilim technology be affected in the same way?" asked Sahrin. "If it happens to the humans, why won't it happen to the Nefilim?"

"That is central to the Nefilim plan," Obirin answered. "Nefilim technology does not rely on electromagnetism as humanity understands it. We use an energy grid that can be created on any planet. Each one has its own character, but by setting it up and finding its nodes of power and manipulating them, it can be controlled, and used for our own ends. The first task of the awakened Nefilim that you saw in the caves was to reactivate that grid. It won't work perfectly to start with, as so many years have passed, and the geometry will have changed, but they will work quickly to overcome the problems, and it will be functioning soon. We are assuming that they will want to put the grid online either during the three days of the photon belt phenomenon, or immediately afterwards."

"When they do, with the human energy systems inoperative because of the belt, they plan to exert total control over the human population. And, eventually, the underworld areas as well."

"And you obviously want to stop them," Sahrin said. "How you plan to do that?"

Obirin and the headless one both started to answer her, but they stopped as the ostrich woman suddenly stirred, flapping her wings in agitation.

"The crystals will be arriving soon. They want us to return," she said.

"We'd better get back then," said the headless one, and they set off along the beach towards the meeting room.

"Now you'll see what we plan to do," Obirin said as they walked. "In short, we plan to disrupt their grid, and replace it with our own."

They had just arrived back in the meeting room when a creature with the head of a rat and fur streaked with patches of scales came running in from the street. It was in a state of panic, speaking through desperate gasps. "…from the outside… flying… they're killing everyone…" It gagged and collapsed face down on the floor. There was a gaping wound in its back. It shuddered once, then lay still.

The sound of engines became audible. Not loud – more like something metallic that whispered. It was a low whirring sound that grew out of nowhere. As the mutant with the chiseled skin came running though the door, holding the dwarf Nefilim woman under one arm and an old army pack under the other, the black profile of a helicopter appeared in the sky, visible through the doorway above the tops of the surrounding buildings.

Machine guns fired insistently. There were lasers as well, their ruby-colored rays sweeping the ground like stilts below circus performers. The firing was indiscriminate. Pieces flew off buildings as they were torn apart by bullets or sliced open by lasers.

A red helicopter paused in front of the building and a laser beam sliced down through the wall and the ceiling, setting it on fire. It passed in front of Sahrin, cutting the mutant with four arms and no eyes in half. Sahrin stumbled backwards into the arms of the creature with a hole in its torso. It took hold of her arm. "Come! We have to get away!"

There was pandemonium everywhere. More mutants came screaming through the door, chased by a hail of machine gun bullets. One of them died in the doorway, its head split open like a melon.

"To the water…!"

"Along the beach…!"

"The basement…!"

There were bodies everywhere. The dwarf Nefilim woman had been hit. She was trying to stand up, but her body was broken. A creature with skin covered with patterns that moved like oil on water lay dead below a collapsed beam, its body seared by laser burns.

Obirin took hold of Sahrin and pulled her out of the room, onto the slope that led down to the water. The survivors had gathered in the shelter of one side of the building. The helicopter at the front was moving down the street away from them. Something exploded into flames several houses away. There was screaming, and the sound of more firing.

The mutant with chiseled skin was with them. He opened the army pack that he was carrying and tipped its contents onto the ground. There were a dozen crystals, all different colors, each the size of a closed fist.

"We don't have much time. You all know where you have to go. Take these…" He handed the crystals one by one to the mutants gathered around him. As each took a crystal they left, running in either direction along the backs of the buildings.

Smoke from burning buildings and flesh was everywhere.

"Come with me," Obirin said to Sahrin as he took a crystal.

"I'll go anywhere, as long as it's away from here."

"Down towards the water. We have to go north." Obirin started off down the slope, towards the beach they had walked peacefully along just a few minutes ago.

They were just clear of the shelter of the buildings when a helicopter came screaming over the burning rooftops. It was on them even as they turned to see it. The helicopter's machine gunner didn't see them until it had almost passed over them. They saw him yell into his headset and swing his gun around as the helicopter turned.

'*Back!*' thought Obirin.

They started running. They were almost at the top of the slope when the gunner found his mark and opened fire. Bullets struck the ground all around them, kicking up clouds of dirt. Obirin staggered and fell to the ground, liquid pouring from a wound in his side. The crystal he had been carrying fell out of his hand and landed at Sahrin's feet. She picked it up and leaned over him.

The Nefilim was dying. "The crystal is your concern now," he gasped, choking as more of the liquid flowed from his mouth. '*One of the others will tell you what to do. Go…*'

Sahrin hesitated, not sure what to do, until the helicopter came back into view and started firing again. She ran back through the building, and kept going, out into the street. She ran towards the center of the town, to the market square, not sure what she was doing. Every second building seemed to be on fire, and the smoke and the confusion made it hard for her to see where she was going.

She reached the square. Dead and wounded lay everywhere. The stalls were in ruins, but a few of the buildings had been spared, and were still intact.

Sahrin felt a hand on her shoulder. She whirled around. It was the mutant with the two dwarfs in its belly.

"Where's Obirin?"

"Dead. He was hit." Holding it out in a shaking hand, she showed the mutant the crystal.

"Oh. Then you'd better come with me."

They passed the market stall that she had paused at on their way to the meeting. It had been demolished. The belt of grenades was lying on the ground amongst the debris. She picked it up and slung it over her shoulder.

Two helicopters appeared above them, firing indiscriminately. Sahrin looked up. The helicopters were only thirty feet above them, and descending. They were going to land.

There was so much to shoot at that Sahrin and the mutant hadn't been noticed. They moved out of the way. The helicopters were still ten feet from the ground when Sahrin swore. In the one that was going to land further away from them, she saw Thead, sitting beside the pilot. He was leaning out of the window, firing a pistol and laughing.

Something about the image made perfect sense. "You piece of shit!" she yelled, not caring that Thead wouldn't be able to hear her. She took one of the grenades from the belt and pulled the pin. She couldn't reach the second helicopter, although she would have dearly loved to, but the first one was close enough.

Her aim made perfect by cold rage, the grenade sailed with unerring accuracy towards the helicopter. Some of the soldiers who were gathered near its side door preparing to disembark saw it coming. Their eyes, visible through the slits of their masks, opened wide as they watched the small gray object arcing towards them. The helicopter exploded in a ball of yellow and orange fire, sending pieces of metal, plastic, and flesh flying.

Sahrin let out a long scream and started to move forward, taking another grenade from the belt. She was going to get Thead.

The mutant grabbed her by the arm and spun her around. "Don't waste yourself," he said urgently, his face only inches from hers. Without waiting for her to reply, he pulled her away.

The second helicopter landed. Soldiers jumped out of it, and began spreading out across the square.

"Quickly! This way."

"Where are we going?" Sahrin yelled above the sound of gunshots and screaming.

The mutant ran into a building. He led Sahrin to a door beneath a staircase and opened it. They descended rough stone steps into darkness. There was a heavy thud above them as the building was hit.

They reached the bottom of the steps and set out along a corridor that twisted and turned, then finally straightened out as it descended deeper underground. The mutant had taken a torch from his pack. The walls were dark and cold, and dripping with moisture.

"Are we under the water?" she asked, not sure whether she had spoken the question or merely thought it.

"Yes, we are beneath the water," came the reply. "We can find safety on the shore. There is an opening onto the surface there."

They walked in silence, the water from the ocean dripping from the rocks above them.

Back at Barker's Mill.

Tommy, Onethian, and Corporal Ortega, who was from Guatemala but would never go back there, had discovered that they shared a peculiar brand of ideology-free anarchism.

Bark, Reina or any of the others would have dismissed it as not giving a stuff, but to the three of them who had been holding their apolitical congress in the lounge bar of the Red Lion Hotel in Barker's Mill, and who had eased its proceedings with liberal application of alcohol, such an uncharitable view of their manifesto was unproductive, unwarranted, and totally beside the point.

"The leaders are all stuffed mate," Tommy was saying to Ortega. "If they gave a shit, they wouldn't have let that gas or whatever it was knock over all your mates, would they? That General of yours sounds like a right asshole."

"They most certainly would not have," Onethian agreed, nodding in a deceptively sober fashion. He was shitfaced. "And you're right, the General *is* a prick." *Prick* and *General* were both new words for Onethian, and he was trying them out.

Onethian was intensely literal, Tommy and Ortega had found. He liked to state facts, and little else. He didn't volunteer much, and they had yet to hear him ask a question. Some might have found him a little flat, but his new friends were having no problem with that side of his personality. Regardless of anything else, he liked beer, had learned how to play pool, and tended to agree with them. For someone who wasn't from this planet, Onethian was a top bloke.

Ortega came from a part of the world where the practice of openly asking questions had been all but bred out of the population by decades of repressive regimes, death squads and UN peacekeepers. To him, there was nothing unusual about Onethian's periods of silence interspersed with short, unadorned statements.

There was a question confronting them that they had not yet discussed; the matter of what they were going to do. They had spent the last few days doing nothing but drink, play pool, and eat fast food. Onethian and Ortega had been staying at Tommy's house, where he had introduced Onethian to fried food, and both of them to the powerful combination of beer and satellite TV.

It was Ortega who raised the subject. Not so much on his own account, but more because of what he had heard the other two saying. Onethian, who had an obvious stake in what was going on because of his crew mates, seemed to know something, and Tommy, of course, had friends who were in the thick of it somewhere. If they were still alive.

Tommy nodded slowly while Ortega put the question. "Well," he answered, "I wouldn't have a clue where they are, and from what you two guys saw down there, things were a bit dodgy. And now the place is crawling with soldiers again. Not looking too flash, I reckon. Be good to do something, but I don't see how it's possible. Maybe we should go ask at the base. Someone there must have an idea."

The corporal shrunk away from the idea. "No, not me, not that. I'm a deserter as far as they're concerned. I'd be history. Shot straight away. I'm not going near the place. And I wouldn't go there if I were you, either. They've got way too much going on to be worried about either any friends of yours, or how nice they should be to troublemakers like you."

"I heard talk in my unit that the scientists have worked out the aliens' science. It was all just talk and rumors, of course. But I heard that the aliens are not going to have it their own way. There are some surprises planned for them."

One afternoon, they went back to the rock ledge from which Tommy, Bryce, and Reina had watched the base before everything went pear-shaped. They sat there, drinking and watching. The base had been re-established. Helicopters were delivering new soldiers and more equipment.

Tommy saw his first Nefilim. The sight sent a chill down his spine. They were being led away in small groups to armored vehicles. There was something about the way the Nefilim were being led, almost herded, that recalled Ortega's comments about them and their plans.

After a while, they got bored with watching the compound, and went back to Barker's Mill, resigned to the fact that there was nothing to be done.

The days went by. It was hardly surprising that Tommy and Ortega happened to be sitting in the lounge bar of the Red Lion when the photon belt arrived.

The difference chimney.

Sahrin had discovered that the mutant's name was Geoca. The two small characters that lived in its torso also had names, but it was beyond her to distinguish between them. Geoca had tried to explain as they made their way along the damp length of the tunnel, but in the end she decided just to call them Geoboy and Geogirl. Daft names, but easy to remember.

Nothing much else was said, so Sahrin used the time to think. She was in a state of shock. Nowhere, in all of her travels, had she seen so much death and destruction in such a short period of time. And she had come to like Obirin.

The passageway was long. It didn't twist or turn; it just keep going, step after step, in a long straight line through the darkness. They splashed through brackish ankle-deep water, hands on the rough sides of the tunnel for guidance.

After what felt like a long time, they came to steps. They were slippery with slime or moss or something, and they changed direction frequently as they rose to the surface. They led up to the back of a small cave set into the base of a cliff.

When they emerged, it took Sahrin a few seconds to get orientated.

The island was still visible out on the water, but it was slowly disappearing, dissolving into a fine mist that was rising from the sea. The beach curved around to form a bay, bound at each end by outcrops of rock that jutted out into the water. Behind them, barring their way, sheer walls of rock reached upwards, their tops far beyond reach.

"Well, this is just fine," Sahrin said out loud and to herself. "What are we going to do now?"

Even as the question left her lips, she had seen it. At the far end of the beach, with its bow listing in the shallows and its prow dug into the loose sand, was the ship. Her ship. *Their* ship.

She hadn't seen it at first because of the mist and the waves that were breaking around it, and, of course, because she wasn't looking for it. It seemed to be in good shape. Too relieved and surprised to wonder at what it was doing here, she started towards it.

She saw people. One was standing on the deck, talking to two more on the sand.

"What is it?" Geoca couldn't see anything. To him, the ship was invisible.

She told him. Geoboy and Geogirl twittered excitedly.

"They're relieved," Geoca said, "because your ship might be a quick way to the surface. We might be able to use the difference chimney."

"The what...?"

"If we use it, you'll see. If we don't, it doesn't matter."

The people at the ship had noticed them. The two on the sand started walking towards them.

It was Bark! And the person with him looked familiar. It was one of the people from outside the place where the tunnels had been. She had seen him on the side of the sand dune, sitting with two other people. She didn't know his name, but he was wearing one of her shirts.

She ran to Bark, and they hugged each other, Geoca and Bryce looking on and inspecting each other at the same time.

"Are you okay?"

"Of course. We're down in numbers, though. And you? Are you all right?"

"Yes. I won't go wandering off on my own again, though. I don't know what possessed me."

Geoboy and Geogirl made some of their chirping noises.

"How did you get here?" Bark asked, at the same time noticing the Geocas, and that there were three of them.

"A longish story. You'll hear it all eventually, no doubt." She introduced Bark to Geoca, and watched as surprise registered on his face. Geoboy and Geogirl must have put thoughts into his head, as they had done to her. That had been only a few hours ago. It seemed like eons.

"Geoca here says there is a way back to the surface. We have to get there; we have something to deliver." She took the crystal from her pocket and showed it to Bark. "It's something to do with making sure that the Nefilim and the human government don't take over. It's part of some kind of energy system. On the island, they called it the Stream."

"Later. Look at this." Bark was curious, but their immediate situation was his first priority. "The ship needs attention."

* * *

As they worked, Bark told Sahrin how they had been dragged into the shaft behind the Pilot's Station and how they had emerged from it to be thrown onto the beach, scattering themselves, their belongings, and the cargo everywhere. There was some reorganizing to be done, but luckily the damage was minimal.

Sahrin, in turn, told Bark everything that had happened to her after she had left them in the caves. She told him all that she could recall of Obirin's history lessons, and what had been said about the photon belt, the Nefilim invasion, and the intentions of the human rulers. And she told him about Thead, and the slaughter on the island.

"None of them sound all that delicate, do they," said Bark, shaking his head and wondering why they had to be involved in this at all.

The sound of gunfire was still coming from the island. Clouds of smoke drifted across the water. They could smell burning.

Geoca didn't help the others work. He sat on the sand, arms folded on his knees, looking at his former home. He stayed like that, unmoving, until the others had finished and Sahrin called him up onto the deck. As he climbed up, she saw that not only Geoca, but also Geoboy and Geogirl had been crying.

"We need your help," she said. They had seen a helicopter flying around again, after a few hours during which nothing had seemed to be happening on the island. The invaders were on the move again. It was time to go.

"Of course," replied Geoca, pulling himself together. "We have work to do."

He paused, his head lowered. One of the small Geocas was speaking to him. "We have the crystal to place. The route from here to the node is simple enough, though. Is your ship functional?"

It was.

"The difference chimney, then," said Geoca.

"What?" Bark asked, as confused as Sahrin had been.

"I'll explain, but in the meantime, head towards those rocks." He raised a thin hand and pointed towards a distant formation protruding from the cliff face.

They raised the sails and tuned them as finely as possible, so as to catch the faint currents that drifted around them. The ship rose, hesitantly at first, as though it needed convincing, but Bark was doing his job well, and as the polarities shortened, they picked up speed. Carefully, so as not to imbalance the flow into the sails, they started towards the rocks that Geoca had indicated.

Rather than sail in a straight line, which would take them closer to the island than seemed advisable, Bark took them near the beaches, and low, gliding over the surface of the water, taking what cover they could in the patches of mist that floated above it.

Their progress was slow, and Geoca had time to do his explaining. Difference chimneys were anomalies in the planet's magnetic field. The result was a pillar-shaped zone of either reduced gravity, or in a few extreme cases, a total reversal of gravity. They were scattered around the planet, with no apparent pattern, and the majority of them began somewhere in the planet's depths and terminated at or below the planet's surface.

There were a few – three, to be precise – that extended above the ground, up into the atmosphere and out into space, where they gradually faded away, along with the rest of the planet's field. These ones were all full difference, in other words anti-gravity, and they were in far too much use by the military, and far too developed with bases and research facilities, for the curiosity of the population to be accommodated. Accordingly, their existence wasn't known to the public, who of course weren't told that there was a lot more going on in orbit around their planet than they suspected. So that it should stay that way, all the known difference chimneys were out of bounds to them.

But the populations of the underworld were under no such restrictions, and they made much use of the chimneys. Among other things, they used them to travel to and from the surface. The chimney they were heading towards, Geoca said, was a major thoroughfare to the surface, frequently used by the mutants and rebel Nefilim. It was also one of the biggest, he said, easily large enough for the ship to fit inside.

While Geoca was speaking, the two smaller Geocas had left their place in his torso, and had climbed up and perched on his shoulders like parrots, looking around at the ocean over which they were traveling. One of them squealed and started pulling Geoca's hair to attract his attention. The mutant leaned over the rail and looked down. Something swimming in the water was in trouble, and floundering.

Geoca turned to the others. "We have to pick up a friend of mine."

Bark, who had come over to look, rubbed his chin and considered the situation. Of course, they could cope with another passenger, but the process would be time-consuming. "We can lower a rope," he said.

They came to a stop. The creature stopped swimming and trod water, looking up at them as the rope descended.

"But he won't be able to hold it," said Geoca. The creature tried to grasp the rope between its teeth, but it couldn't get a grip. Geoca inclined his head towards one of the small Geocas.

Geogirl slipped down his arm and out onto the rope. She swung downwards, letting the rope slip through her grasp until she had reached the mutant. She dropped into the water and disappeared, holding the end of the rope. When she reappeared, the rope had been tied around the mutant's body.

On Geoca's signal, Bark, Bryce, and the Senator began winding the rope in. The mutant at the other end of the rope was heavy, and the winding was hard work.

It was a pig. A large boar, to be precise, with a long, heavy snout and large curved tusks, and massive flanks covered with coarse, black hair. It was almost unconscious when they heaved it onto the deck.

Geogirl scurried to Geoca and climbed back up to join her twin.

Geoca bent over the pig. The others stood back, surprised. This didn't look like any mutant at all. It looked like an ordinary, everyday pig.

The animal stirred, coughing up water. It turned its head towards the circle of faces above it.

"It's you," it said to Geoca. "I thought I was finished. Are we safe?"

"A talking pig?" In a day of firsts, it was yet another one for Bryce.

"Yes, a mutant, he's one of us. And yes, Pig, we will be safe soon." Geoca smiled and smoothed the coarse hair on the animal's brow. "These are friends of ours, and they are helping us."

The ship had begun moving again. Pig coughed more water and sat up. He looked around at the others as they went back to their posts. He felt reassured; this was infinitely preferable to drowning.

Bryce went below deck to check on Reina. She had fallen heavily when they had landed on the beach, and she had a bruise on the side of her head. Luckily there was only a small cut, and not much blood at all, but she had been unconscious since her fall. He went to where she lay and sat down beside her.

She was coming around. He stroked her forehead, brushing hair away from her face.

She opened her eyes. "Shit, my head…"

"You knocked yourself out, mate. You've had a bit of a sleep."

She propped herself up on her elbows and looked at him groggily. "Where are we? Did we make it all right?"

"Yeah. There's no damage to the ship. In fact that bump on

your head is the worst of it. And we're away again now, but we have to be careful; those helicopters followed us here, and they've trashed a whole town full of people and set fire to the place."

"Why would they do that? Are they total assholes or something?"

"They must be. They tried hard enough to waste us, didn't they?"

"Yeah." Reina shook her head and stood up. "Psycho fucks."

"Yeah. And this girl Sahrin showed up just before we took off. She's a friend of Bark's. She seems OK, Pretty cute, actually…"

Reina laughed, almost. "Fuck, my head. Stick to the plot, greaseball."

"She had this total freak with her. Name's Geodesa, or something. You wait till you see him. He's got this hole in him, with these two little dwarfs in it, and they can get out and run around."

"No shit. Somehow I'm not surprised."

"And then we picked this pig up out of the water."

"You mean something almost normal happened?"

"Not quite. The pig can talk."

Reina didn't reply. She was putting her boots on.

"Let's go see what's happening."

They went up onto the deck. The ship was approaching a range of cliffs that was broken up into a labyrinth of dead ends and fjords that seemed to disappear in every direction. "Here," Geoca said as they approached the rocks that he had pointed out from across the water.

Following his directions, Bark steered the ship under an overhang and was about to take it up into the blackness behind it when the Senator, who had been standing at the bow looking back towards the island, called out. Five helicopters were speeding towards them across the water.

"This isn't good," said Pig, standing upright with his front legs on the rail.

"They're onto us," said Reina, forgetting that a pig shouldn't be speaking.

"Quickly," said Sahrin, remembering what had happened on the island. "Whatever we're going to do, we need do it right now."

They floated upwards into the darkness, and were instantly caught up in the difference chimney's anti-gravity. Swirls of light spiraled upwards and around them, heading for the surface like a giant corkscrew.

"Are they below us?" Bark had given up trying to control the vessel. There was no choice but to surrender it to the current. They traveled smoothly upwards, circling around the axis of the vortex as they went.

Bryce and Reina leaned over the side and looked down. The helicopters had entered the shaft and were visible below them. They were rising, accelerating as they came.

"They're chasing us, all right," said Bryce.

"You are so bright it scares me. And they're gaining on us," said Reina. "They've got props. We don't."

But their advantage wasn't doing the helicopters much good. The power of their rotors was interfering with the force of the current, making it unbalanced and unpredictable. They were gaining on the ship, it was true, but they were reeling from side to side, tumbling erratically.

One of the helicopters went too close to the edge of the shaft. Its blades clipped the rock and it spun around and smashed against the surface, exploding in a ball of fire. Pieces of debris flew in all directions. One of them struck one of the other helicopters. It lurched violently, flying straight into the helicopter beside it, sending pieces of glass and metal flying everywhere.

The two machines were tangled together like mating insects rotating around a common center. Fire broke out in one of them. Flames began to spread, slowly at first and then with gathering speed. Soldiers began jumping from the helicopters. Some of them were on fire, and they floated in the current like fairy lights, bobbing up and down as though they were suspended on springs.

"Don't waste any sympathy on them," said Geoca, as one of the soldiers drifted into the spinning blades of one of the remaining helicopters and was turned into goulash. "They've got plenty to atone for. Their abuse of my people has gone on forever."

The burning helicopters were closing on them. Something on one of them exploded, tearing a hole in the side of the fuselage. More soldiers jumped ship and abandoned themselves to the mercies of the vortex.

The two remaining helicopters, one black and one red, hung back, wary of getting too close to the confetti shower of flesh and metal.

The two tangled helicopters passed harmlessly upwards through the hull of the ship, and appeared through the deck. Even though there was no danger to them, it was still disconcerting to have a burning hulk pass so close.

As the helicopters drifted through the deck, a Nefilim, splattered in both human blood and the paler pink blood of its own species, appeared in the twisted door. It clung to the door frame, injured and deciding what to do. From the way it was looking around, it was obvious that it could see them.

Events took the decision out the Nefilim's hands. The helicopter was about ten feet above the deck and still rising when it lurched suddenly, tipping the Nefilim and the bodies of some dead soldiers out. The soldiers floated away towards the outer edges of the vortex. The Nefilim landed gracefully on the deck like a huge ugly swan.

"Oh well, this is very interesting, isn't it," said Geoca.

Before anyone could do anything, the Nefilim reached out and took hold of Bryce. It lifted him off the deck and held him to its chest.

The ship lurched, caught in an eddy in the difference current. Everyone stumbled, holding on to anything that they could. Bryce tried to escape from the Nefilim's grasp, but the creature's grip was too strong and its reflexes too fast. It slashed his throat with a single talon.

The sight galvanized the others. As the Nefilim threw Bryce's twitching body overboard, Pig charged, throwing his mass against the alien's knees. There was a cracking sound as they shattered under the force. Pig dug his tusks in and tore with all his strength. The creature fell, screaming and flailing, but its arms were held by the rest of the crew who had rushed to join in. Pig jumped onto its throat, and sliced it open with his tusks. The Nefilim made a sound like nothing any of them had ever heard before, then it was dead.

Reina hadn't joined in the attack. She was standing still, in shock. "Bryce…" Her friend was dead. She tilted her head back, unwilling to see what was before her. She saw something appearing in the shaft above them, and the sight of it brought her back. She would have to wait until later to think about Bryce.

"Look!" she called to the others. The vortex was splitting like a hydra into smaller paths that branched off the main shaft. From where she stood, it looked like a Mandelbrot set, the pattern repeating itself as it flowed away into ever smaller versions of itself, upwards and away into the darkness. It was though they were traveling up the stem of a huge transparent plant. (Actually, they were, but that is another whole story.)

Geoca gave Bark directions, pointing towards one of the smaller branches. Bark maneuvered the ship towards it, taking care because the rock walls were closer now, crowding in on them.

Behind them, the helicopters, which had been relying on the Nefilim for directions in their pursuit of the ship, now had no idea which direction to take. They disappeared up another of the passages. They'd lost them.

"That's the first good thing that's happened," grumbled Bark.

"It's been a bitch of a day so far," said Sahrin. "I feel as though I've been walking around in a slaughterhouse."

"Let me tell you about it sometime," said the pig.

"Sure thing, Pig. But maybe when we have more time. What do we do now?" she asked Geoca, who alone among them seemed to have any idea of what was happening.

"We are about to… what do you call it with a vessel like this… dock? land?"

"Whatever."

"Whatever. We are near our destination."

"You mean where we have to drop the crystal thing?"

"Yes. I know exactly where to go. It shouldn't present any problems at all."

"That comes as something of a relief. I hope you're right."

The channel had opened up like the head of a giant mushroom. They entered a cavern with a huge domed roof. The trails of the vortex dissipated, leaving them floating calmly in a fine sparkling mist.

"This is one of the terminal points of the difference chimney," said Geoca, "and just over there is our landing place."

They set down on a wide ledge set into the wall. It had obviously seen much use over the ages, and the rock was worn smooth. The area was littered with artifacts and rubbish.

"But this doesn't exactly get us back to the surface, does it," said the Senator, who was becoming less and less keen on this underground stuff.

"Don't worry, we're almost there," replied Geoca. "We're underneath one of their cities. Believe me, this is the safest place for the ship at the moment. Once our mission here is done, you can take to the skies again."

There was a stairwell leading away from the landing area. They climbed upwards, and after a few minutes came to a small, very ordinary looking door set into a brick wall. "We use this route frequently," said Geoca, producing a key. "It's perfectly safe."

On the other side of the door, which Geoca carefully relocked after they had gone through, was a small room. It was empty, apart from another door, and lit by a small grate high in one wall. A barely adequate amount of sunlight filtered through the cobwebs that covered it. Geoca used another key to open the second door, and led them into a much larger room that looked as though it was a storehouse of some kind. It was lit by large, dust-encrusted arched windows. Crates and boxes were stacked in untidy piles everywhere. At the edges of the room, racks of clothes and other props covered in drop sheets hulked in the gloom like ghosts.

"Our dressing rooms," said Geoca. "This is where we disguise ourselves for the surface world. Most of you are all right, of course. But you'll understand if I take a moment to attend to my appearance. My little friends would not be as readily accepted up here as they would like."

He went to a rack and chose a long overcoat and a hat. The coat covered Geoboy and Geogirl, but from the murmuring sounds that came from beneath it, they weren't too happy about it. Looking at Geoca's face, which settled quite comfortably under the hat's wide brim, Sahrin realized that he was good looking, in a quiet sort of way. He had an air of competence about him.

"Pig," Geoca said. "What are we going to do with you?"

"There's no advantage in me coming along with you," the boar replied. "I'd stand out like dog's balls."

"True enough. It would be better if you were to wait here. We'll be as quick as we can."

Shortly afterwards, they emerged from a door in the side of an old theater in the downtown part of New York.

Interlude

The UN observation base on the moon.

Lieutenant Sider was approaching two points of completion.

The first was the end of his shift, which would be welcome enough, and the second would occur in one Earth week, when his tour of duty would end.

He would be going back on the next shuttle, to blue skies, real warmth, and real air, not out of a bottle, and fresh food. Of course he knew that, as always, after a few weeks he would get impatient with the people down there, with their trivial preoccupations and their circuses, and that would be the beginning of his yearning for the stark, unambiguous beauty of the empty lunar landscape. And then he would apply to return to where he felt most comfortable, to his friends in this sealed microcosm on the moon. To the United Nations forward observation base.

The center of a network of satellites and unmanned observation posts, they were the Earth's eyes. They kept watch, waiting and observing. They kept their superiors on Earth informed about what they saw, and kept the data feeds operating.

They had seen only fleeting glimpses on their banks of monitors and scanners, but it was enough to tell them that there was something going on. Whatever was coming from the new planet was somehow shifting through frequencies as they came out of space and headed towards the Earth.

Sider had tried to think it through, but lacking any hard facts, he had only come up with conjecture. That was all that anyone on the station had done. It had begun about a year ago, when one of them had seen it coming, heading inwards, past the orbit of Pluto and heading their way. It was too big to be a comet, or an asteroid.

They contacted Earth, and were asked whether it was a planet. It probably is a planet, they said, and you'll find it's coming to life, unless we're very much mistaken. Keep a careful eye on it, Earth said.

Of course they were going to keep a careful eye on it.

The new planet was about the size of Earth, and it had an atmosphere that was heating up as it approached the sun. They started picking up EM waves and what seemed to be communications or broadcasts. They made recordings, and sent them down to Earth, and never heard anything, except when they were told to keep sending information.

It was going to pass close to Earth. The authorities told the population that it was a comet, and most people never heard any suggestion that it was anything else. Someone leaked something into the newsgroups, but that leak was quickly found and stopped, and Aussie Bloke disappeared so quickly that no one missed him.

But the crew on the station knew that it was no comet. As it came as close to Earth as it was going to get, the EM activity became more intense, and then during one rest period, as Sider slept, dreaming of the plains and mountains that surrounded the base, whoever was on duty at the screens hit the alarm. Bleary-eyed, Sider went down to the control center and joined the others who were gathering there.

A fleet of objects had left the planet and was heading for Earth. During the next twenty four hours they watched as the objects drew closer. There were hundreds of them, arranged in an armada. Like a swarm of locusts, someone described them in a dispatch to Earth.

The authorities on Earth wanted to know everything, and kept a channel permanently open, taking all the images and data the base could send. In return, they told the base nothing.

In no time at all the fleet was upon them, and they could see in their telescopes the light glinting on the flanks of ships. Some of them where as big as the largest UN aircraft carriers that patrolled the seas on Earth. Some of them were bigger.

They tried to communicate with the ships, but there was no reply, or if there was, they didn't know how to receive it.

It was almost a beautiful sight.

Sider and a few of the others were standing in one of the viewing domes, a small transparent hemisphere joined to the rest of the complex by a narrow passageway. They were looking at the fleet, wondering, when they saw three pinpricks of light leave one of the ships.

It was soon obvious that they were heading their way, and they kept coming and coming, and one of the others said we're going to get some visitors, we're going to make contact, and Sider said maybe, but they're not slowing down, and they're getting pretty close.

They stood and watched, spellbound, as the three points of light traced achingly beautiful arcs down towards them, unerringly targeting the complex.

When the missiles hit, they destroyed most of the domes and underground structures instantly and the air exploded out of the others almost as quickly. The side of the hemisphere in which Lieutenant Sider was standing was ruptured by a piece of flying metal, and the last thing that he thought, as the blood boiled from his eyes and the cells in his body began exploding and freezing and he turned into something that was hard and dry and inside out, was that it was a pity that he hadn't met the aliens.

PART 3

Deep shit.

The General had chosen one of the tributaries off the main shaft, and was flying around in a maze of tunnels, looking for a way out.

Thead could tell that things weren't going well for the General. The bitch Sahrin had wasted a helicopter, and with it a squad of his boys, and the pursuit of the freak ship had been a total disaster. Three more helicopters gone, and thirty men, minus the couple of live ones they'd pulled out of the vortex.

The General's face was a ghostly white, and it wasn't just from the reflected glare of the searchlights.

Thead had his own concerns. For a start, he'd realized in the shaft that, like the locals, he couldn't see his old ship any more. And the feeling of being in two worlds at once, the familiar impression of being in a state of continual transference, was gone. He felt totally, undeniably physical. He'd undergone some sort of shift.

The General had turned the radio down, to get some respite from the torrent of abuse that was coming from the Gore twins. "What the fuck do you think you're doin' you little fuck I'm goin' ram your head up your ass old man just you wait till the SG hears about this you are fucking history old man that's what you are history and as for following those Nefilim freaks up here you have got no brains you piece of crap I'm gonna…"

"No one forced you to come with us, Vice-Secretary. You could have stayed on the island and finished your movie." The General flipped the switch on the torrent of abuse, which had just intensified by another degree.

"Not the best time for everyone to get edgy, General," said Thead. "We're in trouble here."

"Do you like the Gores, Thead?"

"That's irrelevant, General. I'm a scientist. And a philosopher of course, dedicated to the truth."

The General grunted. "Crap. You're a nasty little piece of work who would probably be quite happy with those idiots over there." He nodded towards the Gores' helicopter.

"You don't understand me, that's all," sniffed Thead. "Apart from which, no, I have no particular feelings for the Vice-Secretarial personalities, one way or the other." *But it's becoming increasingly obvious that they are more likely to be of use to me than you are, General,* he thought. The General had been under a dark enough cloud before they had set out on this ill-fated mission, and things would be worse, not better, after this.

They were flying above an underground river. The stink of sewage permeated everything, making them gag and stinging their eyes. Their searchlights fell on a wall of cascading water ahead of them. It was a waterfall, issuing from a great vent at least fifty feet wide, high up in a rock face.

"What is it?" asked Thead, immediately forgetting their recent animosity.

"It's not natural. Judging by the smell, I'd say it's a sewer outfall."

They flew into the sewer's mouth, the General not caring whether the Gores followed, but they did.

They soon regretted their decision. Their path narrowed and the roof became lower, until finally they were forced to set the helicopter down. When they climbed out, the General, Thead and six soldiers were standing knee-deep in raw sewage.

"Aw, shit," said one of the soldiers, holding his hand over his mouth. No one laughed.

The Gore twins arrived. As they landed, the wind from their rotors sent a slurry of sewage flying, covering everyone.

"Gas masks," the General ordered, but he was too late. They were all dripping slime.

The Gores emerged from their helicopter, fully outfitted with orgone breathers, waist-high waders, and portable halogen searchlights.

"A lovely evening for a stroll, Theo."

"I think so, Alexis. Very fine. And such bouquet." They were happy, relishing the General's predicament. They shone their lights down the tunnel. It was long.

"Hmm."

"Yes. Hmm. Shall we?"

They started walking, trudging through New York's shit.

How fitting, the General thought. His career, once bright and hopeful, had sunk to a new nadir. He'd lost men and helicopters. Two of the top Nefilim were dead and the strangers on the ship had escaped him again.

"Where are we?" asked a soldier.

"Shut up!" The Gore brother fired into the water and laughed as the soldier jumped.

"Jesus," said the General, "don't shoot at my boys, please, Vice-Secretary. We might need them."

"Awfully sorry, General," replied Alexis. "I'll try to restrain my brother's exuberance. But you must surely appreciate a certain… frustration…" Her icy blue eyes blinked behind her gas mask.

They walked for hours, entering passageways and making turns without having any idea where they were going. Finally, just when Thead was beginning to wonder if they would ever get out, a light came into view, beckoning to them from the distance. It was a welcome sight; even the Gores breathed sighs of relief behind their masks.

Shortly afterwards, they emerged from a stormwater drain into bright sunlight. They were standing in the bottom of a viaduct, surrounded by buildings. The water was cleaner here, a fact for which they were all supremely grateful as they washed themselves as well as they could.

The General tried his radio, but it had stopped working. With no choice, they started walking again, until they found a way up onto a street. They stopped at a pay phone. They would have to get someone to come and pick them up.

The skyline told them that they were in New York. *Ironic,* the General thought. There was a good chance that the SG would be in town. The perfect end to a perfect day. Pedestrians walking past held their noses and kept their distance.

He searched through his wet pockets for change for the phone and found none.

"Who's got a quarter?"

One of the soldiers handed him a coin. The Gores sniggered. The General dialed.

Half an hour later, unmarked vehicles arrived and collected them.

New York.

The group blended into New York easily. The streets were a sea of humanity in which there was no danger at all of them standing out. If anything, they were underdressed. The anonymity was reassuring.

Geoca knew the city well. He navigated their way through the streets and to a subway, where they descended into the maelstrom of the city's subway rush hour. They couldn't move in the crowded carriage. It was hot and claustrophobic, and the air was hardly breathable.

Finally, after what seemed like several hours but which was actually only one, they were walking through one of the poorer neighborhoods. It felt like a different city, with its narrow untidy streets and dilapidated buildings. Most of the shop windows were covered with metal grills, and the streets were watched over by surveillance cameras.

Reina had always supposed that of all cities, New York was the one to visit, and despite their mission, she was feeling like a tourist. For Bark, Sahrin and the Senator, it was just another large city, with the same frantic energy found in large cities in any place or any time.

It was raining, a gray drizzle that had been going on long enough to fill the gutters, causing the blocked drains to overflow, and turning the newspaper hoardings into an untidy pantheon of soggy, disintegrating newsprint.

"COMET APPROACHES NEAREST POINT," said one. "H-19 BEST SEEN TONIGHT," another proclaimed above a grainy blown-up picture of a hazy white object set in a field of black.

"What's going on? What comet?" asked Reina. They had turned down a side street, and were walking along a row of small shops that sheltered precariously beneath a freeway.

"There is no comet," replied Geoca. "It's a lie. It's Marduk, the Nefilim home planet. Which means that the photon belt is near."

They came to an antique shop. Geoca pushed the door open and went in. He waited until the others had followed, then locked the door behind them. It was a typical musty and overcrowded junk shop; shelves and displays were piled high with old ceramics, metalware and things made of old wood.

Behind the counter, which was as crowded as any other part of the shop, sat the proprietor, smoking a cigarette and reading a newspaper. "COMET FEVER GRIPS CITY," the headline read. He looked up and smiled as he recognized Geoca.

"Well, well. I've been expecting a visitor, but little did I expect that it would be you! How are you?"

"Tired, but well enough, old man. And you? How is life here on the surface?"

"I can't complain. Well, I could, but who would listen?" The shopkeeper came out from behind the counter and embraced Geoca. "It's good to see you. As for life here, I've grown used to it. It has qualities about it that grow on one. But I still miss the underworld." He surveyed the group over the top of his glasses and seemed satisfied with what he saw. "Of course, I never lose sight of my real purpose here. You have the crystal?"

"Of course," Geoca nodded. "It's taken some effort and a few lives to get it here."

"I see. Well, we knew it wasn't going to be easy. But we should proceed. There isn't much time."

"Are we close, then?"

"Yes. Very close." He led them through a narrow door out to the back of the shop, into a small and surprisingly neat living room, furnished with as tasteful a selection of items as the shop's stock could provide. From there they passed through another door, and down a flight of stairs to an alley behind the shops.

The place was shared by rubbish and rats that scurried away into the corners, and someone's makeshift bed; an old mattress in a lean-to of cardboard boxes at the end of the lane.

The old man knelt down beside an iron grating set into the wall. "Here it is."

"Here's what?" asked Bark and Reina together.

"The node," replied Geoca.

"This space here," said the shopkeeper, moving the grating aside. "It's been watched over for many years. And this is the moment I've been waiting for, all that time. Now, if I can have the crystal…"

Sahrin reached into her coat, searched among the grenades she still had there, and produced the crystal. With a sense of relief, she handed it over.

"My, but it's beautiful." The shopkeeper admired it for a moment, allowing the antique dealer in him a few seconds of indulgence. His fingers traced its finely cut surfaces.

He placed the crystal into a depression in the floor of the recess. As soon as it was in place, it began to glow with a soft blue light that pulsed gently, like a leisurely heartbeat.

As they watched, gathered around the opening in the wall as though it was a campfire on a cold night, the crystal appeared to expand. Then they saw that it wasn't the crystal itself that was growing, but rather its influence. It was as though it was taking over the rock that surrounded it. The blue light spread out in fine tendrils that slowly solidified, forming into thicker lines of force that disappeared underground.

"The paths of the Stream," the shopkeeper breathed, his voice lowered. "They will keep growing until they meet with the energy lines of the other crystals that have been placed at the other nodes, and between them they will continue to grow, until eventually the Stream will cover the planet. And it will create a new world in the process."

"How long will it take?" asked Bark. He was impressed.

Reina thought it was quite beautiful. "I want one," she said.

"Soon, my dear, everyone will be able to have as many of these as they want," the shopkeeper replied.

"No one knows how long it will take," Geoca said. "The last time this was done was over a quarter of a million years ago. And then, as far as we know, there was nothing competing with it."

"What could be competing with it?" Bark had forgotten what Sahrin had told him about the Nefilim grid.

The shopkeeper placed an old cardboard box over the crystal to conceal the glow, and replaced the grating. "The Nefilim grid. An unnatural thing, an abomination. Hideous in its genesis and hideous in its maintenance. It will fight for its survival, we can be sure of that."

"And we'll fight to destroy it," said Geoca. "Of that you can be equally sure."

They were finished here. They went back inside, where the shopkeeper opened an old bottle of Madeira and disappeared into the kitchen to cook a meal.

And they were all, they realized as they sat down to plates piled high with meat and vegetables covered with a rich sauce, hungry. After they had finished eating, which took quite some time, and were feeling mellowed by the Madeira, which took much not much time at all, the shopkeeper cleared his throat and changed the topic of conversation, which had been relaxed and casual until then. Everyone had enjoyed a respite from the trials that they had been through.

He set his glass down. "As the Stream grows, it will be in ever-greater conflict with the Nefilim grid. There are interesting times coming. There will be much turbulence, and the photon belt will only be the first of it."

"But I'm afraid," he said, filling their glasses, "that there has been an unfortunate occurrence. One of our messengers has disappeared. He was carrying a crystal to the Antarctic. We don't yet know exactly what happened to him, in fact we may never know. He could have been captured, although for his sake I hope not."

"The empty node is a problem. It is a matter of urgency that a crystal be placed there. If the geometry isn't complete, the Stream will not have the balance necessary for it to grow properly, and there is no telling how it will develop."

The others exchanged glances around the table.

"So you want us to deliver another crystal, then?" asked Bark.

"It will have to be a communal decision, of course."

They had all seen enough to know what was at stake. "We'll do it," said Reina, and the rest of them nodded. Having gone this far, turning back wasn't an option.

"Good," said the shopkeeper. "Your vessel is the only way we have of getting to the node in time. I have to confess that we were hopeful, and your answer has been anticipated. There is a courier on her way here from the underworld. She is bringing a new crystal with her."

"How long until she gets here?"

"One, maybe two days. Until then, I suggest that you take some time to relax. There is nothing more to be done until she gets here."

So they finished their evening with another bottle even older than the first, after which they all slept long and soundly, until the sound of the traffic on the freeway woke them late next morning.

Geoca and Bark went back to the cellar where Pig was waiting. They took him some fruit and vegetables, and a bottle of water, which they emptied into a bowl for him. They told him how the crystal had been placed, and then how they had agreed to go to the Antarctic.

Pig nodded solemnly as they spoke. "You'll have to get some warm clothes, then," he said after a while. "I don't suppose I'll have time to grow a winter coat."

The Senator, Sahrin and Reina were all curious about the city and they went exploring, spending the day in the crowded downtown streets. Mall culture confused the hell out of them.

* * *

The next day, the courier arrived. She knocked softly on the door of the shop, and when it was opened she darted in from the street like a mouse trying to get away from a cat without attracting its attention. She wore a long cloak that covered her from head to foot. She kept her gaze towards the ground, refusing to look up.

The shopkeeper locked the front door and they crowded into

the small living room, where she produced a bag from under her cloak.

"Please take good care of this," she said, her voice low. "Not only is it desperately needed far to the South, but it also has lives to be weighed against it. Three of us set out, and I alone have survived." She sank back in her chair, for the first time raising her head enough for them to see her.

She was strange, unsettling and beautiful, all at the same time. Her face was covered with small intersecting planes that glittered like tiny mirrors. It was impossible to tell whether it was a mask, or whether it was what she was made of. Whatever it was, it couldn't hide the underlying softness of her face. She looked like someone's idea of a robot, except that the segments moved easily, flowing like water over her as she spoke. Reflected light sparkled from her like a constellation of stars.

"What happened to your companions?" asked the shopkeeper, who was busy pouring drinks and had his back to her. "Where they taken by surface people?"

"No, we had no trouble from them. We're well used to keeping out of their way. My friends were buried by a rock fall not far from the surface."

"Oh. I'm sorry."

"I've never seen one like you before," broke in Geoca.

The shopkeeper turned to look. "Oh, my! Neither have I. Where are you from, my dear?"

The new arrival stopped trying to hide and pulled the hood back from her face. The mirrors that were her skin reflected the room and its inhabitants in a sparkling blue mosaic of tiny images.

"I am what you are," – she looked around the room – "but my type have kept to ourselves, even to the point of staying apart from the rest of the mutants. We have our own catacombs underground, and we have lived there undisturbed by any, mutant or surface people, since we all went underground after the wars against the Nefilim."

Geoboy and Geogirl were mesmerized. They had climbed out

of their hole in Geoca's torso and were perched, one on each of his knees like a pair of lap dogs, staring wide-eyed at the stranger. Geoca noticed their attentiveness. Silently, he asked them what they were thinking.

'*She's... nothing,*' the male thought back to him. '*There is nothing inside her... no thoughts...*'

'*Or nothing that we can find,*' added the female. '*It is as though she is empty...*' She was unsure of what to say, and her thoughts trailed off. '*But she's so beautiful...*'

The blue woman was still talking. "We know, as you do, the danger posed by the surface people and the Nefilim. Alone or together, the two races are capable of inflicting great suffering. We remember the Nefilim well. That's why we've decided to help you. I'll come with you, if I can."

"Then you should depart as soon as possible," said the shopkeeper to them all.

* * *

They left the antique shop and started towards the basement where Pig was waiting. They hadn't even reached the subway when the photon belt arrived.

"What..?" They looked around, and then up. Great colored bands of light were sweeping across the sky, as though they were inside a gigantic kaleidoscope. The colors of the buildings and people around them shifted and changed, racing to match those in the sky.

"It's happening, then," said the Senator, drawing his coat around him, even though he wasn't cold.

"It's real," said someone else. "Did you ever doubt it?"

"Of course I did. Didn't you?"

Before they could do or say anything else, the great darkness fell on them, dropping out of the sky like a stone. They were surrounded by total, impenetrable blackness. Bark held his hand up in front of his face. He couldn't see it. He could see nothing.

"Everyone come to me. Hold on to each other, and don't let

go." He felt someone take hold of his arm.

"What the hell are we going to do now?" Like all of them, Reina hadn't given any thought to the arrival of the belt. It had seemed too weird.

"Three days of darkness." someone groaned. "And we're stuck in it."

"Where the fuck are we?" Sahrin demanded, sounding a lot braver than she felt.

"Well, we've no way of telling that," said Bark, "but we do need to find shelter. With no sun for three days, it's going to get cold."

"And there are millions of people in this city," said Reina. "They're going to be confused and desperate. And dangerous."

The silence that had fallen around them with the darkness was giving way to the sounds of panic and confusion. People were calling out each other's names, or calling for help from anyone. Some were just screaming.

Cars had crashed and people were injured. A truck had caught fire. In the faint pool of impossibly weak light cast by the flames, they could see bodies lying on the ground. Someone was hurt and trying to get up, but they couldn't. Someone ran out of the darkness, and knelt down to help. From behind them somewhere came the sound of gunshots.

"I'd say keeping our heads is the first thing. This is going to be three days of ugliness. We'd better find somewhere safe."

"Can we get to the basement from here?" someone asked.

"Too far," said Geoca. "We'd get lost, nothing is surer."

"We're lost *now*," said the Senator. He wasn't taking the situation well. He didn't like the dark.

Someone ran up to them, careering blindly through the darkness. They collided with Bark, almost knocking him to the ground. "GET OUT OF MY FUCKIN' WAY!" a bodiless voice yelled, stumbling into a couple more of the group before running off. There was a thudding sound as whoever it was hit something hard and immobile that refused to fall over. A few seconds of stunned silence were followed by the sound of carefully measured footsteps and cursing moving away from them.

The group clung to each other, but didn't move.

"Don't be afraid," said an unfamiliar voice.

"Who..? Oh… it's you…"

It was the blue woman.

"Yes. Can you see now?" They could. Her hands were glowing, and where she held them out, they could see the pavement, bathed in the pale light that emanated from her skin. There was just enough for them to see what they were walking on.

They edged slowly along the road, staying close to the buildings, until they found a doorway leading off the street. They went in. It was some sort of reception area.

"Thanks," Bark said.

"That was a nice trick," added Reina. "What's your name?"

"A name… what would I do with one of those?" she laughed. "Names only get you in trouble. I prefer to travel light."

"I think we might have sufficient idle time over the next few days to deal with propositions as arcane as that." The Senator was looking through some cupboards.

"But practicalities first, I think," said Bark. "Let's see what's here."

It was a doctor's office, or some sort of medical clinic.

"Very useful," said Reina, not meaning it. "A supermarket or a deli would have been closer to the mark."

"If they have something to do with food, you're quite right," answered Bark.

"They do. And I am."

The blue woman sat down on the floor and leaned against a wall. "You need more light." She lowered her head and slid into some sort of trance. "I can keep this up as long as I don't have to move," she said. Her skin lit up as though a switch had been thrown somewhere. She shrugged out of her cape, letting it fall away to expose her bare torso. The room filled with light.

"What do we do now?" someone asked.

"We wait, answered Bark, "for the darkness to pass."

"When it does, there'll be chaos. If what Obirin told me was correct, none of their energy systems will work," said Sahrin. "There will be no electricity. Everything will fall apart."

Geoca sat down next to the blue woman. "There may be no electricity, but there will be the Nefilim grid, don't forget. Of course, it won't be the general population who get to benefit from it, you can be sure of that. There will be a new order. Things will never be the same again. That's why the Stream is so important." Geoca's helpers scurried onto his crossed legs, where they crouched, once again engrossed in the sight of the shining woman.

They slept. When they woke, it was time to think of food. All they had found in the doctor's rooms was a jar of jellybeans.

"A search party!" proclaimed Bark. "Consisting of myself, firstly because it's my idea and secondly because I don't feel like sitting around here doing nothing, and one volunteer. There's no need to expose all of us to what's going on out there."

"You're forgetting something," said Reina, who had just woken up. She had no intention of getting out from under the blankets that she had taken from the doctor's linen supply, which for some unknown but happy reason had been well stocked. It was cold, as someone, she forgot who, had said it would be, and as soon as this little talkie bit was over, she was going to submerge again and go back to sleep. "It's pitch black out there. You can't see zip."

The shining woman lifted her head. "Come here," she said to Bark. "Kneel down beside me and close your eyes."

He did as she said. She placed her fingertips on his eyelids. She held them there for a few seconds and then took her hand away.

"You can open your eyes now."

Bark opened his eyes. Everything was illuminated by an internal light. It was beautiful. *Everything* was beautiful. "Is this how you see?" he asked, looking around incredulously. It was as though everything was made of crystal. It was cleaner, more pristine than anything he could have imagined. The only time he had ever seen anything similar was long ago on a beach on some nameless planet when a stranger had given him some even stranger drugs.

"You should be able to find your way around now," said the shining woman, without answering his question. "Who else is going to go with you?"

"Reina," replied Bark, looking at the light that glowed inside each of the people in the room, pulsing a rainbow of colors and frequencies that was different for each of them. Except the blue woman. When he looked at her, all he saw was a dark black shape, as though he was looking into the emptiness of deep, starless space.

"No way," said Reina. "And thanks for asking. I'm quite comfortable here."

"Yes, but, my dear, while I appreciate – indeed, share – your predilection for your creature comforts, you must agree that you are the only one among us who has any real knowledge of the world out there. Even though it's not your city, it's still your culture. And further, I think it reasonable to propose that the communal good should take priority over your desire for comfort."

Even before he had finished, Reina had said "shit," rolled her eyes, and started pulling her boots on. "I suppose, then," she grumbled. "I want to get a warmer jacket anyway."

She sat down in front of the blue woman and was soon seeing things the way Bark saw them.

* * *

An emerald green sky covered New York like a giant sheet of infinitely thick glass. Beneath it, the city glittered in the diamond light of the vision that the blue woman had given them. Reina felt as though she was on an alien planet. Bark had the same feeling, but in his case that was to be expected, of course.

The streets were virtually empty. There were bodies lying around, and a couple of stragglers wandering around in what was to them total darkness. Bark and Reina helped them indoors and got them set up with food and something to keep them warm.

Mostly, though, people had gone underground, finding their way into buildings, or at least some sort of shelter.

In the distance, a row of office buildings was on fire. The sight of it stopped them in their tracks, even though they were a city block away. The flames were black, and were surrounded by a nimbus of black fog. Above them, radiant blue clouds of smoke billowed from the burning buildings, trailing upwards towards the sky and disappearing into the green surface like the tentacles of a jellyfish. More trails of smoke in the distance connected the ground and the sky like lightning strikes.

A crowd of people had gathered around the flames. In the darkness that the photon belt had brought, fire was the only source of heat or light. A few people were carrying torches made of pieces of wood, but the darkness clung like treacle, and the flames weren't casting anything like the light that they normally would have. A fight had broken out in the crowd.

They stood watching for a couple of minutes, and then decided that they should keep moving. They had to find food and get back, and it was cold, and getting colder.

They found a shopping mall. Reina chose a jacket from a shop, and then they found some backpacks. Reina found another jacket there that she liked better, and swapped them, and Bark found a pair of boots and a black woolly hat. Reina thought it made him look like a cheap criminal, a house burglar or something, but he liked it, so she said nothing.

The age of fashion sensibilities had passed, anyway. Even so, she found a third jacket that she liked even more.

In a supermarket they filled the backpacks with food and drink and anything else that might be useful. The few staff and customers who had been in the place when the darkness fell had set up camp in the aisles. They had candles for light, food to eat, and blankets for warmth, which made them incredibly wealthy by current standards, at least until the light returned. None of the inhabitants confronted the two intruders, except to ask for news of the outside world.

"Don't bother going out there," Bark told them.

"The manager went outside a few hours ago," someone replied, "and he hasn't come back yet."

"Aisle three, on the right about half way down," said a woman when Reina asked her where they could find a can opener. She was making coffee on a gas burner borrowed from the hardware department.

Everything was going well. Laden with supplies, they left the supermarket and set off towards the doctor's office. Reina stopped to pick up some magazines from the contents of a newsstand that had spilled over onto the footpath. As she knelt down to gather the magazines together, idly wondering what someone like Geoca or the blue woman would read or whether they read at all, a light rain began to fall.

Bark grabbed her by the collar and dragged her into a doorway.

"What the fuck! It's only rain! What are you...?" Her protests trailed off as she saw it, coming down the street towards them, moving deliberately and slowly. It was a vehicle, but it was unlike anything she had ever seen before. It was slung low, and had no wheels; it was floating on some sort of field, and whatever it was made of shone brilliantly with a white light, or white as they were seeing things at the moment, anyway. It was uncovered, and on it sat three human soldiers and three Nefilim, all armed, or at least carrying things that looked like weapons, even though they weren't like any guns that Reina had seen before. All of them, human and alien, were wearing visors of some kind. From the way they were looking around, it was obvious that they could see their surroundings.

Reina and Bark retreated into a doorway and crouched down behind some overflowing rubbish bins.

The raft drifted silently past them. As it neared an intersection, a middle-aged man carrying a kerosene lantern appeared from a side street and walked out onto the road. In the meager visibility provided by his light, he didn't see the raft until it was almost upon him.

It would have been the first time he had seen a Nefilim. He staggered backwards, his mouth open in silent shock at the vision that had come sliding out of the darkness towards him. In panic, he threw the lantern clumsily towards the raft. It hit the side of the vehicle, bounced harmlessly off, and rolled along the road. Kerosene spilled onto the ground, where the flame caught it.

The raft didn't stop or deviate from its course as one of the soldiers raised his weapon. There was a thin hissing sound and a beam of light shot towards the man, striking him in the center of his chest. He staggered and fell to the ground. The aura of light inside him flared up like a small supernova. He became totally white, as though he was being consumed. Then he disappeared.

The raft slid silently down the street and disappeared around a corner.

"Shit," said Bark. "That's the word, isn't it?"

"Let's get back," said Reina, looking at the white smudge on the ground that was the only remaining trace of the man.

As they walked, they kept a careful watch for any more soldiers or Nefilim.

"The Nefilim grid," said Reina. "The raft must have been powered by it. And the gun as well."

"I suppose they'd have to be," agreed Bark. "Nothing else seems to be working. They'll be totally in control when the light comes back, if they keep that up."

"That's if the three-day thing is right," said Reina.

"I think it will be. I've heard of things like this photon belt before, in other parts of the universe, even though I've never seen one. They always pass."

"Oh. Do they always kill electricity? It's a bit inconvenient if they do..."

"Well, that's hard to say. You see, this planet is the first place I've ever encountered this electricity that you talk about."

"Yeah? What does everyone else use?"

"Oh... well, there's gravity, water, sunlight, starlight, mental energy, the space winds, such as my ship uses, and the crystals, of course. In the case of the Stream, the crystals are being used to focus the natural energy paths of the planet. Of course, there are other ways to use crystals."

"I know. You can hang them in a window."

"I suppose you could. But crystals have form, and order. The keys to the power of the universe are locked into their lattice structures. Quite literally. The beauty of ratio and numbers is there, and the power of helixes and pyramids and spirals. It's all there."

"Then what about the Nefilim grid? Does that use crystals as well?"

"I know only what the stories about the Nefilim say. From what I've heard, they extract the life energy from living beings and use it to maintain their system. It's totally artificial, and has nothing to do with any of the natural systems of a planet. The Nefilim have created their own geometry to allow this to happen, but it is a geometry that needs to be constantly held in place."

"How do they get the life force out of someone, then?"

"You've seen the light that radiates from inside people? The light that you've been able to see with the vision that we've been given? I've never seen it before, but it's the life force; I'm certain of it. Each individual has their own, with their own stamp on it. It resonates with their own frequency. Somehow, the Nefilim must be able to use that by taking it into their system. I don't know how they do it, but we can assume that it's far from pleasant, and not beneficial to the individuals concerned."

"And the system we're creating?"

"You've seen as much of it as I have, I suppose. The crystals amplify the planet's natural energy. Each planet is like a huge crystal, as you know... oh, well, you know *now* then... with exactly the same vortices as the smaller crystals that you are familiar with. Or not familiar with. When one of the crystals is put in place, it acts as a catalyst, or an amplifier. When the process is complete, and the Stream has grown and developed, like a living thing, for it *is* a living being, in a sense, the entire planet will be bathed in energy, available for anyone and everyone.”

“How do you know that?”

“I’m well traveled, Reina. I’ve seen it done before. I’ve seen most things done before.”

“Sahrin tells me that your ship can travel through time.” Reina was making the most of this opportunity to get some questions answered.

“Well, yes…” Bark hesitated. “But don’t make too much of that.”

“Why not? Sounds pretty good to me.”

“It is, but we can’t just do it at will, which is what you might be thinking. We travel the universe by sailing the currents of the space winds. Think of rivers and how they run through a landscape, twisting and turning around obstacles, narrow in some areas and wide in others, flowing fast or slow, deep or shallow, depending on the terrain. It’s the same in space, and in some of the currents, time varies. You can travel backwards or forwards in time, and to particular places. So it can be that if you take one route to a place, you will arrive in its past, but if you take another route, you will arrive in the future. Like the ports on a river, the main stops are known to all the ship’s captains. And just like a river system, a backwater is a backwater. And this planet of yours is in one of the backest waters I’ve ever come across.”

“No shit. So we can go to the future or the past if we want? That could be useful, couldn’t it? We could go back, to before all this happened, and put the crystal in its place a few months ago, before all these goons started running around killing everyone.”

Bark laughed. “No, but it’s a nice thought. For one thing, this planet is in a pretty wild part of the universe, as I said. We only found our way here because of an old map that we could barely understand. This area hasn’t been surveyed, as far as I know. There might be timeflows here, but if there are, they’re not on any chart that I know of.”

“Pity. They sound great.”

“Oh, they are. You haven’t seen anything until you’ve seen the time drifts as they twist around the Naan nebulae. Or the time banks of the Sentori system, where time has been trapped, and builds up in vast mountains. Perhaps I'll show you one day…"

"Yes… maybe…"

They walked for a while in silence. They passed a wall covered with the same white marks that had been left when they had seen the man shot. There were a dozen or more, as though people had been lined up against the wall. "If this is their new world order," said Reina, "I don't think much of it."

"Neither do I," said Bark, then, his attention on something else, "Look at that. Up there." He was looking up into the sky.

Reina looked. A swarm of shooting stars was moving across the sky. There were hundreds of them, too many to count. Each one appeared first as a tiny point of light, a pinhole in the firmament, then flared in intensity as it floated downwards on a long shallow gradient.

After a few seconds, each light winked out of existence, leaving smaller fragments that fell towards the earth, trails of smoke following them as if they were spent fireworks. It went on for a minute or so, and then the sky was as empty as it had been before, its emerald expanse clear again.

"A meteor shower?" said Reina.

"Best guess, I suppose," said Bark, "although given the current state of things, it could be anything."

They had reached the doctor's rooms.

The Secretary General's New York office.

It was dark outside, but on the fortieth floor of the United Nations building, behind the drawn curtains of the Secretary-General's office, the lights were burning. In the corner, a fax machine purred softly as it accepted a message from somewhere.

The power wasn't coming from the backup power system, for that was as dead as the main system. The building was plugged into the new grid.

The Secretary-General lowered himself into a seat. He was big, and years spent in offices and meetings had only served to make him larger and softer. He almost rippled as he relaxed against the soft antelope vellum of the couch. His eyes were like pissholes in snow, set into skin that hung off him in moist oily folds. He leaned across his stomach and pushed a small onyx box along the table.

"Cigarette, President Veal?"

The President took a cigarette without saying anything and lit it.

"I'm sorry, Theo," the Secretary-General continued. "Do carry on."

The Vice-Secretary picked up where he had left off. "So as I was saying, we filmed our operation. One should always document one's successes, don't you agree? I have it here, if you care to see it…"

"But of course, dear boy, of course," the Secretary-General wheezed. "Into the machine with it. You don't mind, do you, General?"

The General sat nursing a whiskey. "Of course not." He would have loved to say what he thought of them and their habit of filming their exploits, but he and the Gores continued as always to observe the unspoken rule, and behaved themselves in front of the Secretary-General.

The Vice-Secretary hit play. The first segment had been shot from the air, while the helicopters were circling above the island. Missiles and tracer fire spat from just off camera, down onto the buildings and fleeing creatures. The camera zoomed in on a mutant that had been cut neatly in two. Its arms flailed around uselessly, then it was consumed by flame from somewhere. The sound of laughter came from behind the camera.

After a few more panoramic shots, the scene changed. They were on the ground. Alexis Gore was standing outside a burning building, holding a small lizard-headed creature up off the ground. She turned and threw it into the flames, and then reached out of shot and took another similar but larger creature by the neck and dragged it into view.

"Well, here we are in the hottest news spot in the cosmos," she laughed to the camera. "And here I am speaking with one of the local citizenry. Sir or madam – why, you're just such a goddamn freak, I just don't know what I should call you, now do I? You seem to be having a spot of civil unrest here! A bit of bother, some might say! Would you care to comment?"

The creature said nothing. "What? No comment?" She shook the mutant. "Well, shall I just bring it on home to you then, lizard breath? A little first hand experience?" She drew her pistol from its holster and held it to the mutant's temple. "Well? No? Oh well, damn it…" Her shot took the mutant's head off.

The scene changed. Soldiers were herding a group of mutants toward the end of an alley. With nowhere to go, they gathered in a group against a wall. They seemed to know what was coming, and some of them were trying to protect the others. The soldiers lined up, taking their time and joking among themselves, and then someone gave the order. It was finished in a few seconds.

"Damn, those Uzis are just the most excellent things," said Theo Gore, from his spot on the couch beside his sister. "I swear, you could plow a field with one."

There was more. When the tape was finished, the Secretary-General cast the closest thing he had to a beatific smile in the direction of the two Gores. "Well done, both of you. An excellent job. I take it you cleaned the place out thoroughly?"

"We *all* cleaned the place out thoroughly, Secretary-General," interrupted the General.

"Ah yes, General. You were there, of course. And your boys acquitted themselves well, I hope."

"Of course, Secretary-General. There was nothing left standing."

"Except..." prompted the Secretary-General.

"Yes, yes. Except the strangers' ship. It got away. Chasing it cost us dearly. After the two Nefilim were killed, we had no hope at all of finding it. They were the only ones who could see it."

"Goddamn freaks. From now on, always have a couple of them with you when you go out. And in separate vehicles, so they don't both get iced at the same time."

"Yes, Secretary-General." *I might have thought of that myself anyway, asshole.*

"Secretary-General," Vice-Secretary Theo interrupted. "We've all of us been mighty busy keeping law and order and showin' the freaks who's boss, and we're just a touch behind the play. What's happening with those Nefilims?"

"Well," chuckled the Secretary-General, the thought improving his mood, "whatever their plans were, we gave them a few surprises. They were expecting us to be backward, or at any rate a pushover. We had a few tricks that they weren't expecting. We seem to have caused something of a rift in their ranks."

"Well, ain't that a sha..."

"Quiet, boy, I'm talking. There seems to be a faction among the bonies that want to go the full distance and fight us for control. They want everything to be how they planned, with them on top and we humans as their slaves. But they're no problem; we've got the troublemakers put away. We had to kill a few, but the rest are safely locked up. And of course there have been the more sensible ones, who've decided to throw in their lot with us. Some of their leaders have come over to us, and brought their followers with them. A much better option than joining their friends in the deep freeze, they seem to think. They're a screwed up lot, these Nefilim, if you ask me. They're just as bad as us, with their factions and their lack of unity. Why, did you know that there's actually some of them down there with the mutants? They've been there all along. Rebel Nefilim, if you please! Jesus! President Veal... what's the matter, are you not feeling well?"

"Oh... a little dizzy, that's all..." The European President wasn't looking at all well. He was sweating, and fumbling with the buttons on his jacket.

"Well now, you shouldn't work so hard, Veal." The Secretary-General smiled, then continued. "So, the new order is not exactly what our friends had envisioned. They've supplied us with their technology, including their energy grid and their vehicles and weapons, and we, of course, are in control of the situation. When the darkness lifts, the population of the world's major cities will look up into the sky and see the Nefilim craft that are being put into place right now. They will be told that they belong to visitors from space, who have come out of the kindness of their hearts to share their technology and knowledge with we Earthlings. The official line will be that they've come to help us get over the terrible effects and chaos wrought by the darkness and the collapse of the power supply. Of course, the general confusion will demand that we impose strict martial law, especially in the cities and around the bases and grid points. Naturally, we'll get as much mileage as we can out of our new allies. Law and order will be the responsibility of the two Vice-Secretaries, of course."

The Gores beamed. It was good to be appreciated.

"I'll introduce you to your Nefilim counterparts later. There's a lot to be done. There are potential troublemakers to round up, and the transfer to the new energy system must not be held up by any civil unrest."

The Secretary-General turned to the General. "Don't worry, General. I'm not forgetting you. We have need of your services in another area. Even though your recent action underground did a lot of damage to the mutants, they're still causing trouble. It appears that they're trying to set up some sort of energy source in competition to our own. Of course, we can't allow this."

"Once the immediate problem of this grid-making fantasy of theirs has been dealt with, I'm going to put you in charge of solving the mutant problem once and for all. We'll get the public on our side by telling them that the mutants are another race of aliens, bent on our destruction. A few public executions should get the message across. Hangings, maybe. Crowds have always liked a good hanging. We'll use the mobs to track them down. Some blood sport will provide some diversion and be good for public morale. But that's later, General. Something for you to look forward to. First, we have to deal with this system of theirs. We don't know how complete it is, but we know that they're working on it. We captured one of them, not far from the Antarctic. He was carrying one their accursed crystals, but we couldn't get his destination out of him. He's dead now, which is unfortunate. I'm sure we could have cracked him eventually."

"We figure, General, that since we've got their crystal, they'll be sending another in its place. And just in case they decide to send that weird ship of theirs to do the job, I want you to be there to welcome them. You'll be leaving for the Antarctic immediately. I want that ship. I want to know how it works, and I want those people. I want to know where they're from, and how they got here."

"Will we be traveling in the new fliers, Secretary-General?" The General was looking forward to a chance to redeem himself.

"Of course, unless you'd rather walk. Nothing else is working. Three of them have been set aside for you, complete with their Nefilim crew and the human pilots they're training."

"Excellent. I've wondered what those things are like on the inside."

The Secretary-General poured everyone more to drink. "I saw inside one yesterday, actually. They're quite something. Far in advance of anything of ours, of course. But that's irrelevant. We have them now. I wonder how things would have turned out if we'd known that the Nefilim had stored hundreds of them underground for all that time. Just sitting there, waiting for their owners to come out of hibernation. We probably would have ripped the place apart looking for them," he laughed. "We're still finding out what they're capable of. Accept nothing less than total co-operation from your Nefilim crew, General. If you have any trouble at all with them, let headquarters know at once."

The General nodded.

President Veal lurched forward in his seat. "I'm sorry, I'm going to be..." Sick, probably, but he never finished his sentence. He clutched the back of his head and tried to stand up. He failed, and collapsed in a twitching heap on the floor. A few seconds later, he stopped moving altogether.

"Oh dear," said the Secretary-General, without moving. "A dead President! What are we going to do?"

No one moved or spoke.

"Well, it solves a problem, I suppose. I must admit, I had no idea how Veal and his bureaucratic cronies were going to make themselves useful in the future. He shouldn't have been smoking, perhaps. Not these, anyway." The Secretary-General laughed to himself and picked up the box of cigarettes from the table.

"You mean...?"

"Yes, I'm afraid I do, Alexis my dear," said the Secretary-General. "One of the responsibilities of power, as you know, is having to make the hard decisions. Such is the price of greatness."

"Hot damn. Very neat, if you don't mind me saying, Secretary-General."

"Not at all. Neat, yes. The chemists tell me that there will be no trace of anything in his bloodstream or his lungs. A purely academic point, of course, since there will be no autopsy. But it's a nice testament to good work on their part."

His eyes flicked down at the dead President.

"Poor old thing. He looks so peaceful. Oh well, I suppose we'll just have to make Europe a special UN protectorate. No time for elections now. Such is life." A gurgling sound escaped from the corpse's lungs.

"Now, where was I… ah yes, General, find that ship, that's right. Take the boy with you." The Secretary-General flicked a casual finger towards the end of the couch where Thead had been sitting quietly, watching and listening. What a terrible and efficient branch of humanity this was. In all the variants of the race that were scattered among the stars, he had never before encountered anything like this. No one had ever gotten the better of the Nefilim before, but these people had done it.

At that moment Thead knew, deep in his soul, that he was on the right side.

"An absolute pleasure, Secretary-General," he purred. "If the ship and my former crew mates are anywhere near this Antarctica place you talk about, I will make it my first priority to deliver them to you, by any means possible."

"That's a good boy. But make it your first priority *regardless* of where the ship is. And feel free to use all means, including the impossible." The Secretary-General got up and went to his desk. He pressed a button on the intercom and asked for someone to come and take the President away, then spoke to the room again.

"I think that's all we need to cover for now. Thank you all for your attendance. Your co-operation is very much appreciated, of course," he smiled, then added, "Don't trip over the President as you leave. Oh, Thead. Stay a while. I'd like to talk."

As the others left, they passed two soldiers coming into the room with a stretcher. The Secretary-General put a finger to his lips, silencing Thead while the soldiers bundled the President's body into a bag and zipped it up.

"A tragic loss," intoned the Secretary-General as the soldiers departed.

"What did you want to see me for, Secretary-General?" Thead asked after they had gone.

"First, Thead, I want to share a wonderful sight with you. It's almost time."

The Secretary-General pressed a button, and the lights in the room dimmed. Another button, and the curtains that covered the window slid back to reveal the darkness outside. Apart from the hundreds of fires burning out of control in the city below, everything was black.

"Looks like hell, doesn't it? I'm told we've lost a few suburbs. Normally I could offer you an excellent view of the city. It stretches as far as the eye can see. But even though we're blinded, as it were, there's something I want you to see. Wait."

They stood in silence, Thead not sure where to look or what to look for.

"Come on, come on… ah, there it is! Up there, boy! High in the sky! Look at that!"

Thead looked up and saw the same points of light that Bark and Reina were watching from another part of the city. They watched in silence as the lights flared then broke up, falling towards the Earth in thousands of burning fragments.

In a few minutes it was over, and the sky was as dark as it had been before.

"What was that?"

"That, boy, was the last you'll ever see of the invasion fleet from the Nefilim home planet. They just blew themselves to hell on HAARP! We've had it installed for years. As soon as they touched the layer of harmonic scalars, well… they disintegrated. Their craft just fell apart. Alien stir-fry, God knows how many of them!"

The Secretary-General laughed loudly. For now, he was a truly happy man. "If the Nefilim down here were planning on getting any help from home, they're going to be mighty disappointed! It's looking good, Thead. It's looking damn good! We're on top of things!"

He paused for a moment. When he spoke again, his tone had changed. "Can you understand our power, Thead? There is nothing that can stand in our way. With the alien technology, and their help – regardless of whether or not they want to give it – the stars themselves will soon be ours! You've been there, you've traveled through the universe; I don't doubt you for a moment, boy. Your experience will be most valuable. Get me that ship of yours, Thead, and you'll find that my gratitude can be plentiful. I remember those who help me."

"Tomorrow is a bright place, my boy, and it is adorned with the banners and flags of a humanity that has claimed its rightful place in the galaxy. I intend to be remembered by future generations as the leader who pulled Earth back from the brink of disaster and led humanity in its conquest of the stars!"

Thead thought about the universe. Not the whole universe, of course, because that would have taken more time than he had right now, but he did have time to briefly contemplate the state of at least part of the universe as he knew it. Because it was so easy for anyone to go anywhere, there was no fuss made about territory. Borders had long ago ceased to mean much. The galaxy was a fluid, messy place; the many races that shared it tended to co-operate, and for the most part in peace.

The reason the Nefilim were so infamous was that they were, in all the known history of the universe, the only race that had resorted to violent conquest and enslavement. In the face of their fleets of warships, their weapons and their brutality, the scant resistance that the more peaceful races had put up had meant nothing. When the Nefilim horde had come sweeping in from the distant edge of the galaxy (this edge of the galaxy, Thead realized now), they had swept the soft civilizations of the inner star systems ahead of them like dust before a wind.

And when their progress through the galaxy had stopped for no apparent reason, and they had retreated, disappearing as quickly as they had come, they had left behind nothing but an abiding fear of them. Who they were and where they had come from had been lost, if it was ever known, under layer upon layer of myth and legend. *What a terrible, beautiful thing their history was,* thought Thead.

But now the Nefilim had met their match in these humans. Pragmatic, cunning, treacherous, deceitful – no puerile abstractions of compassion or peace for this race. If the Earthmen wanted to take the stars, there was nothing out there to stand in their way. Tomorrow belonged to them, just as the Secretary-General was saying.

"But I didn't just want to show you the fate of our enemies, Thead, as inspiring as it is. After all, you've already seen that at close quarters, and you performed well yourself, I'm told. No, there's something else. A little task I want you to perform during your trip to the ice."

The Secretary-General drew the curtains and turned the lights back on.

"Sit down, Thead."

Interlude

What we did during the darkness at Barker's Mill.

Seventy-two hours after it had arrived, the darkness passed. The sky shuddered and convulsed as though a cover was being dragged away, and in an instant the darkness was replaced by a radiant, uniform light unlike anything anyone had seen before.

The sun had become a pale orange orb in the sky, as though its fire had been washed away. Just as the darkness had been total, so too the new light seemed to have no center. It was everywhere. It was as though the sky and the light had become the same thing.

Barker's Mill came through in reasonable shape. The darkness had come late on a moonlit evening, while most people had been indoors, and being a small town, it lacked the dangers of a big city.

Onethian had been at Tommy's house, wondering whether he should write his memoirs, when it happened. The stars visible through the window in front of him disappeared, and a few seconds later the power failed. He went to the kitchen and rummaged around until he found candles and some matches. Then, thinking that this was as good an omen as any, he began writing, which apart from sleeping is how he spent the rest of the Darkness, as it came to be known.

Tommy and Ortega spent the seventy-two hours of the Darkness in the Red Lion. This was an accident, albeit a happy one. Apart from the barmaid, they had been the only people in the place, so they had a plentiful supply of beer, potato crisps and peanuts for the duration.

None of them had any idea what was going on.

"It's the end of the fucking world, that's what it is," said Tommy. Neither the barmaid nor Ortega could come up with any convincing argument to the contrary.

"Not looking good," lamented Ortega.

"Not looking like anything, is it, mate," Tommy had replied.

Using matches for light, the barmaid led them to the upstairs rooms. There they spent the three days, thinking that time, or the planet, or something, had stopped.

By the time the light returned and the cold began to abate, they had eaten pretty much everything in the place that could be eaten, and had made serious inroads into the bar's top shelf.

And they all knew each other a lot better. "Well," said Tommy, "we won't forget that in a hurry, will we."

Ortega said nothing. He was sleeping off a bottle of vodka. Denise was finding her clothes.

"You won't tell anyone, will you," she said, slipping her t-shirt on. "I mean it was fun and everything, but we thought it was the end, didn't we? We didn't think we'd see daylight again. I sure didn't, anyway."

"I'm not so sure we're seeing it now." Tommy was looking out the window. The dull, anemic disk of the sun hung in the sky like a paper cutout. He wasn't just looking at the sun, though; the window also provided a good view of the harbor, and on its far side, the sand dunes that surrounded the military base.

Hovering above the base, motionless, were two cigar-shaped craft. They were big, and they glowed with a soft orange light that hung around them like an aura. He had never seen anything like them before, and they had no markings on them that might give a clue as to whose they were.

"Don't worry," he said. "It'll be our secret. I don't think anyone'll be caring about what we got up to, anyway."

A pained groan came from Ortega's direction. He was coming around. Tommy smiled. That'd teach him.

Denise went to where Ortega lay. She leaned over and ruffled his hair, then kissed him. She did the same to Tommy and went to the door.

"You're nice boys. Thanks for the good time. You can let yourselves out, okay? I'd better find the boss and see what's happening."

"No worries."

PART 4

Ice.

When the light returned, they left the doctor's office and returned to the basement where Pig was waiting. With the subway out, they had to walk all the way, and it took them hours of navigating their way through streets full of people wandering around in shock, looking up at the new sky with open mouths, before they finally reached the old theater.

*   *   *

They were glad to get back to the ship. Exactly how Geoca navigated them through the network of underground passages and caves and found their way to the surface was beyond any of them. He stayed quiet, as though he was listening to something, and spoke only when he whispered directions to Bark. After several hours, the ship emerged from a cave located high in a cliff face.

This was a place that the surface dwellers rarely visited, said Geoca. It was a wilderness area, supposedly protected for the sake of the environment, but actually used by the authorities for secret research that was carried out in large, isolated compounds hidden in the most inaccessible parts of the park.

Geoboy and Geogirl knew about it. They created one of their mental slide shows and showed it to the others. It began with chalets set in idyllic forest settings and against backdrops of majestic mountain scenery. Inside the buildings, grim-faced men and women oversaw animals in cages or in various kinds of apparatus, or being dissected alive or burnt with chemicals. There were diseases beyond imagination. Animals and prisoners wrapped in tinfoil were being cooked alive with radiation. Humans and mutants were there as well, undergoing the same experiments. They all had numbers tattooed on their foreheads; they weren't going anywhere. There was more suffering here than anyone on the ship could think about.

Bark shook himself loose from the vision. With him not

attending to it, the ship was rolling away from its center. He brought them back onto the right course, still wondering at the local humans. How could they do these things?

The others kept watching as the vision continued. Finally, it finished with the sight of acid baths, in which bodies were being dissolved. When it finished and her eyes had cleared and refocused on the material world around them, Reina turned away without saying anything and walked to where Pig was lying on the deck. She sat down beside him.

"Pig, I saw you just now. When you were young. You were in that place, weren't you? In one of the cages. I recognized you. I don't know how."

The vision, which he had seen as well, had left Pig disconsolate, confronted again by memories he would rather leave behind. "I was there, yes. I was born – no, I was created – there. I am no work of nature. I am the result of their experiments. Not really mutant, not of the underworld, like Geoca, but the product of the surface dwellers and their manipulation. I don't know exactly what they did to make me how I am. I don't much care." Pig was choosing his words carefully. "I was rescued from the vivisectionists when I was young. The recollection that I have of my time there is disorganized, just a string of impressions and feelings."

"Geoca and some other mutants came in the middle of the night, they tell me. They destroyed the place, so that the surface dwellers could not perform their evil there any more, and took away the animals and other victims they found there. I was one of them. They took us underground, and cared for us there."

"So they raised you as one of their own?"

"Yes. But I like the surface, I like the space, and the open air and the freedom. I would very much like to live under this new sky that is above us now, but it is safer underground. With my friends and their kind. What do you think, Reina?"

"Think of what, Pig?"

"Of our situation. Of what you've seen."

Reina didn't know what to say. "Well, I don't know if I'd rather be delivering fruit and vegetables or not. I'm not shedding any tears for the old world, Pig. It was heading for a bad place all along. Now that it's finally there, ruled by idiots with shit for brains; well, I'm not surprised at all. Disappointed, but not surprised."

"But there is hope, isn't there?"

"Yeah, I suppose there is, but you'd have to agree it's a long shot."

Pig lowered his head to the deck. She saw the effect her words had on him.

"Don't worry, piglet." She scratched him behind the ears. "We're doing our best. We're taking the crystal to where it's needed. What more can we do?"

It wasn't long before they were high above the open sea. The receding coastline was nothing more than a distant smudge on the horizon. Pig luxuriated in the smell of brine on the fresh breeze. Open space. His snout wrinkled, this time with pleasure.

* * *

A few days later they were above the ice. The light here was dim, as though they were sailing through a perpetual twilight. It seemed as though the long southern night was falling, but that was impossible. No night would ever darken the planet's surface again.

The illusion was caused by layers of heavy cloud that hung low, obscuring the tops of hills, and blocking the light of the sky. Storms surrounded them as they sailed above the ice sheets and glaciers, looking in vain for the node.

"What do you mean, you don't know?!" the rest of them had exclaimed when Geoca and the blue woman had admitted to not knowing where the node was.

"We should be getting directions sent to us, but we're not," Geoca had insisted. "Each node has a keeper, someone who looks after it and makes sure it is safe. Like the old man in New York. And there should be a keeper here somewhere. We should be able to hear him, but it's quiet. There's nothing. Something has happened."

"Then how are we going to find it? In this weather? We can't see shit!"

After many hours of searching without knowing what they were looking for, they found a small group of huts in the hollow of a valley. There was no sign of movement, and no tracks in the snow around the buildings.

"Let's have a look," Bark said, his mood a little better now that they had something to distract them. His vision of complication after complication stretching out ahead of them like a trail of black holes in space receded a little. They dropped the anchor among some rocks and let the ladder down.

There were three huts. The snow had piled up in drifts against the walls and covered the doors, so that they had to dig their way in. Inside, the huts smelled of cold and damp, the sodden floors littered with empty tins and boxes. Papers were strewn everywhere.

In the last hut, they found the body of a male slumped over a desk and covered in blankets. There was another body on a bunk in the corner.

"Jesus, this place must have been unbelievably cold." Reina tried the radio sitting on the table. It was dead.

"They froze to death," said Sahrin. "A nice welcome to the new age."

"What were they doing here?"

"Some sort of research, I'd say," said Reina. "Geology or something, judging by these." The walls were covered with maps, and there were shelves of books with long, complicated titles.

"It was a long shot anyway. Shall we go?"

"Wait a minute." The Senator looking at one of the maps. He turned to Reina. "Is this a map of the continent we're on?"

Reina looked. "Er… yeah, it is. Look, here's where we are, I bet…" She pointed at a spot on the map that had been marked in red. It was close to a bay they had just flown over. And there was the mountain range that they had seen to the south. "So?"

"And this other map. Is it the whole planet?"

"Yes. It shows everything." Reina explained how the Antarctic was shown on the world map as an irregular white procession of bays and inlets across the bottom of the map.

"I wonder if this could be our answer."

"How's that?"

"Geometry. Structure and order." The Senator went to the desk and picked up a pen and a ruler. "Show me the direction of this planet's magnetic field."

Reina went up to the map. "There it is. That arrow there. Magnetic North."

"And New York?"

Reina showed her. The Senator drew an arc from New York to the red mark on the Antarctic. "Show me where all the nodes you know of are," he said to Geoca. "With a little luck, we might be able to deduce the location of our destination."

They settled down to work. Outside, the winds abated and the clouds began to clear.

An hour later, the blue woman stood up. She'd been sitting on the floor, apparently unworried by the cold. Her eyes were glazed over, as though she was concentrating on something that existed on another plane.

"The keeper," she said. "It's the keeper. I'm getting him. He's been ill, and hasn't had the strength to contact us. He can give us the directions we need." She slipped back into her trance state.

"That's it, do you agree?" the Senator asked Geoca and Reina. The maps on the wall were covered in lines. On the map of the Antarctic, there were two points where the paths came together from five directions and intersected.

Geoca and Reina both nodded. The Senator stood back and smiled for the first time in a long time.

"That's it, then. Our node is at one of those two locations."

The blue woman had come out of her trance. She pointed at one of the points on the map. "It's that one, there. You did well. The keeper is there."

A conversation in New York.

The Secretary-General was talking to Vice-Secretary Alexis. She had just flown in from the west coast, and she had a problem.

"We're suffering overload, Secretary-General. There are just too many people. We've got all the known subversives, and now we're rounding up the potential troublemakers. But there are just too many of them. The rail system can hardly cope. The grid is providing enough power, but there aren't enough carriages. It's fortunate that we planned ahead as much as we did, but twenty thousand carriages fitted with shackles for the North American region alone just isn't enough. And the camps are crammed to the limit. It's the same all over the world. The system is gridlocked in China and India."

The Secretary-General thought for a moment.

"Use freight carriages as well, but only if they have solid sides. No stock carriages, we don't want to alarm the general population."

"Very well. But that doesn't solve the problem of where to put the prisoners. In North America we've got seven million in the camps, and we're adding another three hundred thousand every day. It's worse in other parts of the world."

"Then we'll start the executions earlier than we planned. Get rid of as many as you need to. Just get the numbers down to a manageable level. I'll leave the details to you."

"Of course. Thank you, Secretary-General."

"You're welcome, my dear. Do you have any other problems?"

"Nothing that we hadn't anticipated. Looters, of course. They're being shot on sight. There's chaos in the cities, but that will decline when we get the troublemakers out of the way and the bulk of the population out into the country. We're keeping strict control of food and water. The rationing system is going smoothly, as is the curfew. We're letting them outdoors for eight hour shifts. Anyone found on the street outside their allotted time is treated as a looter."

"Very good." The Secretary-General was staring at her.

Alexis knew what was going on. She arched her back slightly so that her uniform stretched tight across her breasts.

She stood up and came around his desk, unzipping her jacket as she went. In a single efficient and calculated movement she climbed out of her pants and onto the Secretary-General, straddling him in his chair. His stomach made it difficult, and she was balanced precariously on the edge of the chair, her knees on either side of his. She reached down to the side of the chair and twisted a lever. The back of the chair swung back, taking the problematic abdomen with it.

"That's better," she said, sliding upwards, at the same time unfastening the belt on the Secretary-General's trousers. She lowered her face onto his, taking his tongue into her mouth.

"Nngg…" The Secretary-General reached out and punched the intercom. Someone in the outer office answered. "No interruptions," he said, his voice thick. He brought his hand back and put it between her legs, pushing as many fingers as he could into her.

She moved further up, rubbing his face between her breasts, laughing as he moaned and covered them with slobber. Reaching below her, she started rubbing him, slowly and firmly.

"Who's a hard Secretary-General, then," she said, her tongue in his ear now. She pushed his hand away and put his penis between her legs, rubbing it back and forth against her wetness. The Secretary-General moaned and slobbered some more over her nipples.

She thrust downwards, driving him into her. She moved with a hard, insistent rhythm, her hips grinding against the flab that covered his pelvis. A few seconds later the Secretary-General made a loud gasping sound and came inside his Vice-Secretary.

Undertakings on the ice,
and the General meets God.

From the air, they couldn't see anything that might distinguish the site they were looking for. There was nothing except a few outcrops of rock scattered around in a wide expanse of snow. A mile or two away, a range of hills reached for the sky in a half-hearted attempt to escape the monotony of the landscape.

"Are you sure this is the right place?" Bark was asking. "There doesn't seem to be much here."

"It is. The keeper says we are almost above him. He says we should land."

"Land…?"

The blue woman was insistent. "He just says that we need to."

I suppose he knows what he's talking about, thought Bark, taking the ship down. They landed near a small pile of rocks.

"There," said the blue woman. "He says that the entrance is among those rocks."

"I'm not so sure about this," said Pig. "There's something about it that I don't like. I have a feeling."

"I agree," said Sahrin.

"Who am I to argue," said Bark. "We'll leave the crystal on board until we make sure it's safe. I'll go, and a couple of others can come with me. Everyone else can stay on the ship. Any volunteers?"

Sahrin was already lowering the steps to the snow. "Me."

"I'll show you the way," said the blue woman.

A few minutes later, the three of them were standing in front of the rocks. Bark was about to suggest that they look around for an entrance when there was a loud grinding sound, and a section of the rock in front of them slid into the ground, revealing a flight of metal stairs that led down to a set of doors.

"That's pretty obsessive security for such a quiet neighborhood."

"You're starting to sound like an Earth girl, Sahrin," said Bark. "The sooner we get you away from all these bad influences, the better."

"What bad influences?" Sahrin asked, feigning confusion. "They're all so civilized here."

"It's not entirely their fault," said the blue woman as they went down the steps. "They haven't exactly had a free hand." They stopped in front of the door.

"How do we open it?"

"Never mind," said the blue woman, and a second later the door slid open.

They entered and found themselves facing a glass wall. On the other side of it were some doors, and a couple of corridors that disappeared off somewhere. Before they could say anything or wonder what to do next, a section of the glass wall slid away and one of the doors beyond it opened.

"Must be our boy," said Bark. "Let's go."

The keeper was there, alright. He was tied to a table in the center of the room. A Nefilim was adjusting a device that had been put around his head. Lights pulsed, illuminating the man's face like something from a fairground. The keeper saw them enter and tried to twist his head, but the device wouldn't let him. He was held fast. He tried to speak, but couldn't.

Behind the Nefilim stood a couple of soldiers, their guns already trained on Bark, who had walked in ahead of the blue woman and Sahrin.

"I was hoping so much you'd make it, Bark." It was Thead's voice.

Sahrin, who hadn't entered the room yet, thought quickly. They hadn't seen her. She stopped just outside the door, staying out of sight. She kept quiet and listened to what was being said.

The voice she didn't know belonged to the General.

"That's enough, Thead. You. The one in the weird getup. You have a piece of crystal with you. Where is it?"

Bark ignored the question. "Thead, what's going on? What are you doing with these people?"

"Don't worry about your friend, asshole." The General's voice was hard. "He's with us now. He's a bright boy, he knows the winning side when he sees it. Now, what about you? This is the only chance you'll get."

"Forgive me if I seem impolite," smiled Bark. "Thank you for the offer, but your approach leaves something to be desired."

The General made a *tut-tutting* sound. "Such manners… normally, I might be impressed by your spirit. I might even be inclined to play with you. But not today. Where's the crystal?"

Neither Bark nor the blue woman said anything.

"People never learn, do they," said the General. He drew his pistol. "If I were you, I'd talk, now."

"I'm curious, whatever your name is," Bark said. "How did you send those messages to…" He almost nodded towards the blue woman, but she was standing next to him, and he didn't want to give anything away. "…us?"

"You're stalling for time, my friend. No matter. The message you received was just another example of how the new technology can be used. The device we have attached to the keeper allows direct control of his mind. He is a transmitter, if you like. We used him to bring you here. Does that piss you off? It shouldn't; it's just the winners winning and the losers losing. Get used to it. Now, where's the crystal? You're trying my patience."

Bark said nothing.

"Idiot." The General turned his gun towards the blue woman and fired.

Where the bullet entered her, her skin parted, becoming a swirling vortex of liquid blue light. The bullet fell harmlessly to the ground.

"Would you care to try that again, General? I assure you, the same thing will happen," she smiled.

The General did try, a couple more times, with the same result. The robe she was wearing was torn by the bullets, but she was untouched.

The General stared at her. "What the fuck *are* you?"

"One of those that you would hunt down and exterminate like

vermin, General. And before you ask, the chances of me changing sides are less than zero."

He lowered his gun. "Take her."

One of the soldiers went to grab her by the arm. She melted away under his touch, as though she was made of water. She collapsed into a pool of liquid on the floor, and instantly reformed, rising like a summoned spirit.

The soldier backed away in confusion. She stood naked before them, her skin glowing like blue-tinted glass reflecting the sun.

"Jesus, you people are weird," said the General. "But whatever you are, rest assured, I'm going to get the crystal. And I'm going to get that ship of yours. Kill the male."

The soldiers both turned towards Bark. He recognized the weapons they were pointing at him. They were the same as the ones he had seen used in New York.

Shit, he thought.

He heard the hiss of the beam. And then… *he wasn't dead.* Or if he was, it wasn't what he was expecting. He opened his eyes in time to see the soldier nearest to him flicker out of existence.

There was another hissing sound. The second soldier turned into a dark, burning shadow before disappearing.

The General and the Nefilim didn't move. The General raised his hands, palms outwards, as if to caution Thead against a rash action.

"Thead, what the hell are you doing? Are you mad?"

"Oh, I know what I'm doing, General." Thead indicated the keeper with his weapon. "Let the prisoner go. Untie him. And you," he said to the Nefilim, "…take that thing off his head."

The General and the Nefilim did as they were told.

"You'll be sorry, you little shit," the General snarled through clenched teeth. He loosened the clamps on the table.

"Not as sorry as you," said Thead, and fired, turning the General into a black smudge on the floor. He turned to the Nefilim. "Against the wall."

"What's going on?" Bark asked. "I thought you'd changed

sides. What happened?"

Thead looked shocked by the suggestion. "Of course not! I'd never go over to these animals! I was with them because I was forced to. I was held prisoner after I was captured, and if I hadn't pretended to go over, they would have killed me on the spot. You've seen what they're capable of. No, I've just been waiting for the chance to get back with you all. When I heard about this trip, and that the purpose of it was to capture you and the ship, naturally I made sure I came along. I had to make sure that they didn't succeed."

The Nefilim turned towards Bark and the blue woman as if it was about to speak. Before it could say anything, Thead fired. The creature joined the General.

"It was about to attack," said Thead, lowering his weapon. "I've been around them long enough to know."

Outside the room, Sahrin had been listening. She heard Thead's words, but her mind was replaying the scenes from the attack on the underworld – Thead in a helicopter, smiling and laughing as he gunned down mutants. What he was saying sounded convincing, and yet... It doesn't matter what people *say*, Sahrin thought, but what they *do*. But then, he had just saved Bark and the blue woman from being killed. She stepped out into the doorway.

Thead was the first one to see her. "Oh, Sahrin. I didn't see you there."

"It wouldn't have mattered, would it, Thead?"

Tense looks passed between them. Any further conversation was stopped in its tracks.

In different circumstances, Bark might have questioned Thead about what Sahrin had told him; how he had been taking such pleasure in his part in the killing in the underworld. He might have, but the fact that Thead was holding a gun was such a strong and effective distraction that the thought never occurred to him.

Thead saw that Bark and Sahrin were both looking at him in a manner that was altogether too calculating. The blue woman, who had retrieved her robe from where it had fallen, was looking at him with an equanimity that worried him just as much. This was a little less friendly than the reunion he had been planning.

"Here," he said, handing the gun to Bark. "You're the Captain. Please take this thing off my hands."

Bark took the gun without saying anything and turned to the keeper. Behind her back, Sahrin took her finger out of the ring of the grenade she had been holding and slipped it back under her jacket.

"How are you feeling?" Bark asked the keeper.

"I'm... I'll be all right." He looked normal enough, in much the same way that the shopkeeper had. Which, given the relative scarcity of normal-looking mutants, was an indication that this place, whatever it was, had some human traffic, and that the keeper had to interact with it.

"I'm sorry about all that," said the keeper. He was middle aged, a few years younger than the shopkeeper had been. He was dressed in a white coat, devoid of markings except for a small symbol on the lapels.

"Not to worry," replied Bark, choosing not to display his relief at still being alive. "We can get the crystal from the ship, and if you're up to it, you can show us where the node is."

The keeper sat up. "Yes. I've been waiting a long time for this. Quite frankly, I sometimes doubted that this day would ever come. Now, the node. It is in another part of the base."

"Base? Is this an installation of some kind?"

"Oh, yes. It's... how shall I describe it... a scientific and research station. I suppose those are the right words. I've been working here for years, with the other scientists. Now, if you can get the crystal, I'll show you where it must be placed. But it would be best if you..." – he spoke to the blue woman – "don't go with us into the lower levels of the base. Your appearance would attract attention. There are only humans down there."

"Of course. I'm just happy that we found you before they did you any harm."

"I'll go with you back to the ship, then," said Bark. "Sahrin, you stay here with our friend."

Bark and the blue woman were heading for the stairs when they heard footsteps. Someone was coming down, in a hurry.

It was the Senator. He was holding the crystal, and was breathless from running.

"Nefilim ships! Three of them, they came from behind the hills!"

"Shit! What were they doing?"

"Nothing, at first. Then they started towards us. That's when I got the crystal and jumped ship. I thought it best to get it down here, where it's safer. Where I *hope* it's safer, at least."

"Everything's fine. We were just coming up to get the crystal. I'll go back up to see what's going on. This is the node guy. He says that the blue woman shouldn't go any further, so the rest is up to you and Sahrin. And Thead. Go with them and place the crystal."

The keeper stopped looking at the crystal. "If you'll just wait here, I'll get some clothes for you all. Dressed as you are, you'll be noticed immediately."

He left the room. A few seconds later they heard the hiss of a door opening and closing. Bark looked at the weapon he was holding and wondered how much life was left in it. There was probably some way of telling. He wondered what it was. "Let's go."

The blue woman cast a lingering glance in Thead's direction, her opaque eyes giving nothing away, and then followed Bark up the steps to the surface.

A few minutes later, the keeper returned. "Here," he said, emptying the contents of a bag onto the table. "Put these on."

Soon they were all dressed like him. "Not bad," he said. "You could all pass for the real thing." Whatever the real thing was, it involved white lab coats, loose white trousers, and shapeless rubber boots.

He led them into a short corridor, which terminated at a door. He placed his thumb on a panel and the door slid aside to reveal the intersection of several more corridors.

Something was going on. There were people walking everywhere, talking among themselves or shouting to one another in a strange language.

"What is this pla..?"

"Don't say anything!" whispered the keeper. "Your voices – your accents – they will give you away. Now please, just follow me." He led them through rooms full of computers and other equipment. There were more people there, all dressed in the same white coats, and working as though they were engaged in some frantic race.

The keeper led them into another area. It was empty.

"Administration," he said under his breath. "Say nothing. They're very careful here." And so it turned out to be.

They were approaching an open elevator when two men lacking the ubiquitous white coats appeared from around a corner. They blocked the way, and spoke to the keeper in the language that neither Sahrin nor the Senator nor Thead understood.

The keeper replied with a sentence or two and gestured towards his three companions. He was using them as some sort of alibi. The strangers, obviously guards of some kind, appeared satisfied. One of them stood aside to let them pass.

Sahrin breathed a silent sigh of relief. Apart from her grenades, which would be dangerous if she used them down here, they had no weapons with them. They had almost passed the two guards when one of them grabbed Thead by the arm.

The guard spoke again, this time with a different and more demanding tone in his voice. When Thead said nothing, the guard tightened his grip and started to reach for his gun.

The keeper tried to place himself between Thead and the guard and started to speak, but they were having none of it. The other guard grabbed him and pushed him against the wall.

Something had to be done. While Sahrin and the Senator jumped the guard holding Thead, the keeper reached into his coat and pulled out a small device. He slapped it against the side of the guard's head. The guard sighed and collapsed, staring blankly at the ceiling, his eyes wide open.

Sahrin had taken out a grenade. She held it in her closed fist like a knuckleduster and swung as hard as she could. The guard who had been holding Thead staggered backwards, then came lunging towards her. She hit him again.

They heard footsteps, several, running. The noise of the struggle had probably attracted attention somewhere, or perhaps they had been seen on some monitoring system. Thead was already heading down the corridor, away from whoever was approaching.

"Let's move!" The Senator grabbed the keeper by the sleeve and dragged him after Thead.

The footsteps were closer. Sahrin grabbed the guard and spun him around. He was grappling for something on his belt. She pulled his trousers open at the waistband and pulled the pin out of the grenade with her teeth. "I'm sorry if this seems unfair." She pushed the grenade down his pants, then pushed him away and ran to the elevator where the others were waiting.

She made it just as more guards appeared at the far end of the corridor. They started firing as the elevator door slid shut. Sahrin crouched down as bullets smashed into the plastic and metal around them, sending splinters flying. As the elevator started downwards, the explosion of Sahrin's grenade shook the corridor. The firing stopped.

"A harsh measure, but that should shake them for a while," said Thead.

"Thanks for your help," said Sahrin, looking at him grimly. Thead's courage seemed to be inversely proportional to the ability of his opponents to fight back.

The keeper had been hit. He was slumped down on the floor, sitting against the wall. His chest was covered in blood. "Look, I've been shot," he said, as though he was only mildly surprised by the fact.

"Press hard on the wound," the Senator said to Sahrin as he tore the keeper's coat to make bandages.

"That won't do any good," the mutant said through a froth

of bloody bubbles. "Don't worry about me, I'm not important. Worry about the crystal. It must be put in place."

The elevator slid to a stop.

"We should put the elevator out of action," the keeper said as they got out. He was leaning heavily on Thead, who was relieved to have something to do.

Sahrin pocketed the gun she had taken from one of the guards and took out another grenade. She threw it between the closing doors. "But how do we get back up?"

"Don't worry about that," the keeper said. "I'll show you when we're done here."

There was a muffled explosion, followed by the grinding of tortured metal as the elevator made its final stop. They looked around. They were surrounded by the base's plumbing; heating, water, and power.

"Their systems are operating?"

"Sporadically, but yes. They're in the process of changing over to the Nefilim grid," the keeper replied. "That's the reason for the activity you saw going on up there. There are some problems, and the work that is underway here will be adversely affected if the power supply is not made reliable soon. Through there." He pointed to a doorway.

"Good work or bad work?" They were walking between rows of humming pipes.

"Good if you're one of the scientists. Bad if you're one of the subjects."

"Who are they? Are they with the authorities... the... what is it... the UN?"

"No," the keeper coughed. "But they know about each other. And they exchange information. They co-operate, but they don't trust each other."

"Are they mutant, then?"

"God, no. Apart from myself, the only mutants here are being experimented on. It's here." They had reached some large vats, and the keeper was pointing between two of them, towards a rock wall. "Please put me down there."

Thead did as he was told. The keeper busied himself in a corner, pulling at a panel in the side of one of the vats. At first it resisted, but then it gave way, protesting with the sound of corroded metal.

The keeper coughed blood again. "Have a look. Get down here with me."

The others squatted down and looked into the recess under the boiler. The only thing visible in the blackness was the top of a rusting iron ladder.

"It doesn't go far down. There's a ledge, about ten feet down. One of you must take the crystal down there and place it."

"I'll do it," said Thead.

"No, I will," said the Senator. "I'll go." He climbed into the opening before anyone could argue, turning around and placing his feet on the rungs of the ladder. He looked down. "It's dark down there."

"You'll have to feel your way. Just next to the bottom of the ladder, two or three feet to your right, you'll find a depression in the rock. It's well defined; you'll know it when you feel it. The crystal will fit into it."

"I know, I remember the one in New York."

"Good. And don't move away from the ladder. The ledge is narrow, and it's above a chasm. If you were to fall, we could do nothing for you."

"Don't worry," said the Senator, disappearing into the darkness. "I won't be doing any sightseeing." He descended the ladder carefully, probing the darkness each time he transferred a foot from one rung to another. Eventually he found the ledge. With one hand firmly holding the ladder, he stood for a moment and fought off a wave of vertigo. He looked into the darkness, hoping that his eyes would become accustomed to the weak light coming from the opening above him.

He could almost, but not quite, make out shapes that were as insubstantial as ghosts. Swarms of tiny points of light swirled around him. Perhaps his mind was creating them out of the darkness. Not knowing what was around him made him feel uncomfortable. He shook his head, and told himself to concentrate. He dropped to his knees, and started searching. The rock was rough, and slippery with moisture that permeated the air and chilled his skin.

He found the cavity easily enough. Running his fingers around its inner edges, he could tell that it was the same as the one he had seen in New York, except that this one was full of ice-cold water that quickly numbed his fingers.

He took the crystal out of its bag and soon found that if he positioned it wrongly, it would almost, but not quite, fit. It would rock like a loose piece of machinery, or it would be too big, and refuse to go into the cavity at all. Displaced water spilled over the ground around him.

Suddenly, after what seemed like forever, he felt it jump into place, as though the rock was taking hold of it. A blue light appeared inside it, soft at first, then with greater intensity, skittering across its faces and twisting into spirals and whorls of light. It was quite beautiful, he thought, as the tendrils of light began to spread outwards, growing stronger with each second, turning from thin feathery trails into braids of luminescence that were as thick as his forearm.

It was done. He swung back onto the ladder and started climbing. Someone was calling him.

* * *

Sahrin had heard them first. Someone was coming. She scouted around and saw their searchlights scanning the aisles as they approached.

She ran back to the others. "They're here!" She bent down near the top of the ladder and whispered as loudly as she dared. "Senator! Get up here now! We've got company!" A muffled reply came from below.

"The way to the surface is not far from here," the keeper said.

"This way." Weak now, he raised a bloodied hand and pointed down one of the aisles.

"As quickly as you can, then," said Thead, taking the keeper's weight.

Sahrin hung back, waiting for the Senator and looking anxiously in the direction of the approaching lights. Just as their pursuers appeared around a corner, the Senator arrived at the top of the ladder.

"It's done. It's working."

"Good! Come on, they're onto us."

The soldiers saw them and started firing, the beams from their guns weaving a web of light around them as they ran. Thead and the keeper had disappeared around a corner. Sahrin got there and dived behind a drum.

"Hurry!" she screamed at the Senator, and fired at the advancing guards. One of them dropped. Realizing that their fugitives were armed, the others took cover and started firing again.

The Senator had almost reached Sahrin when the full blast of a beam hit him squarely in the back. He flew forward into her arms. She pulled him around the corner. His back had been laid open by the blast. It was a mass of mangled and burnt flesh. Sahrin turned him over.

He was dead. Sahrin lowered him to the ground and took out two of her grenades.

"Eat this," she hissed, pulling the pins and hurling both grenades down the aisle. She turned as they exploded.

There was no sign of either Thead or the keeper. She started running, looking down aisles as she passed them. Four, five… nothing. Just as she began to hear the sound of running footsteps behind her – fewer now, she must have taken out a few of them – she saw movement in the gloom at the end of a row of storage cabinets.

It was the keeper, leaning against the wall. She ran to him. "Where to, where to?"

"Here, right here," he replied, and in the depths of a corner she saw the faint outline, just discernible, of steps.

"Lean on me," she said, and she half carried, half led him onto the stairs.

"Stop… there's a board, to hide the steps… they don't know – no one here knows – that this is here." Sahrin slid it across, hoping he was right.

"Where's Thead?" she asked as they climbed towards a beckoning patch of daylight.

"He said that I should wait for you. To show you the way. Then he went up the steps. To see that the way was clear, he said."

Great Maker, Sahrin thought. *The guy is a worm.*

A few minutes later, they emerged among some debris at the bottom of a pile of rocks. Sahrin helped the keeper out and laid him down in the snow. He was bleeding from his mouth now.

She stood up and swore softly. Of all the sights that could possibly have greeted her, this was the one she could have done without.

The ship had been destroyed. It was lying on the snow, its back broken, its hull shattered and its contents spread around it like confetti. Flames had consumed the bridge and were working their way across what was left of the deck. The masts were broken and protruding from the wreck at every possible angle, giving it the appearance of a dead insect impaled by toothpicks.

Sahrin squatted down beside the keeper, her eyes brimming with tears. There was no sign of anyone.

There was another crashed vessel as well. The prow of a flier was visible above the ridge of snow its impact had thrown up. It was burning as well, thin wisps of acrid smoke trailing upwards and mingling with the black clouds billowing from the ship.

Then she saw another one. It had crashed further away, close to the hills. The place was a battlefield.

What happened here? Even as she asked herself the question, she was formulating an answer. Somehow, Bark must have taken down the two fliers before their own ship had been destroyed.

Which meant that there might be more of them.

And here she was, stranded on the ice with a dying stranger, and an underground base full of thoroughly pissed off people who were no doubt looking for her. And as far as she could tell, her friends were all most likely dead.

Thead. He had to be here somewhere, he had only come up a minute or two ahead of her. She turned, looking for him, and instantly her heart sank. She could see Thead, but the brightly colored saucer-shaped vessel hovering just above the snow a hundred or so feet away laid a greater claim to her attention.

It was the same as the ones that had crashed. She didn't know for sure, because she had never seen one, but she could guess what it was. She'd seen the shape on steles and in ancient art in other parts of the galaxy. It was a Nefilim flier, or a disc of the sun, if you took the old translations literally. And Thead, his back to her, was walking towards a flight of steps that reached from the side of its glistening hull to the ground.

We've been set up. She started towards him, rage growing in her like a storm. She lifted her gun and steadied herself, feet apart, and took careful aim. This time, she wouldn't miss. It was an easy shot. She pressed the trigger. Nothing happened. She cursed and shook the gun, and aimed and pressed again. Nothing.

Thead had seen her and was running up the steps.

The gun's grip grew warm in her hand. Before she could wonder what was happening, the warmth became a searing heat that sent a shock of pain through her. She threw it to the ground, where it hissed in the wet snow, melting a hole and sending clouds of steam into the air. She leapt away, half expecting it to explode.

Someone had appeared beside Thead at the top of the steps. In the glare of light reflecting off the snow, she had difficulty seeing what was going on. She squinted as hard as she could, her hands shielding her eyes. It was a Nefilim. There was no mistaking the tall gangling form. It was looking in her direction.

She pulled the pin from her last grenade. Thead and the Nefilim watched as she lobbed the grenade in a long arc that would take it straight to them.

The grenade never made it. It stopped, suspended in the air. Sahrin stared in disbelief. The grenade floated slowly to the ground, and landed gently on the snow as if it was being carried by an invisible hand. It sat there, as inert as a rock.

She was defenseless, and too close to the ship to run. If they wanted her, they had her. A third figure had joined Thead and the Nefilim. It was pointing and waving in her direction.

It was Bark. He was yelling something. He ran down the steps and came across the snow towards her.

"Sahrin!" He stopped when he was close enough to see that she was looking at him warily.

"Are you their prisoner? What's going on? Shall we run for it?" She was ready to go.

"No, I'm not a prisoner! It was close, but everyone is OK."

"Not quite. The Senator's dead."

"Oh." Bark and the Senator had known each other for a long time. "We're falling by the wayside, aren't we."

"It's getting that way. The old guy's wounded. He's over there, I don't think he'll last long."

"Let's have a look."

When they got to the keeper, he was lying peacefully, looking up at the sky. He didn't seem to be in any pain.

"You again," he said when Bark's face appeared above him. "We did it. We placed the crystal. Or your friend did. I suppose she has told you."

Sahrin realized that she hadn't. "Yes. We did. Or the Senator did, anyway."

"Let's get you back to the ship." Bark lifted the keeper up. A deep gurgling sound came from somewhere inside him. They began walking back to the Nefilim ship.

"What happened? To our ship?" Sahrin asked.

"They were hiding behind the hills. When I left you and came up here, the ship was out of control. Reina and Geoca and the blue woman had tried to get away from the Nefilim, but of course they don't know anything about sailing a thing like that..." – he nodded towards the burning wreck – "…that was a nice ship, you know. It was older than some of the civilizations we've visited. Anyway… one of the fliers crashed soon after they appeared. I got to the top just in time to see it. The other fliers must have thought that our ship was firing at them. The Nefilim have a sound beam, I'm told, that heats material up and makes it disintegrate at the same time…"

"Is that what happened to my gun?"

"Yes. You're lucky they have good aim. I tried to fire at the two fliers that were moving in on the ship, but they did the same thing to me that they did to you. Our weapons were useless. I couldn't do anything. All I could do was watch and wonder what was going on."

"What do you mean?"

"Well, one of the Nefilim fliers fired on our ship. Luckily, we were near the ground, and didn't have far to fall. It was almost a graceful landing, actually, but as soon as we hit the ground, we caught fire and started to break up. No one on board was hurt. We were all able to get off."

They had reached the steps. Sahrin looked up at the Nefilim, who was still standing waiting in the doorway. Thead had gone inside.

Sahrin stopped. "Are you sure about this?"

"As sure as I can be. When the other Nefilim ship destroyed ours, this one opened fire on it. The culprit is over there…" He nodded towards the second wreck. "These Nefilim seem to be on our side. Or at least not on the other side, which is enough for now. There must be something going on between them. Some sort of faction thing."

"Have they said anything to you?"

"In that strange way they have of talking to us, yes. But only a little. Come on. We haven't got much of a choice."

They went up the steps. The Nefilim extended its arms and took the keeper from Bark. Words appeared in Sahrin's mind. She was used to it.

'My name is Anak. There is no need to worry. We are not going to hurt you. Come. Your friends are inside.'

Pig appeared beside the Nefilim. "Come on. You're letting the cold air in."

Inside, the vessel seemed bigger than it had from the outside. Everything was built for the Nefilim. There was more headroom everywhere, the seats were bigger, and everything was further off the floor than it would have been in a ship designed for humans. There were none of the drab, antiseptic colors that the local humans used. Everything was made out of rich, translucent materials that shimmered and held their colors like resin. The walls were covered in embossed patterns of spirals and complex, interwoven shapes that twisted and turned upon themselves.

Everyone was there. Geoca was bathing a scratched arm in the light emanating from some Nefilim device. The blue woman was absorbed in one of the designs on the walls, as though she was reading it.

The Nefilim carrying the keeper laid him on a bunk and began adjusting controls on the wall nearby. A violet light descended on him. There was a sound like the tinkling of brittle bells.

Two other Nefilim were at the ship's controls, looking at a map being projected into the space in front of them. They were talking between themselves in low voices, ignoring what was going on around them.

Sahrin saw Reina. She was looking out of a view port at the burning wreck of the ship.

"Hey."

Reina turned and smiled. "You! Great!" She went to Sahrin and hugged her. "Are you OK?"

"Yeah, I'm OK. We did our job, I guess. The Senator's dead, though."

"Oh. Shit. I'm sorry. I'm sorry about the ship too. It was my idea to try to move it when these flying saucer things showed up. I thought I'd seen you guys doing it enough to have some idea."

"Well, there is a knack to it, I guess. Don't worry; what's done is done. It looks like we've still got transport, anyway. Do you know what these Nefilim are about?"

But Reina wasn't listening. She was looking at the coat that Sahrin was wearing. Then she looked at the keeper, and over at Bark, who was having a mind-speak session with one of the Nefilim.

"What are you wearing? I mean, where did you… What the *hell* is down there?"

Sahrin didn't know what Reina was getting at. "Just some scientists, and some guards. And a whole lot of equipment. Some sort of research place. And totally unfriendly. We were lucky to get out. Why?"

"That." Reina pointed at the emblem on the coat that Sahrin was wearing. "Geoca, Pig, come and look at this."

Sahrin didn't know why the design had caught Reina's attention. In fact, she hadn't even looked at it properly. She twisted the sleeve of her coat around so she could see it; a black twisted cross, set at an angle, in a white circle, in a red rectangle. She'd never seen it before.

"What is it?" she asked.

"Nazis," said Geoca.

"Fascists," said Pig.

"Make up your minds. Which one? I've never heard of either of them."

"Both. Either. Same thing," said Reina. "They were around years ago, though, in the middle of the last century."

"Sorry?"

"About eighty years ago, I mean."

"Where they are a race of aliens or something? Or mutants?" Sahrin had never heard of them.

"Well, some might have called them mutants, but no, not in the way you mean," said Pig. "In fact, that would be doing the rest of us a grave disservice."

"They were all wearing it," said Sahrin, remembering that the symbol was everywhere down there, on uniforms, on walls and doors.

"So, what are they doing down here, after such a long time?" Geoca looked over at the keeper. "Let's ask him. He'll know."

They went over to where the keeper was lying. He looked up at them as they gathered around.

"I heard your discussion. It's not surprising that you haven't known about them. They've been there since the 1940s. And I should point out that I'm not one of them, although of course they don't know that."

"There was a big war. Almost every country on the planet was involved in it, so it was called World War Two," Reina said to Sahrin. "One of the main countries was led by a group called the Nazis. This was their symbol." She touched Sahrin's sleeve. "The swastika. And since then, the only people who have used it have been a few extremists and nutjobs."

"Quite so," said the keeper, "but the people here are not part of any fringe group. They are the real thing."

"After all this time? What have they been doing down there?"

The keeper coughed, but there was no blood now. Whatever the Nefilim technology was doing, it was working. "Let me tell you a story. In the final months of the war, as the enemy was closing in on all sides, and the final result was a foregone conclusion, the Nazis dispatched a fleet of submarines to the Antarctic. It was all done in the utmost secrecy. Anyone left in Germany who knew about it disappeared, except for the people at the top, of course. The submarines arrived here just as the war was ending."

"What were they carrying? It must have been something important."

"It was. In those submarines, the Nazis had spirited away their most advanced technology and the very best of their scientists. Not the ones that were working on the conventional weapons, though; those scientists stayed on, to be shared between the advancing enemy armies as war booty."

"No, the scientists that were spirited down here were working on the most secret, most advanced of the Nazis' projects. Earth energy, strange flying machines powered by water, contact with other races – their enemies initially had no idea that these projects existed."

"When they got here, they moved into the base below us. It had been set up in the years during the war, using slave labor that was exported from Europe and never sent back. While their homeland was being overrun, the scientists set to work. After the war, the victorious countries slowly pieced together fragments of information from confiscated records and interrogations, and a year or two later, not sure what they would find, they sent an expedition of ships down here."

"And did they find them?"

"Yes. But of the four ships that made the journey, only two returned, and of six hundred soldiers that landed, barely fifty survived. When they returned home, they disappeared. No one, except those that sent them, ever heard their story. This part of the continent was never visited again. The powers to the north learned very quickly that the people in this place wanted to be left alone."

"What are they doing here, though?"

"They want to leave. The planet, that is. They've got no future here, and they know it. Even though many of them are young, being the descendants of the men and women who originally arrived here, they know that history has moved on, and there is no place for them or their ideology. They want a homeland of their own, and they know they'll never get it on this planet. So they want to find it – or create it – somewhere in space."

"You sound almost nostalgic for it yourself."

"Do I? I don't mean to. These people have nothing that I want. The only reason I'm here is that they built their base on one of the Stream nodes – deliberately, of course, they have a good understanding of planetary harmonics, you see – and they killed the original keeper. So I was sent, hidden in a group of stragglers from their homeland, and I've been doing double duty ever since, working among them and keeping the node safe for this day. For when it would become part of the Stream."

"Wow," said Reina, not sure whether her horror should be mock or real. "Nazis in space."

"Nazis in space indeed," added Geoca, thoughtfully. "It's one way to get rid of them, I suppose."

Sahrin wasn't sure what they meant. Nazis must be a bad idea.

"And soon. They're almost ready to go." The keeper lay back and closed his eyes, weakened by his storytelling.

Bark had joined them. "We're leaving. All of you should find a seat, or at least something to hold on to. I've just been conferring with our Nefilim friends here, and they tell me that the ride might not be as smooth as we would like. These ships are powered by the Nefilim grid. That would normally be a guarantee against any power failure or mechanical breakdown, but it seems that the advent of the mutant Stream has thrown their system into some confusion."

Geoca and Pig looked at each other and smiled, Geoca obviously, and Pig, being a pig, less so.

"You might as well tell them that it will only get worse," said Geoca. "As the Stream grows stronger, which it will do even faster now that the last of the crystals is in place, the two systems will disrupt each other as they fight for control of the planet's fields. It's happening already. The disruption began a few days ago and is getting stronger all over the planet. As well as anomalies, there will be geological transformations – earthquakes, floods, new land rising out of the oceans…"

"The religious nuts will be loving it," Reina smirked, thinking how readily Bryce would have agreed with her. "The end of the world, Armageddon. And throw in some aliens! Jesus!"

"Well, I don't know about that, but chaos is spreading, from what Nibat says," said Bark.

"Niba… who what?"

"One of the pilots. He's in charge, as far as I can work out."

"So, back to the point…" Geoca and his miniatures were restless. "We're leaving, yes?"

"If we can. Nibat tells me that the first ship that crashed here did so because it ran into a break in their grid. Which suggests that we might have problems of our own. Our flight will be erratic, to say the least. They can scan ahead, they say, to check that the grid is there and intact, but that won't provide protection against any irregularities that develop suddenly."

"Thin ice, then," said Pig, who had found a spot of spare mattress near Reina's feet.

"I don't know what you mean by that, but it's got the right tone to it." Bark was already wondering where they would go now. He was no longer in charge, or even almost in charge, as he had been when they still had their ship; now that they were cast into an alliance with the Nefilim on this ship, nothing was certain. Not that anything had been certain before.

Without warning, the flier lurched suddenly to one side and then rose into the air. The pilots were scanning the energy fields around the ship. Above the smoking grave of the first Nefilim flier, the tear in the grid was still visible. One of the monitors showed a piece of the grid's energy field flapping like a broken wing, buffeted by the currents of the Stream that were eating into it.

The pilots said something to each other in their own language, then realizing that Bark was behind them, one of them turned towards him.

Bark nodded. "Let's do it, then."

The pilots were about to slide onto the grid when an explosion beside the ship knocked it to one side, sending them sprawling.

"What...?" Sahrin picked herself up off the floor.

The Nefilim said much the same thing, but in their own language. The three of them bent over their consoles, scanning the ground below them and the sky around them, while their passengers rushed to the view ports.

The base had seen them. Or more correctly, someone in charge of its weaponry had seen them. Almost directly below them, the cover of a silo was sliding back into place. As it closed, another opened and there was a flash of light as a second missile streaked towards them. Almost too late, the pilot activated the ship's defenses. The missile was already too close for comfort when its circuitry was scrambled by a massive pulse of energy that drained the ship's power, dimming the lights on the control panels. The missile veered to one side and exploded further away from them than the first had.

Whoever was in charge on the ground realized that they were wasting hardware. There was a pause of a few seconds, then a beam shot upwards from an outcrop of rock. The ship's defenses blocked it, setting up a field in its path so that its energy was absorbed. Its owners, shocked that one of their latest inventions could be so easily brushed aside by the alien technology, indignantly fired twice more, then stopped.

"Can we go?" Bark asked.

'We cannot move onto the grid while our defenses are engaged,' one of the Nefilim replied. *'And if we let them down, we will be vulnerable to further attack.'*

'We'll wait to see what they do next. Perhaps they're just encouraging us to leave. Or perhaps they want a fight.'

There wasn't long to wait. Another beam sliced up towards them, followed quickly by another of a different color, then a third, the same as the first. It worked. Unable to identify the frequencies and react to them quickly enough, the ship's system struggled to keep up, and the second beam almost made it through before it was blocked. The third got through. It was a glancing hit to the side of the flier, melting a searing hole in the hull. Tiny pieces of superheated metal floated down to the ground like glowing pollen.

'The damage is tolerable. But unfortunately, it appears that we must fight,' Anak thought to Bark.

A second later the missile silos and the rocks from which the beams had been fired disappeared, their molecules disrupted by a Nefilim ray. There was no noise or fireworks, just sudden eruptions of fine dust being showered through the air like so much fungus spore.

Whoever was giving the orders below didn't know when to stop. More silos opened their black eyes to the sky, and missiles poured out of them like a pack of hounds eager for a hunt.

The missiles were easy enough to deal with, but the distraction they created was almost too much. More heat beams surged upwards from the ground. Most of them were intercepted as the ship's defenses learned from what was happening and its reactions grew faster, but a few of them got through, tearing pieces from its hide as though it was an animal being flayed.

'It hurts!!' The words tore through Pig's mind. 'It hurts! The fire! Make it stop! Please!'

Pig jumped to his feet. For some reason, he knew what he was hearing. It was the ship; he was hearing the ship. The ship had consciousness...

"It's speaking to me! The ship... this ship!" he said to Reina.

Reina was well past being surprised by anything. "What's it saying?" she asked.

'Let me, let me... Give me control of the weapons! I can do it! My defense array is young and inexperienced, it is struggling. I can do it! Please!!'

Pig told her.

"Then I hope it succeeds. If it fails, we'll all be dead very soon," she said. An explosion rocked the ship. Another missile had come too close.

"I don't think the ship is talking to me, though," Pig said. "I can just hear it, that's all. I think it's talking to the pilots. It wouldn't be asking anyone else for control of the weapons." Pig was right. The ship was indeed talking to the pilots. It screamed as another beam cut like a scalpel into its skin.

'Yes, yes, time to try anything,' the pilots replied, and took the defense system offline. 'Do what you can, ship, and quickly.'

The ship's intelligence leaped into the spaces left by the younger entity of the defense system. The alleviation of its agony was the only thought in its mind as it wrapped itself around the terminals of the weapons and without pausing lashed out, firing first and then taking control of the rays as they randomly traced powdery paths of dissolution across the landscape.

It was as though the surface below had been put into a blender. Clouds of snow flew into the air as the ship searched out the sources of its pain and turned them into dust. Bit by bit the surface weapons disappeared into the chaos of the rays, and the attack on the ship grew less, until suddenly it stopped as the last of their weapons disappeared, and the gray dust drifted slowly away in the wind.

The ship contemplated its wounds. *'I'm hurt,'* it said to the pilots, who knew what had to be done.

The ship released its control of the defense systems and allowed itself to be moved, slowly and painfully, a few hundred meters away from the enemy base. It sank onto the ice and sighed deeply to itself.

'How long?' asked Nibat.

The ship replied, and the pilots swore softly to each other. They would rather be away from here, but if the ship needed time to repair itself, there was nothing they could do about it.

"Can we help?" Bark asked. "Is there anything we can do?"

'No. The ship can do it by itself. We will help when we are asked. Apart from that, we just wait.'

"The ship hurts, doesn't it," said Pig. "It feels pain, just as we do."

One of the pilots looked at Pig. *'Yes, it does. The intelligence is distributed throughout the ship. It feels everything that happens to it; it is sensitive to any change in itself or its environment. How do you know this, animal?'*

Pig wondered about being called an animal, but replied without commenting on it. He told the Nefilim how he had heard the ship talking.

'I see. We communicate with it in the same way. You're a mutant, yes? Otherwise you wouldn't be speaking.'

Pig agreed. He was going to say he was as mutant as you could get, but then he remembered Geoca and thought better of it.

'*You could help us, animal,*' thought another pilot. '*We can only converse with the ship while we are at the controls. We need to be connected with it. For us it is not a natural ability, as it seems to be with you. We need to look at the damage, though. Would you be our...*' The Nefilim paused. '*...medium? Ears...? Would you tell us what the ship says?*' The pilot paused, searching for the word, rubbing the gray dome of its head.

'*Say yes!*' It was the ship. '*You can talk to me!*'

'*I can?*' Pig thought. '*Oh, I can...*'

'*Yes, you can...*'

"Of course," Pig said to the pilots. '*Are you badly hurt?*' he asked the ship.

'*No worse than has happened in the past.*' The ship had regained its composure. '*I can repair some of the damage, but there are some parts of me I can't see. I have a darkness inside me, as though it is something living and has grown out of the corners into which light cannot reach. I'll do what I can. Most strange... it must be the damage.*' The ship sounded calm now, almost philosophical, as though the matter was merely of intellectual interest.

'*Oh.*' Pig was thinking about light, and the blue woman. The others had told how she had provided light for them during the darkness, and how she had given Bark and Reina the ability to see when they had gone out to get provisions. Since then, there had been several occasions on which he had watched her sitting quietly, the strange hues on her skin rising and falling in tides of color flowing across her. Pig's thoughts spiraled in a decreasing orbit around the problem that confronted them, and it wasn't long before his snout was twitching in the way it did whenever he had an idea.

He went to where she was sitting motionless, her eyes closed. This was something she did a lot. She had never offered any explanation, no one had pressed her for one, and she was allowed to sit in silence, communing with whatever it was that she communed with. He was just opening his mouth to speak when she opened her eyes and turned to him.

Her eyes were white orbs. The pupils and irises had disappeared, as Pig had occasionally seen them do when she came out of one her trances. If she had been an ordinary person, there could have been no question that she was blind, but then, Pig knew as they all did that she was no ordinary person, and she was most certainly not blind.

"I've been following your conversation with the ship's mind, Pig. You have a special gift."

"Well, so do you then, if you heard it as well."

"Not so special, for me. But something new for you, I think."

She was right, of course, but Pig couldn't see anything to be gained by dwelling on the fact. "You heard the ship, then, when it said that it has darkness inside it. Places that it can't see. It has been hurt."

"Yes, I heard."

"Can you help? Could you give it some light so it can see to do its work, just as you did to Bark and Reina?"

For a few seconds the blue woman sat in silence, so that Pig began to suspect that she was going to ignore him. Then she stirred.

"I see no reason why it wouldn't work, but I can't communicate with the ship myself. Although I can hear it, I can't talk to it. That seems to be an ability that you alone possess. I would need to have direct contact with the ship in order to give it light. Unless..."

"Unless what?"

"It might be possible for you to be the intermediary, the channel between the ship and myself. A bridge, if you like."

"Then I'll ask the ship?"

"Yes. Ask the ship."

Pig closed his eyes and sought out the ship with his question.

'Yes,' said the ship, its voice again rippling with urgency. 'It is impossible for me to tell how damaged some parts of me are unless I can see them. Let's try. What's your name?'

'Pig.'

'Pig... tell your strange friend I'm ready. She must be unusual, *if she can give me light to see by, mustn't she?'*

'*Oh, yes,*' thought Pig. He told the blue woman.

"Close your eyes, then, Pig," she said, and just as she had done in New York with Bark and Reina, she reached out and placed her fingers over his eyes. In an instant the darkness behind Pig's eyelids fled, replaced by a flood of pure light that poured into the most remote corners of his mind. Just as Bark and Reina had been able to see everything in the external world with absolute clarity, so Pig was able to do, except that his vision was directed inside himself.

He could see the pathways and meeting places where his thoughts gathered and conversed with one another, where they combined and created his mind. Hidden, forgotten places were illuminated as the light swept through them. Pig was clearly visible to himself, down to the smallest detail, as though he was made of the hardest and purest crystal, shot through with rays of light that might have come from the stars. He felt a calm detachment from the processes of his own mind. He had become an observer, fascinated with this overview of his own mental processes.

The ship's intelligence was swimming beside him, humming with anticipation.

"It sees the light," Pig told the blue woman.

"Good. Now I need to enter your mind, so that I can pass from you to the ship."

'*There's no need,*' said the ship, entering Pig, playing in the light it found there, wrapping itself in it like a cat amusing itself with sheets of paper.

The ship led Pig over the space that had once divided them. The light followed them, flowing in their wake like a river. In contrast to his own mind, which had no strict order and which was built out of structures he had created himself and which had no reason for existing other than that he had made them, the ship's mind was a vast and ordered labyrinth of paths and connections and nexus points that possessed none of the comfortable chaos and disorder that Pig had seen inside himself. This mind was like an irrigation system that kept branching off again and again, decreasing in size, until the pathways became impossibly fine threads that wove through the physical body of the ship like a nervous system.

'I like this light!' The ship was happy. 'I can see everything inside myself the way it really is; look, Pig, here's where my pilots are when they talk to me!'

Pig saw two empty spaces, recesses in a featureless black surface that seemed to be nothing more than the absence of the all the other things that surrounded them. It reflected no light, and seemed to mark the border of the ship's internal world. It didn't feel hard, or soft, or anything. It just seemed to be behind everything, in the same way that the ground is below everything. Around the depressions the ship was talking about, columns of light stood arranged in groups, waves of some kind of energy pulsing through them. A low noise grumbled in the background, as though somewhere far away gears were grinding together, their teeth wearing down slowly and inexorably.

Pig looked into the closest of the columns and saw shapes shifting, moving in and out of focus. It was impossible to tell what they were; perhaps it was some landscape, but there was no way of telling whether it was an internal one or an external one, or whether it was just some part of the ship's functioning which was incapable of having any meaning for him. He was on the verge of turning away when the image shifted, as though it was adjusting itself to him, and suddenly the scene was suspended in space before him as clearly as if he was there.

He was looking at the landscape around the ship. In the distance, the wrecks of the two Nefilim ships were visible. Closer, the remains of Bark's ship lay, still burning. The ground in front of the wrecked ships was pockmarked with craters from the small war that had just been fought. Snow was falling. Something was moving through the floating drifts; he couldn't tell what.

When he looked more carefully, he could see nothing, and thought that he must be imagining things, or that the movement of the snow was playing tricks on him. It was just the ambiguous shapes that the snow was creating, swirling as though they were being disturbed by the passage of something through them. A mirage of light and shadow, he told himself.

And yet… he wished that he could see more detail, and as if his thoughts were being read, the scene flickered again, dissolving momentarily into a blizzard of static and snow, before presenting him with another, magnified view.

He had been right. There was something there. The realization came to him suddenly out of a chance combination of snow, wind, light and a group of the invisible objects. The snow was being caught against them, attaching itself for an instant before being swept away.

They were people, or at least humanoid. Their shapes were almost disguised by the fact that he couldn't see them, but was instead looking at the holes they made in the falling snow. But it was clear enough. They were carrying objects that could only be weapons, and they were heading this way.

'Ship, look at this! Can you see? Can you see what I see? People in the snow?'

'Yes. They must be using some sort of cloaking device. Wait, while I scan through the frequencies. I doubt that they would be cloaking anything but the visible spectrum.'

The image flickered again, and the colors changed swiftly, racing up and down a rainbow of hues, causing the scene to contort wildly as energy fields appeared and then as quickly fell back into oblivion. Pig was wondering what it would feel like if he were to get a headache while he was inside someone else's head, when the ship found what it was looking for, and the image suddenly settled down.

'Found it. They were more thorough than I thought…' Almost in negative, the picture was hard to decipher at first, but after a few seconds Pig's mind stumbled on the key, and the flickering mosaic of heavy purples and yellows suddenly made sense. They were soldiers, and they were wearing the same symbol as the one

he had seen on the coats that Sahrin and Thead had returned in. And they were definitely coming this way.

'*I'll tell my crew,*' said the ship, and it alerted the pilots, letting them know that it wanted to talk with them. One of them would go to a console and activate the link that allowed the ship to communicate with them.

Within a few seconds a circle of color appeared in one of the depressions. It grew, like liquid rising, until it resembled a shining translucent lens set into the floor. It trembled slightly, resonating in sympathy with the low sound that rumbled through the distance. The ship told what it had seen, and passed the image of the soldiers in the snow to the pilots. The pilots asked a few questions, which the ship answered, but they were technical, and Pig couldn't follow what was being said.

When the conversation had finished, and the substance that appeared to be more liquid than anything else had retreated back to wherever it had come from, the ship's intelligence moved away, down a passageway. Pig followed. He imagined them both to be blood cells traveling down an artery, and that at any moment they might meet some other blood cells coming the other way.

Pig could see the damaged areas ahead of them. The black surface was twisted and torn, thrown up in folds and convolutions so misshapen that it looked as though a volcanic eruption had taken place, or some fungus had taken hold. Some of the torn edges glowed sullenly, while others appeared to be covered with gray ashes, as though they had gone cold. Sparks flashed across the gaps, as though struggling to maintain a connection, but mostly they failed, falling away to become dwindling threads, sucked into the dark vacuum of the outer world. *Whatever or wherever <u>that</u> is,* Pig thought.

'*Here is where my power is going, leaking away,*' said the ship. '*But it's not as bad as I feared.*' Without saying anything further, the ship wrapped itself around one of the wounds and worked its way into the torn edges, making itself thinner so that it spread out.

'*It looks bad enough to me. Can you fix it?*'

There was no reply. The ship was busy. Where it was moving over them, the broken edges were reaching out, straightening themselves and joining together. The angry colors of the wounds faded, and when everything was as it should be, the ship moved on, selecting a new section and setting to work on it. There was nothing he could do here. Pig had time to have a look around.

A short distance down the passageway, he came to a large opening in a wall. He entered and found himself in a large room, the center of which was taken up by a huge whirlpool of blue and white light. It moved lazily as it spiraled towards its center, where it disappeared into the depths, its mass draining away somewhere. A narrow ledge ran along the outer wall to a point on the other side of the room. There, another exit led to another passageway.

Pig stood on the edge of the whirlpool, wondering what it was. He looked up. Suspended high above him was another whirlpool. It was a mirror image of the lower one, moving in the opposite direction. It was, Pig decided, very impressive, an awesome spectacle. But he still didn't know what it was.

He was still wondering when the ship appeared beside him.
'Fixed?'
'Yes, all done,' the ship replied. 'Everything should be fine now.'
'What is this?'
'You like it? When the currents are running, I sometimes come here just to watch. This is the vortex. My power source. This is my point of contact with the grid. In fact, what you are looking at now is the energy of the grid itself. It is calm now, because we are stationary, and my need for power is not as great as when we are in flight. But you should see it when the vortex is operating at its maximum. I never tire of watching the display. It is like looking into the heart of the universe.'

Pig realized now that the vortex was the source of the sound he had heard. The low, mechanical growl was coming from the depths in front of him. And it would be that sound, he surmised, that would rise in pitch and intensity as the vortex sped up to provide the ship with power.

'Well,' said Pig, tearing his attention away from the psychedelia in front of him. *'If you're done, I should be getting back, I suppose.'*

'But you will come again, won't you? You are the first visitor I've ever had. Come again, and I'll show you some things that will amaze you...'

Pig felt some affection for the ship. It seemed young and enthusiastic. *'Of course, I'd like that.'* He was beginning to feel disorientated by the physical impossibility of his situation. *'But right now, you've got things to do.'*

'I have. I'll take you back to yourself.'

Seconds later, Pig shook himself back into the real world and opened his eyes. The blue woman was still sitting beside him, and the keeper was lying unconscious nearby.

Apart from that, the ship was empty.

* * *

Outside, the snow wasn't helping. It was clouding Reina's sights, obscuring her view. It was difficult, searching out the fleeting hints of corporeality that wove through the snow before her, but occasionally one of the advancing soldiers stopped to fire, or paused to negotiate some obstacle, and in those few seconds, Reina was able to take aim.

They fell easily enough. They were physical, despite their invisibility. When she delivered a well-aimed burst from the Nefilim weapon that had been thrust into her hands, the unreal, indefinable forms – that she knew were soldiers only because the pilots had told Bark and Bark had told her – lurched backwards and fell over. They didn't get up again, but there were plenty more to replace them.

It took some machine gun bullets kicking up the snow in front of her for her to realize that they were using old-fashioned guns. She wondered how they'd managed that. Guns weren't supposed to work any more.

"Hey, Geoca," she called. The mutant was lying belly down in the snow a few feet away from her, using a weapon identical to hers, but not with the same effect. He was no marksman. In fact, he was a lousy shot, something that had never bothered him until now.

"Keep firing, it doesn't matter," said Reina. "Just give them something to worry about."

Even that was asking a lot, Geoca thought as he pressed the firing stud and watched as a few rocks disintegrated harmlessly in the distance. He had never been good at this sort of thing. During his childhood, he had felt no attraction to the various cruelties that amuse children of all races. His two miniature selves had been responsible for that. He had learned early on that it was easier to do without their silent, brooding disapproval as they slipped away into their distant meditations, removing themselves from his mind and leaving it feeling as lifeless as an empty street. Geoca grew up loathing violence of any kind, and the situation here didn't sit well with him at all. Geoboy and Geogirl were hiding somewhere near his feet, chattering their panic and their disapproval to one another.

There was a sound behind Reina. A loud... *whump*... followed by the sound of air being exhaled quickly. She whirled around, thinking that some of their enemy must have come around behind them, but it was one of the Nefilim. It had been hit. Pale blood gushed from a neat hole in its chest. It looked at her, shock registering on its face as clearly as if it was human. Something that was almost words appeared in her mind, and then the Nefilim pitched forward into the snow, limbs twitching.

Another bullet plowed into the snow, uncomfortably close to her. She saw one of them heading for some rocks. It ran down a shallow slope, giving her a clear view of the line of footprints as they formed in the snow. *Unlucky*, she thought, then fired.

Bark was proving to be almost as adept as Reina at this shooting business. Their new weapons were easy enough to use, but they were made for Nefilim-sized hands, and felt large and unwieldy. It was easy to overcompensate for the unaccustomed weight, but Bark was quick to adapt. He had to be. They were running out of time.

The ghostly shapes kept coming, pouring out of holes in the snow. The Nasties, or whatever they were called, must want them real bad, he thought. Or the ship. They were probably after the flier.

If only the Nefilim ship could help them; but it was busy, repairing itself. And doing it quickly, Bark hoped, as he heard some commotion on the other side of the ship. It sounded as though they were surrounded.

Anak came up to Bark and grabbed him by the arm. *'Ready,'* the Nefilim thought, and pointed towards the ship. *'Go.'* He moved on to the others.

Bark edged up the steps, firing as he went. Reina and Geoca came after, doing the same. Anak followed, carrying the body of his dead companion slung over his shoulder. The last one in was Nibat. He was carrying Sahrin. He lowered her onto a bunk beside the keeper.

The ship's defense field was working again. The metallic clamor of bullets striking the hull suddenly stopped. Pig, now thoroughly recovered from his experience, felt a wave of elation and gratitude as the ship flexed its mind.

'Lovely,' the ship said. *'Let's fly.'*

The soldiers on the ground, cursing whatever had given away their existence, turned off their camouflage fields and watched helplessly as the ship rose into the sky above them. They watched as a pair of missiles was launched from a silo that had escaped destruction. The missiles were only halfway to the ship when they were met by something that incinerated them in an instant, turning them into showers of sparks and burning fragments that fell back to earth.

Colonel Kalstend's heart sank. His superiors would *love* this. He didn't know what they had lost, or who they had lost to, but he knew they had lost. He and his surviving men were surrounded by bodies, a pall of gray dust, and smoke and fire.

The flier kept rising and moved away to the north, diminishing in size until it had become a tiny speck.

Bark's dream.

It was quiet inside the ship. They were cold, wet and exhausted, and no one had any idea what they should do now. Reina stood beside Sahrin, stroking her hair and wiping blood from her face. This made no difference to Sahrin, who was unconscious. Pig stood with his front hooves up on the edge of the cot. He leaned over her, his snout quivering.

Sahrin was in a bad way. A bullet had mangled her shoulder, and she was so covered in blood that it was impossible to tell whether she had other injuries as well.

Bark felt as though he hadn't slept in days. He collapsed in a corner, and the scene in front of him faded into blackness as he fell into a fitful sleep. Almost immediately, he found himself in the middle of a dream.

Colors swirled around him like a whirlpool. He feared for a moment that he was about to be carried away somewhere. Just as his fear was about to subside, the kaleidoscope shattered with a noise that reverberated through his mind. Its pieces fell away like a collapsing hillside.

He was standing on a flat plain, surrounded by a mass of people that reached to the horizon in every direction. They were crowded together so tightly that it would have been difficult for any of them to move, but none of them were trying. They were standing still, as though waiting patiently for something to arrive or something to happen. The air was heavy, boiling with an expectancy heated by a sun that burned high in the clear sky.

Not far from where Bark stood, a pyramid rose out of the crowd, towering above everything around it. It emanated a sense of mystery, something slow and heavy that caused Bark's head to throb as the waves resonated inside him. He felt drawn to it, and began pushing his way through the crowd. They didn't resist him, but just stood still as though they were incapable of even registering his presence. They swayed like trees as he forced his way through them, the call of the pyramid urging him on.

Finally, he was at the base of the pyramid. It was large, much taller now than it had seemed before. He ran along the length of one of its sides. The crowd made way for him now, clearing a path as if to encourage him now that he was close to his goal.

At the corner of the pyramid, he came to an area enclosed by a stone wall. He found an opening in it and looked down a flight of steps into a sunken courtyard. The sun burned his skin. A woman in a flowing gown stood in the middle of the courtyard. She had one hand on the head of a large animal standing beside her. Both of them, the woman and the animal, were looking up at Bark.

In the next instant, he was standing beside them. The woman took his hand.

"Come with me, Bark. I want to show you something." The animal nuzzled his other hand and licked his fingers with a warm, rough tongue.

Together they led Bark to an opening in the base of the pyramid, and stood aside as he entered. It smelled of dust, and age, and neglect. When Bark became accustomed to the meager light coming from the doorway, he saw that he was not alone. There were a dozen or so people lounging around on the dirty floor. In front of each of them, a screen flickered dully, showing a listless gray static that seemed entirely at home in these surroundings. The place smelled like a urinal.

"What is this place? Who are these people?" he asked.

The woman didn't answer. One of the figures on the floor looked up at him and spoke.

"You must come here very quickly; as soon as you can. There is no time to waste. It is very important. Bad things will befall us all if you don't come."

Bark was confused, and in his dream state, the confusion was amplified, so that it became vague and sharp and relentless, all at the same time. "Come where?" he asked.

"To save us all, and to save yourself," said the figure.

"But from what?"

"From those who seek to impose a new order. From the future."

"A lot of things seem to need saving. Where are you?"

"At the center."

The center... Bark thought of the place underground where the mutants had been attacked. "Are you underground? Where the mutants live?"

"No," the figure said. "The mountain!"

Bark didn't know anything about any mountain. Before he could ask what the figure meant, he was outside again. The woman was beside him again. The pyramid was gone, and where it had been a hill now stood, looming over them, its peak hidden among clouds that now filled the sky.

"What's this?" he asked. "Is this the mountain?" The animal circled him, it head lowered towards his feet.

"A mountain like the one you must go to," replied the woman.

"Oh. I see."

"No, you don't. But when you wake up, ask your friends."

"You mean this isn't a dream?"

The woman laughed lightly. "Of course not," and then as though the two statements were connected, "...look around you."

Bark looked. Through the clouds, he could see the mountain erupting, spewing clouds of ash that spread out and settled over the surrounding plain.

Where before the plain had been covered with people, it was now covered for as far as he could see with bodies. They had been dead for a long time. Flesh gray and slippery with decay fell from bones into a thick soup of putrefying liquid, which Bark, suddenly horrified, realized he was standing up to his knees in. His mind reeled. This had to be a dream, despite what the woman had said. The smell of rotting flesh was so strong that it stung his eyes. He felt his throat convulsing. The mass of bodies disappeared over the horizon in every direction, as though there could be not a speck of land anywhere that was not covered by it.

He spun around towards the woman, but she was gone. He

looked for the mountain that had been the hill that had been the pyramid, somehow expecting to find comfort in its presence, but it too was gone. Then he threw his head back and howled, so loudly that he thought he would tear something in his throat, and he hoped that the noise and the agony and the stench would wake him, but when he lowered his eyes from the dark clouds above him, nothing had changed except that a warm sickly rain had started to fall.

The slime in which he stood had become warmer as well, but it was the heat of decay, and it made his own flesh, the only living matter in the universe, shriek and shrink, and try to crawl away from the sensation.

A dark shape appeared on the horizon. It was heading towards him, growing in size as it came gliding across the sea of bodies.

Then the object was much nearer. It was his own ship. Its boards were broken, and its hull rotten and wet with the same dark decay that ravaged the bodies through which it sailed, as though they were the waves of a dark ocean.

There was no one on board. It was a ghost ship, piloted by no one, and propelled by a wind that did not exist. Even if there had been a wind, it could have had no effect, for the sails were rotten rags hanging from the masts.

As Bark watched the apparition move past him, the memory of his ship – the real ship, the one that was lying in pieces on the ice – rose in his mind. The realization caught him like a trap, and he was instantly thrown out of the vision as though some god had found him watching something he should not have seen…

His eyes sprang open. He sat up with a start. His skin was cold with sweat, and his heart was pounding. For a few seconds, the reek of the sea of bodies lingered in his senses. Reina and Thead were leaning over him.

"What is it?"

Bark quickly overcame his confusion. "A dream, that's all. Nothing. It was nothing."

"A bad one, by the sound of it." Reina touched his arm. "We've been through the mill, haven't we?"

"We certainly have," said Thead.

Reina turned and looked at Thead blankly, without saying anything. She shared Sahrin's distrust of him. She didn't have anything concrete to base her feeling on, but she had felt it, nevertheless.

Bark sat up. "Do either of you know anything about a mountain?"

"I was held prisoner inside a mountain," said Thead. "It was hollow, and they had built an entire city inside it. There were thousands of people there. Scientists, soldiers, and workers. It was impressive."

"Will Anak or Nibat know where it is?"

"I should think so. It's the center of the UN operations. Why?"

Bark turned towards the pilots. "Because that is where we are going."

"No, no," stammered Thead, suddenly worried. "You don't want to do that."

But no one was listening to him.

The Secretary General's
happiness comes under a cloud.

The past few days had been full of heady excitement. Everything had gone according to plan; the Secretary-General couldn't remember a time when he had enjoyed life so much.

With his new emergency powers, he had been able to settle many old scores, and he had found it wonderfully amusing to see those who feared that they might be on his list run for cover. He'd never suspected that there would be so many of them. Of course, once they ran, he had them hunted down, just to see what they had been hiding.

But more importantly, the Nefilim had been contained, and split into factions. For a race with their level of technology, they had *no* idea of tactics.

And the bulk of the Earth's population, confused by the photon belt and terrified of the vessels that had appeared above the world's cities when the light had returned, had been only too happy to believe what they were told. Apart from which, most of them were getting hungry. There had been those who hadn't played along, of course, but the process of rounding up the dissidents and troublemakers was going smoothly.

But this morning, things had taken a turn for the worse. The Secretary-General had been awakened early by reports of problems.

A delegation of nervous generals came into his office while he had been in his daily meeting with the Nefilim leader. There were problems with the grid.

Sections of it were falling apart, the generals said, as though it was being distorted by some influence. It was almost as though it was unraveling, said the squat, chain-smoking general Nguyen, who had distinguished himself a few years ago by subduing the Siberian region, and was now proving his worth in the southern parts of what had once been the United States.

The Secretary-General folded his hands behind his head and narrowed his eyes into tight, untrusting slits. That the grid should function properly was vital to his plans. He asked the generals what had been going on.

Fliers had been crashing, and some of the new equipment, including weaponry, was failing, they said. It hadn't been widespread at first, so initially it had been thought that the equipment was at fault, but in the last few hours there had been more crashes, and the pieces of the puzzle were coming together. It was obvious now that the cause of the problems was the grid itself. The Nefilim scientists had confirmed it.

"But *why* is it the grid?" hissed the Secretary-General, looking sideways at the Nefilim and wondering darkly whether there might not be some treachery afoot.

'Our old enemies,' the alien thought. *'They've been a problem for us since we created them. It is the mutants and their stream. You have not been successful at stopping the seed crystals being put in place, and now it is growing, pushing our own grid aside.'*

"But we only found out about the fucking thing by accident!" the Secretary-General raged, spraying the alien with spit. "And if we hadn't tortured a few prisoners we took during the raid on their underground shit hole, we still wouldn't know about it!"

The Nefilim, who thought that the Secretary-General was a particularly disgusting specimen, even for a human, said nothing, and kept its thoughts to itself.

"You mean their system is more powerful than yours?" the Secretary-General added, belatedly realizing the implications of what the alien had said.

"The mutant stream grows." The alien was using its voice. "It is its nature, it is like a living thing. Our grid needs control. Theirs grows."

The Secretary-General dismissed the generals, sending them back to their commands. He sent the Nefilim away as well. The alien gave him the creeps, with its dry leathery skin, its black eyes and gaunt features, and the way it could read your mind and put its own thoughts into yours. *But,* he consoled himself, *the Nefilim haven't been so clever after all. Our satellites had been ready for the invasion fleet from their pox-ridden planet.*

He wondered how the Nefilim would react to the visit they would be getting in the near future. When they saw a fleet of their own ships coming towards their planet, of course they wouldn't suspect anything, especially when some of our Nefilim contact them and tell them that they're coming home. *And then we'll show the boneheads how to organize an invasion,* he laughed to himself.

His smile faded. He was getting ahead of himself. These problems were serious. With the old technology useless because of the belt, the Nefilim grid was essential. The mutant thing would have to be destroyed. The mutants would have to be destroyed. Every last one of them.

He leaned as far towards to the intercom as his bulk would allow him. "Get me the Vice-Secretary."

There was a slight pause, then "Which one – which Vice-Secretary do you want, Secretary-General?"

A moist smile curled his lips. Which one, indeed? They were both so dedicated, and so sweet. "Either one," he replied, his mood briefly elevated by recollections of warm flesh.

When the call came through a few minutes later, it was Theo. He looked tired.

"Good morning, Vice-Secretary," the Secretary-General crooned.

"Good afternoon, Secretary-General."

"How are things going, Theo?"

The Vice-Secretary paused and looked at the screen for a second. "Well enough. There was some resistance, but it's being… what…?" – he smiled off camera – "yes… neutralized. As we speak." There was laughter from somewhere beside him.

"Very good. Do whatever is necessary. And the camps?"

"Filling up, Secretary-General. The trains have been running around the clock. The resettlement areas are filling up, but the prison camps are already overcrowded."

"Then execute a few."

"Already happening."

"Then get rid of more. No one is going to miss them. It just means less mouths to feed."

"Very good. Are there any more railway carriages?"

"Where do you need them?"

"Central Europe, India, and Australia, and Mexico. That's where we need them most."

"I'll see. If they can be found, I'll see that you get them. It's having the locomotives converted to the grid that takes the time. How are the Nefilim behaving?"

"No problem at all. They're playing their part."

The Secretary-General smiled. "They don't have much of a choice, do they?"

"No. The ones who came over to us did a good job of rounding up the others."

"I'm glad to hear it. But if they betray their own kind that easily, we have no reason to trust them."

The Vice-Secretary nodded agreement and changed the subject. "We've been having some trouble with the power supply."

"I'm not surprised. That's the purpose of this call. What's been happening? Weapons failing?"

"Among other things. Transport systems as well. Not much at first, but more of it today. It's only in a few locations so far."

"Is it a big problem?"

"Not yet. Nothing that a few forced marches won't overcome. And we're just resorting to more traditional methods of dispatching surplus prisoners. But we wouldn't want to get any more of it. What's going on?"

"We've got some gremlins in the works, Theo. It's the mutants and their friends. There's another power system, interfering with the Nefilim grid. I'll get all the relevant information sent to you, but the short version is that we need to dismantle the other system. If we don't, things will get much worse."

"Now, young Thead has let us down," the Secretary-General

continued. He was supposed to get us that time ship, but it's been wrecked. We know he's with some of his friends and some mutants, and they're all with some rebel Nefilim, in one of their fliers."

"I've heard that there were some Nefilim that had gone over to the mutants. Or do you mean loyal to their home planet?"

"Neither. As far as we can tell, there are some that have been with the mutants all along. They've been hiding underground with them for god knows how long. Which would explain why they've eluded us so far. We'll get them when the time comes."

"What's Thead got to do with this mutant system?"

"His friends have been helping the mutants set it up. If we can get them and the mutants they're with, we can find out exactly what it is, where its control points are, and how to destroy them."

"Very good. Do you know where Thead is now?"

"Yes, of course. He's wired; we've been tracking his movements. They're in a Nefilim flier, heading north. I want you and Alexis to intercept them and take them alive."

"Can Thead be trusted?"

"It doesn't matter. But I must say, he performed the first part of his mission well enough. He got rid of that insufferable General for me. And I don't suppose that we can really blame him for their ship being destroyed. For that, we would have to talk to one of our own trigger-happy pilots, but he's dead, I hear. You'll need to be careful, Theo. I'm told that Thead's friends made a real mess of a Nazi base in the Antarctic."

"Did they, now?" The Vice-Secretary was impressed. "It was an uneasy alliance between us and the Nazis, but they did have their uses. I never had any problem with them."

"Me neither, actually. But we've got more to worry about than a few eccentrics living under the ice, even if they do have some good technology. How's your sister?"

"She's well. She's here, actually, but she's busy conducting an interrogation. She sends her love. As do I, of course." The Vice-Secretary bowed his head and put a hand on his chest as if he was swearing some kind of oath.

"Ah, Theo, you and Alexis are everything to me."

"And more," smiled the Vice-Secretary. "I'll expect the information."

"And remember, we need them alive."

The Vice-Secretary pouted but said nothing as he reached out and cut the connection.

* * *

Alexis Gore had almost finished the interrogation when her twin entered the room.

"How's it going?" he asked, stepping around the blood on the floor.

"Almost done," Alexis replied, wiping her hands. "She hasn't said anything, and I don't think she's going to. I was told she might have something for us on those refugees that are going underground in Poland."

"We'll get some more in, but it'll have to wait until after we've done the little job Uncle Albert's just given us. May I? You're done here, aren't you?" he said, cradling the prisoner's head in his hands.

"Yes. What's the job?" Alexis asked as Theo snapped the prisoner's neck.

"He wants us to catch some freaks."

"Freaks, freaks… which freaks?"

"Thead's friends."

"Ah, Thead! Stupid little fucker."

"Why, how singularly observant of you, dear sister."

"Hell yeah. When do we leave?"

"As soon as the info gets here."

The presence of death in the room was making Vice-Secretary Alexis horny. She unbuttoned her shirt.

"You wanna do it to me, brother?" she breathed.

"Of course I do, little sister. Get over here."

* * *

The information from Mount Weather arrived a few hours later. Thead was on a Nefilim ship that had left the Antarctic and was heading north, passing over South America.

"Too easy; just too damn easy," Theo said as they walked towards the group of fliers they were going to take. They were met at the steps of the first flier by its Nefilim pilot.

'There are problems with the grid.'

"Well, fuck! Wouldn't that be right? What does that mean, bonehead? Can we go, or not?"

'I don't know some of the words you use, but I assume that they are derogatory. Be careful, human. I could snap you like a twig.'

"But you won't will you," sneered Alexis. "Now answer the freaking question."

The Nefilim looked at her for a few seconds before it replied. *'Irregularities in the grid are increasing. We can leave, but there is no guarantee that we will get far. Also, it is not advisable to take all six fliers. That will put more load on the grid, and increase the chances of a breakdown. I suggest that we take three.'*

The Vice-Secretaries thought for a moment, then agreed. "Whatever. It's your toy. How many of our boys can we take?"

Minutes later, three fliers rose into the sky, each containing its Nefilim pilot and a cargo of humans.

"Where to, sister?" Theo was sitting in the co-pilot's seat with his feet up on the controls.

Alexis, in one of the other fliers, was looking at the map that floated in front of her. A small glowing point showed Thead's location.

"They're about halfway across Brazil, still heading north."

"Then let's head them off up Mexico way."

"Sounds ideal. Do we have to take them alive?"

"Afraid so. If we can, anyways. Ain't that a bitch?"

Yucatan.

Rio de Janeiro was in chaos when they flew over it. Buildings in the city center were on fire. Large areas were already reduced to ashes. Streams of people were flowing out of the city, along the highways to the countryside.

Reina and Geoca looked down on the scene from the same viewport. Geoboy and Geogirl sat on Geoca's shoulders and watched in silence. Bark looked over their shoulders for a moment, then went to Nibat.

"Can we get a better look at what's happening on the ground? Can we go lower?"

'There is no need. Is this what you want?'

One of the screens zoomed in on the ground below them, panning slowly as the ship passed overhead. Soldiers were herding the population out of the city. Wreaths of black smoke drifted across the columns of refugees.

A group of people, separate from the main column, lay in a field beside the road. They might be resting, or ill, Bark thought, until he realized from their contorted poses that they were dead. Then as if to underline the fact, soldiers opened fire on a group lined up beside a ditch.

Reina and Bark recognized the few vehicles on the road. They were the same as the one they had seen in New York during the Darkness, and they were carrying mixed crews of humans and Nefilim. If the idea was to make sure that the plebs knew who was in charge, it must surely be working well.

Further on, they passed over a small village. There were no Nefilim in sight, but soldiers were gathering the population together in the town square.

"I wouldn't want to be down there," said Geoca. No one disagreed with him.

"Just think how long you and Pig and our blue friend would last, Geoca, if this is how they're treating their fellow humans," said Bark.

"I'd be keeping my mouth shut, that's for sure," said Pig.

Geoca nodded. "Those of us who are caught won't be faring well, but we know how to keep out of their way. We've been doing it for thousands of years, after all."

They left the city behind and continued northwards, over the jungles of the Amazon. As they crossed Central America, the flier's lights suddenly failed for a few seconds, and they dropped in altitude, falling along a gradient that was too steep for comfort. The ship corrected itself almost immediately, but a few minutes later the same thing happened again. This time it was worse.

'The grid,' thought Nibat. *'It's failing.'*

"Will it get any worse?"

'Wait, I'll ask the ship.'

"The ship says it can see ahead," said Pig, who had already asked it, "and that the grid to the north is irregular. Our Stream is growing there, and it is hampering the Nefilim grid, distorting it."

"Will waiting benefit us?"

Pig slipped into his talking-with-the-ship state for a moment and then opened his eyes.

"The ship says that the grid is getting weaker. But if we can stop for a while, it will try to rearrange its power system so that it draws from the Stream instead of the grid. It's not sure that it can be done, but it will try."

'Then we should stop, and let the ship try,' thought Nibat.

"If we have to stop," said Bark, "we should find the safest place we can. Somewhere out of the way, where we're not going to be harassed."

"But we should find it quickly," said Pig. "Ship says that the way ahead is weaker, and more dangerous."

They were somewhere above the Yucatan Peninsula.

"Then we'll just take the first place we can find," said Bark, and he and Nibat began looking on the screens for somewhere to land.

"Wait," said Pig. "The ship says it has made contact with

another flier. It is nearby, and there are people there. It's on the ground, in a safe place. Here." The ship passed the location to one of its display panels.

Ten minutes later, they were hovering above their destination. Hidden in dense jungle on the top of a high plateau was a small town, fifty or so buildings, all worn roofs and enclosed courtyards, interspersed with garden plots and uneven paths that had never seen a vehicle. Everything was as you would expect to find in an isolated country village, except for the Nefilim flier that sat at one edge of the town, where the jungle had begun to encroach. They landed beside a derelict building on the opposite side of town.

"The ship will set to work now," said Pig. "It can't help us, nor can we contact it, while it is busy."

Leaving Nibat in charge of the ship, and Sahrin and the keeper who were still recuperating, the rest of them emerged onto a dusty street. A few dogs gave them cursory glances and then carried on with whatever they were doing. People had come out of their houses and stood in groups looking at the strangers.

"I wonder what they're thinking," said the blue woman. They were an unusual collection, after all; Bark, still in his traveling attire, a blue-skinned woman, a pig, a tall dark-skinned woman, a man with a hole in him, a nervous looking man wearing a white coat, and Anak.

Two men came up to the group and stood in front of them. They looked as though they were trying decide which one was the leader. They looked carefully at Anak, and moved closer to him. *Perhaps they were expecting such a visitor*, Bark thought. After all, there was a Nefilim ship here. From the way they looked at the alien and spoke in brief snatches of their own language between themselves, it was obvious that they were communicating with him.

"Can you tell us anything about the other ship that's here?" Bark asked. "The one that looks like ours?"

The locals looked at him blankly, and then looked back to Anak.

'*They say that they don't speak your language,*' the Nefilim thought to Bark. '*Leave it to me.*'

Bark was confused. Never before had he had any trouble being understood by any race of people. That's how it was anywhere in the universe. The various races had their own languages, of course, but they could all understand each other. It was just the way it was, and no one questioned it. On that level if no other, minds worked together. So he hadn't been surprised that he understood everyone he had met here, and had been understood by them, that was just the way it should be – but now here were these people with olive-colored skin, broad faces with high cheekbones, and long, shining black hair shot through with beads and strips of colored cloth, and they couldn't understand him. What was going on?

While the conversation between the Nefilim and the two men proceeded, Pig had noticed another pig, smaller than him and covered with white hair rather than black. It had its snout in a pile of vegetable scraps below a kitchen window, oblivious to the gathering that was going on only a short distance away. Pig went over to it. The other animal looked up and grunted.

"Hello."

There was no reply.

"Can you tell me why there's a Nefilim ship here in your town? Is it safe here?"

The pig looked at him again, and gave another grunt, this time a warning one, and put its nose back among the scraps.

Pig realized that it didn't understand him. "Well, *excuse me*," he said, and returned to the group, leaving the pig to its foraging.

The others had come to some conclusion. They were setting off, with the two locals in the lead. As they passed between the buildings, they saw that there were more people here than just the Indians. A young couple came out of a house and approached them.

They spoke, and again Bark could not understand. He looked

at Thead, who was standing next to him. Thead shrugged; it was gibberish to him as well. What was happening to them?

The couple, a man and a woman, had much lighter skin than the two local men, and they were dressed differently as well. They were resigning themselves to not being understood by the new arrivals when Reina spoke up.

"There's no need to worry about us," she said, answering the question they had asked. "We're not here to cause any trouble. We just need somewhere quiet to hang out for a while. Our ship is making some adjustments. We'll be on our way as soon as we can."

"There's no drama about how long you stay here," the man said. He was tall and wiry, his hair bleached by long hours in the sun. "As long as you're not bringing trouble, you're welcome."

"That's right," said the woman. She was shorter, and looked as though she was used to hard work. Her long brown hair was turning into dreadlocks, and her arms were swathed in bangles and tattoos. "From what we've just heard, we're all on the same side."

Reina was relieved. "Good. We need some time out."

"I suppose that's why we're here as well, in a way," replied the woman. "Hi. I'm Sarah. This is Steve."

"I'm Reina." She introduced the others.

"Can we have a look at the other flier?" asked Thead, but neither the two Indians nor the young couple could understand him.

"It's already organized," said Reina.

A few minutes later, they were standing in front of the flier. It had been there for a long time. The jungle had grown over it, winding its tendrils and vines through the ship's undercarriage and around the drives.

"Where's the pilot?" asked Reina, but Anak had got there first, and already had the answer from the two Indians.

'They're surprised that we don't know,' the Nefilim thought. *'The pilot left years ago, saying he would return. He was with the mutants. He went to work on preparations for the changes that*

are happening now, and he left the flier here. Because of that, they regard the Nefilim as their protectors. I see no advantage in acquainting them with any of the complexities of the situation in the wider world.'

Bark, Pig and Anak entered the flier. Leaves and dirt had gathered in the corners, and a bat flapped its way noisily outside, irritated at being disturbed. Other than that, everything was as it should be. The controls were working, their lights winking slowly in the gloom. After a few seconds, the ship realized that they were there, and the cabin lights came up.

Anak went to the pilot's station. The ship responded, sensing a familiar form, even if it wasn't its own pilot. Anak worked in silence for a few minutes, then turned back to the others.

'The ship has been waiting for its pilot for eight Earth years. It has used the last of its power reserves to maintain itself, and has protected the village during that time. It has distracted and deterred unwelcome visitors, so that the existence of this place has been kept a secret.'

"It appears that there's nothing for us here, then," said Bark.

"Not that there should have been anyway, of course," added Pig. "But it does leave open the question of why rebel Nefilim should be wanting to protect a small village in the middle of nowhere."

"True."

It was getting cold. Even though the temperature was falling as if night was coming, it wasn't getting dark. Perhaps it was getting dark somewhere beyond the sky's endless new light. They left the ship and found Steve standing outside, waiting for them.

"The others have gone to their homes. There will be a meal soon. Do you want something to eat?"

"Excellent," Bark said, after Pig had translated for him.

They followed him along one of the dusty streets to a large house badly in need of painting. The others were inside, along with several families of Indians, and others who looked as though they were from a mixture of places. Reina, when she had walked in a few minutes earlier, had thought that the place was like a cultural club; there were whites, blacks, Asians, a family of Arabs, and a couple of Polynesians.

A few minutes later, food appeared from a back room. As they ate, and the local beer was poured, the talk relaxed. Everyone had something to say.

Pig had some beer poured into a dish that had been set in front of him. A talking Pig was obviously a novelty here, and he was holding court in a corner of the room, surrounded by a group of children. They were laughing at his stories of life underground and the strange creatures he described, thinking that they must be fairy tales, but they became unsure of that when they remembered to look wide-eyed at Pig's strange companions.

Only the blue woman chose not to take part. She stood outside, impervious to the cold or just ignoring it, looking up into the sky.

Reina was talking to Steve and Sarah. Bark sat beside her, not wanting to be left out, but forced to rely on Reina for a summary of what was being said.

"So how long have you been here?" Reina had asked the couple.

Steve answered. "We only arrived a few months before the Darkness came, but there are others who have been here for a long time. This community has been going for years. This area, this whole peninsula – it's a high energy place, you know. It's been known for a long time that there are certain places that would have an important role once the earth changes began. This is one of the safe places. One of the places where we can begin again."

Sarah spoke. "And now the changes have begun, just like the seers and prophets said they would. I never thought things would be quite this messy, but we knew it was coming."

"Yeah," said Steve. "Those who have wanted to know have known. There are places like this all over the world."

"The Indians here are great," said Sarah. "They've known about all this for centuries. They're Maya, you know, and according to their calendar, we're on the cusp of two ages of the cosmos. The old system is falling apart, and the Earth is cleansing itself as it makes way for the new order. The photon belt and what it did to the sky is just part of that process. It was all foretold in their calendar. The death of the old technologies, as well."

Reina had heard a little about this sort of stuff, but she had always written it off as New Age crap. She was still inclined to. She'd never heard anything about a Mayan calendar. "You mean you've known all about the mutants and all that?"

"No, not down to the details, although of course word has come in from the outside," said an older woman who had been listening. "But why should that interest us, except in the most general sense? If we knew all about their struggles, we might be drawn in."

The others nodded agreement. "That's right. What's important to them isn't important to us. We want to live in peace with the Earth and in peace with nature. Power doesn't interest us."

Anak had been listening as well. "That's an admirable ideal," he said aloud, taking care to articulate his words clearly. "And there are those among my own race, myself included, who would agree with you. But it is an ideal, and reality is a harsh place at the moment. Unfortunately, we are in a difficult situation. Elements of your race and mine have both attempted to obtain degrees of power to which they have no rightful claim. In the case of the Nefilim, those who would have enslaved – and still would enslave – your planet have come unstuck at the hands of your own rulers. Treacherous and dangerous though my race can be, it appears that they have met their match in what your humans have become. And your leaders, using the Nefilim and the effects of the photon belt as an excuse, have turned on humanity itself, and seek to bend it to their will. Whether you like it or not, my friends, you have a role in this."

Sarah didn't look convinced. "And if we refuse, for the reasons you've heard?"

Anak found speaking difficult, but he persisted. "Even to refuse is to participate. By refusing them your acquiescence, you deny them the very thing they desire. You are doing the right thing, for the alternative is to be like an animal going to the sacrificial altar, just as my race taught yours to do long ago. When there is no blood on the ground, the power of the gods disappears. You will see."

"Why are *you* involved?" Sarah asked.

"During the long contact between your race and mine, every possible political viewpoint has at some stage been held by individuals and groups among the Nefilim. We're much like you in that respect. For the most part, though, the dominant view has been the aggressive one, which sees the Earth as a natural colony of the Nefilim, on account of its history and its proximity to our home world. These are the Nefilim who see the reconquest of Earth as the first step in our race reclaiming its empire."

"But there are also isolationists, who want us to keep to our own world. The universe is vastly changed from the time when the Nefilim empire controlled thousands of star systems."

"And there are also Nefilim – Nibat and I among them – who for a long time have had good relations with the mutants, and with a few elements of humanity. This has been difficult at times, because of our history as a race, and it is difficult now as well, but we do what we have to. Our aim is to foil the ambitions of both the Nefilim and human ruling elites. Our own planet's population suffers under a terrible weight, just as yours does, and we will do all we can to help the masses of the ordinary Nefilim, just as we are helping the ordinary people and the outcasts of the Earth. I suppose you could say that we are the Nefilim underground, just as the mutants and you people are the human underground. It is vital that we frustrate the designs of the UN and its agents, including the Nefilim who have gone over to them. And there will be more trouble from our home planet, you can be sure of that. They won't have taken the destruction of their invasion fleet well. I'm afraid that your ideals will be sorely tested."

When Anak finished, everyone sat thinking about the past, the present and the future, and how screwed up it had all become.

Reina got up. "I'm going to check on Sahrin and that keeper guy." She pulled a blanket around herself and went out.

* * *

When she got to the ship, it was open, and the lights were turned off. That was strange; she couldn't imagine that Nibat would have left it like that when he had come to the house. She climbed the steps. The control room was empty.

A muffled sound came from the rear of the ship, where the crew area was. She stood still, listening. She heard it again. It sounded like a stifled voice.

She was getting paranoid over nothing, she told herself. It was probably Sahrin. She went to the doorway that led to the sleeping quarters. There was a dark shape standing beside one of the beds.

"Sahrin," she said softly, not wanting to alarm her.

The figure whirled around and something dropped to the floor with a hard metallic sound. It hesitated for a moment then rushed towards her. They collided, and Reina fell back against the wall. The figure lashed out, hitting her on the side of the head. Dazed, she struck out, connecting with something, but her assailant recovered his balance and ran past her, out into the main cabin. As Reina slumped to the floor, disorientated but still conscious, she heard the sound of someone hurrying down the flier's steps. She struggled to her feet and found the control panel for the lights.

The floor was covered in blood. The keeper's throat had been cut, so recently that his arms and legs were still twitching. She rushed to where Sahrin was lying. She wasn't moving. For a moment Reina thought she was dead as well, then she noticed the rise and fall of Sahrin's chest as she breathed; she was just unconscious, drugged so that she could sleep through the pain of her wounds.

Who would do this? It wasn't the Nefilim; the murderer had been human, or at least the size of a human. It could have been

253

one of the locals, but there was no way of telling. Thead… but would he be this stupid? He was on thin ice already, and if he was planning no good, surely he must be aware that something like this would just make everyone suspect him even more. But then, he could be relying on the confusion to cover his tracks…

She didn't know what to do. She knew that she wanted to run back to the others and raise the alarm; but what if the murderer was outside, waiting for her to do just that, so he could come back and finish his… or her… work?

Reina went to the flier's door. She stood at the top of the steps and breathed in so much of the cold night air that her lungs hurt. Then she screamed, as loudly as she could.

* * *

"From now on," said Bark, "we must make a point of never being alone. If there is a murderer about, he'll be less inclined to strike again if he's outnumbered."

"True enough," said Geoca. "And if one of our group is the culprit, he will find less opportunities coming his way. Unless, of course, he chooses to do away with the person he is with."

Sahrin was awake now. She watched in silence as the keeper's body was covered.

"I was lucky, wasn't I. Thanks, Reina." Her voice was small. "If you hadn't come along, I suppose there would be two bodies."

"Most probably. And you're welcome." Reina's head was throbbing now. Whoever had belted her had got her a good one.

Bark was thinking out loud. "Who wasn't in the house when the body was discovered? The blue woman, she was outside… who else?"

"Any number of the locals," Geoca said, then added "…and Thead. He said he was going out for a piss."

Thead had just arrived. "Well, I was," he said. "Of course, Reina wasn't with the rest of you either, was she?"

"That's true," replied Reina. "And I suppose I knocked myself around just to make it look convincing. Shit, Thead, if I was

254

going to ice anyone, I'd do it a bit more subtly than this." *And I'd probably start with you, prick.*

Thead said nothing.

Sarah and Steve exchanged glances, each of them knowing what the other was thinking. It couldn't be a good sign when the guests started murdering each other. This was exactly what they had feared.

There were two bodies in the ship now: the keeper, and the Nefilim, whose name they had never learned, that had been killed in the Antarctic. Anak and Nibat took the bodies and put them in an alcove set into the wall at the back of the ship. A transparent door slid down and sealed the enclosure.

A veil of light descended on the two corpses, and slowly at first and then with gathering speed, they began to dissolve like ice sculptures melting in the sun. When the last trace of them was gone, the light faded.

"What was that? A Nefilim funeral?"

"I suppose so."

"Where have they gone?"

"Nowhere, that would be my guess."

Anak turned to face them. *'Yes, it is a kind of funeral. Layer by layer, their energy bodies have been absorbed into the ship, where they will be utilized. Their personalities have merged with that of the ship, and they will live for as long as the ship survives. When the ship ceases to exist as an entity, they will pass on.'*

"Pass on to where?"

The Nefilim shrugged its shoulders. *'To wherever it is that spirits go. And who knows where that is?'*

"Do you think it's fair?" Sahrin asked, feeling a little closer to death on account of her recent experience. If recent events had gone just a little differently, she would have had a leading role in the ceremony they had just witnessed. "I mean, they haven't exactly been given a choice, have they?"

Pig thought of what he had experienced in his encounter with the ship's entity. "I don't think they'll be unhappy," he said. "In some ways, the view from inside the ship has more going for it than life out here. It's like being connected with everything inside yourself."

"A crash course in integration?" said Sahrin. "I suppose we'll have to take your word for that, Pig."

Before anyone could say anything else, the lights in the ship flickered and the monitors came to life. The ship was with them again.

Nibat went to the controls. *It's done.*

"Then it's time to go," said Bark. "As soon as we get organized." During the few hours of sleep he had been able to snatch after the murder had been discovered, the dream had come again. They needed to go there; he felt that more strongly than ever.

"Then that should be soon. According to the ship, there are fliers approaching this area. Three of them, and they're not ours," said Pig.

"Not Nefilim?"

"Nefilim, yes, but not rebels. If they were ours, they would be transmitting a signal we could identify them by."

"Then we should get out of here," Bark said. "If there's going to be any trouble, it shouldn't happen near this village. These people have no part in our fight."

Minutes later, the flier rose into the air. They set off northwards again, the ship reveling in the novelty of its new power source.

'It's wonderful,' it told Pig. *'It's clear, pure energy. It's like – no, it is – radiance. I can see now that the Nefilim energy was hard, and forced, and sometimes it burned, if I held it too closely. Now, I feel as though I am connected with the whole Stream, and with it the world. I can feel it reaching around the planet and into the earth. Wonderful!'*

"That's good," replied Pig, envious.

They were traveling well now, skimming low over the jungle, staying close to the contours of the hills and valleys. They flew on, feeling a new sense of purpose, towards the mountain of Bark's dreams.

Somewhere over Mexico.

The Gore twins, on the other hand, were not enjoying their journey. Their fliers were finding it hard going. They were lurching, falling and rising in the irregularities of the besieged grid.

Theo was being thrown around in his seat like a rag doll.

"Fuck! How are we supposed to work in these conditions?" he yelled. "We should have been able to take them on the ground, when they were in that freak village," he complained to the Nefilim pilot sitting next to him. "Now they've taken off again, and we won't catch them at the speed we're going!" His voice rose to the pitch that he used only when he was thoroughly pissed off. "Can't you go any freaking faster?!"

'We're going as fast as we can,' thought the pilot.

"Where are they?"

The alien replied, but the unit of measure it used meant nothing to the Vice-Secretary. "Perhaps you might care to answer the question in a form that might just mean something to me, skullface," Theo hissed.

'They are a little more than two hundred of your miles away. They are approaching the place you call Mexico City.' The Nefilim's thought had a cold edge to it.

Theo sat back in his seat and drummed his fingers impatiently.

"Open me a channel to the other ship. Not the one with my sister on it. The other one."

In a few seconds the officer on the third flier came on line.

"I want you to go back to that shit hole village they were in. Find out whether anything went on there that we should know about. Once you've got what you want, you can trash the place."

"Prisoners, sir?"

"What would we want with prisoners? Kill them all," the Vice-Secretary snapped, and cut the connection.

Shortly after the flier had headed off towards the village, Theo felt his own ship give one small, final jump, and then it settled down, flying smoothly and picking up speed.

'The grid is strong from here on,' the pilot informed him. *'The way ahead is smooth.'*

The Vice-Secretary breathed a long sigh of relief. "Then hit it, bonehead. We've got lost time to make up for."

* * *

Mexico City was in chaos. The city was so covered with smoke from burning suburbs that it seemed as if night was falling. The UN might have been in control in Rio de Janeiro, but the same could not be said here. There was fighting in the streets, and near the city center a new volcano was erupting, spewing clouds of gas into the sky and covering everything around it with flows of spitting lava.

"I always wanted to come here," said Reina as she watched the flames and the crowds on the streets. It reminded her of a medieval painting of hell she had seen once.

Thead was beside her. "Well, you've finally made it then, haven't you."

At the controls, Nibat turned to Bark.

'They're coming again, only two of them now, and too fast for us to outrun them. The Stream may be more stable, but it can't give us the speed that the Nefilim grid provides when it is strong. We may be able to lose them lower down. The smoke from the fires might confuse their ships.'

"Then let's do it," said Bark, who had no better idea. They swept downwards and disappeared into the black smoke.

The two fliers behind them followed, the Vice-Secretaries howling with joy now that their prey was in their sights. Their soldiers sat ashen-faced behind them, gripping the edges of their seats.

Meanwhile, back in Yucatan.

The flier appeared suddenly over the village.

It should have been easy for them, but the ship on the ground had been warned from somewhere above Mexico City, and it was ready. The instant the UN flier appeared, firing randomly among the houses, it flew into a gaping hole in the grid that had been carved out by the flier on the ground. The UN flier fell like an animal tumbling into a trap, and was only a few feet from the ground when it was met by a barrage of rays.

Before its pilot could do anything, the ship's hull began to shimmer like a mirage. Its weapons fired haphazardly, into the town, into the jungle, and up into the sky. The glow increased, swallowing the entire ship, and it became incandescent, so bright that it was hard to look at.

By the time it exploded in a shower of white sparks that rained down over the village like a light fall of snow, its occupants had ceased to exist. Their molecules had twisted in on themselves, each one falling into a tiny black hole of its own, winking out of existence like a collapsing star.

The villagers gazed up in wonder at the falling white flakes. Steve and Sarah looked at each other, each knowing what the other was thinking. The alien ship had saved them again. They felt blessed, in a way that their visitors would never have understood. There would be a puja tonight. Some buildings were burning; they hurried to put out the fires.

The battle of Mexico City.

"Shit!" Alexis Gore watched the screen in front of her as the dot of light that represented their third flier winked out. She settled back in her seat, her brow furrowed and her eyes dark. "Never mind. We'll get back to those pissants later."

The initial thrill of the chase had worn off. The sky above the city was a mess of smoke and heat and radiation from destroyed nuclear facilities, making it impossible to track either the beacon implanted under Thead's skin or the ship itself.

"Have you seen them?" The radio was crackling, breaking up from the interference. It was her brother. He was flying around in circles high above, in case the fugitives made a break for it.

"No!" she shouted. "I have not!"

No sooner had she said it than a break appeared in the smoke ahead of her. The troublemakers were flying slowly above a wide plaza littered with bodies and wrecked vehicles.

"We've got them!" Alexis called to her brother. "Get down here!"

She took the controls from the pilot and put the flier into a manic descent. It fell like a stone out of the sky towards the other ship.

* * *

By the time Nibat realized what was happening, it was too late. A cloak of glowing mist shot from Alexis's ship and enveloped them. The ship tried to accelerate, but it was held firmly in the force field. It bucked and strained, and then hovered, motionless, held like a pinned insect.

They started to sink towards the ground.

"Can we shake this thing?" A violet light flickered madly outside the viewports.

'If we had enough velocity when it was applied, yes, but we were traveling too slowly. It has us.'

"Weapons?"

'No. Nothing. This is a stasis field.'

The ship settled noisily onto the gravel surface of a road.

A short distance away, Alexis had already landed. Her soldiers were on the ground in seconds. The Vice-Secretary herself followed, smiling, her mood greatly improved. "Come on, you naughty, naughty people. Let's have a look at you. You've caused so much trouble!"

Inside the ship, Reina and Bark were beginning to regret that they had ever become involved in this war, or whatever it was. *This is what we get for sticking our noses into someone else's fight,* thought Bark.

"We're not going down without a fight," Geoca said. "Let's arm ourselves."

"Yes, yes!" Pig shook his head from side to side, his tusks carving the air.

"Oh, but you *are* going down without a fight," said a voice behind them. Everyone turned.

Thead had picked up one of the Nefilim weapons and was aiming it at them. A dark smile curved his lips.

Reina clenched her fists. "You piece of shit. I should have fragged you ages ago!"

Thead laughed. "Well, you might well think that, and you might well be right, but where you're going, I don't think you'll be getting any more chances." He pointed the gun at Nibat. "Now open the door, Nefilim, and we'll go and say hello to my friends."

Nibat thought something that took the smile off Thead's face for a few seconds.

Alexis stood waiting outside. She watched as Thead followed the others out, and smirked. He was a good boy. These fools should never have trusted him. She certainly wouldn't have.

"Stop there," she said when they were on the ground. "We'll just wait until my darling brother gets here. On your knees, all of you."

They knelt down.

"Thead, check them for weapons." She looked upwards for any sign of her brother while Thead did as he was told.

"Nothing in your pockets, dear?" Thead said as he leaned over Reina.

"Fuck you, jerk," she hissed as he ran his hands over her breasts. He moved on to Geoca and reached down and snatched up one of the little Geocas from where they had been cowering in his torso.

"You little rats irritate me, did you know that? And do you know what I do to things that irritate me?" He held the squealing creature at arm's length and put the muzzle of his gun up against its head. "*Frag*, I think is the word they use here."

"Thead!" barked Alexis. "Stop that! The little prick might be useful! You can do what you want to it later!"

Thead threw the creature onto the ground in front of Geoca. "Later, maggot. I know where to find you."

Pig was sitting quietly on his haunches, his eyes closed. He tried to contact the ship, casting around for the telltale signs of its consciousness, but there was nothing. The field was still holding it. But there *was* something. He could feel it, faint and in the distance. It was the unmistakable presence of another ship. It was calling, looking for contact. It came to him more as an impression than anything definite, but once he knew it was there and he focused on it, it became a small but clear voice in a silent part of his mind. It was the flier, back at the village.

'*Where are you? WHERE ARE YOU? I can't feel your ship any more...*'

Pig told it what had happened.

'*Then you are in trouble.*'

'*Big, serious trouble,*' thought Pig. '*I fear that we are about to die.*'

There was a pause, then: '*Death is not that bad.*'

'*Whatever. That's easy for you to say, but it's not what we need to hear right now. We're surrounded by soldiers commanded by a mad woman, and there's more trouble approaching.*'

Many miles away in the village, the flier thought and calculated more quickly than it had ever done before. The lights on its control panel went out and the air around it became cold as it pulled all of its energy into a small tight core.

Pig felt the ship slip away. It was gone for two or three seconds, and then it was back.

'I can see what is happening around you. This is all I can do, but there is danger. Working with the Stream is new to me. Good luck, friend Pig!'

Immediately after the ship had finished, the ground began to shake. Pig's eyes snapped open. The sky above them twisted as though it was being wrung into a ball. The smoke from the burning city was carried along, like trails of dye swirling in water.

A central point formed, and the trails gathered together into a vortex. The Gore brother's flier rode one of the arms of the spiral, caught up in the Stream, swaying from side to side like a leaf buffeted on a churning river.

Pig could only guess what was happening. The flier in the village was somehow manipulating the Nefilim grid. It was forcing a section of the grid into a smaller area, winding it up like a spring, tighter and tighter. The ground continued to shake, protesting at the forces that were being dragged out of it.

Everyone forgot what they were involved in and stood looking up at what the sky had become. There was a sudden loud crack that seemed to come from everywhere. In that instant, the spring unwound and the center of the vortex shot towards the earth like a thunderbolt sent by an angry god. Where it struck, the earth convulsed like an animal being electrocuted, rearing up with a great tearing sound. Buildings collapsed and were thrown aside like toys.

A trench appeared in the road near Alexis's flier. Its landing gear collapsed and it fell onto the ground, where it rocked like an unbalanced top, its hull cracking and bending.

The trench grew, a gaping mouth opening onto the depths. Sparks leapt back and forth between the surfaces of fractured rock. A couple of soldiers standing near the edge disappeared into the chasm without a sound.

Another section of the earth suddenly tilted upwards. Alexis had been standing on it. She was thrown forward, scrambling madly as she slid towards the pit. For an instant it seemed as though she had found something to hold on to near the lip of the crevice, but the earth twitched, almost as though it was aware of her, and she was thrown screaming into the void.

Theo's pilot was good. He kept things together as his ship was thrown around by the tightening spring of the vortex, and it was only when the trap was released that he lost control. The flier slid sideways, thrown aside by the bolt of power that sped downwards. As the earth below opened up, the ship spun out of control in a wild corkscrew motion. The pilot was just beginning to regain some control when the flier hit the ground and skidded along, losing parts of itself as it went. The ship came to rest on the edge of the crevice, in front of the sister's wrecked craft. It balanced precariously, on the verge of tipping over into space. The door, which was on the safe side of the vessel, opened, and figures spilled out onto the ground.

When it had started, Bark and the others had stood still at first, not sure what was happening. But then Pig had yelled "This is for our benefit! Let's move!", and they had come to their senses.

Thead tried to maintain his balance, and fired at Pig and Bark as they ran towards the ship. The blast burned a glowing scar on the ground in front of them. They changed direction, and ran towards the burned-out shell of a nearby building. Thead turned and was about to fire at the blue woman when he was hit. He pitched forward onto the ground, his back smoldering, and didn't move.

Sahrin was standing in the doorway of their flier. She slumped heavily against the bulkhead and lowered her weapon. "This way," she tried to call, but she was weak, and her voice was little more than a hoarse whisper. The others had seen, though, and came running.

Their ship was conscious again. With the damage to Alexis's flier, the stasis field had disappeared, and it was preparing to fly.

Someone was still firing at them. Sahrin peered, her vision blurred with perspiration that stung her eyes. She felt like crap. It was one of the soldiers near the other craft. She tried to fire, but what little strength she had was ebbing. As the blue woman came up the steps, Sahrin fell forward into her arms.

Pig and Bark were the last ones in. As the door closed behind them and they took off, the Gore sister's ship started firing. Sparks flew from the ship's hull as it rearranged itself against the attack, the ship's mind rushing to the areas that were hit and doing its best to hold the damage as soon as it happened.

As they took off, the earth stopped heaving. Slowly, it groaned its way back into place, leaving only the gaping hole in the ground as evidence of what had happened.

'Where now?' Nibat asked. 'There is some damage that needs to be attended to.'

Bark ran his hand across his brow. "Where now? Away from here, for a start. They will have help coming."

'Then we can do without being around to meet them.'

"Exactly."

"There is a node in the Stream near here, on the outskirts of the city," said the blue woman. "The ship could repair itself in flight, but it could be done more quickly if we were at the node. It would save us time in the long run."

"Whatever you say," replied Bark. "Let's do it."

They changed direction and followed the banks of a new river that flowed through the ruins of the city.

* * *

Theo Gore lay sprawled face down on the ground. There was dust in his mouth and eyes. As he struggled back to consciousness, the sound of confusion and voices came back to him in fits and starts as the veil of darkness fell away.

He struggled to his knees. Around him, his soldiers were

doing the same. He spoke into the band on his wrist. "Alexis! Where are you?"

Silence.

"Alexis!" He looked across at her flier. It sat like a discarded broken toy, surrounded by rubble.

There was some static, and then he heard a small voice coming from his wrist.

"Get me off here, fuck it!" It was her, alright.

"Ah! Alexis, where are you? Are you in your ship?"

"Cut the shit! I'm stuck down here! Get me out!"

"Stuck where? Down where?"

"Down here! Down the fucking hole, idiot!"

"Settle down, sister." He walked to the edge of the pit and looked over the edge. It gave him vertigo, looking into blackness that seemed to go down forever. She was there, sitting on a narrow ledge protruding from the rock face forty or fifty feet down.

"Are you hurt?"

"No. Well, my foot. I suppose I've hurt my foot."

"Mmm. Can you walk?"

There was a pause, and then in measured, even tones, her voice heavy with sarcasm: "You... dumb... fuck... I don't know, do I, because there's nowhere to walk down here, is there? Just skip the medical profile and..."

"Yes, sister, yes..." He turned to one of his soldiers.

A few minutes later, the Vice-Secretary was dangling from a line and clinging to a harness designed for a Nefilim. By the time she was being pulled up over the edge of the precipice, her brother's attention was elsewhere.

"Well, thank you for the lovely welcome," she grumbled, brushing herself off.

"Look," said Theo, without looking at her.

She looked. A crowd was approaching. It was a large crowd; there were hundreds, maybe thousands. It was hard to tell, and no one was going to count.

He didn't know it, but Theo Gore had been recognized by

the younger brother of a Mexican resistance fighter. The boy had seen the Vice-Secretary's picture on the wall of his brother's room, alongside the pictures of various presidents, industrialists, Central American dictators and other enemies of the people.

The boy ran to a meeting that was going on in the car park of a burned out supermarket, and whispered in his brother's ear as he sat with the rest of the District Committee of the Revolutionary Council. The Committee immediately deferred its plans for the re-establishment of order in the city, and decided instead to greet the Vice-Secretary.

Gore was infamous in Mexico, even more than he might have expected. He had made his name during the uprising that had begun in Chiapas and Oaxaca a few years before, when the people of those areas had risen up yet again against the multinational corporations and their sympathizers in the government. The government, its own forces divided by the revolt, had called on the United Nations for help.

It was given, of course. Tens of thousands of blue-helmeted soldiers were sent from all over the world to contain the uprising, which had quickly spread all over the country. The UN gave itself a mandate to make Mexico safe for democracy.

The UN peacekeepers were led by a young and enthusiastic Gore, eager to prove himself in his first major command. He tore the place apart. His forces descended on the population like a plague of insatiable locusts. The slaughter was terrible, and it went on for weeks. Prisoners were taken by the thousands, and few were ever seen again.

The people's army fought back, but they were standing up against the military might of the world's richest nations, and they didn't have a chance. By the time all opposition had been crushed and a brooding, resentful order had been restored, Gore had earned himself a place at the top of the local pantheon of hate and fear.

In the years that followed, the locals would remember Vice-Secretary Gore whenever they passed the stadiums that had been used for the executions, or the landfill sites that had become mass graves.

The crowd saw that it was indeed Gore. A roar went up and they began to run, pausing only to pick up rocks or anything else that could serve as a weapon.

The Gores looked at the scene in disbelief. Why would peasants dare confront them like this? They snapped out of their inaction as the first rock thudded to the ground a few feet in front of them.

"Don't just stand there, you idiots! Open fire!" The soldiers started firing deadly pale rays into the crowd, cutting swathes of powdery disintegration through it.

They kept coming. Part of the mob surrounded the flier that Alexis had arrived in and dragged the pilot out. The alien tried to break through the crowd and run, but there were too many of them, and they followed the Nefilim as it staggered and then fell under the hail of rocks and blows from clubs and farm implements.

Someone threw a Molotov cocktail into the flier, and soon flames were streaming from the open doorway and the viewports. There was no explosion; the flier's hull just crumpled, as though it was made of plastic melting in the heat.

Theo realized what was happening. "Clean-up time!" he screamed, running towards the advancing crowd, firing into them as he went. His soldiers, conditioned to the end, followed him.

"Theo! You're mad! There's way too many of them! Come back!" called Alexis, but if he heard her, he didn't take any notice. "Stay here," she said to the men around her. They stayed. It was wisest to obey the Vice-Secretary closest to you.

Many of the crowd were falling, but they were too great in numbers, and within seconds Theo and his men were surrounded. Iron bars and rocks fell on them relentlessly. Grasping hands pulled at their clothes, their hair and their flesh. The last thing the Vice-Secretary saw was a blood-covered machete swinging towards his face. He didn't understand the last thing he heard. If he had known even a little Spanish, he might have understood it, but it wouldn't have helped his appreciation of the situation.

Alexis watched in disbelief. There was nothing she could do; she had a handful of soldiers left with her. The crowd kept coming, the bodies of her brother and his men carried aloft, like bloodied trophies. She looked around. They couldn't stay here. Retreat was the only option, but behind them their way was blocked by the pit that had almost swallowed her.

They had to put the pit between them and the crowd. They made their way to one of its ends, where it narrowed to a thin crack in the ground, and went around to its far side. They kept going until they were opposite her brother's flier, still perched like a cartoon character on the edge of a canyon.

"This gives us a little time. This way, we divide them."

"That's one way of looking at it," said a burly sergeant. "They also get to come at us from two directions. You might say that we're surrounded."

"Thank you, sergeant. You might say that. Your lack of enthusiasm is noted. Just do your best to convince this rabble that they're wasting their time here." The sergeant scowled, then turned and lifted his weapon towards the mob.

The crowd had rounded the two ends of the pit, and were converging on them again. The soldiers were firing and people were falling, disappearing in bright incandescent flashes. It wasn't enough, though. Alexis admired their determination. *We must have touched a nerve,* she thought. *What a pity they're not on our side.*

Part of the mob had surrounded the flier and were rocking it back and forth. The ship activated its propulsion system, but it was badly damaged, and it merely shuddered further towards the edge, making the crowd's job easier.

Alexis fired into them and a few fell, but it was useless. The craft toppled over, sliding into the void. It fell gracefully, almost in slow motion, taking a small shower of rocks and dust and a few people with it. There was a muffled tearing sound as it broke up on the rocks on its way down.

There was nothing to do but fight and go out with honor, Alexis thought, shooting a ten-year-old between the eyes. The closest building was a factory of some kind, and most of it was still intact. They ran to it and started up an outside staircase.

"Stay here," she said to a short fair-haired soldier who looked as though he might be the type to obey an order that meant certain death. "Slow them down."

She was right. He stayed at the bottom of the steps while the rest of them went on. As the howling crowd converged on him, they made easy targets, and many were killed before they swarmed over him.

He had bought them the time they had needed. They made it onto the roof. From here, it would be easy to pick off anyone stupid enough to put their head above the top of the staircase.

We're lucky that the old guns don't work any more, she thought. Too many people had them, too many of the low-life like this rabble. If this lot had been able to use their old shotguns and rifles, there would have been no contest. It was just as well that they were reduced to tearing up fragments of rock and finding pieces of rubbish to use as clubs. Fucking neanderthals!

As if to argue the point, she heard a soft ripping sound behind her. She turned to see the sergeant reach clumsily for an arrow protruding from his neck, and then pitch forward over the side of the building. There was a cheer from the street below.

She thought of her brother, and a cold, dead anger welled up inside her. She went to the edge of the building and shot a few people, more for her benefit than theirs, but she soon grew tired of that, and besides, the charge light on her gun was dimming. She crawled back to where it was safer, and sat down.

She could smell something burning. A soldier, bleeding from a head wound, came up to her. "Vice-Secretary, they've set fire to the building. Judging by the way it's spreading, I'd say that they've used accelerants."

She said nothing.

"Vice-Secretary?"

"What can we do, private?"

The soldier said nothing.

It wasn't long before they could feel the heat, and not long after that the smoke began to make breathing difficult. Below them, the crowd was chanting something in Spanish.

She was gasping for breath, and was on the verge of losing consciousness, thinking that this was a shit of a way to go, and how unfair it was that both her brother and she should die before they had been able to make their real contribution to history, when she heard a new sound.

It started as a distant thrumming, then quickly became louder until it seemed to fill the sky.

Lying on her back looking up through the smoke, she saw something. It was big. If there had been a sun in the sky, it might well have been blocked out by the object that was hovering above her.

PART 5

The Secretary-General sees a glimmer of hope.

The lookout at the top of Mount Weather was isolated and small. It reminded him of the observation tower of a submarine, open to the elements and swept by the wind. The view from the mountain's peak was spectacular. Forest covered peaks stretched away until they met an ocean in the haze of the distance.

But the Secretary-General was oblivious to the view. He was pacing back and forth, his clasped hands twitching nervously behind his back. He was in a dark mood. *Damn them all to hell* – the Nefilim and their treacherous technology, that infernal Thead and his incompetence, not to mention losing one of his Vice-Secretaries!

It was falling apart. *Everything* was falling apart. The grid's failure was accelerating. Even as he thought it, the earth shook, and a deep rumbling came from somewhere in the distance.

There was something new going on in the sky as well. It had become darker, turning a heavy shade of indigo as if night was falling. It seemed restless, as though it was somehow acting in sympathy with the travails of the earth. Lightning flashed intermittently, illuminating the hills with violent flashes of white light. Seconds later, heavy thunder rolled across the hills.

The Secretary-General found himself wishing that it would rain. It would help him believe that what was happening was somehow natural.

Not even attending the morning executions had helped his mood. The grid had failed totally in most of Asia and large parts of South America. There had been mass breakouts from some of the camps, and not surprisingly, the population had turned on his armies. In areas where the grid was down, their weapons had been useless, and it had been no contest. It wasn't fair.

The few reports that were still coming in told of bands of soldiers roaming the countryside, trying to escape the vengeance of their former prisoners and subjects. In Europe, rivers had changed their courses and obliterated whole cities. Japan had disappeared into the sea, as had the southern half of England.

What was to be done? It was a good thing that the Nefilim had sent their invasion fleet when they did. If they had come now, it would have been too much.

The Secretary-General felt as though he was at some sort of terrible nadir. Things could only get worse. He heard the soft hiss of the doors of the elevator behind him, then footsteps. Whoever it was, there were two of them. One human, one not. What was it now? He turned around.

It was one of the scientists who had been working on the grid, and his Nefilim counterpart. God, he was starting to tell the boneheads apart...

"What is it?" His voice was flat.

The human scientist spoke. "We think we have a solution to the problem with the grid, Secretary-General."

"A solution...? What sort of solution?"

"Well, we now know for a fact that the cause of the problem is not in the grid itself."

"Of course, it's that fucking mutant system, isn't it?" the Secretary-General snapped. "That's hardly news. Haven't we known that for a long time?"

The scientist shifted his weight nervously. The last thing he wanted was to appear redundant. "Well, yes, Secretary-General, we have supposed that to be the case, with good reason, of course, but now that we've done the work, we can confirm that it is."

"Can you now, Einstein. Well, I'm so relieved I can hardly speak. So what? Or should I say, now what?" *Little weasel*, thought the Secretary-General. *He's shitting himself.*

He turned to the Nefilim scientist. "So what's happening?"

'*What your man says is correct,*' the alien replied. '*The answer lies in destroying the mutant stream...*'

"The what? What 'stream'?"

'*Their answer to the grid. While ours is static, theirs grows, like a living thing. They describe it as a stream, because in some respects it behaves like flowing water.'*

"Then why don't we just get control of this stream of theirs?"

'And how would you propose that we do that? It would do you no good, things have gone too far. No, it must be destroyed.'

"I'll have to take your word for that. How do we destroy it?"

'If we leave things as they are, our grid will literally be eaten alive. But if we strengthen it, by giving it a large enough infusion of energy, we should be able to make it strong enough to destroy the other system.'

"Ah, a king hit! My kind of tactic. And how do we provide our grid with this much-needed power?"

'In the same way that it was activated a few weeks ago, Secretary-General.'

He hadn't seen the process, but he had read the reports. "You put people into it. It ate them up, somehow, it used them as some kind of fuel."

'A primitive understanding, but close enough. We propose using the same process, but on a much larger scale.'

"Last time, you used two individuals at each of your control points. What sort of numbers are you talking about this time?"

The Nefilim paused for a moment. *'One hundred and eight. At each control point.'*

The Secretary-General smiled. "That's the one thing I admire about your race. You never do things by halves. So we'll do it as soon as possible?"

'Yes. As soon as possible.'

"Any one hundred and eight?"

'Yes. Fifty-four males and fifty-four females.'

"Fine. Anything to satisfy your predilection for symmetry." The Secretary-General was in a better mood already.

'The requirement is technical, not aesthetic.'

"Of course it is, bonehead. We should be able to do it within twelve hours. Where we can, we'll get the necessary numbers from the camps. And in areas where that's impractical, we'll just round them up. There are people everywhere. They're like maggots."

The Secretary-General's cell phone buzzed at him. He answered it and listened in silence, then said "Yes. Very well."

A Nefilim heavy cruiser had just reported in. That was news enough in itself, as there were only a few of them on the planet, and the Secretary-General hadn't seen one in the flesh before, but of more importance right now was the fact that his one surviving Vice-Secretary was on it. The ship would be arriving in a few hours.

"I'll see that your requirements are met," he said, and dismissed the two scientists.

* * *

The Secretary-General was there to meet the cruiser when it arrived. He hadn't seen much of the Nefilim technology for himself. He'd been stuck in his office, issuing orders and listening to reports. The cruiser was an impressive sight. At least a hundred yards long and twenty wide, it was covered in intricate, brightly colored patterns that made it look more like a work of art than a warship. Attached to the rear of the ship were large diaphanous fins that swept forward, reaching halfway along the length of its body. As the ship settled to the ground, they folded close to the body, like an insect's wings.

It was quite beautiful. The Secretary-General dreamed of the day that humanity would be able to build such marvels for itself. And then the universe would learn all about humans...

Steps had descended from the side of the ship, and people and aliens were disembarking. His surviving Vice-Secretary was among them.

"Alexis, my dear!"

"Secretary-General." She'd looked better. She was limping, and her hair had been singed. She had a bruise on her forehead, and she looked tired.

"So, things didn't go well for you," said the Secretary-General. "Theo..."

"...is dead, yes," she hissed through clenched teeth. "The

fucking grid let us down, just when we needed it most. There was an earthquake. Something in the sky caused it, something weird. And we were attacked by a crowd. There were too few of us, and too many of them. We didn't stand a chance."

"Yes, Mexico City was never a very civilized place."

"It's no sort of place now. That's why I'm late. I was almost unconscious when we were picked up. When I came around, we were well away from the city. I ordered the commander to turn around and go back."

"Really? To what end?"

"We trashed the place."

"You mean where you were attacked?"

"That as well, of course. No, we trashed the city. We took out the whole place. Where it used to be, there's now just a lot of ashes. You know, these ships have got some great weapons." She managed a tired, thin smile.

"Well done, Alexis. I don't think we had any special plans for Mexico City. A firm hand, that's what is needed, and that's what you've got, my dear. I wish I could have been there with you."

The Vice-Secretary's smile was a strange one now. "So do I, Secretary-General."

"You know, I thought for a while that you might be losing your touch, my dear. Another failure, after all. And our fugitives are still… well, fugitives…"

"Yes, but through no fault of our own."

"Of course, through no fault of your own. Don't worry, dear. I'll look forward to reading your full report, but I'm not cross with you. Everyone has problems these days. And I *am* sorry about Theo." He was, too. The Vice-Secretary had been excellent.

Despite herself, Alexis felt some relief at being let off the hook. "What now, then?"

"We're going to fix things up." The Secretary-General sounded confident. "But there's time enough for that. Come to my quarters for a drink later. You can cry on my shoulder."

Some things never change.

The Secretary-General wanted to witness the process. It was time to take a more personal interest in things. It meant traveling to the closest control point.

He was almost late. The grid under the flier he was on screwed up. Luckily, it had happened when they were literally within sight of their destination, and even more luckily, they had been able to land safely. The Secretary-General and his entourage had made the last part of their journey in horse-drawn carts commandeered from a farm.

He was in a terrible mood by the time they arrived. He felt like having someone – it didn't matter who – executed. But he didn't; instead, he reminded himself that there were matters to be dealt with that were more important than his own frustration, no matter how consuming it might be. And he'd read somewhere that one of the components of emotional maturity is the ability to delay gratification.

The Secretary-General reflected on his wisdom and sagacity as he was led underground to the cavern in which the scientists and Nefilim were assembled, waiting to begin. The victims – no, the volunteers – were there, as many as the Nefilim had said were needed, and they were evenly divided between male and female.

The Secretary-General took the seat that had been set out for him. He leaned forward, rested his hands on his walking cane, and looked over the scene in front of him.

"You are all about to make a great contribution to the future of the human race," he said in a loud voice that reverberated off the back wall of the cavern. "Of course, you haven't been given a great deal of choice in the matter, but don't let that disturb you." He smiled broadly. "You can rest assured that those that matter will benefit greatly."

"Eat shit, you fat fuck!"

The Secretary-General stopped, his mouth hanging open. He

was shocked, but strangely elevated. No one had dared to speak to him like that in years.

He smiled again. "Who said that?" he asked genially, waving back the soldiers who had begun to move into the crowd.

"I did. What the fuck are you going to do about it, shithead?" The speaker was a young male.

The Secretary-General toyed with his cane. "In ordinary circumstances, citizen, I would do nothing, of course, because there would be nothing I *could* do, being merely a duly appointed servant of the people. I might, of course, be tempted to see that you came to the attention of some of the more enthusiastic members of the security community. But in this most special of instances, I think I'll ignore your indiscretion, and be satisfied that you are going to share the fate of the rest of this rabble. Perhaps I'm learning some self-control in my old age!"

"Asshat."

The Secretary-General's smile widened. "Whatever you say, citizen." He hadn't felt this alive in years. Contact with the people was so invigorating. He must do more of it.

The guards – some of them Nefilim because they looked so intimidating and had proven on that account to be effective at crowd control – made the prisoners lie down in pairs, male and female, in a grid that had been marked out on the floor. There was a little trouble, but not much. Anyone who resisted was clubbed unconscious, but it was mostly abject fear that did the job.

Columns of light appeared, reaching down from the ceiling onto each of the couples. There were some incongruous pairings here, the Secretary-General sniggered to himself. He could have made them fornicate, but this wasn't the time for such frivolity. It was a home movie idea that could wait for another time.

Technicians moved among the victims, attaching probes. It was a visceral process, and there was some blood, but no complaining. Something was anaesthetizing them. Or paralyzing them. When it was done, the Nefilim technicians did something to a device that had appeared from the floor, and the process began.

The victims started melting into the floor, as though they were made of salt and the rock below them was a pool of dark water. It took just a few minutes, during which the Secretary-General watched, enthralled. *Science! How marvelous!* Standing up and crossing over to the nearest victim, he looked down into the melting face. It was streaked through with something the color and texture of granite. The eyes were the only thing that still looked human; they looked back up at him.

After a few minutes, it was all over. The last traces of the bodies had disappeared into the rock. The columns of light flared, suddenly intense as they assimilated the new energy, and then disappeared.

"Is that all there is to it? When do we know whether it's worked?"

One of the Nefilim turned to him. *'We know now. There is enough power in the grid not only to reclaim what has been lost, but also to destroy the mutant creation.'*

"Excellent! How long? And it will stay like this?"

'Yes. The process will begin immediately, and within days, everything will be as it should be.'

Ah, science!

Battlefield Earth.

The Nefilim sent another invasion fleet. This time it was mainly transports and their escorts, instead of the large cruisers that had made up most of the first fleet. They were planning a different kind of war. And this time, they were prepared. They paused out of range of the defense satellites whose orbits enveloped the globe, and sent in unpiloted drones that destroyed them, one by one.

With the space defenses gone, the invaders had free access to the Earth's skies, but when they appeared above the cities in their battle groups, they found to their surprise that there was plenty of resistance.

When groups of their own fliers came up to meet them, they didn't know what to think; perhaps they were being welcomed. In the first few minutes they lost ships, but they learned quickly.

The invaders were repelled from some cities, but Paris, Beijing and Cairo fell, and other places besides, and these became their centers. Other cities didn't survive the fight for them, and became worthless piles of ash.

When the Nefilim who had gone over to the humans realized what was happening, most of them changed sides again. It was a messy process, and many were killed. Those that didn't make it away were rounded up and put in safe places deep underground, well away from the fighting. The humans were left with the bulk of the Nefilim weapons, and they made good use of them.

The war for Earth had begun in earnest. The humans, deducing that the Nefilim had set up their main command center in Beijing, destroyed the city. The invaders retaliated by wiping out Chicago and what little was left of Germany.

The war was fought in the oceans as well. Cruisers, crewed by both Nefilim and humans, hunted each other in the expanses of the Pacific and beneath the ice of the polar seas.

After a few days, the human government in general and the Secretary-General in particular were happy with the way things were going. The fighting was hard, and the casualties were high, but the aliens were fewer in number, were playing away from home, and they were being confronted by their own technology.

When the war was in its second week, most of a supply fleet from the Nefilim home planet was destroyed as soon as it entered the Earth's atmosphere. After that, the balance shifted even further away from the Nefilim.

The Nefilim prisoners were given an ultimatum – work with the UN, or not at all. Those who refused were executed.

The grid had grown strong, just as the scientists had said it would. The Stream had resisted, but now it was falling back, like a plant giving way to a withering drought.

For a few days, the Secretary-General was happy.

* * *

But it didn't last. A few days later, Alexis and the few generals who could make the trip converged on Mount Weather.

It was bad. Once again, everything was in chaos.

"WHAT THE FUCK IS GOING ON? I want to know what's happening!" the Secretary-General bellowed. He suspected a plot. He had some scientists tortured, but it changed nothing. *What was happening?*

The grid was writhing, like an animal having a seizure. Spikes of energy were sweeping through it, causing power systems to overload and craft to drop from the sky like stones. Weapons were failing. The earthquakes started again. The military campaign was falling apart.

"It's the invaders!" ranted the Secretary-General.

"It can't be. The same thing is happening to them," came the reply. "They're no better off than we are."

Even without the technology and the weapons, the fighting went on. The armies on both sides took up clubs and made shields and spears and bows and arrows. The population, instead of being turned to ashes or incinerated, was soon fleeing before medieval hordes.

The war clattered and moaned like a re-enactment of the Crusades. At this, the Nefilim had a natural ability that was more than a match for the humans, and the tide of war turned in their favor.

More ships arrived from their home world, dropping reinforcements by parachute before they lost power and made suicide dives into human-held areas.

"So...? what is happening?" yelled the Secretary-General, leaning over a map of the advancing Nefilim lines.

"There is something in the grid," replied the scientists.

"What do you mean?"

"Entities – consciousness – something alive is *inside* the grid. Whatever it is, it is fighting us."

"Find a way to put me in there," said Alexis, whose thirst for revenge was consuming her. "If you can do it to the plebs you use for energy, you can do it to me. I can find out what's happening, and then you can bring me back out."

It was agreed.

The Stream, and how the grid came to be in trouble.

It had taken them five days, but they finally found the node the blue woman had talked about.

It was well past the outskirts of the city, isolated at the end of a small valley, near a cluster of houses and surrounded by trees. They landed and followed a worn path to an old adobe building set into the side of a hill.

The house was well past its best times. The steps that led up to it were hollowed with age. On the portico in front of it, a couple of thin dogs scratched themselves under bare wooden benches.

They went through a pair of unpainted doors into a room that appeared to be some sort of shrine. Against the far wall a cluttered altar was covered in photographs and paintings and an almost impossible number of burning candles. On a table stood ritual objects, pieces of plants, and a couple of skulls that had been fashioned out of some black material. On the walls hung paintings of people in saintly poses. A few wooden benches like the ones outside were arranged in front of the altar.

There was room here for maybe a dozen people, twenty if it was going to be crowded. The place smelled of burnt fat, mixed with a heavy, sweet aroma.

"What is this place?" Bark had never seen anything like it. This planet kept coming up with one surprise after another.

"Some religious cult thing," said Reina. "Voodoo or something. This part of the world is big on weird religions."

"Weirder than other places?" asked Pig.

"Nah, probably not. They're all pretty strange if you ask me," Reina replied.

A bead curtain beside the altar parted, and a middle-aged woman came into the room. She stood uncertainly beside the altar, her hands clasped in front of her, and said something in a language that none of them understood.

"Sounds like Spanish," Reina said.

"Why is it," said Bark, who had had enough of the mystery, "that I can't understand her? Sahrin, can you?"

"No, I can't. It's weird. What's going on?"

"It's the photon belt," said the blue woman. "Out there in the rest of the universe, you can all understand each other" – they nodded – "but the photon belt has its own rules. This planet is undergoing some special reconstruction, and it will have its own ways from now on. It's going to be a special place. You can understand the rest of us because you met us before the belt arrived, but from now on, for as long as you're on this planet, you won't be able to understand anyone you meet who speaks a language different from any that you've already heard."

"Could be difficult." Bark shrugged his shoulders.

"Well, at least that explains that," said Sahrin. "You sure know a lot about what's going on."

The blue woman held Sahrin's gaze and nodded, but didn't reply. Instead, she spoke to the local woman in her own language. Before she had finished, a voice came from behind the bead curtain. It spoke in Spanish, and then changed to English.

"Come through! Enough formalities and introductions!"

The local woman looked relieved. She pulled the beads aside and gestured that they should enter.

"At least someone here speaks a language we can understand," said Sahrin.

The room behind the altar had no windows. A few candles worked hard, pooling their resources in unsure battle against the gloom. The walls were lined with shelves of props that no doubt had turns of duty in the shrine room. In one corner sat a bench, at which the woman had obviously been working. On it figures of deities, no bigger than children's dolls, were in various stages of construction. Limbs, torsos and heads were piled together, the aftermath of some toy armageddon, waiting to be resurrected.

The voice spoke again from the far end of the room.

"Down here. Don't be shy."

They approached, their eyes gradually becoming accustomed to the light. There was no one there. Just a large pile of something that appeared to be mud.

"That's right," said the voice. "It's me. Or should I say, I'm it!"

Bark turned to the blue woman. "Could you…?"

She nodded, and shrugged out of her robe. Soon there was enough light for them to see by. The voice was coming from the thing in front of them. It was alive.

"Not just a parlor trick for the locals, I assure you," it said. "What you see is what you get."

It was about five feet high, about five feet wide at its base, and tapered towards the top as though it had been poured onto the ground and then allowed to set. Its pink surface bulged unevenly, as though it was covering mounds of fat. Set into it were eyes, noses, ears and mouths, as though the whole thing was the result of a collection of wax figures being allowed to melt together on a hot day.

"I can guess what you're thinking. You're quite right, I wouldn't be winning any beauty contests, would I?" said one of the mouths.

"What *are* you?" Geoca asked the question for all of them.

"One of you," another mouth replied. "A mutant, just like you. I have a special job, though. I'm here – well, mobility isn't my strong suit, so I'd have trouble being anywhere else, wouldn't I? – to look after the node. Actually, you could say that I'm part of the Stream, rather than a keeper. Remedios here is the keeper, even though she doesn't know it. She thinks I'm the oracle for this shrine. She looks after me, and the Stream flows through me."

"I've never come across a mutant like you before."

"No, you wouldn't have. They broke the mold when they made me!" The thing seemed to find that funny, and most of its mouths laughed. "I've been expecting you," one of them said above the chorus.

"I don't think so," replied Bark. "We've only come here because our flier needs fixing. If it didn't need repairs…"

"I know all that," the creature replied. "But as I told you, I'm part of the Stream, and since your ship changed its power system, so is it. And therefore I know what's been going on. No magic, I assure you, no magic. As I said, I've been expecting you. There are no secrets." It laughed to itself again. "I also know that you're planning on going to Mount Weather."

"Mount Weather?"

"Their headquarters. You know what I'm talking about, Bark. Your mountain. Am I right?"

"You're right."

"Of course I am. Now, there have been some developments that you might not be aware of. The Stream is in serious trouble."

"What…? The last we knew, things were going well…"

"Oh, they were, and I wish it was still so, but I'm afraid you're a little behind the times. The Nefilim grid is growing again, and at a rate much faster than before. It seems to be unstoppable."

"They've changed something, then."

"They most certainly have. They've charged it up. Given it some juice. The Stream is falling away before it, and nothing that we've tried has made any difference."

"How? What have they done?"

"I may have the answer." Anak was using his voice. "They have probably put a large number of individuals into the system. Their energy would have been used to make it much stronger than before." He explained how it was done.

"That's fucking inhuman!" Reina flushed with anger.

"You can see all this happening?" Bark asked the pile of mouths.

"To an extent. I can see and feel that the Stream is being attacked, and I can see the places where the grid is in contact with it. They are very different in nature, you see. I can't see into the Nefilim grid, though. It's not part of my domain. Are you hungry? Remedios will get you something to eat."

"Later perhaps, thank you. Can't you do anything about this?"

"There's nothing I can do myself, but I can help *you* do

something. As I said, I'm part of the Stream. It's possible for you to enter it by using me as a gateway. For a heap of body parts, you know, I've got my uses."

"We wouldn't doubt that," said Sahrin. "How do we do it?"

"Oh, it's easy. We just have to join up a little. It's no big deal. I think our young cloven-hoofed friend here knows the score. It's much the same as when you were inside the ship's mind, Pig."

"You do get around, don't you," said Pig.

"And we'd be able to change things?" asked Geoca.

"I wouldn't have a clue. But you'd have a much better chance than me, I can tell you that much."

"And what's to stop us from getting caught up in the Nefilim grid? If it's as strong as you say?" Sahrin asked.

"Oh, it is, believe me. It's causing a lot of trouble, and the humans are making the most of it. But to answer your question, there's nothing to stop you from being caught there, apart from the fact that if I sense that you're in trouble, I'll try to bring you out. That's about as far as travel insurance goes, I'm afraid. I can't make any promises."

"I don't know," said Bark. "It sounds risky."

"Well, I haven't tried to hide the fact. But it could be important."

"I'll do it," said Geoca. "I want to see what the Stream is like. We've done so much for it, but we know nothing about it."

"Me too," said Sahrin. "Geoca shouldn't go in on his own."

"But you're injured," said Pig.

"Tell me about it," Sahrin answered. "It's giving me the shits."

"Your injuries won't affect you while you're in the Stream," said the pile of mouths. "It's a mind trip. In fact, while you're in there, I can do a bit of repair work, if you like."

"Sold," said Sahrin.

"But I'm afraid that I haven't told you the full story." The creature sounded more cautious now. "The problem with the grid isn't the only recent development."

Bark looked at the ceiling. "That would be too much to ask,

wouldn't it."

"True. A few days ago, a Nefilim invasion fleet entered the Earth's atmosphere."

No one said anything, so the mutant continued.

"They've made up for the disaster of their previous attempt. They succeeded in getting past the satellites. This was apparently a surprise to the government, who were distracted with domestic matters, to their detriment as it turns out. The Nefilim ships have attacked many cities, and the fighting is fierce. Fortunately, though, there's nothing in this area that they want, and I doubt that we'll see them down here, for some time at least."

"I'll go as well," said the blue woman, without offering a reason.

"The war makes this attempt to help the Stream more urgent," said the pile. "You see, both sides are using the grid as their power source. If it fails, their war will suffer. They won't have anything to fight with."

'Then I want to go as well,' thought Anak. 'We have to do it before they wreck everything.'

It was agreed.

A few minutes later, they were ready. The four of them sat around the mutant with their backs to it. When it told them to, they leaned back, and its surface opened up beneath each reclining body. As they sank into it, the mutant's flesh wrapped itself around them like a placenta, a thin layer of translucent skin growing over them so that soon they looked like nothing so much as pupae inside their cocoons.

* * *

It was shining, filled with the pure light that stars produce. They were floating in sparkling blue and white waves that washed through them and over them, carrying them along. They knew who they were, but their physical bodies were gone. Their minds had taken new forms.

Geoca felt his miniature selves merge into him. His separation from them disappeared, their voices became his, and his theirs. He saw his own mind, clear and radiant, and he saw his thoughts clearly, as if each one had its own existence. *This is how it is meant to be,*' he thought to himself, and then for good measure agreed with himself.

They saw why it was called the Stream. It was warm, suffused with a soft bubbling energy that made them want to bathe in it forever. It was an intricate fabric of channels and pathways, and their minds flowed out into the fine tendrils that spread out into the earth like the roots of a plant.

It was there that they saw that the Stream was in trouble. They saw it being attacked, and as they dissolved more thoroughly into it, they felt its pain. They saw that the Stream was nowhere near the size it should be; it was being torn apart at its edges, eaten alive by something totally alien to it.

Something floated past them. They felt its awareness, felt it observing them. It hesitated for a moment, then slowly moved away. It thoughts were different; none of them understood it.

'*What was that?*' someone asked.

'*An elemental,*' answered the blue woman. '*You might call it a nature spirit. There are many of them, many different kinds. They love being in the Stream. They will use it to reinvigorate the planet, if they get a chance.*'

'*Then we'll just have to give them the chance, won't we,*' thought Sahrin.

'*Should we see where the damage is being done?*' thought Anak.

'*Yes.*' Sahrin was feeling better. Here, her pain was gone. '*Where is the grid?*'

'*All around us. Come with me.*'

The blue woman led them to a place where the Stream was heavily disturbed by turbulence. It was writhing around, seeking escape from its pain. The grid was visible beyond the divide that separated it from the Stream. It was a churning mass of darkness, creeping forward, eating into the Stream like acid.

As pieces were eaten away, they were thrown back into the grid and carried away.

'This is how it is happening, then. Look at that!'

'We can't do much from here. Can we get through?'

'I say yes. Let's do it.'

'But we don't even know whether we'll survive in the grid, let alone be able to enter it. We might just be foreign bodies to it. It could reject us. It might just chew us up, like it's doing to the Stream.'

'I doubt that it will reject us outright,' thought Anak. *'Remember the method that's used to power it.'*

'OK, I'm remembering it. What if we end up in the same boat?'

'We've come this far...'

They pushed against the grid. There was no resistance at all; it was as though it wanted them. As they crossed the threshold, something pulled at them, as though it would have liked to dismember them, but it didn't have the strength.

Suddenly, they were inside. It was different here. Where the Stream had been full of light, here everything was underpinned by a static that hissed relentlessly.

A flood of tiny shards of artificial light swept around them in a blizzard, stinging them like pieces of glass. It felt strong, but it was a harsh strength, a composite of other things that had been pulled apart and reassembled in new combinations. The grid was a kaleidoscope on the verge of disintegration, continually fragmenting and being forced back into place.

They looked different here. The glowing bodies they had possessed in the Stream were gone; their physical bodies had been partially remade, flickering as if they had been created from the static itself. They looked like holograms that hadn't been focused properly. Their minds were closed off again. When they spoke, it was almost with their physical voices.

"It hurts..."

"It wants to cut us..."

"Yes, it hurts!" It felt as though it wanted to flay them alive with its countless tiny needles.

"Wait," said the blue woman. Something here had changed her blue coloring to a bright, burning red. She put her hands on them, one by one, and the pain stopped.

"It can't hurt you now. It's not that strong, it just needs balancing. It feels worse than it is." She withdrew from them, but the healing she had given them remained, protecting them.

"I don't like it. Look at it, it's ugly."

From here, they had a new view of the effect it was having on the Stream. Shafts of darkness plunged into the Stream and spread out, like the branches of a tree. Once inside it, they started twisting and turning, tearing the Stream's body apart and throwing pieces of it back into the grid. When that was done, the static moved in to fill the empty space that was left.

"It's awful."

"It is. Let's see what's going on."

The grid was constructed of broad, long corridors, intersecting at right angles. On top of it was superimposed another finer grid of smaller pathways that divided the main squares into smaller ones.

"I know where we need to go," said the blue woman.

"Where?"

"To the control points," she replied, "where it began. There are four of them."

"I know how to find them," said Anak. "I know this system. There will be one near here."

He led them to one of the main corridors. They paused at the intersection, looking at the torrent as it roared past them like an endless horizontal waterfall. They leapt into it, and it picked them up, sweeping them along. It was much faster than the Stream. After a while, Sahrin noticed that the grid was empty. "There are none of the elementals here, are there?" she yelled above the noise.

"Of course not," answered the blue woman. "Would anything live here by choice?"

"We're almost there," said Anak. "Soon you'll see the only life form that the grid is home to."

Something had appeared ahead of them. It appeared first as a distant glow, like daylight at the end of a tunnel. As they approached it, they saw a gigantic mass. It looked like a huge ganglion of nerve tissue, some cell that had grown out of control and become a tumor.

The current entered the cavern that surrounded the object. It was suspended in the center of the space, held in place by thin tendrils that grew out of it like tentacles. The force of the flow diminished, leaving them floating in front of it.

"Jesus! Is that thing meant to be here?"

"Of course," said Anak. "It creates the power that keeps the grid going. It is the gateway – the contact between the physical world and the grid."

It was beating slowly, like a heart, as the currents flowed in and out of it. There was sound coming from it, some kind of voice. As they got closer, and moved in among the outer branches, they realized that it wasn't one voice, but a cacophony of voices. There was whimpering, and moaning and screaming. It was a choir of pain.

"Where's that coming from?" asked Sahrin.

"You'll soon see," Anak replied. "I thought it might be like this."

They were approaching the thing's center. The branches had become thicker, and attached to them were objects that looked like air sacs in ribbons of seaweed. They stopped in front of one of the pods. Something was trapped inside it.

"What is it?"

The thing in the pod moved, straining against its imprisonment. A face turned towards them.

"This is what happens to the grid's power source," said Anak. "Their life energy is drained from them, until finally they become empty husks. Then they are replaced."

They looked around. There were scores of the cocoons scattered around them.

"If we can get them out, the grid will lose its power," said Sahrin. "Does that sound right?" She reached out and started pulling at the pod. The material came away in sticky strips.

Anak followed Sahrin's example. It came away easily, falling from the body in large clumps. As they threw it aside, it was carried away by the current, disappearing into the distance.

It was a boy, probably just a teenager. As they pulled him out, his eyes opened. His mouth opened and closed as though he was trying to say something, but no sound came. He looked back and forth in confusion at the strange apparitions floating around him. They asked him who he was, but there was no answer, just the blank questioning look in the eyes. He began moaning.

"He's not all there."

"Literally. The grid has been eating him alive."

"First, we should free them all," said the blue woman. "Then we take them to the Stream. It's this place that is hurting them. In the Stream, their pain will cease."

They set to work, moving among the closest arms of the ganglion and freeing all the prisoners they found. Then they herded them like sheep along the current, until they reached a point where the grid and the Stream were touching.

"Here you are," they said, and pushed them through, one at a time, delivering them into the Stream like midwives delivering babies. It was an easy birth. The grid seemed unaware that it was losing something, and allowed them to pass through easily. Sahrin and Geoca went through with them, and watched as the tortured bodies transformed into glowing spheres of light.

'I think they'll like it here,' thought Geoca. *'How do you feel?' he asked one of them. 'Are you all right?'*

There was no answer, but Geoca felt a wave of happiness flowing from it. It reminded him of a dog wagging its tail.

'They may have been people once,' thought Sahrin, *'but they're something different now.'*

'They seem simple,' thought Geoca, watching them drift away. *'But they're happy. Let's go back.'*

They went back into the grid, where the blue woman and Anak were waiting for them. They went back to the ganglion and searched thoroughly, freeing the rest, taking them to the Stream and releasing them.

It was a long time before they put the last of them through. By then, the grid was reacting to what was going on. The current was growing erratic. By the time they took the last group to the Stream, the grid was no longer advancing on it. Its strength was gone, and it was retreating, falling back before the advancing effervescence like dark sand being covered by the incoming tide.

Anak pushed the last of the newborn through. "There are three more control points."

"Then let's find them. We must be giving someone a few headaches."

Anak agreed. "If that's what you get when your world starts collapsing around you, yes."

* * *

They found the second control point, and then the third. They cleared both of them out, removing all of the prisoners from each and setting them free in the Stream. They lost track of time.

"They just feel, don't they," said Sahrin, watching the last of them float away. "I wonder if that's all they'll do."

"There's one more control point," said Anak.

"And then they'll be history." Geoca was enjoying himself. "I wonder what's happening out in the real world?"

"I'd say that we have their attention by now," the blue woman answered.

"Let's go." Anak knew the way.

Sahrin had been thinking. "What's to stop them just putting a whole lot more people in here, and reactivating the whole thing?"

"Nothing at all," Anak replied. "An important detail, and one that can only be attended to in the physical world."

"A bit of wanton destruction?"

"Totally wanton, I'm afraid."

"Break a few gadgets…"

"*All* their gadgets…"

"Then let's finish up here as soon as we can. The sooner we kill off this pile of shit, the better."

The last control point soon became visible, glowing like a nebula in space.

"This one's bigger than the others."

"This is the main control point," replied Anak. "This is the one we have to destroy for real."

The blue woman stopped. "Wait. I can feel something. There's someone in here with us."

"But there hasn't been anyone or anything here, apart from the prisoners."

"Well, there's someone here now, and they're heading this way…"

* * *

Alexis saw them. They were entering the outer reaches of the primary ganglion. There were only two of them, a male and a female, both human. This was too easy!

"Go and get them," she said to the two Nefilim she had brought with her. "Alive preferably, but if things don't work out that way, I don't care…"

The two aliens swept forward, Alexis floating behind them like a dark Madonna.

A Nefilim diving towards you is a frightening sight. They came screeching out of the clouds of static, their arms outstretched and their jaws gaping, looking like demons from some witch burner's nightmare.

"Shit," said Geoca. "I hope this was the right thing to do."

"So do I," replied Sahrin. "But it's too late now. Let's go."

They sped away, down between two converging arms of the ganglion. Their pursuers were gaining on them; they were too close for comfort. Sahrin felt something clutch at her foot. She kicked herself loose as Geoca took hold of her by an arm and threw her to one side. She landed against one of the cocoons in the web. Its occupant began thrashing around, making it hard for her to free herself.

As Geoca launched himself feet first at the closest Nefilim, the blue woman and Anak came flying out of the shadows. Their trap, such as it was, was as sprung as it would ever be.

The blue woman stopped in front of the two Nefilim. She turned herself into a burning star, redder and brighter than any fire, and then an instant later became a whirlwind, spreading out into arcs that rotated in space like flaming swords, threatening to incinerate everything in their path. The glare was so strong that the attackers were blinded. They reeled backwards, shielding their eyes. Taking advantage of the confusion, Anak had come up behind them. He grabbed the closest attacker around its neck and twisted. Its death squeal disappeared in the noise of the grid and the moans of the prisoners.

The blue woman wasn't able to keep up her display for more than a few seconds, and the other Nefilim could soon see what was going on. It lashed out with a foot, reaching past the body of its companion and hitting Anak square in the face. He reeled backwards, struggling to stay conscious.

Geoca and Sahrin leapt forward. Each of them grabbed one of the Nefilim's arms and pulled as hard as they could, stretching the alien out as though it was crucified in space. It flailed around wildly, trying to shake them off, but they both knew that they wouldn't be getting any second chances, and they held on. The alien finally dislodged Sahrin by bringing a foot up and kicking her in the head. The Nefilim swung its free hand around, driving its talons into Geoca's face. It took hold of him and swung him around, close to its mouth. The blue woman leapt onto the Nefilim, but she was too late to stop it from ripping into Geoca's body with its teeth. It threw him aside and was turning on her when Anak came charging at it.

He drove a fist into the Nefilim's body. The blue woman sprang away as the Nefilim doubled over, unable to resist as Anak sent it spinning away like a bowling ball, where it became caught up like an insect in the web that surrounded them. It lay there, trapped, its head twisting back and forth as it looked for some escape.

Alexis had been watching from a safe distance. *Damn, I'm such a fool,* she thought. *I've fucked up badly.* She should have let them talk her into bringing more than just the two aliens with her. But no, she had to prove that she was capable, and she was regretting it already.

Anak, the blue woman and Sahrin were looking in her direction.

I can't fight here, Alexis thought. *Shit!* There was nothing else to do. She turned and pushed herself away into the first current she could find. She would flee to the center of the ganglion, and get back to the real world. And then she would come back with enough help to waste these vandals.

But the current wasn't fast enough, and Anak was. Alexis felt a strong grip close around one of her legs. She spun around. "Who the fuck do you think you are? Do you know what you're doing?" she yelled, looking around desperately for a way to escape.

Anak knew what she was thinking. "Don't bother," he said. "There's no way out of this."

"That's right," said the blue woman. "And as for who we are – we're your future."

Alexis sneered. "That's a little melodramatic, don't you think, freak?"

"Not at all, considering what we're going to do," said the blue woman.

Sahrin had stayed with Geoca. He was unconscious, and his wounds were bad. His body was mangled. It was obvious that he wasn't going to survive. Unless... she took hold of Geoca, and moving him as carefully as she could, found a fast current to the Stream.

As they were approaching it, Geoca stirred. "It's OK," she said as he tried unsuccessfully to speak through the mess the Nefilim had made of his face. "It'll be better soon."

She eased him through the barrier between the grid and the Stream, gritting her teeth as he strained against the pain of the transition. "Hang in there," she said, and then he was part of the Stream again. She stayed close as he floated, conscious but not moving. After a few minutes, he was able to communicate.

'Better?'

'Much better. I can feel the healing. Thank you.'

'Not a problem. I know you'd do the same for me.'

'Of course I would. What happened?'

'You got hit in the face, but I expect that you knew that, and you got a bad Nefilim bite. You're a mess, I'm afraid. Well, your body is, anyway. I thought you were done for.'

'I don't feel done for. Strange, isn't it, that I should feel so much better here.'

'Not so strange, perhaps. I'll go back and see what's happening. Don't go too far away, OK?'

'How far is too far? I'll stay here.'

She went back to Anak and the blue woman. They were where she had left them, which was good; she didn't like the idea of hunting for them in the confusion of this horrible place.

"Geoca's fine."

"Good. We have more problems, though. The Vice-Secretary and her friends have forced our hands," the blue woman said. "If they hadn't come, we could have removed the prisoners, and then had time to think about our next move. But it's clear now that they know that something's going on, and they're prepared to do something about it. They wouldn't have sent her" – she indicated Alexis – "otherwise."

"And when she doesn't return, they'll send more…"

"Exactly. We've had one lucky break, and it would be too much to hope for another one. They won't make the same mistake twice. They'll send real numbers next time. We have to act quickly."

"What, then?"

"What, then? You want to know what then, bitch?" snarled Alexis, who was still being held by Anak. "I'm going to take your…" Anak put a hand over her mouth. It covered most of her face, but it had the desired effect. He turned her around so that she was facing him and sent her a thought. When he turned her back around, she lwas silent.

The blue woman continued. "We have to get to the physical plane and disable the installation at the control point. They won't be able to get in here or resupply it after that. Here's the problem. The transformation process is slow. When they see that it's us coming through, they'll have plenty of time to deal with us while we are helpless."

"And even if we did get through, we'd most likely be outnumbered," added Anak.

"Big problem," said Sahrin. "So what are we going to do?"

"The prisoners here need to be freed. That's your job, Sahrin. Anak and I will make the transformation into the physical plane."

"But you just said…"

"I know. But they won't be seeing me. I'll be in disguise." She moved in front of Alexis. "You're going to serve a purpose, Vice-Secretary. That should be something new for you."

Alexis found her voice again. "Fuck off, skank!"

"Let go of her, Anak."

The blue woman dissolved into a cloud of sparkling stars. Before Alexis could do anything, the cloud had enveloped her. She looked puzzled and tried to move, but her limbs wouldn't obey her. The cloud began to grow smaller. At first it seemed as if it was condensing, but it wasn't. It was soaking into the Vice-Secretary's skin as though she was a sponge. As the last of the cloud disappeared into her and her skin returned to its normal color, Alexis's agitation ceased and her face became calm.

The Vice-Secretary spoke. "This is my disguise."

"Is it…" Sahrin hesitated – "you?"

"Until I leave this body, yes. Whoever is waiting on the other side shouldn't find my appearance alarming, I think."

"What about her? Where is she?"

"She's here, and as you might expect, she's communicating

her displeasure to me. She's very direct."

The blue woman/Alexis turned to Anak. "Anak, do you think you'll pass for one of them?" She pointed at the Nefilim that was stuck in the web. It had stopped moving.

"As long as they don't look too closely."

"Good. Sahrin, release as many people as you can. You'll have to be quick, because there's no way of telling what will happen once we get to the other side. And equally, we don't know what will happen here if we disable their controls."

"Oh, great. That makes me feel real secure. Give me what time you can." Sahrin didn't enjoy the thought that this might turn out to be a suicide mission.

The blue woman/Alexis and Anak turned away towards the center of the ganglion.

Sahrin set to work. There were so many of them. The pods were everywhere, and the task was even bigger now that she was doing it alone.

The other two reached the center of the mass. It was calm, in the way that the eye of a hurricane is calm. There was no static, just a ball of light suspended before them.

"That's the entrance." Anak moved towards it and put his hand on it. It rippled and changed color, like oil floating on water.

"Then let's use it."

They pressed against the surface. It resisted them briefly, stretching inwards, then parted. As they entered, their minds were thrown back and forth between consciousness and unconsciousness. Alexis felt it, and surged against the intruder, fighting her with all the strength she could muster. The blue woman struggled to maintain control over her host.

* * *

Small bubbles formed on the floor in the control center then joined together, creating a thick slurry of foam. The ground began stretching upwards as shapes formed under it. As it continued to rise, the rock didn't crack or break, but dissolved slowly into the forming bodies, like water soaking into dry earth. Finally, their features became visible, and as their skin absorbed the last of the rock, their eyes opened.

The blue woman's grip slipped, and Alexis made a break for it. She rushed into the space in her mind that the blue woman was grappling for, and planted herself there as strongly as she could. She pushed as hard as she could, and the blue woman was almost forced out. The cloud, blue again now that they were out of the grid, began to appear around her body as Alexis sat up. She looked around at the human and Nefilim scientists who were watching.

"Don't just stand there!" Alexis yelled, jumping to her feet.

The blue woman rushed back into her. In an instant, she re-established control, pushing the shrieking Alexis back into her corner. The scientists looked confused. One of them stepped forward.

"Vice-Secretary, what's going on? What was that blue light?"

She ignored him. *Don't just stand there...* "Don't just stand there!" she said. "Get on with your jobs!"

She looked around the room. They were in an underground cavern. Its ceiling was lost in darkness and the floor was covered in pieces of rock, some of them large, but most of them small, strewn across the floor like gravel. There were more scientists, soldiers and other hangers-on here than she had hoped. A few Nefilim were busy at the controls that she and Anak needed to get to, and there were some human scientists watching every move the aliens made.

A dozen or so human soldiers were standing around. They looked agitated, and were all looking in her direction. Two officers approached. A couple of scientists followed them, eager to talk to her, but they hung back, waiting their turn and whispering to each other in worried tones.

"Vice-Secretary, thank god you're back," said one of the officers.

She said nothing; she just looked at him, hoping that her

silence would draw more information out of him. It did.

"About an hour ago we got word that a Nefilim carrier is on its way here," he said. "They've been active in this region, but this is the first time they've moved towards the control point itself."

"Did you organize reinforcements?" she asked, hoping it was something that Alexis would ask.

"We asked for them, but the commander of this region said it was impossible to fly troops here. It's getting too dangerous. While you were in there" – he pointed at the floor between them – "the grid has gone further out of control. Many areas have lost all power. And the regional headquarters are under siege. All they could send was a couple of companies, and they're traveling here by road."

"But what about the Nefilim carrier? Won't it be here soon?"

"A few minutes ago we learned that they've gone to ground, a few klicks from here, on the other side of the sand dunes. The grid gave out on them."

"And so they're heading this way on foot?" Alexis was frothing with rage while she spoke. It was distracting.

"We can only assume so. The grid in this area is far too unstable for them to use. But they have other craft approaching. They're a while away yet, and we don't know how close they'll get before they're forced to land."

"Then we'd better see to our defenses." She walked over to a soldier. "Give the Nefilim your gun." She nodded towards Anak. The soldier handed his weapon over. "Let's prepare. All military to the surface."

Just as the soldiers were about to enter the tunnel that led to the surface, a private, breathless from running, came hurrying out of the darkness. He spoke briefly to an officer, who cursed quietly and then came over to her.

"The Nefilim are at the perimeter of the compound. We're dug in, and we're holding them, but there are more of them than we thought."

She looked over at Anak. He read her thoughts and nodded,

just enough to show that he understood.

"Let's get up there," she said.

* * *

She half expected to hear the sound of gunfire as they approached the surface, but the alien weapons that both sides were using had made warfare a quiet business. Something exploded just before they emerged, and there was some yelling, but that was all.

When they came out into the light, she saw the remains of vehicles scattered around in burning pieces. The perimeter fence was in tatters. It had been holed in many places by fire from both sides, but the Nefilim hadn't entered. They had taken cover in the rocks and dunes, and were firing into the compound from there.

"Get me a gun," she said, and took the weapon that was offered to her. "Are they showing any signs of advancing?"

"No," a sergeant replied. "They seem to be content just to sit there and snipe at us. They're waiting for their backup to get here, I'd say."

A beam burnt a trail across the ground between them. They scattered, and she found herself behind a building. Another ray shot from the dunes, and the upper half of the soldier next to her flew apart in a cloud of powder.

This was definitely more Alexis's scene than hers, and Alexis knew it. The Vice-Secretary was throwing herself around in the prison that had been made for her, hurling herself against the walls that confined her.

'You'll be free soon enough, Vice-Secretary, but bear in mind that if this body is destroyed, it won't affect me. You, on the other hand...'

Something exploded close by. There was screaming, but it soon stopped.

"How long until our reinforcements get here?"

"About two hours, Vice-Secretary." The colonel wiped soldier dust from his face.

"And theirs?"

306

"If they have to walk the same distance as the ones here, about an hour, perhaps. That's a guess, of course."

The real fight was ahead of them, then. She wished that Anak would hurry up. As she thought it, one of the soldiers near her turned to an officer.

"My gun's fucked," he said. "Jammed, or dead, or something. Bonehead crap!"

"Same here," said another one. "What now?"

She knew what now. Anak had come through. The grid was dead. All around her she saw soldiers cursing their weapons, trying to shake life back into them.

An officer ran up to her. "The guns are dead! All of them!"

She looked across at the dunes. The firing from there had stopped as well.

"I'll check the grid," she told the officer. "Something must have happened down below. Do whatever it takes to keep them out."

The officer turned away. "Get anything you can!" he yelled. "And bayonets! Pass out the bayonets!"

She entered the tunnel and went down just far enough to be out of sight of the surface. She didn't have to wait long until Anak appeared.

"It's done."

"The scientists?"

"Unconscious. The controls are destroyed, beyond repair. When they come around, they won't be able to do anything. The grid is dead. They have no power, and no way to restore it."

"Then we're done here." She went to the part of her mind in which Alexis prowled like a caged animal.

'We're done. Thank you for your help.'

'Screw yourself, freak!'

'You have appalling social skills, Vice-Secretary. I'm afraid that I have to render you unconscious. We don't want you complicating our departure, and I'm sure you would try. When you come around, I think you'll find your hands will be full.'

With that, she reached for the Vice-Secretary's mind and

pulled it into unconsciousness. She left the body. Alexis again, the Vice-Secretary slumped to the ground, fast asleep. The blue cloud that had drifted out of her skin quivered, shifted, and shifted again until finally it took the shape that Anak was familiar with.

The blue woman opened her eyes. They were once again the blank white orbs that Anak knew. She was naked, though.

"I can't stay like this, can I? I'd attract too much attention, and the only clothes I could take would be hers." She looked down at the Vice-Secretary. "Even then, my skin color…"

'Enter me, as you did with her,' thought Anak. 'I can carry you out.'

"I've never tried it with a Nefilim. I don't know if it will work."

'Then there's only one way to find out. Hurry.'

Anak was right. She dissolved, again becoming the cloud. She surrounded Anak and entered him.

A Nefilim mind was softer than a human's. It was full of colors that flowed and shifted like a thousand tidal pools. It felt like clay, waiting to be shaped, but she could feel a strength beneath it as well. It might be malleable, but it would never break. She drew back from the interior, closer to the surface of Anak's mind. She wasn't here to do anything; she was just a passenger.

Anak found a side tunnel where they wouldn't be disturbed. All they could do now was wait. If he showed himself on the surface now, the soldiers would assume he was one of the enemy. It would be a while before the Nefilim reinforcements arrived, and when they did, they would hopefully be able to slip out of the base in the confusion that would ensue.

'So we wait,' he thought, and sat down in the darkness. He didn't mean to, but he soon drifted off into a fitful sleep. He dreamed of Marduk. He was there, even though he had never been to his home planet, and he had no idea what it was like. He was an Earth Nefilim. He had been born among the mutants, and had been raised in the underground labyrinths. Whenever he had this dream of his home world, he had no way of knowing how accurate it was, or even whether there was any truth in it at all. But it was the same every time…

He saw fleeting images of a cold, dark sky above vast plains of gray ice, bounded by freezing black mountains. Under the ice his race waited, frozen solid, until the feeble rays of the approaching sun warmed the air enough for the ice to start melting. It was the Marduk spring, stirring after the long sleep of deep space. The ice melted and flowed away to create short-lived oceans, and the sleepers emerged from their cocoons. They stretched their rejuvenated limbs and looked up to the sky. The sun hovered in the dark gray depths, sullen and weak. Anak was with them. They turned towards him, welcoming him home.

Just as he opened his mouth to speak to his own people in his own language, he woke, just as he always did.

Something was happening on the surface. There was yelling, and the unmistakable sounds of battle. The Nefilim were attacking.

He went to the tunnel entrance. They had come out of the dunes and had fought their way through the perimeter fence. The Nefilim were swinging their weapons like clubs, while the humans were either doing the same or slashing at the aliens with bayonets. The humans had fallen back towards the center, where the fighting continued between the buildings and around stranded vehicles. Dead and wounded lay everywhere.

Anak moved carefully, using the buildings for cover whenever he could, and keeping as far from the fighting as possible.

'Behind you!'

The voice in his head was clear and loud. He turned. A human was rushing towards him. The soldier lunged, thrusting his bayonet forward. Anak knocked it aside, deflecting it from his body, but it continued downwards, slicing into his leg. Taking hold of the rifle, he drew the bayonet out and pulled the weapon towards him.

The soldier, who either forgot or refused to let go, came with it. Anak seized him by the arms and held him up against the side of a building. He put his face in front of the soldier's. A terrified teenager looked back at him.

'*I am not one of your enemies, human.*' He drove the thought firmly into the boy's squirming mind. '*Your battle here is lost. Stay hidden until the fighting is over. That is your only hope of survival.*'

He lifted the boy into the air and threw him up onto the roof of the building. The youth lay motionless where he landed, looking up into the sky as though it held the answer to something that puzzled him deeply.

'*We need to hurry,*' thought the blue woman. The fighting was moving towards them.

Anak slipped through a hole in the fence, and limped towards the sand dunes. When he reached them he slumped down behind some rocks. The wound in his leg was bleeding badly.

'*I can't lose much blood. It affects our race badly…*'

'*I'll do what I can,*' she thought. '*It will only be temporary, but it will have to do for now.*' She flowed down his body to the wound. A blue salve appeared over the cut, and the blood congealed before his eyes. He stood up and tested his weight on the injured leg.

It was a long climb to the top of one of the highest dunes.

They were near the sea. Below him, the compound was already hidden among the sand dunes. In the other direction there was a small bay, and on the other side of it a town. A road wound around the bay towards the town. He was looking at Barker's Mill.

As good a place as any, he thought, and headed for the road.

Karma is a shit.

The Secretary-General was exhausted. He was sitting alone in the gloom of his office, surrounded by the quivering shadows of the candles that provided the only light in the room. Nothing at Mount Weather worked any more. There were no weapons, no vehicles, and the air conditioning was out. The air was turning to shit. He wouldn't able to stay here much longer.

"It's not fair! None of this is fair!" He struggled to his feet and swept the contents of his desk onto the floor. A candle landed in a waste paper bin, and a few seconds later flames were licking at a pile of maps lying on a table.

The Secretary-General stood looking sullenly at the flames. He'd show them. The mutants and their freak friends might think they'd won, but he'd show them. As soon as he'd dealt with the Nefilim.

He had to go. A meeting of what was left of his war council was about to begin. He lit a kerosene lamp and left his office.

"There's a fire in there," he said to the guard outside, without looking at him. "Do something about it."

"What shall I do, Secretary-General? The water pumps aren't working."

"I don't give a shit what you do. You can throw yourself on it, for all I care."

The floor of the war room was awash with water. He didn't ask why. The few generals and bureaucrats who hadn't run away or been killed or captured were there, waiting for him. He sat down and looked around the table. *Jesus, what a miserable collection.*

"Where are the Nefilim? *Our* Nefilim, I mean?"

"Gone," said a man in a black suit who rivaled the Secretary-General in bulk. "The last of them ran off a few hours ago. All we have left are a few prisoners."

"Rats leaving the sinking ship," said the air chief, who had been without his air force for several days now.

The Secretary-General looked at him. "Who said anything about a sinking ship? I very much hope that our enemies are underestimating us to the extent that you are, Field Marshall."

The Field Marshall shuffled his papers and looked away. "The Nefilim armies have closed the circle around us," he persisted. "The mountain is surrounded. Our troops have fallen back to defensive positions in the foothills. We should be able to hold them for a while…"

"You'll hold them for as long as I say. What about weapons? And casualties?"

"Nothing is working any more," said a General. "We've been using rocks and bayonets, and the men have been making spears and bows and slingshots. The other side is doing the same. Basically, we're fighting a medieval war down there. Casualties have been heavy on both sides. And there are thousands of wounded in the foothills around the mountain."

"Never mind the wounded. I want you to send agents out through the enemy lines and into the surrounding countryside. Tell them to recruit the locals and organize whatever stray troops they can find. And then they are to attack the enemy from behind."

The other members of the war council looked at each other. The local population would never lift a finger to help them.

"Yes, Secretary-General," they murmured, knowing that it was a futile mission. Everything was lost. They were cut off and surrounded. Of the three relief columns that had tried to fight their way in, only one had made it. One had been repulsed, and the soldiers had scattered, fleeing into the forest. Another had been ambushed within sight of the mountain, and the few survivors captured.

The situation was even worse than the war council knew. On every continent, the population had turned on both the UN armies and the Nefilim. Armed with farm implements or tools or whatever else they could find, the mobs were now evenly matched with their tormentors, and were hunting them down wherever they could be found. It was worst in the areas around the largest cities, where millions were roaming the countryside, desperate for food and shelter. The cities, looted and burned, were controlled by marauding gangs. Cannibalism and disease spread. Violence was everywhere.

There were places that fared better, though. In isolated and remote areas, many communities had held together. They watched from a distance as the rest of the world slid into chaos.

But the Secretary-General and his councilors had more pressing matters to attend to.

"...the mutant thing has grown into this area..." someone was saying. "You can see how the plants have changed, they're growing so fast that you can almost see it."

"I've seen it," said someone else. "You can see the path it takes, right under us."

The Secretary-General started paying attention. "That grid thing of theirs? It's here?"

"Well, it's not actually a grid, Secretary, not literally, it's more of a..."

"Christ, shut up... it's here, under us now?"

"Yes, Secretary. There have been some strange side effects, too. Like this condensation. It just appeared out of nowhere." The speaker made small waves in the water on the floor with his foot.

The Secretary-General was thinking. A smile formed. "God, yes, yes," he said. "A gift from God." Here it was then, proof that the universe was on his side, despite everything that had happened. The scales of justice had clicked back into place. He leaned forward.

"Do we still have any scientists among the Nefilim prisoners?"

"Very few, but there are some, yes, Secretary."

"Then put them back together with our scientists."

"Why, Secretary? Surely we can't trust them, with their own armies outside."

"Firstly, we have no choice, Field Marshall. Secondly, any of them that give even the slightest sign of resistance, deception or anything other than what we want from them are to be executed on the spot. Slowly and in front of the rest of them. We have one more chance, gentlemen."

* * *

The scientists were put to work, adapting Mount Weather's power and weapon systems to the Stream.

The Secretary-General, for his part, put away the ceremonial sword that had been presented to him several months ago by the civilian governor of the East Asian region. If everything went well, he wouldn't need it.

Then he slept, and as he slept he dreamed of Vice-Secretary Alexis. Strangely, there was no sex. She was running, breathless and wild-eyed, up and down hills of sand, pursued by dark shapes that looked like black shadows cast against a wall. He thought that she got away, but he wasn't sure. Then he thought that he had become one of the dark shapes and was chasing her himself. It was all very confusing. He was talking in his sleep, mumbling incoherently, when his aide shook him awake.

It had worked. The Stream was online. They had power again. By the time he got to the war room, it had come alive. The screens on the walls flickered with panoramic views of the surrounding countryside. Icons that represented units of soldiers glowed steadily on the map set into the table in the middle of the room. Radios chattered in front of their operators.

"Armaments?"

"Almost, Secretary. They've taken some time to charge up, but the main weapons systems are online. The hand weapons will take longer, because we can only charge a certain number at a time, but we've done some, and they're already in use."

"Very good! Very, *very* good! Now let's get rid of our first encumbrance!" He gave the order, and sat back to watch the screens. Seconds later, lasers began slicing into foliage and Nefilim alike, burning both like dry paper.

The Secretary-General's alterations are noticed.

Bark was getting restless. It felt like it had been days since the others had disappeared into the creature.

Reina and Pig were getting jumpy as well. They'd gone back to the ship and told Nibat what had happened, and he had come back with them. They all sat on the seats in front of the shrine room and watched exotic birds flying in the jungle. They ate the food that Remedios brought for them, and after that they slept. But that had been hours ago, and now more time than they cared for had passed, and they needed to know what was going on.

Finally, Remedios emerged from the shrine room. She said something they didn't understand, and pointed towards the door. The creature wanted to see them? The woman nodded, not sure what the question had been.

They went in. Geoca and Sahrin were still visible under the creature's skin, but there was no sign of either the blue woman or Anak.

"What happened to them?" asked Bark, gesturing towards the empty spaces.

"Two of your friends went into the grid and haven't returned," the pile replied. "The other two have come back into the Stream, though. They are fine. They're coming this way; they'll be here any minute. They'll be able to tell us everything that has happened. But I can tell you now that they must have been successful. The Nefilim grid went down several hours ago, and there hasn't been any sign of life from it since. The Stream is growing everywhere… Your friends are here now…"

The bodies stirred, and the membranes that covered them dissolved into transparent threads, falling away as if they were dissolving in the air. A few seconds later their eyes opened, and Geoca and Sahrin sat up.

They looked around as though they were disappointed with what they saw. Geoboy and Geogirl opened their eyes as well, then whimpered and closed them again.

"Everything is so... *hard* here," said Geoca. He looked disappointed.

"We did it," Sahrin said slowly. "We closed their grid down." She told the others how they had taken the victims and freed them into the Stream, and how she had barely released the last of them when the grid had suddenly disappeared altogether, blinking out of existence like a light being turned off.

"You did well," said the pile. "Both they and the Stream will benefit greatly."

"I believe that," said Geoca.

"I want to stay there," Sahrin said suddenly.

"I thought there was something up," Pig said. "Is the Stream good, then?"

"Absolutely... *beautiful*. Like nothing else. I can't put it into words now. Maybe later..." Her voice trailed off.

"It is a wonderful place, I know," said the pile. "I know I look like a monster to you all, but I regard myself as being lucky, living in the Stream as I do. I would want it no other way. You know, if you really want to do it, you can. You can stay there. But there is something else," the creature continued. "The Stream is growing everywhere, now that the grid is gone."

"That's great!" Reina was happy. If it was all over, she was looking forward to going home.

"But as I said, there is something else. Something is drawing power from the Stream. Something large."

"What is it now?" they asked, their smiles fading.

"Their headquarters. Mount Weather. A few hours after the grid failed, they started taking power from the Stream."

"They must have attached themselves to it, just like our flier has. Just there? Nowhere else?" Reina asked, her spirits sinking.

"Just when it could have been the end for them," said Geoca.

"I suppose it's no surprise that they should refuse to give up." Bark kicked at a pile of dust on the floor. It squealed and ran off under the bench with the dolls on it.

"We'll go back into the Stream." Geoca looked at Sahrin, who nodded her agreement without hesitating. "We'll see what can be done at Mount Weather. We'll see if we can pull the plug on them."

"Good," said Bark. "And we'll approach the problem from a different angle. We'll continue on our way there."

"Good luck to you all, my friends," said the pile as it prepared to take Geoca and Sahrin back into itself. "As long as that place exists, it is a danger to all of us. And to everything."

Bark, Reina, Nibat and Pig left for the ship, wondering what the Stream was like, and where the blue woman and Anak were.

Interlude

Sahrin flew in wide soaring arcs through the Stream. Geoca, united and whole again, followed. They skirted the edges of the whirlpools of silver bubbles that tossed them from side to side, and laughed at the waves of pleasure that surged through them. Soon they remembered that they had a mission, and they stopped playing. They extended themselves out into the Stream, letting it carry them along. It was repairing itself, flowing into the places that had been left by the grid.

They soon found what they were looking for. It was a piece of night. Waterfalls of blue light cascaded into it, disappearing into the darkness like stars flowing into a black hole. They circled it slowly, not sure what to do. Leap into it? Into what?

'It doesn't look appealing.' Sahrin skirted around its edges, keeping a safe distance away.

'I suppose we know what comes next, don't we...'

'There's no immediate rush, is there? It will take the others time to get there...'

'It will...'

Geoca felt Sahrin come nearer to him. He reached out towards her and she came even closer, laughing. They swam around each other, teasing and probing. Finally they joined, flowing through the Stream, two currents that had come together.

'You feel... like I thought you would,' Sahrin thought. *'Like I hoped...'*

'And you,' he thought, flowing through her. They entered each other with sighs that had no voices. As she wrapped herself around him he softened, feeling her resonate through him. Around them, crystals of light condensed out of the Stream and sparkled like stars in space. They became a helix, spiraling slowly around each other, creating a veil of ecstasy that enveloped them in silence.

They stayed like that for a long time.

After time had passed, they stirred. *'Time to go,'* they said, and unraveling from each other, they leapt into the torrent and were swept into the black hole.

PART 6

Geoca does theater.

They were inside Mount Weather's power system. Stretched out into long thin trails, they squeezed into the labyrinth of narrow channels. In the Stream they had been unaware of dimensions, but here the narrow confines of the circuitry pressed in on them from all sides as they flew along its wires and fiber-optics and raced through the masses of chips and connections.

'Look at their devices... all their machinery! We can get into it...' Sahrin swept through the food refrigeration units and turned them off. Laughing, she locked a few doors, and stopped some elevators from working. She looked through the security cameras, using them as eyes to see the results of her work. *'We can do anything we want here.'*

Geoca found the radar screens and covered them with snow, so that the operators wouldn't see the approaching ship.

Sahrin moved into the radio network and filled it with harsh static, then watched as the operators threw their headsets off. *'Marvelous!'* She overloaded the machines that were charging the guns that the soldiers would use. They exploded in a shower of sparks.

'The others must be getting close by now.'

'What are they going to do?'

'Who knows?' Sahrin felt a sudden wave of doubt. They had no plan. *'What are we going to do?'*

'A distraction,' thought Geoca. *'We'll give them something to look at. I know just the thing. You do what you can with their lasers.'*

'Lasers?'

'Look.' He showed her one. There were a dozen of them, large powerful weapons concealed in bunkers around the circumference of the mountain.

'But don't touch the one I'm using...'

'Yes...' Sahrin took off towards the closest of the lasers.

Geoca entered another one, and looked through its sights.

It was trained on a mound of rocks, which it was laboriously burning away, bit by bit. There must have been something behind it that they wanted to get at.

'*Time to put a stop to it.*' He found the amplification circuits. Hurled back and forth between the reflective elements, he grew in power, becoming a mass of searing, burning light.

The soldier sitting in the gunner's seat cursed as the laser faltered. He swore and punched the side of his console in frustration. The laser's beam faded out as though something was blocking its path, then suddenly a cloud of red-colored light shot from it, as though it was an obstruction being expelled. The soldier's mouth hung open as the cloud stopped halfway to the rocks he had been firing at. It hovered fifty or sixty feet above the ground, then surged outwards like an exploding nebula. It flared, a seething transparent mass, then collapsed in on itself, congealing into a form that took the shape of a figure hovering above the no-man's land between the human and Nefilim lines.

Geoca was putting on a show. He was fifty feet tall, a figure of fire burning so brightly that it was hard for anyone on the ground to look at him. He raised his arms, and a huge pair of wings grew out of his back, so that he looked like some angel from hell, a Marian vision from the other side. The two small Geocas floated beside him like oversized demonic cherubs, casting balls of cold fire towards the ground from their open mouths.

The Geoca-angel reached out and swung a mighty arm along the length of the ground that separated the two armies. A stream of fire flowed from its fingers, creating an impassable lake of molten rock.

The soldiers on both sides drew back and then turned and scattered, the Nefilim disappearing into the jungle, and the humans either bolting into the tunnels that led back into the depths of the mountain, or fleeing to either side of their positions around the base of the mountain. A few stood frozen where they were, unable to move.

Geoca grew six more pairs of arms. Each of them threw

shining spheres down onto the ground that shattered when they hit, sending showers of sparks and smoke into the air. He moved on around the mountain, his eight pairs of arms weaving like snakes, as if he was a religious idol that had come to life.

Sahrin, watching through the monitors, was impressed. It was a spectacular sight. Geoca's sense of scale and theater was superb. But she had her own work to attend to. She flowed into the hardware of the laser she had chosen and told the gun's computer that it was about to explode. When the computer relayed the news to the operator, he scrambled down the ladder to the access way as quickly as he could, swearing all the way.

Excellent. She swiveled the gun around and looked through the sights. Not yet having had the benefit of a visitation by a vengeful deity, the opposing lines of soldiers here were still intact, and still going about their bloody business.

A couple of tanks went rumbling through the human ranks, on their way towards the Nefilim positions. Arrows bounced harmlessly off their iron flanks. A fireball was thrown towards one of them, and was extinguished instantly by a jet of foam. *An unfair fight,* she thought. There had been a time in the recent past when Sahrin would have had no hesitation at all in destroying the lot of them outright. But that felt like the old Sahrin, the one who hadn't experienced the Stream. Now, she felt pity for the soldiers from both sides below. They were nothing more than pawns. She didn't want to kill or hurt anyone.

Aiming carefully, she fired a long laser burst into the ground in front of the tanks. They stopped instantly, their drivers wondering who on their own side would be firing on them. She traced a ring of fire around the tanks, surrounding them with a trench of fire. The soldiers on the ground looked on in confusion as she neatly sliced the barrels off both tanks. Then she did as she had seen Geoca do, and separated the armies with a reminder that they should not try to cross the land that separated them.

It was time to move on to the next laser bunker and see what could be done there. As she was about to leave, Sahrin's attention was caught by something in the distance.

A small silver streak was approaching, moving quickly and low, skimming above the treetops. It was a ship.

The battle for Mount Weather.

As they approached the mountain, Bark had been feeling even more strongly attracted to the place. It seemed almost to have acquired a voice, heard in brief snatches in the way that a conversation in another room might be heard.

Mount Weather rose out of the jungle before them.

"What's that?" There were flashes of red light on the face of the mountain.

Nibat made an adjustment to his monitors. *'Lasers, the locals call them. A basic but effective form of energy beam. We will need to be careful.'*

As they drew closer, a larger light the same color as the lasers came into view from the far side of the mountain. Without being asked to, the ship focused in on the object until it filled one of the screens.

"Geoca!" they all said simultaneously.

"He's not exactly doing things by halves." Reina was impressed. Geoca had formed clouds around himself, and heavy rain was falling on the soldiers below. They wallowed in mud, trying to get away. The two smaller Geoca angels swooped at them like burning harpies, adding to the chaos and confusion.

'Whether he means to or not, he's providing us with a most welcome distraction,' thought Anak.

"For what, though?" Now that they were here, Reina made the same realization that Sahrin had. They had no plan.

"I want to get in there," said Bark. The closer they got, the clearer the voice in his head was becoming.

"Whatever it takes. I'm with you. This place has got to go," said Pig. "We've been living underground long enough."

'We'll find a place to land,' thought Nibat.

They flew in close to the surface of the mountain. Near the summit they found a plateau big enough hold the ship. It was high above the fighting, and close to something that looked as though it might be an entrance to the mountain's interior.

"That was easy," said Bark, and went to get the guns.

* * *

The Secretary-General watched on one of the few working monitors as the ship landed. He touched a key on the desk in front of him.

"Security. Some unwelcome guests have just arrived near Exit 23. See to them. I'm not interested in anything that they might have to say. Just dispose of them."

His brow creased by ever-deepening furrows, the Secretary-General went back to watching the battle, such as it was, that was going on outside.

* * *

Nibat wasn't happy about staying on the ship, but he was the pilot, and he had no choice. Bark, Reina and Pig stood at the edge of the plateau and looked at the chaos unfolding far below them. If they were going to find a way in, it would have be up here somewhere.

"Let's have a look." Bark led them away from the ship, along a track that had been cut, a long time ago by the look of it, into the side of the mountain.

'*You must destroy this place. I'll show you how.*' Bark started as the words appeared suddenly and clearly in his mind. He spun around, expecting to find that Nibat had followed them.

Reina and Pig looked at him. "What's wrong?"

"It's nothing."

The path wound across the face of a steep cliff and then up towards an escarpment. They were climbing through a maze of boulders and old lava flows when there was movement ahead of them, near the crest of the incline.

"What's that?" whispered Pig.

"A missile bay? A door?" said Reina.

"Let's look," Bark said, and they started climbing towards it. It was slow progress. There were boulders in their way, and

330

everything was wet with condensation, so that they found it difficult to get a good footing. Pig did better than the others, and was soon ahead of them. He paused, his ears pricked up, then turned and hurried back.

"Voices, up there," he whispered, pointing with his snout.

They listened, tightening their grips on their guns. There was movement; a few fleeting glimpses of uniforms between the rocks.

"Down!" Even as Bark said it, a ray flared against a rock near him. They had been seen.

"Bark!" a voice called. "Give yourselves up!"

Bark recognized the voice. "Thead! We thought you were…"

"Dead? Ha! Fuck! Yes, I'm sure you did. But I'm far from dead, I assure you. A little sore, for which I owe Sahrin, but apart from that, I'm quite happy in my new position. You see, Bark, people here appreciate my talents."

Reina snorted. "We appreciate that you're a prize asshole," she called out.

There was a pause before Thead answered. "Shut up, bitch! Now, if you'll all just drop your weapons…"

"And if we don't?" said Bark, buying time, trying to work out where Thead was.

"No matter, really. I'm just in rather a hurry, that's all. We've got a lot on at the moment, you see, and the truth is that you're something of a nuisance."

A rock tumbled somewhere behind them. Bark knew instantly what had happened. While they had been distracted by Thead, his men had been working their way around them. They were surrounded.

Reina moved closer to him. "Sounds like…"

"I know, I know."

A beam flashed among the rocks again. A grenade arced over and flared a short distance away.

"Shit, Bark," said Reina, keeping her head down. "We're not even in there yet, and they're onto us! And where's Pig?"

Pig was gone.

* * *

Sahrin had noticed what was happening. She rushed to Geoca.

'They're here! But they're in trouble!'

'Then let's see what we can do.' Geoca finished his display by turning into a giant cobra that reared up, spreading its hood and spitting fire. The apparition moved quickly, slithering through the air above the battlefields. It traveled around and up the mountain, followed by two fiery dragons, each twice the size of a man.

Sahrin found a laser near the mountain's peak. It gave her a good view of the surrounding countryside, but more importantly, she could see her companions, edging their way through the maze of rocks that surrounded them. She could also see Thead and his soldiers. *Thead!*

The cobra appeared above them, twisting like a Catherine wheel. Thead's soldiers began panicking, shooting into the sky at it. Some of them turned and ran.

"You idiots!" yelled Thead. "It's nothing! It's just trickery! It can't hurt you!" A few of them stopped, uncertain. The rest kept going. "I want those mutants dead! Now!"

Sahrin could see Reina and Bark. They were surrounded. She started firing the laser, melting the rock near Thead's men.

'I'm not going to kill any one,' she thought.

'I know. But do your best to scare them off,' replied Geoca.

The laser fire revived their fear of Geoca's cobra spectacle. To Thead's men, it was all part of the same package. They turned and ran. Sahrin kept firing, herding them like sheep. But she couldn't see Thead. And now she couldn't see Bark or Reina either.

* * *

Bark and Thead had almost collided, coming around the same corner from opposite directions. Thead had the advantage; Bark had been balancing himself near the edge of the ravine that the narrow path skirted. He had just enough time to say "Thead!" loud enough for Reina, a few feet behind him, to hear. She stopped, staying out of sight. Thead leveled his gun at Bark's chest.

"You've turned into a nasty piece of work, Thead…"

Thead's expression didn't change. "There's no time to waste on talk, Bark. Time to die."

As he pulled the trigger, there was a clatter of falling rubble beside him. Something charged out and hit him, throwing him off balance. The gun fired harmlessly into the air.

Pig collected Thead in the thigh with a single thrust of his tusks. Thead staggered, waving his arms and hovering on the edge of the cliff like a tightrope walker in trouble. His good leg buckled under him as Bark swung out with his foot, and he fell headfirst into the ravine, screaming as he went.

Bark went to the edge and looked down at the trail of bloodied rocks that descended into the shadows. He felt no pity at all for Thead.

"Thanks, Pig. We're better off without that one around."

Pig shook blood off his tusks. "That's OK."

"You know, I used to like Thead. He was only a boy when I took him onto the ship."

"Well, I didn't know him long enough to ever like him. He was a prick." Reina picked up Thead's gun. "And it's too late now. Let's go."

They waved to the Geoca-cobra, and watched as it slid off down the mountain. They climbed up to the door that Thead had emerged from. As soon as they entered, it hissed shut.

A speaker near the door crackled.

'Don't worry. It's me, Sahrin. I'm in their system. We both are.'

"Can you control all the doors?"

'Some. Most, I think. It's just a matter of finding them. I'll call Geoca. He can help. The boss man, the Secretary-General, he knows that you're here. I've been keeping an eye on him. He's not happy.'

"That's understandable. Hopefully he's going to be even less happy."

'Come to the holding cells.' It was the voice. Bark was hearing

things again. *'Near the landing bays.'*

"Sahrin, where are the cells? I mean the prison, I suppose." Bark figured that he'd better do as he was told.

There was silence for several seconds. They started to wonder whether something had happened, then Sahrin came back.

'I'll show you. I'll make the lights flicker. Just follow it. I'll use the doors as much as I can to keep the guards away from you.'

* * *

The Secretary-General was watching over the shoulder of one of the computer operators. She had been searching for whatever it was that had been disrupting the system, and she had finally found it.

"What are they?"

The operator did that thing where you suck air in over your teeth, and shook her head.

"I see. Well, either destroy them, or kick them out of the system. I don't care which one. Just stop them from interfering. We're fighting a war here."

"Enclosing them is the only option, Secretary-General. Ordinarily, we might be able to find a way to eliminate them or expel them from the system, but we have neither the time nor the resources," she replied, nodding sideways towards the empty seats in front of the other terminals.

She began setting up internal firewalls around Geoca and Sahrin.

"There they are." The lines of code and icons that scrolled down the screen meant nothing to the Secretary-General.

"That's lovely. Just make it quick."

* * *

The doors to the cells stretched along a corridor, one side of which was taken up by large windows that looked out into the mountain's volcanic shaft. The inside of the volcano was covered with lights, windows, walls and reinforcing. Floodlights pointed downwards, dispersing the darkness for a few hundred feet.

"You could fall a long way down there." Reina leaned against the glass, looking as far down into the gloom as she could.

"Some have," said Pig. "It's one of their favorite methods of getting rid of problems. There are a lot of bones down there."

Bark was looking through the peepholes in the cell doors. The rooms were packed with mutants, Nefilim and humans, all segregated. There were twenty or so cells, with no room to spare in any of them.

"Sahrin, can you open the cells?"

Her voice, thin and distant, came from a speaker above them. *'I'll try. I'll have to hurry, I think they're on to me. I've lost contact with Geoca.'*

One by one, the doors of the cells slid open and their occupants emerged. Some ran, hurrying away before whoever had done this could change their mind. Others hesitated, not sure what was going on. Two soldiers went running past in a panic that was so blind that they didn't seem to notice the group. If they did, they didn't care enough to do anything about it.

"All of you, out of here," yelled Reina, pushing the nearest of the prisoners towards the exit.

'If you could just let me out... We have things to do.' It was the voice, loud and clear in Bark's mind. Its owner was here somewhere. Bark walked along the corridor. There was one door that hadn't been opened. Unlike the others, it had no locks or timing devices. It was welded shut, sealed by gobs of metal that held it tight in its frame.

"They really want this one to stay shut, don't they?" Reina aimed her gun at the door. "Shall I?"

Bark nodded. Most of the door collapsed in a shower of dust. There must have been some sort of field as well. Terminals sparked, tiny bolts of lightning spitting through the air where they had been cut.

The room was bare except for a single bunk. The figure sitting on it stood up and faced them.

"Thank you. It's been a long time since that door was open."

"No problem." So this was the owner of the voice.

"You don't know me, but I know you, Bark. And the rest of your crew."

"You're right, I don't know you at all, and since I'm not from here, I find it hard to see how you know me."

The stranger came out into the corridor. His skin was black; but it was a real black, like night, not at all like Reina's dark brown skin. His eyes were entirely black, without a speck of white in them. And when he opened his mouth to speak, his teeth were black as well. It was like looking into a shadow. The only color on him was the pale blue of his prisoner's uniform.

"A long time ago, Bark, I gave a map to a member of the crew of the ship that you are now the Captain of – or *were* the Captain of, I suppose I should say, since it has been destroyed. That was thirty-nine Captains ago."

"Well, if you are who you say you are, you're something of a legend. There have been all sorts of stories about you."

"I don't doubt it. But for now, you'll have to trust me. We can talk later."

"Agreed." There was a muffled explosion in the distance. "What are we doing?"

"One of the reasons I've been locked up here is that I know too much. If we destroy its power facilities, we destroy this place. And believe me, we *must* bring it down. I'll show you the way."

The speaker in the hallway hissed urgently. *'It's me! I think they've got me! Yes, they've got me, I...'*

Reina leaped to the intercom. "Sahrin! What's going on?"

There was no answer. Just a low, grinding static.

"We have to go," said Bark.

"There's someone we need to bring," said the black stranger. "We'll need him." He went to a cell a few doors along, and stood in the doorway.

"You can come out now, William. Thank you for waiting. It's time."

A disheveled man came out into the corridor.

"It's you! The voice was real, then."

The black stranger nodded. "Yes, it was real, William. And now it's time to do as we discussed."

* * *

They had been cornered, but Geoca and Sahrin had done their work. Communications were a mess, working only intermittently when they worked at all. Half the monitors weren't working, and most of the troops were locked out of the main part of the complex. And now the prisoners were loose, causing havoc. A group of them had overpowered the guards at the armory.

The war room was in chaos as well. With the communications down, everyone was coming in person to deliver their reports and get their orders. One of them, a sergeant, had come from the loading bays. His hair was caked with blood.

"Prisoners have taken two fliers, Secretary-General. We fought the rest of them off, and now they're trying to get out through the ground exits. And the ship we sent to the control point is on its way back. We got a message saying that they found the Vice Secretary and a few men wandering around near the base."

"And the control point?"

"Apparently it's gone, Secretary-General. The Nefilim took it. A relief column got there too late. We lost that as well."

The Secretary-General snorted. "They're welcome to it. Bring the Vice-Secretary to me as soon as she gets here."

* * *

The dark stranger knew his way around. "There," he said after they had used a service elevator to get to an area a few levels above the landing bays. They were in front of an unmarked door.

"What's in here?"

"Backup terminals," said William. "We can access the system from there."

The single technician in the room went into a state of shock when they entered. The black stranger picked the young woman up by her shoulders and put her on a seat near the back of the room.

"You don't mind if we borrow your computer for a moment, I hope?"

She said nothing and nodded.

"Hello, how are you," said Pig, and sat down in front of her.

She nodded again, this time slowly.

"Now William…" The black stranger pointed at the vacated seat. "You remember what we discussed, don't you?"

William, who until now had appeared slightly bewildered by everything, came to life. He set to work, and soon the screen in front of him was a clutter of menus, dialog boxes and scrolling lists of options.

"What's he doing?" Bark looked at the screen and quickly became confused. "Anything we should know about?"

"William here was one of their top system administrators, before falling out of favor," replied the black stranger. "They found out that he had been sending information to the mutants. Of course, no one but a select few were supposed to know that the mutants exist, so he was doubly damned. They didn't want to do away with him, because of his knowledge of the system here, and also because of anything he might know about the mutants. In case he might be useful some time, they threw him in jail."

"Over the last few months, I've been in contact with him, just as I was in contact with you, Bark. I've been preparing him for this day. If anyone can bring their system down, it's William. William, how are you doing? We will be having guests any minute."

Reina had left the door ajar and was standing by it, listening for anyone approaching.

William nodded. He was reciting a stream of code into the headset's microphone. A few seconds later he looked up.

"It's done. I've released the bots. They have already started self-replicating, locking up all the free space on the storage devices and memory. Bit by bit, the system will freeze, until finally the whole thing will go into gridlock. By that time, BabyMutator will have wiped every CMOS in the place. They won't be able to do a thing to fix it."

"I don't know what you're talking about," said Bark, "but it sounds convincing."

William smiled. "Oh, they'll be convinced, all right."

Reina heard footsteps approaching. "They're coming. We need to go…"

Pig got up from in front of the computer operator.

"I'm sorry about your job. I think you'll find that the labor market here is about to suffer a major contraction. If I were you, I'd leave this place as soon as possible." He followed the others out of the room.

They were out in seconds and found a stairwell. Above them, soldiers ran from room to room, kicking in doors and shouting to each other.

"How long until the system starts failing?"

"It's already started." Now that he was away from the computer, William had reverted to his soft-spoken self. "They should start to notice it in a few minutes. With the bandwidth that's used here, it won't take long to spread."

"Then there's no rush, is there," said Bark. "We can just sit tight, and wait for it happen. Then when they're all running around trying to figure out what's happened, we can slip out."

"It would be nice if it were that easy, but unfortunately it's not," said William. "The lighting will go soon, and this whole place will be plunged into total darkness. But more importantly, the power system will melt down. The storage units will either go dead or explode, depending on which part of their cycle they're in. And the safeguards on the weapon systems will go down. They're all that's holding them…"

"Thanks. I think we get the picture. It's time to go."

"I know how to get outside," said the black stranger.

The center cannot hold.

The power was failing. The computers were failing. Damn it, *everything* was failing.

"What is it?" demanded the Secretary-General. "Is it those things that you locked up in the network? Have they got loose?"

"No, they're still where I put them." The operator looked nervously up from her screen, wishing that she didn't have to tell the Secretary-General about the other strange things that were happening. The links with the fliers and cruisers that were in flight had disappeared. Internal and external communications were frozen, as though they were choking on something. The lights flickered. Something rumbled deep underground, making the room shake.

"Fuck! FUCK!" The Secretary-General went to the monitors. He was sweating. Through the static and streaks of the disintegrating images he saw streams of soldiers, technicians and bureaucrats pouring out of the exits into the foothills, smoke billowing after them.

"Secretary-General, I think the lighting's starting to go."

The Secretary-General looked around the war room. The few people that were left were watching him, waiting for guidance. *Waiting for help. Imbeciles. They didn't even have the sense to run.*

"We're done here," he said. "It's time to leave."

They went to the landing bays, through corridors full of smoke and empty of people. The lights flickered on and off in celebration, spurring on the Secretary-General and his followers.

The situation in the landing bays was no better, and quickly getting worse. As they walked onto the deck, an overloaded flier tried to take off. It floated clumsily in the air, bobbing around like a ship on a swollen sea, then slid slowly, almost gracefully, down the volcano's shaft. It veered to one side as the pilot struggled to regain control, and ploughed into several levels of offices and laboratories.

There were only two fliers left. The Secretary-General looked around at the soft, weak-chinned bureaucrats who had come with him. He didn't need them.

He turned to a lieutenant. "Bring some men and come with me."

The bureaucrats surged forward, confused. "But Secretary-General, what about us? What are we going to do?"

"You? You can die." The Secretary-General turned to the lieutenant. "You heard me."

The bureaucrats turned and tried to run, but they had no chance of getting away. A couple of the more sprightly ones almost made it to the exits, but the rest fell where they stood. The soldiers were from the Secretary-General's private guard. Their conditioning was working hard now, straining to overcome the obvious and increasing challenge to their instinct for self-preservation, but it was holding well. They lowered their guns and stood still, their minds frozen. They would die before they would respond to any stimulus other than a direct order from him.

The other flier took off. It rose to the top of the shaft, and was just about to accelerate away when another ship appeared in the sky above it.

The Secretary-General watched as the new flier hovered for a few seconds, then swooped down, firing as it came. A beam sliced the lower craft in half and the two sections fell away, disintegrating against the walls. Bodies spilled out, tumbling into the depths. The new flier hovered in the circle of sky above them, spinning slowly, its lights blinking.

The fires were spreading now. On the other side of the shaft, the inner part of the complex was collapsing towards the center. It teetered in space, a sagging mass of girders and debris, lurching further downwards with each explosion.

"We should get to the surface, Secretary-General." The deck buckled beneath the lieutenant as he spoke. "We need to get you off the mountain."

The Secretary-General looked around at the fire and twisted

metal. His world was disintegrating around him. Someone was going to pay for this.

It was time to go.

Somewhere in cyberspace.

Geoca could sense that Sahrin was nearby, but that was all. They were being held apart by something. He couldn't define what it was; it was harder than anything he had ever felt before, as if there could be no question about it at all, no qualifications; it was just there. It was all around him, so thoroughly and perfectly that he couldn't move, couldn't resonate, couldn't do anything.

Unable to move, he had time to think. They'd done well. They'd stopped the fighting, which for some reason seemed more important now than it would have before. And Sahrin had helped the others to find their way through the base.

The trap had been sprung on them just after she had opened the cell doors. They'd felt it teasing them, probing, as if it was confirming their existence, then it had circled around them, forcing them into a small corner. When there was nowhere left for them to run, it had closed in, snapping shut like a trap.

Geoca would have been pacing up and down in frustration if he could, but he couldn't. He was trapped, like an insect in amber.

The ship turns peacenik.

Nibat was relieved when the others emerged from the interior of the mountain, but his relief was to be short-lived. He would soon be arguing with the ship.

As soon as Bark, Reina, Pig and their two new acquaintances were on board, they took off. Nibat was glad to be doing something again.

"It's got to stop here," the black stranger said. "The Secretary-General must be stopped."

Nibat took the flier up so that they had a good view of the mouth of the volcano. Within minutes, a flier appeared. The dark stranger was at his shoulder.

"Intercept it."

Nibat put the flier into a steep descent towards the other craft.

'They've seen us,' the ship said. *'They've armed their weapons.'*

'Then take them down.'

Instinctively, the ship obeyed the order and fired. It was a clean hit. The flier fell away in two pieces.

The ship came to a halt above the volcano.

'What have I done? Who did I just kill?'

'What do you mean? What are you saying?' Nibat asked. The ship had never talked like this before.

'I didn't want to do that. We shouldn't have done it. I won't do it again.'

'But they were going to attack us!'

'We were flying towards them! Of course they were going to fire on us!'

'Ship, what is this about?'

'I won't kill any more. It's the Stream. It's the way it flows through me. It's taught me – or I've seen for myself – something different. All this fighting and killing... I won't be part of it.'

'Not now, ship. It can't be now. First, we must deal with the situation confronting us.' Nibat knew that the ship was right. But

philosophy would have to come later.

'Pilot, you don't understand.' The ship sounded sad.

"The Secretary-General must be stopped," the black stranger repeated.

"Circle the mountain and watch for anyone on its surface," Bark said to Nibat. "Do you know what that Secretary-General person looks like?"

'Of course,' replied the Nefilim. 'Everyone does.'

"Watch for him," said the black stranger.

William was looking worried. "Their weapons systems will be redlining any minute. I suggest that you keep your distance. When it goes, it will be big."

They went into an orbit around the mountain. All around its circumference, on its slopes and in the foothills, confused and panicking people were fleeing the angry, smoking god that it had become. The ship scanned them, zooming in as close as it could, comparing each fugitive with the images of the Secretary-General that it had recovered from its memory.

'There's the chairman of the Security Council... and the president of the Food Bank...'

"Don't worry about them. They're nothing without their leader. Keep looking."

A few minutes later, the ship spoke again. 'There's another ship approaching. It's about ten minutes away.'

"Complications we don't need," Bark said when Nibat told him. "Who is it? What can you find out about it?"

Before the Nefilim could answer, the ship interrupted.

'I've found him. Your man. He's there, on the side of the mountain...'

"That's him all right," said Reina. "I'd recognize that slob anywhere."

The familiar figure on the monitor wobbled over the rocks, barely keeping its balance. Its face was bright with sweat. Reina could almost hear the wheezing. He was with half a dozen soldiers.

The black stranger stood looking at the image on the monitor with his arms crossed. "You have to kill him."

That's fine with me, thought Nibat, and passed the order to the ship.

'No! I've killed enough. You've all killed enough. You're as bad as each other!'

Nibat struck at the control panel with his fist. *'This is not the time for this! Do it!'* The others looked on, Pig alone among them understanding what was going on.

'NO!!'

"Then we'll pick him up," said Bark, when Pig told him what had been said.

The soldiers with the Secretary-General had noticed them and started firing. The ship deflected their beams easily.

The display caught the attention of the approaching flier. It swung towards them.

* * *

Alexis, returning from the disaster at the control point, saw the Secretary-General cowering among the rocks.

"Not MY Secretary-General, you don't!" she screamed, sweeping down on an attack path.

* * *

'They're attacking!' Nibat tried to put the weapons online, but the ship refused.

'I'm sorry, pilot...'

A beam from Alexis's ship burned a long painful welt on the flier's skin. If they weren't going to fight, they had to run. Nibat accelerated away, weaving like a corkscrew, evading the beams that kept coming towards them.

The wound on the ship's hull hurt. *'Why do they do this to each other?'* It kept going, until they were a safe distance away, then it slowed, diverting energy to the repair of its damaged skin. *'Why do they do this?'* the ship asked again, but there was no answer.

346

The one that just won't go away.

Alexis brought her flier down so that it hovered above the surface of the mountain, a few meters from where the Secretary-General was hiding. She put the external speaker on.

"Well, bubble boy, it sure looks like things haven't been going your way. You could even say that you've fucked up something chronic."

"Wha…??" The Secretary-General stood up, his face working itself into the closest thing resembling a smile that he could manage. "Alexis, my darling, you're a gift from heaven. Quickly, now, get me off here." He felt an ominous rumbling beneath him. Something inside the mountain was about to shit itself.

Alexis continued as if she hadn't heard him. "You prick. You let me go to that control point knowing what was going to happen. You knew there was fuck all chance of me surviving! You slug!"

The Secretary-General was almost speechless with shock. She wasn't making any sense. "M… my dear, I…"

"Don't *dear* me, asshole. You didn't give a toss whether I lived or died."

"But Alexis, I sent a ship – that ship – to collect you! It was the second time I've had to send someone after you!"

"You sent them to see what was going on, that's all! It was just good luck on my part that they saw me, scrambling around in the sand like some fucking savage, trying to hide from the boneheads. They slaughtered us!" She swiveled the camera around, panning over the mountain and the surrounding countryside. "What a mess. What an absolute, total fuck up! You're an incompetent, dangerous old…"

"But I…"

Alexis pressed the firing stud that she had been fingering impatiently. When the smoke cleared, there was only a crater to mark the spot, and something wet and visceral hanging off a nearby shrub.

"Damn, that felt good! So long, shithead!" She turned to the pilot, who was watching with his mouth hanging open. He was young, and from Idaho. He didn't get this. "Find that other flier's trail. Let's find out who we're dealing with."

"Yes, Vice-Secretary." The pilot was reaching for the controls when the ground below them heaved, convulsing violently and surging upwards. Above them, a rock face gave way, disintegrating under the forces that tore at it from below. Boulders the size of houses slid down towards the flier. Caught in the avalanche, it was flung downwards onto the settling rocks. It lay trapped, humming desperately like a pinned insect.

Alexis grappled her way towards the exit and palmed the panel beside the door. It scraped halfway open and refused to go any further. She squeezed through the narrow gap and looked down at the rocks that waited hundreds of feet below. The flier was pinioned on the brink, held like a flea in a pair of tweezers. The ground shook again, and the ship tilted even closer to the abyss. There was a ledge not far from the door. She reached out for it, dangling for a few seconds above empty space, hanging onto the edge of a viewport, and then swung herself to safety.

"Come on!"

Apart from the pilot, there were four soldiers on board. One of them began edging out of the door, and had just got a foot onto the ledge when more rocks came crashing down. The soldier, the ship and its contents were swept away in a torrent of rubble and choking volcanic dust.

Alexis leaped out of the path of the avalanche. She staggered, struggling to keep her balance as the ground settled. "Shit!" She kicked at a boulder.

She heard a footstep behind her. As she spun around, she took a knife from her belt and swept it upwards, pressing it against a throat, the blade tight against the skin.

"You!"

"There's no need for that, Alexis."

Thead reached up and gently pushed the knife away. "It's good to see you. And you should be pleased to see me. You need some help, it seems."

Alexis suppressed the urge to take a step backwards. "Somehow I'm not surprised that you've survived all this, Thead."

"You're not? I am. Well, I *almost* am. My former friends pushed me off a cliff and left me for dead. They left me with this rather nasty wound." He looked down at a blood-soaked bandage wrapped around his thigh. "There's loyalty for you. Now, time is short. You must come with me. There's something that will interest you."

He turned and limped towards a nearby ridge. She watched as he began climbing. *I haven't trusted him before,* she thought, *but that was mainly because he was a dork, and not for any particular reason.* He'd never been less than eager, she had to give him that. And what else was she going to do? She was glad she'd wasted the Secretary-General, even if it had terminated that particular career path. The oversexed slob. The thought of servicing him made her flesh crawl.

She started climbing after Thead. Beneath them, the ground was shuddering constantly now. The meltdown in the power section was accelerating, turning the mountain's interior into a mass of molten rock and steel.

She reached the top of the ridge. Thead stood waiting for her, a broad smile on his face.

She stopped, gaping. "Oh, sheeyit…"

They were looking down on a ship. It was hovering just below the crest of the ridge, so close that it was almost possible to reach out and touch it.

It wasn't a Nefilim ship. She had never seen anything like it before. It was large, easily as big as one of the Nefilim cruisers, but not as sleek, and not as colorful. It was bulkier, and covered with external probes and attachments that looked as though they had been stuck on as an afterthought. And where the Nefilim ships were covered in detailed patterns, no two alike, this ship was painted a dark featureless gray.

Even though she'd never seen anything like it, she knew instantly and exactly what it was. On the side of the tower that dominated the top of the hull, there was a red rectangle, and inside that a white circle. In the white circle was a black swastika.

"Nazis!!??"

"I think that's what they're called, yes. They found me shortly after I'd dragged myself out of the ravine. We'd just seen the Secretary-General when the other flier arrived on the scene. We were about to intervene when you came along and drove them away. And of course, we were watching when you moved your motion of no confidence in the Secretary-General's leadership. Come. Time is running out."

He led her down to a ladder dangling from the belly of the ship.

"It seems that they've never been great fans of the Secretary-General," he continued as they climbed. "You, on the other hand, have earned their approval. Along with myself, of course. Just put it down to our winning ways." He turned and smiled down at her.

Alexis grunted and said nothing. Yes, if Thead was anything, he was a survivor.

Sahrin and Geoca.

Sahrin felt the heat increasing around her. Everything was shuddering, as though a force somewhere was building, pushing at the barriers that had been holding it back. A crack appeared in the walls of her prison. Bright light poured in through the gaps left by the pieces as they fell away.

The current outside was more turbulent than it had been before. Piece by piece her prison fell apart, the fragments carried away in the torrent of the mountain's gathering collapse. She emerged from her cell like a hatchling from its broken shell. Geoca was waiting nearby, pulsing with impatience.

'We have to go. It feels strange here. There's something going on.'

'Yes. Quickly.'

They sped along the buckling, twisting pathways of the system. It threatened to block them, distorting and collapsing, and more than once they were forced to retrace their path until they found another way. Finally, they saw the entrance ahead of them. The Stream was pouring in even faster than before, feeding the fires that were consuming the complex. They struggled against it, fighting their way towards the vortex.

They were thrown back. They tried again and again, and were repelled each time.

'It's no good. It's too strong.'

'Oh, no...'

The current around them began to boil. It became hard to think.

'We're finished?' thought Geoca. He was beginning to fade.

Somewhere behind them there was an immense explosion, many times larger than any of the previous ones. Its pressure created a tidal wave that rolled over them, picking them up like leaves on a raging river. It flung then forward, searing them, threatening them with disintegration, and pushing them against the incoming flood of the Stream.

They didn't know it, but they were participating in Mount Weather's final moment. The gate to the Stream began to collapse, closing like a camera shutter. They crashed through an instant before it snapped shut.

They floated unconscious in the cool flow of the Stream, its current running through them and around them, healing them as they slept.

Sahrin and Geoca were home.

Reina decides to go home.

The mountain was still visible, a small hill in the distance in Nibat's monitor, when it erupted.

The screen was filled with a blinding white flash. Seconds later, the light was replaced by a rolling pillar of cloud, lava and fire. The lava surged towards the sky in slow motion, then curled over and collapsed on the disintegrating slopes of the mountain. The cloud took on a mushroom shape, as if a nuclear explosion had occurred. Bolts of lightning cracked through its upper reaches, reaching down to the destruction below.

Reina whistled slowly. "That's gotta be it, I reckon."

Nibat fed more power into the engines. *We got away just in time. If we were there…*

"We're lucky that we didn't hang around dealing with that other ship. I wonder if Geoca and Sahrin made it out."

"You heard Sahrin," said Pig. "She said they were trapped. It sounded like that, anyway. I doubt that they could have got away."

The black stranger, who had been talking to Bark, heard what they were saying. He came over and looked at the inferno that the mountain had become.

"Don't give up hope. And remember, it was important – no, *vital* – that an end be put to their activities. There was more at stake than you know. I can't tell you more. I'm afraid that once again, you'll have to trust me."

Bark wasn't totally convinced, but there was nothing to be gained from arguing now. "I suppose we will, won't we. Where to now?"

"I don't know about the rest of you," said Reina, "but I'd like to go home."

Barker's Mill.

Reina was looking down on Barker's Mill.

"Home," Bark said. The place felt almost familiar to him as well. Across the bay, the sand dunes above which they had moored the ship when they had first arrived shimmered under the clear sky. The memory of their ship, lying wrecked and burning on the ice, came back to him. For the first time, it brought pain with it. There had been an almost impossible amount of history wrapped up in that ship, and now it was just a slurry of charcoal and debris.

"Yeah, home," Reina replied. It looked the same. The same houses, solid and respectable, the same small grid of streets sitting hard up against the edge of the bay, separated from it only by the road that came around the coast and continued on through the forest and around to the dunes. She wondered how Tommy was. "I know a good place for us to land. It's just a little way out of town. A friend's place."

She showed Nibat the way. The ship made the expected impression on the inhabitants of the town, sending them indoors to look up through the gaps in drawn curtains at the humming brightly-colored disk that passed slowly over their rooftops.

They landed behind Tommy's house.

Denise, the barmaid from the Red Lion, heard the noise and felt the vibration. She came out onto the veranda and saw the flier just as it was settling down onto the grass. She ran to the back door and called out. Tommy emerged a few seconds later, cradling his shotgun under his arm.

"No shit! What the fuck is this?"

The flier's door opened and Reina stepped out. "Hi, stranger!"

"Reina! I thought you was history, mate!" He leaned the shotgun against a pile of firewood, went over to her, and gave her a long hug.

"I just about was a few times over, bro. And Bryce is. He's gone."

Tommy looked at the ground. "Oh. You know, I had a feeling." He raised his head and looked past Reina, towards the flier. "Who's that lot?"

Bark, Nibat, William and the black stranger were standing in front of the ship. Pig had jumped out as well, and was investigating one of the local hens, standing nose to beak with it, sniffing cautiously.

"Them?" said Reina. "They're my friends. I think we just saved the world."

"Ha! Yeah right. Of course you did. Tough work, I bet. Do you reckon they want a beer? It'll be a bit warm, though, there's been no electricity here for a while. Or what about a smoke?"

"Thanks, but later perhaps," said Bark.

"Oh, mate, I'll go the smoke," said Reina.

"Sure. So you been flying around in that thing? It's one of those alien things, yeah? Does it belong to that one there?" He pointed at Nibat.

'Yes and no. I'm its pilot, so I suppose you could say that if anyone owns it, I do. But the ship has a mind of its own.'

"Mm. So does my truck. Well, it did. It don't go no more." Tommy didn't seem to be at all disturbed by the Nefilim's use of telepathy. "You know some folks reckon you alien types are all trouble, but the ones I've met have been OK."

"You've met others?"

"Sure. There's a few of them, staying down at the Hanson kid's place. We thought it was a good place to shove them. Quiet and out of the way, you know, what with all the soldiers and everything that's been going through here. Like a railway station, man. There's been some total idiots running around the place."

The hen gave a loud squawk and raised itself up, flapping its wings. Pig came running over to where the others were standing.

"Is that yours?" Tommy nodded in Pig's direction.

"I'm not *anyone's*," Pig said, sitting down heavily. "I'm *with* these people. I don't *belong* to them!"

"Jeez, sorry, mate." Tommy finally looked surprised. Behind

him, Denise laughed.

The Hanson farm was a twenty minute walk away. It was as Tommy had said; humans, mutants and Nefilim, over a dozen of them, were all happily coexisting, and busy repairing old farm equipment and buildings.

A Nefilim who had been carrying old planks of wood that had been scavenged from somewhere saw them coming. He left what he was doing and limped over to them. It was Anak.

"We weren't expecting to find *you* here," said Bark after Nibat and Anak had finished doing whatever it is Nefilim do when they greet each other. "We had no idea what happened to you after you left Sahrin and Geoca in the Stream. We assumed you'd done your job, though."

"Yes, we did what we set out to do," replied Anak. He was speaking aloud. "It wasn't as we expected, though, in fact we didn't know what we were going to do, but things worked out well. Their grid is dead, and there is no way they'll be able to revive it. Where are Geoca and Sahrin? They're not with you?"

"No. They're… We don't know. They could be dead. But we can't be sure. They helped us at Mount Weather, but we think they were trapped in it when it blew up. It's gone, totally. The UN won't be reviving their headquarters, either."

Anak looked sad, an expression you might miss unless you knew a Nefilim well. *'I liked those two,'* he thought.

"I know," said Reina. "We all did. We can only hope that they died quickly."

Bark nodded. "There are still armies to worry about, you know. Human and Nefilim. They might be reduced to throwing stones and swinging sticks, but they could still be a problem. For everyone, not just each other."

"It wouldn't be a problem at all if they could just confine themselves to wiping each other out," Pig said and turned away, going off to talk to some mutants. The closer to finished that this whole thing was, the better he liked it. He'd never had a chance to be a real pig before, and he wanted to get on with it. He'd seen a good looking mud hole on the way here. He was going to have a crap in the grass, then a roll in the mud.

"The Nefilim armies aren't such a problem, actually," said Anak. "They didn't stay long after they took the control point and the base in the dunes. That attack was probably one of the last coordinated actions that their armies performed. A few hours later they melted away. They just disappeared into the forest or the dunes, and a lot of them turned up in places around here."

"Here? Why? It's not some sort of trick, is it?"

"I don't think so. It seems that after their communications and weapons failed, the Nefilim soldiers realized what their leaders hadn't; that they were fighting for a lost cause. There was a rebellion. Many of them have gone into hiding and changed into the cocoon state. They'll stay that way, if they're left undisturbed, until the home planet approaches again."

"But Marduk won't be close again for another thirty-six hundred…"

"Yes, but time like that is nothing to a hibernating Nefilim. Accidents or misfortune will befall many, it's true, because Earth is a much more volatile place than Marduk, but you can be certain that many will survive. But there are some that have come here, rather than hibernate. They were treated with great caution at first, as you might expect, but they had been misled by their leaders, just as the human soldiers were misled by theirs. As soon as they realized it, and realized that the home planet had given up on them, they lost the will to fight."

"You will find that there's a new energy on this planet now," said the dark stranger. "The time for fighting is passing quickly."

"Sounds a bit new age for me," said Reina, "but if it's true, I'm all for it. I suppose I'll believe it when I see it."

"You'll see it," replied the stranger.

Pig interrupted. "Where's the blue woman? Is she…?"

"Oh yeah, that blue chick." Tommy looked around. "She was here yesterday…"

"She's inside," said Anak. He led them towards the barn.

She was waiting for them. She smiled at them all, but it was the black stranger who caught her attention and held it.

"It's been a long time."

"Far too long. But it worked." The black stranger sounded relieved. They touched hands. Glowing auras the color of their skins spread out between them and mingled. It lasted for only a few seconds, and then faded away.

"You know each other, obviously," said Reina.

"Oh yes," they laughed. "For a long, long time."

"Somehow I'm not surprised."

* * *

A few hours later, the blue woman and Reina were walking through the forest near the farm.

"I can't tell you where I'm from," the blue woman was saying. "And I can't tell you why I can't tell you. I'm not much use, am I? I'm sorry. I can tell you that you'll understand one day, though. And sooner than you think."

"But you're not from here, are you?" Reina paused and looked at the blue woman's face. It was shifting and changing beneath its blue surface, as though something was shimmering, just beyond the edge of perception. She seemed almost familiar, Reina noticed for the first time. But from where?

"Don't be impatient, Reina. You'll understand everything in time, I promise. Now, this is important. You must stay with Bark. There's a future there."

Reina laughed and felt her face flush. "I had a feeling there might be. We'll see…"

"With you two together, the others will stay, and you'll need them. And they'll need you. You'll see."

* * *

At the same time, Bark and the dark stranger were having a similar conversation.

"I gave the map to your ship because I had to make sure that

358

you were here to release me, and to see that the work here was completed," the stranger was saying.

Bark was slightly more confused than he was going to admit. "It sounds far-fetched, but I'm not going to disbelieve you. And I suppose our work here is done."

The stranger smiled, a slow smile that hinted at things that he wasn't going to discuss.

"Here, yes… for now. What you say is true, strictly speaking, Bark, but there will be more to do. It's not all bad, though. The future, I mean."

Bark felt as though he was being singled out for something. "Why are you choosing me? You know, I was quite happy as a simple trader. It was a good life."

The stranger laughed. "I know. Believe me, I've got no choice in the matter. Your life as a trader is over. Now, you must build a new ship. I know it's what you were thinking about doing anyway, so just accept this as confirmation, or encouragement if you like. It has to be done. Reina will help. The others will help. Even the flier we traveled here in will help, you'll see."

"You're right, I *was* thinking about a new ship."

Bark was looking up into the sky at the pale sphere that was Marduk. It was growing smaller now, only half the size of the moon. It was swinging around into the outward leg of its orbit, out toward the long dark night that would last three and a half thousand years.

"Good. One more thing. You should know this – Sahrin and Geoca are safe. It'll be a while before you hear from them, but you will. Now, shall we go back?"

They returned to the farm.

Bark realized that the blue woman and the black stranger had deliberately spoken to Reina and he separately, getting them away from the others, and impressing on them both the need for co-operation and a new ship. He didn't doubt their good intentions; he could feel that they were to be trusted, but what was motivating them? And who were they? *What* were they?

The blue woman said it was time for them to go.

"Go where?" Pig asked. Bark could have told him not to bother.

"Just go, that's all," said the blue woman. She leaned closer. "I have to admit, Pig, that I misled you. I'm not really a mutant. Not in the way you might expect, anyway."

"I thought as much," Pig replied, even though he hadn't.

"I'll be seeing you again. Stick with those two…" she nodded towards Bark and Reina. "They'll be needing you." She went and stood beside the black stranger.

"You'll understand one day."

Bark looked around. What was supposed to happen now? There was no ship; not even a device of any kind. He looked into the sky above them. Nothing.

He looked back to see the two figures slowly turning transparent. After a few seconds, they became ghosts, growing fainter and fainter, until finally they were gone altogether.

No one said anything for a few seconds.

"Well, fuck me," said Tommy.

"You get used to it," said Reina. "I have no fucking idea."

Sinus Roris, the Moon.

Out near the moon, the black ship went into an orbit that would take it over the Sinus Roris area.

An officer had taken Thead and Alexis to the viewing area, a bubble that hung from the underside of the ship like the cabin area of a zeppelin. The moon's surface slid silently beneath them.

They saw markings that stood out among the natural chaos of rocks and craters. They had been partially covered by drifts of sand and dust over eons of time, but were still visible. There were small grid patterns, larger rectangular objects, and other things that looked like designs carved into the surface.

Alexis felt like a fish out of water. She was used to being in charge, but here she had nothing to do except be a passenger. She asked the officer whether the objects on the ground had anything to do with their destination. The officer laughed and said no, those were ruins that had been there for thousands of years. No one knew exactly how old they were, or who or what was responsible for them. As for their destination, they would be seeing that soon.

When they did, they knew why he had laughed at her question.

The ship came flying in low towards the bottom of a large crater. In the cliff face ahead of them was a huge set of doors, four of them, each framed by lights that blinked in slow steady rhythms. Embossed in shining metal in the center of each door was a gigantic swastika.

The base had been there for more than sixty years, the officer explained. Our little secret, he said.

Not so little, Alexis said, admiringly.

One of the doors opened, spilling yellow light across the landscape in front of it.

"Home," the officer said, and went to prepare for the landing.

Thead and Alexis looked at each other solemnly without

saying anything. After a few seconds Thead arched an eyebrow. A thin smile curved his lips.

Alexis smirked and nodded slowly. She'd had stranger bedfellows, after all.

They contemplated the entrance to the base as the ship drifted towards it.

Home? Hardly, thought Thead. A place to gather their strength, that was all. And then out. There must surely be some wonderful prizes hidden among the stars in this strange, weird part of the universe...

Epilogue.

Things would be different now.

The water in the streams and rivers flowed with a new, vibrant energy, and the plants and trees were growing as they never had before. The bird song had a new brilliance. Even the air seemed to hum with vitality.

The only machines on the planet that were working were the few that had been adapted to the Stream. It would take time to adapt more, and many conversions would never happen. A lot of the old ways suddenly seemed silly, pointless, or both. When life settled down again, it would have little resemblance to the old ways.

Above the new world, the sky shone with its new eternal brilliance, with no night waiting in the wings to claim the light. But the photon belt had left more than just a never-ending day. Inside the body of every living creature, the DNA was rearranging itself, shaping itself to the new frequencies. In time, people would begin thinking differently. In time, there would be new races.

"So, we'll build a new ship?" Reina asked several days later, knowing that their lives would change forever if they went ahead with it. *Bark is looking different today, she thought. It must be the light.*

"Yes," said Bark, who had been thinking about the future as well. "We'll build ourselves a ship. And then I'll show you the stars as they should be seen."

"Cool," said Reina, noticing for the first time that her own skin had a new tint to it. "Yeah, awesome."

THE END

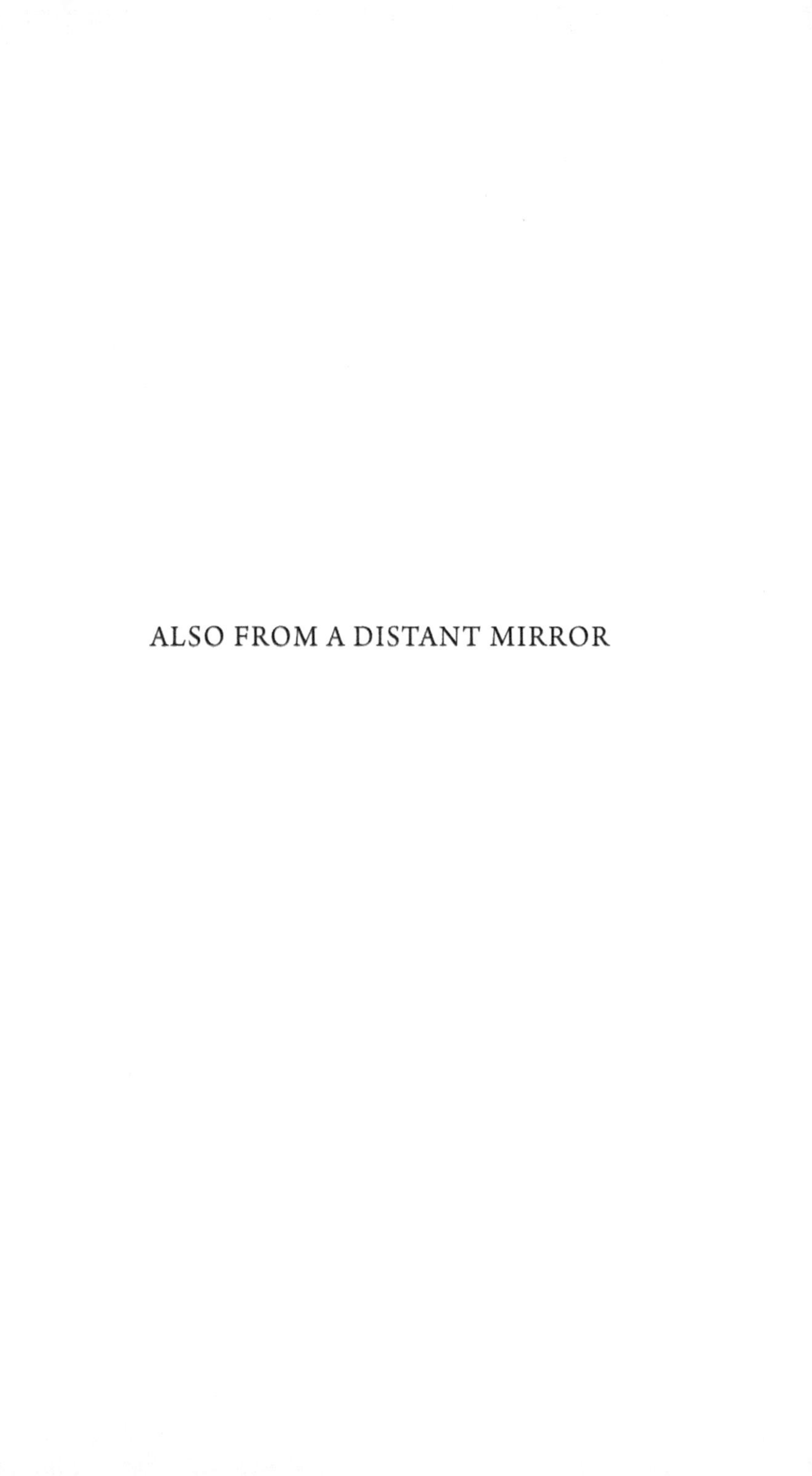

ALSO FROM A DISTANT MIRROR

Béchamp or Pasteur?

A Lost Chapter in the History of Biology

by **Ethel D. Hume**

352 pages
ISBN 978-0980297607

This volume contains new editions of two titles which have been available only sporadically in the decades since their publication.

R. Pearson's *Pasteur: Plagiarist, Imposter* was originally published in 1942, and is a succinct introduction to both Louis Pasteur and Antoine Bechamp, and the reasons behind the troubled relationship that they shared for their entire working lives.

Whereas Pearson's work is a valuable introduction to an often complex topic, it is Ethel Douglas Hume's expansive and well-documented *Bechamp or Pasteur? A Lost Chapter in the History of Biology* which provides the main body of evidence. It covers the main points of contention between Bechamp and Pasteur in depth sufficient to satisfy any degree of scientific or historical scrutiny, and it contains, wherever possible, detailed references to the source material and supporting evidence.

Virtually no claim in Ms Hume's book is undocumented. The reader will soon discern that neither Mr Pearson nor Ms Hume could ever be called fans of Pasteur or his 'science'. They both declare their intentions openly; that they wish to contribute to the undoing of a massive medical and scientific fraud.

The text of both titles has been extensively re-edited so as to modernise the use of English, and make the book easier to read than has been the case with previous facsimile editions. Included are new renderings of all the diagrams that were included in the original edition of *Pasteur: Plagiarist, Imposter*, plus there is a small collection of what photographs of Professor Bechamp are available.

AIR FOR FIRE

David Major

While *The Day of the Nefilim* was a meandering trip through some of the world's great conspiracy theories and New Age tropes, *Air for Fire* is a collection of short stories and poems that happen in every timeline but this one. Shameless historical revisionism, with a chronic disregard for physics and progressive nonsense.

Paperback and ebook

A DISTANT MIRROR